Ocean City Seagull Series, Book One

WELCOME TO SEAGULL STREET

ALISSA ARFORD

Red Hill Creek Enterprises
Ellicott City, Maryland

Published by:
Red Hill Creek Enterprises, LLC
Ellicott City, Maryland
www.redhillcreek.com

First Edition: May 2025
ISBN: 979-8-9985299-1-7

Edited by: Malory Wood
Cover art by: Marc Emond

Disclaimer
This is a work of fiction. While the story references real locations and events, all characters, dialogues, and interactions are entirely fictional. Any resemblance to actual persons, living or dead, beyond those explicitly acknowledged, is purely coincidental. The book may also reference real historical or news events as part of the setting, but these elements have been interpreted creatively and do not represent an official or definitive account.

For more information, visit AlissaArford.com.

DEDICATION

To my parents, Cheryl and James:

You filled my childhood with books,
my heart with adventure, and my life
with love and unwavering support.

This book exists because of you.

PROLOGUE

Everybody was anticipating the summer of 2023, a summer that would finally be "back to normal." No masks. No hand sanitizer. No social distancing. People were tired of living the lockdown life. The pandemic was effectively *canceled* by public opinion. Vacation vibes activated!

The COVID-19 pandemic, which forced the U.S. to shut down in March 2020, wasn't actually over, and it would never really be over, they say. People would keep getting the virus and spreading it as new variants mutated and became more resistant to the various brands of vaccinations. It wouldn't be enough to be double- and triple-vaxxed and boosted. People would need to get vaccinations every fall, just like the flu shot. *Did you get Pfizer, Moderna, or the controversial one-and-done Johnson & Johnson?*

There would be peaks and valleys in the number of cases. Some people would experience long-term effects, things we aren't able to imagine today. Many years from now, scientists will be studying the effects that COVID had on individuals and society at large. Not just the physical, but the mental as well. Say goodbye to all-you-can-eat restaurant buffets, and hello to concerned looks every single time someone coughs.

However, this isn't a story about the actual pandemic at all. It's a slice-of-life look at a handful of twenty-somethings, their families, friends, and one rebel—a *boy* that's maybe a little too *proud.* It's about how people are emerging from the pandemic with varying perspectives.

Still in isolation? Cautiously venturing out, mask in hand? Jumping back into the crowd headfirst? Or maybe you never changed your behavior to begin with. Whatever the case, anticipation of the possibilities that summer can bring are limitless. New beginnings. Love. Success. Fun. *Revenge.*

"Welcome to Seagull Street" takes place in a small beach town on Maryland's Eastern Shore called Ocean City—a vacation resort island that many millions visit each summer, but less than 7,000 call home on a permanent basis.

Look back at the culture, happenings, and the propaganda from the summer of 2023. Some of the Ocean City hot spots you'll read about are real to add some local flavor and make the ambiance as delicious as a handful of Old Bay seasoning on some hot steamed all-you-can-eat blue crabs. Let's go down the ocean, hon! It's almost summertime, and nothing soothes the soul like a peaceful walk on the beach.

PART 1
Monday, April 24, 2023

CHAPTER 1
Rachel "Ray" Anders

Ray lifted her hands to rub the sleepiness out of her eyes, and the cold wet nose of her exuberant rescue dog immediately pushed into her armpit. Charlie had been patiently looking at Ray, willing her to wake up, waiting for that first sign of morning movement to pounce. He started feverishly licking her armpit, knowing he would have only a few seconds to savor the taste and smell of Ray's powder-fresh deodorant before she swatted him away.

Charlie got up at the first sign of daylight, which meant Ray was an early riser in the summer months and only got a reprieve in the darker winter months. Ray needed to get darker blackout curtains or shades for the bedroom to try to trick Charlie into sleeping later.

As much as her body wanted to stay in bed, her mind loved the early morning walks on the beach. She often thought that rising early was destined to be her routine because of her nickname, "Ray." Her parents joked that she was a ray of sunshine when they shortened her first name of Rachel to Ray when she was going through her terrible toddler years. Truth be told, Ray never had a bright and sunny disposition, so the name was an inside joke to the family.

In school, she never told her friends about her nickname and was known as Rachel all throughout school and into her career. Only her family and close friends still called her Ray or Ray Ray. This led to a parade of sun-related gifts throughout her life—mostly from her mom, which she had secretly come to like and even began to collect on her own.

"Good morning, Charlie," Ray said as she cupped his furry black and white head into her hands and gave his nose a quick kiss. "How's my favorite boy this fine day?" Charlie snuggled into her body and nosed her legs to get her out of bed. He knew that he'd have to wait until Ray went into the bathroom and got "morning ready"—which during springtime meant leggings, a sports bra, a long-sleeved t-shirt, a baseball hat, and slides.

Ray sat up, swung her legs over the side of her queen-size bed, grabbed her mobile phone from the nightstand, unplugged the charger, and walked to the bathroom. She scrolled through her alerts and took a quick look at her weather app. It was 54 degrees and partly cloudy, a normal morning temperature for late April in Ocean City, Maryland. It was supposed to go up to the high 60s. It was 6:02 a.m., so that meant 15 minutes until sunrise.

Ray flipped on the light and walked over to the toilet. Then she washed her hands and grabbed her toothbrush. As she looked into the small medicine cabinet mirror over the sink, she realized that her short black hair needed a trim. It was sticking out behind her ears. She liked low-maintenance hairdos, but her hairstylist mom, Gloria, was always begging her to grow it out.

While on lockdown, Ray cut her hair by herself as so many people had done during the pandemic. She hadn't meant to make it so short, but she kept cutting it so unevenly that it just ended up that way. And she liked it. It was a "happy mistake" as her favorite TV painter Bob Ross would have said.

She felt like her pixie hairstyle gave her a confident Scarlett Johansson or Rihanna vibe. Having short hair made her more self-conscious, though—she couldn't hide behind her hair. Any blemish was front and center. She had to be more thoughtful about her earrings and necklaces. She had to remember to put sunblock on the back of her neck. It took a while for Ray to get into the different routine of having short hair. Maybe it was easier, but it was definitely different, and that took some getting used to.

Ray's deep brown eyes were beautifully framed by her bangs, but soon she would pull her hair back under her favorite Baltimore Orioles baseball hat and pop on her prescription sunglasses. These early morning walks with Charlie did not require her to be photo ready. And she was not exactly a selfie-taking kind of girl, anyway.

As she dressed, she cursed the sports bra padded inserts that had become twisted. She'd sworn off underwire bras when she started working virtually, and nowadays, comfort was her main priority in all her clothing options.

She heard a water drip coming from the shower and thought for probably the hundredth time that she needed to upgrade this bathroom. The entire townhouse needed a makeover, but the bathroom was stuck in the 1980s with the bulky vanity and small boxy medicine cabinet with yellowing built-in lights.

The worst part was the peeling seascape wallpaper with lighthouses, pelicans, and sailboats. The place had been furnished with typical beach house decorations, shell creations and nearly a dozen seaside paintings from the famous Ocean Gallery on the Boardwalk. Ray actually loved the beachy look, but it needed some upgrades to bring it into the 21st century. So far, the only artwork she'd added were two charming 8x10 drawings of seagulls from the nearby Raggamuffin Boutique, which was owned by a local artist and cartoonist.

Ray's home was a three-bedroom, two-level townhouse, and she used one of the bedrooms as an office, but it also had two sets of bunk beds in it. Most beach houses crammed in as many beds as possible for potential rental income and to have places for all of the vacationing family members to sleep. Her primary bedroom had a queen-size bed and French doors that opened onto a small balcony with a good water view of the island's bayside, Assawoman Bay. The bay's name made her smirk, remembering how her dad would pronounce it to emphasize the "ass" part of it. The main bedroom was the only room that she had truly made her own since moving in about two years ago. Although it was Ray's house now, it would always truly be her grandparents' home.

"Ready to go, Charlie?" Ray asked as she grabbed the long retractable walking leash. Charlie started barking with excitement, but Ray quickly reprimanded him. Just because they were up at the crack of dawn didn't mean the entire complex was awake. She kept a spray bottle with water in it to use if Charlie got too noisy. He loved water in general but was afraid of the spray and the reprimand that came with it.

They walked down the stairs to the ground floor and out the front door. Ray gave a silent wave to a neighbor angler getting his boat ready to launch at the private dock. Two seagulls were perched on a piling, squawking a friendly "hello" as Ray and Charlie passed by the last dock and through the parking lot to the main street.

They walked east toward the ocean and had to wait for the traffic light to change to cross Coastal Highway, and then crossed over one more street. Seagull Street was located between 26th and 27th Streets, and Ray would have to walk half a block either north or south to get to a light to cross the street in a crosswalk.

Jaywalking on this road was frowned upon because there were a lot of pedestrian accidents in town. The city had a huge ad campaign to encourage visitors to only use the crosswalks. In some areas further north, they put up barriers so people could only cross the road at traffic lights. Ray was a rule follower, so she always went to the crosswalk, and always waited for the light to turn red before stepping out into the street—even if there was not a car in sight. She would press the crosswalk button at least half a dozen times, though. Who knew if that made any difference, but it was a key part of her routine.

This part of town was at the end of the famous Ocean City Boardwalk, which went up to 27th Street. As they walked across the boards and got to the beach, the sun was peeking up over the horizon on the Atlantic Ocean. They only allowed dogs on the beach from October through April. Just a few more days to go.

The bicycle rental operators were just putting out bikes and trolleys and called out a friendly, "Good morning" to them. It was still early in the season, so there weren't many people renting bikes on this chilly morning.

The sun, now fully visible, was speckled orange with a spattering of small low clouds reflecting the first light in a truly picturesque feast for the eyes. She looked over and saw a family of four, smiling excitedly, taking photos or videos with their phones, and posing for selfies. Tourists who were beguiled by the beauty of their first ocean sunrise.

Ray thought back to when she was a preschooler, jumping the waves with her toddler sister, Brenda, both wearing inflatable arm floaties and squealing with excitement as each wave crashed down and sprayed them with water. Her grandfather would laugh and say, "Are you going to swim all the way across the Atlantic Ocean to Portugal, Ray Ray?"

Her grandmother would chime in and say that she'd rather dig a deep tunnel in the sand and crawl all the way to China! Ray must have heard these quips a hundred times, but she never got bored by them. Brenda would always scream in delight that she could smell the Chinese food whenever they dug motes around their elaborate sandcastles.

As Ray walked down the beach, two familiar seagulls landed in her path, alertly jerking their heads from side to side, looking up at her, studying her. Charlie gave a lazy bark and startled them away about 20 yards.

It would have been Ray's grandmother's 85th birthday in a couple of weeks. Her paternal grandparents had lived near Baltimore full-time but spent much of their retirement years right here in Ocean City. Well, that was until they both died from COVID complications in the summer of 2020.

Ray's eyes started welling up at the thought of her grandparents. She pushed her sunglasses up and wiped away the wetness from her eyes. It's something she didn't want to think about right now. Their faces were always right there in her mind—and living in their beach house made it impossible to go a day without thinking about them. It was still hard to comprehend how intensely the pandemic had directly affected her family.

Ray had been close to her dad's parents, Joseph and Elizabeth Anders. When they were sick, she wasn't able to visit them in the hospital due to the strict pandemic restrictions, but she would go to the parking lot and call them on the phone, conferencing them in from their separate rooms. She made a few signs with generic sayings like "I Miss You" and "I Love You" and "Get Well Soon!"

Their nurses—outfitted in what looked like hazmat gear—would walk them over to their respective windows and position the chairs so they could comfortably look out. Their hospital rooms were not on the same floor but were close enough that Ray could see them both from the same parking spot. She would enthusiastically wave back, smiling, even though inside, her heart was breaking. They looked frail with oxygen masks and breathing tubes. It would have been hard to see them up close, but from a distance, it was tragically unfair, Ray thought.

Sometimes Ray's parents would come with her, but they clearly felt awkward standing or sitting in camp chairs in the parking lot for longer than a few minutes. Brenda was trapped in the U.K. due to travel restrictions. Ray went to the hospital alone—almost every day at lunch or after work.

The scene at the parking lot was sometimes sad, sometimes happy, but always emotional. Ray recognized other regular visitors and would chat with them, always keeping at least six feet for social distancing. A few times, groups of visitors would come to the parking lot to visit a mother who just gave birth—they'd bring balloons and signs. One family brought a speaker and did a flash mob dance to *Sweet Child O' Mine*.

Ray's grandparents couldn't see each other before the end, which was perhaps the worst part of it. They ended up dying within two weeks of each other. Their funerals—if you could even call them true funerals—had been streamed online for family and friends to watch. It was heartbreaking for Ray, but her dad had been inconsolable. Seeing him so upset for the first time in her life was the biggest shock of all.

After they passed, Ray came to the beach house with her parents, and they packed up most of her grandparents' personal items for donation. Although the majority of their possessions were in their senior-living apartment outside of Baltimore, most of their summer clothes were at the beach house.

Ray was much smaller than Grammy, so she hadn't kept many of her clothes other than a few cardigan sweaters, some beach cover-ups, three sun hats, and various pieces of jewelry. Her dad had packed away a good amount of his dad's clothes, though, since they were roughly the same size. Pop-Pop had an immaculate sense of style, along with an impressive collection of canes.

Pop-Pop was a bonafide American war hero. While serving in the U.S. Army during the Korean War, he was injured in a night raid. He broke his leg in two places, and all of his toes on his right foot were crushed and had to be amputated. He normally carried a walking stick wherever he went. When Ray and Brenda were little, they'd take all of the canes out of the hall closet and line them up on the floor, examining the carvings and decorations, selecting their favorites. Ray was partial to the cane with the bird's head handle. They remained safely stored in the back of the entryway closet to this day.

Her grandparents were not the sentimental type, and there weren't a lot of personal items to sort out. Sometimes, Ray would pull out an old notepad and see her grandma's perfect handwriting with grocery lists or appointment reminders. Ray's favorite piece of artwork was a beautiful painting of a beach sunrise with two seagulls that hung over the sofa. Ray's family had given it to her grandparents as a 50th anniversary gift many years ago.

Before and during the first part of the pandemic, Ray lived in Washington, D.C., where she worked for a government contractor as a cybersecurity analyst. Like most jobs pre-COVID, she went into the office every single weekday.

Due to the type of work she did, it was hard for someone like her to work from home and maintain a secure working environment. She couldn't take her personal mobile phone into the building where she worked, so she was completely cut off from outside communications during working hours.

The pandemic changed everything, and she ended up working from home most days on a secure laptop, but she still went into the office for some top-secret meetings. She was regularly tested for COVID prior to those meetings, and of course, they all had to sit at least six feet apart from each other and wear N-95 masks due to the regulated pandemic restrictions.

After her dad's parents died, Ray's parents went to Brooklyn, New York, from Baltimore to help her mother's aging parents. They were all worried that they would suffer the same fate, although nobody had ever actually said it out loud. Secretly, they were afraid of jinxing them.

Due to underlying health and mobility issues, her maternal grandparents were immuno-compromised and considered high risk, unable to care for themselves adequately once everything shut down. Ray's parents had intended to be in New York temporarily, but after three years, they'd only been back to Maryland a handful of times. Ray's mom, Gloria, had grown up in Brooklyn and frequently talked about wanting to move back to the big city.

Ray's sister Brenda was 25 and had been living in London for a few years now with her husband, a Brit named Greg, who she met at college. They married right after their college graduation and had a lavish reception at a charming vineyard in central Maryland. The next day, they flew across the pond and had another wedding reception in the village of Arford, which was located in the East Hampshire district of Hampshire, southwest of London near Headly.

Ray figured now that Brenda was 14 weeks pregnant, her parents would stop bugging her about settling down. At only 29 years old, Ray still had plenty of time to figure out her life's plan, right?

Ray had been living alone at the beach for two years now. With no family members left in the area, and her grandparents' beach house sitting empty, making the decision to move to Ocean City permanently was a no-brainer. Given her technical skills and experience, finding a new cybersecurity analyst job with a 100% virtual working environment wasn't difficult. Cybersecurity was the one niche that wasn't slowing down in the shaky post-pandemic economy.

Ray occasionally visited her family up in NYC and had to travel to Fort Meade, Maryland, once a quarter for in-person meetings. Otherwise, she was always at the beach. Her parents had been trying to get her to move to NYC, but the bustling and stressful city life just wasn't for her. Some people loved the excitement of a crowd. Ray loved tranquil moments like watching the waves roll in and how each rise and crash was completely different.

"Time to go back home, Charlie," Ray said as she checked her watch. "But enjoy the view while you can. Soon, no doggies are allowed on the beach."

On the walk back to the beach house, Ray's stomach growled, and she glanced longingly over at the Fractured Prune storefront, which was closed for the season. It was a local donut chain where they freshly fried the donuts and dipped them into a variety of delicious toppings.

Ray liked to keep it simple and would normally get the "French Toast" donut along with an iced coffee. It would be open in a few weeks, but by then, she wouldn't be able to take Charlie onto the beach, so her morning routine would be changing anyway. There was a Dunkin' Donuts within walking distance, along with McDonalds and Burger King. Starbucks was further. The 7/11 convenience shop was the closest of all.

As Ray waited for the light to change to cross back to her place, she checked her phone for the time and any alerts. She had five new notifications in just the short time she'd been walking on the beach.

Being a cybersecurity analyst meant that she could get a notification at any time about potential cyber incidents to investigate. Most of the time, it was not "drop everything" urgent, but you never knew what would come up.

Ray and her teammates took turns monitoring the night shift once a week, so she wasn't "on call" until 8 a.m. today, but they worked very closely, and if something big started happening, all the analysts on her team would jump into their virtual war room for a briefing and to prepare the necessary incident response efforts.

As Ray walked back into her house, it was not yet 7:30 a.m. She went into the living room and turned on the TV. She tapped a few icons on her phone and brought up the YouTube channel for her favorite online yoga instructor, *Yoga with Adriene*. She found a 30-minute course, cast it to the TV, and unrolled her yoga mat. Charlie was eating his breakfast and seemed distracted. Hopefully, Ray could get through it without him jumping all over her. She closed her eyes and took a mountain pose.

Just as Ray was about to sit up from the resting pose of Savasana, Charlie stood on the sofa and started barking as he looked out the front window. Ray stood up and peeked outside.

"Interesting! Looks like a cleaning crew is working in the place next door, Charlie," she said. "Maybe a renter is coming soon?"

CHAPTER 2
Evan Michaels

Evan's alarm was set for 7:30 a.m. every weekday morning. Typically, his internal clock woke him up around 7:15 a.m. and he would grab his phone and turn off the alarm so his girlfriend Ellie wouldn't wake up. This morning, when he opened his eyes, he looked around and struggled to remember where he was at first. The clock on the bedside table said 8 a.m. He had 30 minutes before his first virtual work meeting. His phone was plugged in now, but it had been dead when he got home so he hadn't been able to set the alarm before he fell asleep.

He stared up at the ceiling of his childhood bedroom, which still had glow-in-the-dark star stickers placed in arrangements loosely reminiscent of constellations. All but one of the hanging planets had fallen over the years. Mars was still over in the corner, dust-covered and faded to light pink.

It was all coming back to him. He and Ellie broke up yesterday when he found out that she'd been cheating on him with her high school sweetheart. She claimed she hadn't even seen "Bob" since high school graduation, nearly seven years ago. But from the text messages he'd read, the fact that they hadn't been physically in the same room—at least recently—was no consolation. She clearly wanted to get back together with him. She had never written anything like that to him, and they'd been together for five years, (since college) and living together for three of those years (since college graduation).

Ellie had been sitting at the kitchen table, listening to music on her earbuds, drinking a green protein shake, and tapping frantically on her phone, giggling, and smiling. She hadn't realized Evan had gotten home and was standing right behind her. He leaned down and was about to grab her shoulders and give her neck a kiss. Then he glanced down at her phone and saw a text stream with a photo of a man in his underwear. Evan's head shot back and he squinted to read the entire sultry exchange. He cringed as he recalled the texts.

Ellie to Mystery Man:
Your abs look so hot in that pic. I haven't been back home to VB in so long. Wish I was there right now to rub some sunblock on your rocking bod.

Mystery Man to Ellie:
Me 2 babe. When R U going to dump that loser BF of yours and move back? xoxoxo

Once Evan had seen more than enough, he pointedly tapped Ellie on the shoulder. After the initial shock, and realizing she couldn't make any valid excuses, Ellie admitted that she was no longer in love with Evan and wanted to break up. It was almost like she'd planned it. No emotion. No second thoughts. *How could she be so heartless?*

Evan thought they were just going through a temporary rough patch—both were busy working, and they had different sets of friends. They didn't spend every waking minute together. They were both non-confrontational and were not great at communicating. After five years together, Evan hated to admit that he wasn't sure if Ellie was "the one." They probably stayed together during lockdown because it was convenient and too hard to figure out a way to break up.

Evan took it all in stride after his initial angry stampede around their shared apartment, throwing random stuff into his backpack and grocery totes. He purposefully used the nice ones he knew she liked best. He'd texted his mom that he would be crashing at home as a heads-up, but he'd be there very late.

After he loaded his car with a mess of overflowing bags, he sped out of the parking lot with no particular destination in mind. After driving for a few minutes, he pulled into the nearby Food Lion parking lot. Coincidentally, his Aerosmith playlist started streaming *What Could Have Been Love*. He grabbed his phone and skipped the song. He had a few notifications from Whatnot—the live auction app that was a mash-up of eBay, QVC, and TikTok. He entered a giveaway, sat back in his seat, and waited for the drawing. Evan was what they called a *givvy goblin*. He'd been banned from entering the freebies numerous times because he'd won so many times. *So what* if he was lucky, he thought. After waiting a few minutes, he lost the giveaway and started driving again.

Evan ended up drinking too much and staying out too late. Not exactly a smart thing to do on a Sunday night before a full workday. He didn't drink much normally—or really ever—and his tolerance level was low, even given his substantial (all muscle) weight. He ended up going solo to watch a band at the local bar and grille right down the road from his mom's house. The band ended early, but Evan stayed until last call and was practically thrown out of the place. But in a nice way because he knew the owner… the brother of his high school football coach, who gave him a ride to his mom's home.

Now, Evan tried to open his eyes, but his head was pounding, and he hadn't shut the curtains. It was so bright. He blinked his eyes a few times but could barely focus on his phone screen.

Evan designed websites for a boutique marketing agency located on the Eastern Shore of Maryland. They mostly worked with small business owners who needed basic websites and didn't have a lot of money to spend on marketing. They relied heavily on social media to bring in customers.

Since the pandemic, he worked from home almost 100% of the time, but occasionally he went out to meet with the business owners they designed for, and his own co-workers. He took photos, recorded videos, and got a good feeling about the vibe of the place to help come up with the brand identity for the website and marketing materials.

He was part of a small team, and he enjoyed the hands-on work and the ability to be creative. It didn't pay as much as he'd like to be earning, so he had a side hustle (well, a couple of them). He occasionally helped his Uncle Jack, who owned a bayside restaurant and bar in Ocean City, on some evenings and weekends.

Evan had to log in and start work at 8:30 a.m. for his weekly Monday Morning Marketing Meeting. He momentarily thought about calling in sick, but he still had plenty of time to get set up for the call. He had 11 new text messages since 2:15 a.m. when he went to bed.

Seven text messages from his mom, Mary, who would already be at work at Salisbury University, which was about 30 minutes away from home in Berlin, Maryland. When he told people where she worked, most people thought she was a professor. They didn't realize there were hundreds of non-teaching types of jobs at a university. She was a manager in dining services, which was more complicated than you'd think.

While he was in school there, he'd only see her occasionally around campus, but they'd made a point of having lunch once a week at The Commons. Since his mom had worked there for so long, Evan was able to get tuition remission. Some kids might have been bummed about having to go to a particular college, but Evan looked at it as a Godsend since otherwise he would have undoubtedly had to take out student loans for college.

Evan, his mom, and his brother lived a comfortable life when he was growing up, but after his dad died in a car accident about 10 years ago, things had never been the same. Money was always a consideration in everything they did. Fortunately, their modest house had been paid off even before his dad died but they were always on a tight budget.

His phone pinged. His mom was texting to make sure he was feeling okay and to tell him there were fresh strawberries and blueberries in the fridge and to eat them or they would go bad.

He texted a quick "Thanks" back to her so she would stop texting and know that he was alive.

Mom to Evan:

BTW there's Tylenol in the hall pantry, top shelf.

Ohhhh. And I forgot to tell you that I got two cute little kittens! They were found on campus and were very sickly. I took them to the vet, and don't even ask me how much it cost!

They're probably wandering around the kitchen. I tried to gate them in there. I named them Cookies and Cream.

Kittens! His mom got pets now that he was gone, after he'd spent his entire childhood begging for any kind of furry pet? Of course she would do that. She was probably empty nesting.

Evan quickly scrolled through his other promotional texts. One was from his credit card. As he was checking his credit card statement, two more texts came in from his older brother Brandon who had heard about the break-up from their mom. Brandon texted their mom nonstop 24/7 with a running commentary about everything from the weather to reality TV recaps. They had no secrets. Well, almost no secrets. Evan had no texts from Ellie.

It was going to be a long day. The sooner he got up and drank some coffee, the better. He stumbled over his shoes, tote bags, and backpack, which he'd thrown in the middle of the floor last night, and walked down the hall to the bathroom.

Now that Evan and Brandon hadn't been living at home for many years, the bathroom was spotless. He guessed that it was rarely ever used. Back when he was in school, the upstairs bathroom was an obnoxious mess, except for the one day a month when his mom made them clean it up and threatened to take away their phones if they didn't help. His mom kept the first floor immaculate but had given up trying to keep the upstairs clean when he was in middle school and his brother was in high school.

He looked into the mirror. *Nasty.* He would need to shower before he was Zoom-ready. He always wore his dirty blonde hair on the long side, but that just accentuated its messiness if he hadn't washed it or styled it in a few days.

He hopped into the shower and realized the shampoo options his mom had in there were too complicated for him. Couldn't she buy something normal? He didn't have time to read the fine print about the benefits of each type of product. He just randomly picked one that said "Shampoo" and used it. And why didn't the manufacturers have "Shampoo" and

"Conditioner" in larger print on the bottles? *Truly mind-boggling.* Next, he grabbed a bar of soap to lather up.

"What the… this must be some kind of goat milk soap," he said to himself, cringing at the potent smell.

Evan was always talking to himself. Singing to himself. Whistling. Humming. He had never thought it was weird because it was something everyone in his family did. Ellie said it was beyond annoying. She would stare at him with a look that screamed… "What's wrong with you? Can you be quiet for even one second?" Now Evan could sing whenever he wanted with no judgement.

Evan was smelling very fresh. Way too flowery for a 25-year-old guy who was 6'3" and worked out at the gym most days. *Whatever.* He was just going to a Zoom meeting. Nobody would be able to smell him. He went back into his room and grabbed a wrinkled company polo shirt from his bag. He walked over to the small table desk at the window, the same one he'd had since he was in elementary school. It had a bunch of round water glass stains on it and spots of paint from his model airplane building phase.

He pulled out his laptop and set it up. He'd been to his mom's house enough that the Wi-Fi automatically connected. He clicked through the screens and opened up his email, his calendar, and Slack. All ready to go. Now he had just enough time to make some coffee and grab some fruit.

When he got to the kitchen, the two kittens were curled up together in a ball sleeping on a towel. "Ok, that is seriously cute," Evan said as stepped over the makeshift gate. His first thought was to take a photo and send it to Ellie. Then he remembered the current situation and swore at his bad luck. The kittens stirred, and one approached him tentatively with a tiny, "Meow." It must have been the one his mom was calling "Cream" since it was mostly white. Evan didn't have time to spare to play with kittens right now, he thought, as he put in a coffee pod and started his brew. Props to his mom for leaving it on so the water was already hot.

"Yes. You're ridiculously cute little kittens. I'll come back and see you soon," he promised as he hopped over the gate and went back upstairs with his coffee and fruit.

CHAPTER 3
Olivia McNalley

It was still early in the morning when Olivia pulled out of the driveway from her family's home in Ellicott City, Maryland—a suburb to the west of Baltimore. She was excited and scared. She was about to embark on a new life for herself after what she now considered her "missing years" of 2018-22. She'd just finalized her divorce from Luke, whom she married right after they had both graduated from college nearly five years ago.

Olivia's family had lived in the same neighborhood since she was in kindergarten. Once she left for college, though, she hadn't lived at home full-time until her separation last year. At the time, she'd felt like such a failure. But she *was not* a selfish, sheltered, and spoiled brat, like Luke regularly claimed. She had a good support system, and he didn't.

Her parents had left for work only minutes beforehand, after a prolonged and tearful goodbye from her mother, with multiple hugs, kisses, and important reminders. Olivia had been eager to get on the road herself, even though her mother warned her that it would take much longer with the morning rush hour traffic. She'd have to drive south, down past Annapolis, and then east over the Chesapeake Bay Bridge, which was a scary four miles long.

Olivia backed her filled-to-the-brim white Honda CRV out of the driveway and pulled over to the side of the road as she remembered to start her music playlist she'd called "OCMD New Life 2023." She used a photo she'd taken of her dog Ruby as the cover pic. She made the playlist the previous night and had more than three hours' worth of road trip music ready to go.

She flipped on her windshield wipers and they screeched, removing some raindrops from the thunderstorm that had gone through during the night. A couple of the neighborhood kids walked by her on their way to the bus stop. She used to babysit them back when she was a teen, and they were toddlers. "Way to make me feel old," she mumbled. Olivia was 27… and a half. Late 20s, she guessed people would call it.

Olivia never quite liked her name growing up. A lot of people didn't like their names, though, from her experience. She was named after an ancestor on her mom's side of the family. Growing up, Olivia Newton-John was always her go-to-name twin. Olivia's mom loved the movie *Grease* and watched it all the time. Once, Olivia had dressed up as Sandy for Halloween—not sexy Sandy, but the poodle-skirt wholesome version. When she was growing up, there was Olivia Benson in *Law & Order: Special Victims Unit*, but Olivia was too young to watch that.

Later on, she was ecstatic that the main character on the television show *Scandal* was named Olivia. She sometimes wondered if it became her favorite show because of Olivia Pope or if she'd have loved it as much otherwise. During that time, she tried to get people to call her Liv or Livvie. It didn't stick. When One Direction came out with the song *Olivia*, that was also a major win for her name! Then, even more recently, along came singer Olivia Rodrigo, and it was much cooler to be named Olivia.

When she had children, she would make a concerted effort to pick a name that wasn't different enough to be weird but was different enough to be distinct. She had already picked out four name possibilities for her children, but those were top secret. She was worried someone would steal them before she could use them herself.

The neighborhood kids waved to Olivia and said, "Hi, doggie!" to Ruby. She wondered if they remembered that she used to be their babysitter. Ruby whined and tried to stick her nose out of the partially open car window.

Over the pandemic, everyone had gotten to know their neighbors in a much more personal way than just reading the gossipy neighborhood Facebook group. They probably got more facetime than most of them would have liked.

Many of the neighbors with small kids hosted driveway parties during lockdown, trying to get some socialization for their house-bound kids. When her family would take Ruby on her daily walks around the neighborhood, Olivia would get nostalgic for the time when she was playing on that same road with her childhood friends, who were now long gone. There were four kids in the neighborhood who were in Olivia's grade, and they would ride their bikes and scooters around the secluded neighborhood without a care in the world. She was still connected with them on Instagram, but hardly ever saw them in real life.

She laughed aloud as she recalled how the old biddies— who were probably only in their 40s, now that she thought about it—would stare out their windows or sit on their front porches and watch the kids loitering and the cars driving by too fast. They'd yell out at them and then open up the printed neighborhood directory and call the parents on their home phones. Nowadays, the busy bodies would secretly take photos or videos with their phones or use Ring doorbell footage and post on Facebook to publicly shame the kids and their parents.

There was no such thing as privacy now. Want to take a walk with your boyfriend? Your mom would get a photo texted to her immediately from her friend down the street. Your mom was probably tracking your phone anyway and already knew where you were.

Today, Olivia was heading to Ocean City to move into her parents' beach rental—her new home. Ruby was in the backseat, looking out the window and ready to go… ready to go anywhere, really. She loved to take a car ride. Olivia had given her some motion sickness medicine in a piece of cheese before they left, just in case. She took an extra few minutes to make a video for TikTok for that viral trend called the "Cheese Tax," whereby every time you open the cheese drawer in your refrigerator, you have to give your dog some cheese. That was facts. Dogs loved cheese. This would be the longest ride that Ruby had ever taken, and starting a new life amid the smell of dog barf was not part of Olivia's plan.

Olivia would begin her new job as a third-grade teacher in Ocean City in the fall. Over the summer, she hoped to get a waitressing job at a local restaurant to meet people and make some extra money.

Olivia stopped by a McDonald's drive-thru and ordered an iced coffee (with sugar-free vanilla syrup, which made her feel moderately better about her diet), and a Sausage McMuffin with Egg, her favorite breakfast sandwich since childhood. She snapped a quick selfie with Ruby in the backseat and posted it to her Instagram story as she waited to pay.

Her ex hated fast food, and stopping there made her smile a little bigger as she placed her order. She was her own boss. She could eat what *she* wanted. Watch whatever *she* liked on television. Go to whatever movies *she* felt like. And she could—and would—listen to three hours of Taylor Swift, boy bands, Jimmy Buffett, and pop music as she drove to the beach.

Those all seemed like small and inconsequential incompatibilities, but Olivia knew it was the bigger things that made her and Luke split up. He had become a dictator in their relationship. It was always his way or the highway. The condescending words he used: "Olivia, stop being so stupid. Are you really that dumb? You're so selfish. You're so useless. No, you're remembering it wrong. I didn't say that."

The mean jokes, the sarcastic comments, the patronizing questions, the frequent interruptions, and the constant eye-rolling. The constant gaslighting had been exhausting and demoralizing.

Of course, it hadn't always been that way. In the beginning, it was a truly idealistic romance. Flowers for no reason, fancy dinners, and thoughtful gifts. Then, slowly, with a series of unfortunate events, it all came crashing down. The point of no return was right smack dab in the middle of the pandemic, during one of the most stressful times in history. Olivia had blocked it from her mind. The person Luke had become scared her. However, the bottom line, the last straw, the tipping point, was that she hardly recognized the person she'd become as his wife. She needed to start over and rediscover herself.

Olivia's parents were both professors at the University of Maryland in College Park, right outside of Washington, D.C. Her father Danny was a professor of government and politics. Her mother Mariana was a professor of marketing. Attending UMD was an easy decision for Olivia; however, her siblings hadn't felt the same way. Her younger brother Daniel worked as a sous chef at an up-and-coming restaurant in New York City after graduating from the Culinary Institute of America. Her younger sister Paula was finishing her junior year in college at Salisbury University, which was close to Ocean City. Hopefully, they could plan to meet up more regularly going forward. Paula hadn't gotten into UMD, and there was a bit of animosity between the sisters, to say the least. The overachiever versus the underachiever, among other things.

If Olivia had to describe her family dynamic, it would probably be "advocates of human rights." They always had candidate signs in their yard for Election Day. They would work at the polls for their local "Teacher Endorsed" candidates. They'd sometimes canvas neighborhoods and make phone calls. They regularly demonstrated at political rallies in Washington, D.C., and had attended multiple Presidential Inauguration Day parades. Olivia's parents would let them skip school, and they'd meet up with some of her parents' students in a restaurant afterward to discuss the challenges and opportunities for the next administration.

The only other time Olivia's parents had let her skip school was for the Baltimore Ravens Super Bowl Victory Parade in 2013. Talk about the cold! They were frozen to the core that day, but it was still one of the most memorable experiences from Olivia's childhood. She was 17 at the time, and she remembered it vividly. Her mom had probably taken 300 photos, which she'd plastered all over social media. Sometimes, Olivia would go back and scroll through them and repost them during the football season.

They had found seats in the stadium, which was at the end of the parade route, and had gotten to go onto the field to take photos. They brought homemade double-sided signs with shoutouts for Ray Lewis, Joe Flacco, Jacoby Jones, Ed Reed, Anquan Boldin, and Torrey Smith, who had played football at the University of Maryland. Olivia's dad had taught him in a couple courses. *Let's go Terps!*

After the Super Bowl, her dad bought everyone in the family Torrey Smith Super Bowl #82 jerseys, to wear on Purple Fridays at work, and then again on game-day for good luck.

When Olivia met Luke at college, she realized right away he was more conservative than she was. That was back when the labels of "conservative" and "liberal" were more mainstream and didn't come with as much baggage, though.

Luke grew up in rural Virginia, the kind of area that didn't have cable television, or high-speed internet, or even garbage pick-up. His family liked to go hunting and had a gun safe in the basement full of firearms. There wasn't anything wrong with that, as far as Olivia was concerned. Different strokes for different folks. As long as they didn't put family photos with everyone toting semi-automatic weapons on their Christmas cards, she could deal with it. They were a typical rural American family.

Neither politics nor religion were part of Olivia and Luke's relationship or discussions in the early part of their time together. She always believed that politics was a non-factor. They were a true love match! They both wanted children. They both were professionals with the potential to bring home solid salaries that would enable them to live a comfortable lifestyle, even in an expensive D.C. neighborhood. They were frugal with money. They were physically fit. They loved living in D.C.

Luke wasn't one of those workaholic types who never took a vacation day. They'd go biking and hiking around the DMV (D.C., Maryland, Virginia). They had a kayak they'd take out on the Potomac River. She considered them to be an outdoorsy couple. If it happened to give her great content for her social channels, bonus points. They hadn't traveled much, which was one thing that irked Olivia. The whole perfect life plan was to get married and travel before having kids, right?

Luke played a lot of violent video games, which she didn't love. But what 20-something-year-old guy didn't? He would spend hours on his phone playing games, and Olivia would spend that same amount of time on social media. To each their own way to relax, she thought.

Neither of them were deeply religious. They didn't go to church regularly, even though they had both grown up going to church most Sundays, and always for Easter and Christmas. They were married in 2017 in a church service because it was important to their parents. The wedding vibe was somewhat awkward—city slickers and country folks mingling together. Olivia's family was so outgoing, nobody noticed the underlying tensions. It was a fun wedding reception. The photos with their smiling happy faces proved it.

Over time, however, Luke became distant and detached, preferring to sit alone in his home office rather than spend time with Olivia. They had made it well past the honeymoon phase, but was living separate lives normal? Olivia was not even close to being happy. Her parents' relationship had always been very cohesive. They were constantly chatting, debating, or hypothesizing on some random topic or another. Sure, highs and lows were expected. She knew that marriage wasn't easy. The vows said *in good times and bad*, right?

Older people were always saying that younger people didn't take marriage seriously anymore and gave up too soon. But Olivia thought that younger people knew better in this case—life was short, and if you knew something wasn't working, why suffer? You've only got one life to live.

Olivia was no psychiatrist, but she did know that Luke's behavior had spiraled out of control over the past few years. Why did her beloved husband act like a totally different person? After having to drag him to the voting booth in the past, he became completely obsessed with politics. And, out of the blue, he started quoting the *Bible*. It didn't make any sense.

The start of the downfall of the marriage was around 2018. Olivia started actively avoiding any kind of gatherings with friends or family members because of Luke's erratic behavior. He was completely obsessed with politics, and she was embarrassed by the conversations that would inevitably happen at each and every gathering they had with friends or family members.

At first, when the pandemic hit, Olivia thought it was almost a blessing to have it as an excuse to hide away. Over time, things got worse. So much worse.

Luke was active on social media during that time—mostly Facebook, Instagram, and Twitter—and was always sharing what Olivia considered to be propaganda or "Fake News." It was really embarrassing for her, her family, and friends. Luke's Dad was conservative, but not vocal about his views, and he also seemed embarrassed by the political outbursts. For the older generation, political leanings were almost as private as annual salary.

Most of their friends had silenced Luke's social media posts, changing their user preferences so they wouldn't have to see all the conspiracy nonsense he posted. Olivia wondered if Luke actually believed the things that he was sharing. She shared political things on social media too, but she was always careful to make sure they were factual first.

In the summer of 2020, Olivia had come to the conclusion that she was not destined to be with Luke long-term. However, she felt like she was stuck, and the lockdown made things exponentially worse. They were together 24/7. Her job as a teacher became more stressful than ever, trying to teach class remotely for third graders. The kids could barely type and sit for longer than 10 minutes on the school-provided laptops. The parents were frazzled trying to balance their work-from-home situations, or lack of work, trying to make ends meet.

Luke was able to do his job as a financial planner from home without much change. He had regular virtual meetings, but mostly did his work on the computer from 8:30 a.m. to 5 p.m. each day. He was set up in their office, and Olivia had a makeshift office in their formal living room, which they hardly ever used anyway.

Luke had the TV tuned to his favorite pseudo-news station 24/7. Olivia had gotten to the point where she watched no news on TV. She kept her earbuds in full-time and listened to music, podcasts, or audio books. She couldn't watch the morning network news shows or late-night talk shows anymore. The pandemic, politics, the endless debates, and propaganda. It all made her so sad and angry.

Each night, Olivia would pretend to be asleep when Luke came into the bedroom well after midnight. What was he doing on his computer until the wee hours of each morning? They hardly talked about anything except the logistics of life. Their love life was nonexistent. They ate dinner together, but that was their only time together in the same room. She had to get up extra early to prepare for class, and she took her lunch early, too.

They were together in the same house every hour of every day, but they were more distant than ever before. Occasionally, they would message each other over a chat app. That was mostly about what to order on DoorDash for dinner or what items to put on the weekly Instacart grocery store order.

Speaking of food, and eating, Olivia had gained about 20 pounds since COVID started. Once she got to Ocean City, she planned to go on daily walks with Ruby. Maybe even get a bike. Also, moving around as a server would help increase her activity level. She had started back on birth control pills as a precaution about two years ago—without telling Luke—which was likely another cause of her weight gain.

Luke had bought her an Apple Watch two birthdays ago, and she hardly wore it, but she had it on now and would make more of an effort with her health now that she was back in the dating market. She always balked at wearing it because it would vibrate and startle her with all of the various notifications. She'd taken the time to turn off most of the random app notifications and only keep the important things like calls and text message alerts on her watch. Now she didn't jump each time it vibrated. That was progress.

As she settled into her car seat and cruised down the highway, she took a deep cleansing breath. She began to sing along with her favorite Backstreet Boys song, *I Want it That Way*. She was finally doing what she wanted… and this new adventure was on page one.

More than an hour later, Olivia reached the town of Easton and pulled into another McDonald's. That large, iced coffee went right through her. She got another drink because it was still early, and it was only 0.99 cents. How could she pass it up? She looked at her mobile app to see if there were any other deals she could use. Next, she walked Ruby around the parking lot, but the dog was too distracted to pee.

Back in the car, they were only a few miles down the road when Olivia heard a frantic, "Yelp!" coming from the back seat, followed by a high-pitched whine and a scratching noise.

"Holy guacamole, Ruby! What have you done?" Olivia pulled over to the side of the road to assess the situation and saw that Ruby had somehow stepped on the lever and gotten her head trapped in the window. Fortunately, Olivia was easily able to lower the back window from the driver's seat, but she would need to pull over and make sure Ruby was ok.

Olivia checked her side mirror, and it was clear. She opened the door to dart around to the other side of the car. Ruby seemed a little shaken up, but honestly, how could Olivia really tell if something was wrong? She felt around her neck, looked into her eyes, gave her a kiss on the nose, and said, "You're okay, Ruby Scooby Doo!" She shut the car door and stepped to the back of the car to assess the traffic.

"Oh, shoot. This could take a while, Ruby!" Olivia reached to the back of her head to gather her hair and redo her falling ponytail.

She'd only stopped paying attention to the traffic for an instant. But that's all it took. A huge truck blew by and splashed water from a large puddle right onto her.

"Oh. My. God. Seriously, dude? I'm covered in muddy water!" She jumped back and stepped to the other side of the car to take cover from the approaching vehicles. She shook off her shirt and tried to brush off the blobs of dirt from her white skirt. She waited until the coast was clear and sprinted back into the driver's seat. She grabbed some napkins from her center console and tried to wipe off the dirt from her face, arms, and legs. Next, she used a dry area on her shirt to carefully wipe off her dirt-speckled designer sunglasses. Feeling tense and annoyed, she closed her eyes, rolled her neck in a circle, took a deep cleansing breath, and slowly slid her glasses back onto her face.

Olivia turned to check on Ruby again before merging back on Route 50, which was two lanes each way in this stretch. Maryland had that new law where you were supposed to pull over into the passing lane if there was a car on the right side of the road, but most people ignored that, especially during times of heavy traffic.

Olivia picked up her iced coffee to take a sip as she looked into her side mirror, waiting for a break in traffic so she could pull back out. Suddenly, the cup slid out of her hand and dropped into her lap with a quick swoosh, the lid popping off. The cold coffee and ice dripped off her lap and onto the seat in between her legs. Olivia shrieked in frustration. Her day had to get better, right?

CHAPTER 4
Evan

Evan slid into the wobbly office chair by his desk right at 8:28 a.m. with a steaming hot cup of coffee. He put his coffee mug on a coaster that he'd made in Sunday School eons ago that said: "Let your light shine before others. Matthew 5:19." He clicked on the Zoom link on his Google Calendar and it opened up right away.

As Zoom was opening, he clicked over to Slack and did a quick check to see if any messages had come in from his boss he'd need to address during the meeting. Two new messages.

He squinted at the screen and rolled his eyes as he began to type in a response to her lengthy questions. "So. Umm. Evan," his boss Mary Ann asked over the video call "Where are you this morning? It doesn't look like your normal set up?" He was on mute, and he'd need to switch windows to unmute.

Evan quickly finished typing his responses and then clicked back into Zoom and unmuted himself. He didn't want to get into the Ellie break-up story during this meeting with his entire team. They had all met her at various team happy hours and parties over the years. "Good morning, Team! I'm at my mom's house. I decided to stay over last night after I was visiting with her for dinner."

"That's always nice to spend some quality time with your mom," said Mary Ann in a voice that was much more sing-songy than usual. And she had a weird smile on her face. Why was she acting so strange this morning? Everyone seemed to be giggling.

Then, Evan's eyes focused on the meeting attendee video grid—and he noticed it. He leaned into his laptop. What was in the background of his Zoom video? His eyes widened and he drew in a huge breath. It was his huge Ashley Graham *Sports Illustrated Swimsuit Edition* poster from like 10 years ago. His older brother Brandon had given it to him as a birthday gift. Ashley even signed it.

Evan jerked his head back with embarrassment and said, "Oh my God. Sorry. Having some technical issues. Be right back." He turned off his video. Then he muted his audio. Evan's face was flaming, and he was starting to sweat. "Oh, snap! Why didn't I check my video before I entered the Zoom room! Dude. WFH Etiquette 101. So damn stupid. Like I don't have enough drama in my life," he said, shaking his head.

He could hear the rest of his team trying to hold back their laughter. He looked back at the poster, took a deep breath, and realized it was not *that* big of a deal. She wasn't naked; she was just in a revealing bikini. His team would be cool with it. He pulled out his desk from the wall and turned it 45 degrees, so he was facing his bed, and his camera was facing his closet door. His very plain white and closed closet door.

His team had continued on with the meeting, and when he turned his camera back on, he got a few smirks from his teammates. But the rest of the meeting progressed like nothing out of the ordinary had happened. Although, he had three Slack messages from his best buddy at work, Greg.

Greg to Evan:
DUDE! Now THAT'S how you start a Monday morning looking at that seeeexxxy poster!!

Evan to Greg:
I'm mortified – DO NOT message me again today

Evan sent a GIF of a melting SpongeBob SquarePants.

Greg sent a meme that said "Einstein Approves" and:
Nice hair, BTW. LMAO.

Evan leaned into his laptop monitor again to look at his video stream. His hair was huge! WTF. His mom's shampoo? *It must have been "volumizing" shampoo, of course*, he thought. He brushed his hands through his hair to try to tame it down, without much luck.

Mary Ann was explaining they had a new prospective client called WAFN Industries to build out the website and online marketing for *Local Update News Stories*. Not a local client like usual, but someone had contacted her via LinkedIn and asked for help making a website with local news for the Eastern Shore of Maryland. Apparently, WAFN had these kinds of websites around the country and focused on local news stories that were promoted geographically on social media and via email. It was a free news service that was paid for by sponsorships and advertising money.

Evan was nodding along with Mary Ann's list of things to do regarding the new account and taking some notes. Then, without any warning, his head jolted forward and a screeching "Meoooooow" rung out in his ears.

"What the—!" he yelled, shaking his head and trying to grab the kitten off of him while it dug its tiny claws into his cheek. His extra puffy hair made the scene even more ridiculous. "My God, can this morning get any worse for me?"

There was a huge rumble of laughter from the rest of his team, and some of them turned off their cameras and muted their microphones to hide their extreme amusement of the situation. His boss finally said, "So, Evan, you have a cute little kitty helper at work today? Who is that precious little thing?"

"Yeah. It turns out my mom rescued two kittens from her work the other day, and I guess the gate she put up in the kitchen didn't work. This one here, she's calling Cream. The other one is Cookies," he explained as he held up Cream to the camera, his face bright red from embarrassment.

His teammates spent a couple minutes oohing and ahhing over her, and Evan noticed he had a bloody scratch on his forehead. He saw no tissues, so he grabbed his black t-shirt from yesterday and rubbed it on his head to wipe away the blood. Cookies was MIA. He'd have to find him and secure them both either in the kitchen or in his room.

"I hope you were recording this meeting, Mary Ann; it could go viral!" Evan laughed.

Before the meeting ended, each person at Berlin Creative Marketing Agency was assigned their weekly deliverables by Mary Ann. Next, after trying to corral the kittens back in the kitchen, Evan began to do some research on WAFN Industries. He and Mary Ann would give a virtual pitch to them early the following week. He would design the slide deck and creative concepts, while Mary Ann provided him with bullet points and ideas and would deliver the presentation. He'd be on-hand for technical questions about the website back-end, form functionality, sponsored ad content, etc…

It was always fun for Evan to work on a new pitch. His day-to-day work was maintaining websites and posting and scheduling social media and blog content. He wasn't a great writer, and he got most of the written content from their on-staff writer, Kerry. Then, Evan would design the related graphics or videos or animated GIFs, or sometimes take some photos to illustrate the concepts for the digital marketing efforts.

He searched on Google and found that the WAFN Industries corporate website was kind of basic. He viewed the site source code. It was a WordPress template. He had gotten to the website from the organic search, and it didn't look like they were doing any brand defense ad words for their own company name. Evan went to the *About the Company* page and saw there were five executives listed with names, photos, and short bios. The photos were all top rate with great lighting and crisp resolution. This was probably the best page of the website. The rest was a bit boring.

The site had links to a few dozen community news websites like the one they'd be designing for the Eastern Shore. It was a little odd to Evan that they didn't use the same agency and a consistent template for each community and change up the details for each town. It would have been much cheaper and easier for them to manage with a template. But who was he to complain? Mary Ann made it sound like they had this lucrative job in the bag if their pitch went well.

Next, he checked out their social media pages on LinkedIn, Facebook, Instagram, TikTok, and Twitter. They were all underwhelming as far as content went. But he guessed they weren't trying to publicize their main company, just the local news sites.

The weird part was the social media accounts had thousands of followers. It didn't seem possible to have that many legitimate followers in the rural counties that were being targeted. Evan looked through the followers and they seemed like real people—not obviously fake like those sketchy sex-cam or political spam accounts.

Evan clicked back to the list of their other news sites. He clicked on the *Southside Virginia* link. This was interesting. A lot of political articles: *Democrats are on their way out. Another local COVID vaccine-related death suspected. Baby killers at the local women's clinic. Gun auction next weekend. Victory Day Parade in Russia.*

"Okaaay. This is creepy," said Evan to himself. How could anyone call stories about Russia local news? He clicked on one of the stories and read it. It was hard to read it because it was filled with annoying pop-up ads. As he finally read some stories, he realized they were poorly written with grammatical errors and typos all throughout. It was redundant and seemed like it was SEOd [search engine optimized] to death. *What kinds of keywords were they going for here?* Evan wondered. There were dozens of comments on each article, too, and they seemed a little too positive. Fishy, for sure.

He rolled his shoulders, stood up, sang along to some blink-182 songs, and did 20 jumping jacks to get the juices flowing. Then, he sat down again and read the daily Arnold Schwarzenegger *Pump Club* email. He'd just subscribed to it recently, and it was more interesting than he had anticipated. It had various health related tips—nutrition and workouts.

He'd gotten out of the habit of doing the daily Wordle, but he was now obsessed with the newer Connections game from the *New York Times*. Everyone in his family did it and would text around if they got it, and if so, how many mistakes they had. His quest was not to just get the solution; he wanted to solve it with zero errors.

He continued to look at the other community news websites and found more of the same. Some were poorly designed. Others looked pretty slick. He filled out his research benchmarking spreadsheet with the various links and notes about content and branding.

He'd work on this on and off for two more days and then touch base with Mary Ann. He shared the work-in-progress document with her and then signed off for the day. He had about 30 minutes until his appointment to view a short-term apartment rental at 3 p.m. and was taking off work a couple hours early and then would come back home for dinner with his mom.

After lunch, he'd brought the kittens into his room—along with their food, water, and litter box—to keep an eye on them. He glanced over at them, and they were curled up in a little ball together on his bed in a spot of sunlight from the window.

He smiled, grabbed his phone, and took a few photos. They looked so cute. He opened up his text messages and clicked on Ellie's name and let out a big sigh. Then he texted the photos to his mom. He had been able to keep remarkably busy up until that moment, but his mind started racing. Did he overreact? Why was he looking for an apartment only one day after the breakup? He needed to slow down and try to better plan out his next steps. He was a spontaneous guy, but he had to think rationally.

As Evan's brain was in overdrive, his music playlist started streaming Aerosmith's *Moving Out*. Apropos. Yes. He knew that word and how to use it. *Stop questioning his intellect!* he thought. *Who do you people in my head think you are, anyway?* Evan would classify his internal dialog as *intellectually stimulating*.

His phone alarm beeped. It was time to walk to the bar to get his car for his appointment. As he reached the apartment complex, which was about five miles away from his mom's house, his phone started to ring through the car stereo. It was Brandon, so he answered it. He rarely answered the phone unless it was his mom or brother. His friends always texted and never called, which was how Evan preferred it.

"Hey. Mom told me what happened with Ellie," said Brandon, completely skipping greetings and going right to the purpose of the call. His modus operandi. Yes, Evan knew what that meant, too. *You didn't have to be a Rhodes Scholar to effectively utilize colloquial cliches. Come on brain, keep up!*

"I'm meeting about a short-term apartment lease in eight minutes, dude. It's not a good time. I'm in the car now," said Evan.

"I'm busy for the next few nights, but let's meet on Thursday night for dinner at Uncle Jack's bar and you can tell me all about it," said Brandon.

"Okay. Okay. By then maybe I'll be more inclined to talk about it. See you there, Bro Bra. Later. I gotta go."

Evan called his brother Bro Bra, short for Brother Brandon. He had no idea when it started, but it had stuck. And Brandon hated it, but he tolerated it. Only Evan could call him that, though.

Lately, he'd been changing it up a bit to be more current, saying "Bruh Bra." He'd gotten him a shirt from the Boardwalk last year that said, "Bruh, Did You Even Read The Directions?" Brandon was a typical first-born, Type-A personality, always the over-achiever, doing things the *right way*.

Brandon always claimed that Evan was spoiled by his parents, as the baby of the family.

Evan didn't believe that, though. He always felt like he had been smothered and sheltered up until his dad died, and then his mom started working full-time. At that point, both brothers had to become independent almost immediately. It had been a harsh shock.

Evan pulled up to the apartment complex with three minutes to spare. He should have cancelled the appointment, but he was too lazy to call them and do it. He needed time to think about his next steps. Working virtually, he could literally move anywhere. Why should he keep living in the town where he grew up?

CHAPTER 5
Ray

As far as today went, it was pretty much a status quo day at the virtual office. Ray spent most of her time trolling the Dark Web to make sure none of her top clients were involved in the latest telecom ransomware data breach. This was all billable time, so her boss would be pleased.

She made a sandwich for lunch, and her plate and apple core were still sitting on her desk. She stretched and knew it was almost 3 p.m. and it was time for Charlie's mid-afternoon walk. This was what Ray considered the short walk. Charlie got to go on three longer walks (morning, lunch, and evening). This would be the *Let's go around the corner to the doggie poop grassy area* walk.

As Ray rinsed off her plate in the kitchen, she glanced out the window over the sink and noticed a woman walking down the dockside pathway with a brown dog. She knew all the neighborhood dogs, as did Charlie. Charlie was on the sofa, looking out the family room window, and started barking excitedly. Ray couldn't hide now. The woman was less than 10 feet away and looking directly into the family room window at Charlie. Her dog was barking now, too. *Great.* This was undoubtedly going to spark the attention of her older, long-time neighbor Andrea who lived right next door and was not a fan of Charlie's barking. Andrea frequently called him "Chatty Charlie."

Ray dried her hands off and walked over to the window, pulled back Charlie, and waved, "Hello! Sorry about that. He's not used to seeing many dogs walking back along here."

"Hi! I'm just moving in next door," the woman said excitedly. She carried a backpack and a grocery tote bag. "I hope they'll become friends! Ruby here is super friendly," she said, giving the big brown labrador retriever a pat on the head. "I'm going to drop off my stuff and get situated but I hope we can have a proper greeting soon?"

She disappeared up the steps of the house to Ray's right. Each townhouse had a few stairs leading up to a small wooden front porch. The front door went straight into the family room and the kitchen was next to it. All of these beach houses had the same layout. There was a second-floor balcony over the front porch to look out onto the bay. The sunset water view was what made this particular complex so desirable.

The beach house she was going into was a rental property... or at least it had been. Ray had seen an older couple visit a few times over the two years she'd been living there but they only came for a few days here or there, and she'd only met them one time. That was during the worst part of the pandemic, and they'd all been in masks, so she didn't get a good look at them. They had only waved a quick greeting in passing.

Ray stopped by the downstairs bathroom and then grabbed Charlie's leash and walked out the door, hoping to avoid running into her new neighbor. She only had 15 minutes until her next virtual meeting. Just as she turned the corner from her front steps, her new neighbor bounded out of the door with her dog with a great big, "Howdy, neighbor! I'm Olivia, and this is Ruby. It's great to officially meet you!"

Ray put on her friendly face, which she hardly had to use all winter since the summer resort town was practically deserted since last fall.

"Hi! Welcome to Seagull Street. I'm Ray, and this is Charlie," she said with a fake smile plastered on her face, patting Charlie on the back, then pulling his head back to try to get him to stop sniffing Ruby's butt.

"I'm taking Charlie for a quick potty break over to the doggie area around the corner." Ray paused and took in Olivia's disheveled appearance and hesitated before adding, "Do you want me to show you where it is?"

"That would be great," said Olivia, who also had a huge smile on her face that actually seemed authentic. "Oh. Excuse my clothes! I was splashed with muddy water by a passing truck, and then I spilled my iced coffee. What a huge mess!"

They started walking down the path. Olivia was taller than Ray and was quite pretty. She had a cheerleader vibe going on with a short white—well, splattered—tennis skirt and a tight purple Under Armour t-shirt. She had wavy light brown or dirty blonde hair that seemed like it was freshly trimmed and maybe highlighted. She looked fit, though she was not supermodel skinny.

As they walked down the wooden dock, Olivia said, "My parents own this beach house and were renting it out for about five years. I've never even been here before, which is such a shame. Now that I see it, I can't believe it's been sitting almost empty during the pandemic. I'm a teacher so I was teaching remotely until this past year. But the real reason I haven't been here is that my husband— well, my ex-husband now—doesn't like the beach at all."

"Sorry about that, or else congratulations on your newfound freedom?" Ray responded. "I've been living here for about two years."

"Great! A local!" Olivia said, choosing not to elaborate on her divorce. "I need to get the deets on all of the gossip so I can fit in!"

"Well, my dad's parents originally owned this place, and they bought it long before I was born. I've been coming here my entire life," said Ray. "I work virtually, so I decided to move down here permanently since it was sitting empty. I really love it for like nine months out of the season, but the summer is crazy crowded. I'm not much of a people person. This year, I'm sure it will be way more crowded, post-COVID. So, I'll probably hide out here all summer long."

"Oh, you seem perfectly friendly to me," said Olivia with a hearty laugh. "Now that I'm here and we're both living alone, and we both have dogs, hopefully we can become friends!" She paused for an instant, her smile momentarily turning down. "Sorry. I know I come on strong. My ex-husband always thought I pushed myself on people. But I can't help it." She smiled and gave a short giggle. "I *am* a people person!"

As the dogs sniffed around the grass, Ray said, "Honestly, it has been a little lonely around here. During all of the pandemic restrictions, I basically hermitted myself away. My parents moved to NYC to look after my maternal grandparents. My only companion has been Andrea, who lives by herself on the other side of me. She's older, and I *try* to look out for her. But I don't always do a good job of it."

Olivia nodded and smiled. She looked out onto the water of the bay in the distance. "So this is, like, the bay, and the ocean is that way? How far is it to walk to the beach?"

"It's about three blocks away. Depending on the traffic lights, between a five to 10-minute walk." Ray considered saying that she took Charlie over to the beach most mornings, but she wanted to keep that private time, well, private.

"I need to learn more about the history of Ocean City this summer. When I was a kid, we came here most summers and stayed in various hotels. But all I ever really thought about was splashing around in the ocean, playing mini golf, and obviously going to the Boardwalk and eating things like Thrasher's fries and Dumser's ice cream—my favs." When Ray nodded and didn't respond, Olivia continued, "I'll be teaching third grade in the fall at the local elementary school, and I'd like to include some local history lessons."

"As much time as I've spent here, I never actually studied the full history; except that the inlet was created by a hurricane long ago, in 1933 I think it was," said Ray. "Over the years, I've taken some boat tours where they talk about the history, so maybe you should do one of those? They take off from around the M.R. Ducks bar, bayside, where Route 50 comes onto the island."

"'Em Are Ducks.' Yes! I definitely know that place! My parents have bought so many t-shirts from there over the years!" Olivia held up her phone and tapped a few icons. "Speaking of ducks… are you into birds?" Olivia asked, changing the subject. "Well, bird watching. Or bird listening, really," she clarified.

"Well, I like birds, I guess," Ray said. "But I'm not exactly what you'd call an avid bird watcher, if that's what you mean."

"Honestly, I can hardly believe *I'm* a bird watcher now! So dorky, right? But I just got into it recently over the pandemic with my family. There's a bird app where you can have it listen to bird sounds and it tells you what they are. Anyway, it looks like these two cuties right over there, they're called Laughing Gulls," Olivia said, tapping away on her phone.

"Really? That's interesting. I guess I normally lump all these beachy birds into the generic 'seagull' category," said Ray, turning to take a closer look at the two familiar birds.

"These two are super friendly! They must think we have food," said Olivia. "They're not even bothered a bit by the dogs!" She snapped a few photos of them. "And look! That little guy there is missing a foot! Poor thing. And the other one has a huge growth on its beak. You know, I read that seagulls can live more than 20 years. Can you believe that?"

Ray looked at her watch and realized she needed to get ready for her next meeting. "Oh, shoot. I need to run back and get ready for a Zoom meeting in a few minutes. Look, it was great meeting you, Olivia and Ruby. Welcome to the neighborhood, and I'm sure we'll be running into each other soon!"

As Ray quickly walked away, she looked back at the two seagulls and shook her head, trying to clear her mind and refocus on reality. Ray was a scientist and did not believe in fanciful things like signs from the afterlife, but these two seagulls truly mystified her. They were always around. At first, she didn't really notice them—they blended in with the rest of the beach life routine. The first day she moved into the beach house, two seagulls were sitting on the front porch as if to welcome her. She didn't really think much of it at the time, only in hindsight did she recall that first encounter.

As if waiting for her, when she came back out to walk Charlie later that first day, the seagulls seemed to be flapping their wings directly at her. She didn't have any food on her— no fries in sight, and it was a somewhat startling encounter. Over time, she noticed these exact two birds were always hanging around. One with a missing foot, and one with a growth on its beak. At the beach house, on the beach. They were watching her very closely, it appeared.

As Ray turned to walk up her front stairs, she looked over at Olivia, who was tapping on her phone as Ruby sniffed around. Ray was friendly with a bunch of people online, but nobody was local. Having a friend had its pros and cons; especially one that lived right next door. Once, or *if* she decided to become friends with Olivia, every movement in and out of the house would be a potential conversation. Olivia looked like she could use a friend right about now, too.

Enough about that for now, Ray thought. She had to turn her thoughts to election integrity and the upcoming webinar she would be working on for local government election officials, not spooky seagulls or fresh friends.

CHAPTER 6
Olivia

"That went well, didn't it, Ruby?" At least Olivia thought that meeting her first new neighbor was a triumph. Olivia talked to herself all the time—well, to Ruby. Ruby was still happily sniffing around the grassy area, which was not huge, but it was a relief to have somewhere close by to walk the dog. "I think we're going to like it here," Olivia said.

In Washington, D.C., it was always crowded with grassy areas few and far in between. She had lived in Dupont Circle when she was married and normally took Ruby to a cute little neighborhood park called Mitchell Park. If she was still living there, the flowers would probably be in peak bloom. She opened the photos app on her phone and checked out the memories…

"Yep," she reminisced. "Look at those gorgeous azaleas and tulips from two years ago. I know, Ruby! I need to get some flowers and pots for my front steps!"

Olivia was easily distracted—she always had been—and the ability to use her phone at any moment made it so much worse. If she had a thought or question, she could immediately find out the answer. But was that a blessing or a curse?

Back to the matter at hand. Would she and Ray become friends? She thought that Ray seemed friendly but reserved. She gave friendship a 50-50 probability. Ray looked a few years older than Olivia and appeared to be athletic. You could really see her well-defined leg and arm muscles. She was wearing no makeup, or very little. So she was low-maintenance—it wasn't a crime. They probably wouldn't be going clubbing together. But Olivia was probably too old for that anymore, anyway.

Olivia did a 360 turn to take it all in. This was her new home! The complex was really nice. It was older, but the owners were keeping it up pretty well. The wood decks needed a good power washing, but it was so picturesque. The docks with boats on the bay. Boaters out in the shallow bay water, which was literally at her front doorstep. She could see fish and crabs down there! Maybe she should get a crab pot? A fishing rod? A boat? She could catch her dinner! Wait a minute, didn't her mom say there was a paddleboard and a kayak under the front porch storage area? *Oh goodie*, Olivia thought. *This was going to be so much fun living at the beach!*

So far, the only negative thing she noticed was the parking lot was not right near the entry to the house. She would probably need to get one of those rolling carts so many people around here had to lug their stuff to the beach. She could use it for groceries, too. First, she would have to search the house to see what was in there! Her parents had been renting it out, but there was a storage closet behind the kitchen with a lock that had all of their personal items. Her mom had given her that key before she left this morning.

She tugged at Ruby, and they walked down the dock further toward the bay. Olivia opened the map app on her phone to check out the layout of the land. Seagull Street was one of the wider parts of the island. At most streets, it was only a few blocks wide. The lower street numbers were all the way at the southern part of the island. There were actually a handful of streets before 1st Street. There were two roads that ran north and south on the island below 33rd Street: Philadelphia Avenue, which was closer to the bay, and Baltimore Avenue, which was closer to the ocean. Above 33rd Street, they combined into one main street called Coastal Highway, also known as Philadelphia Avenue.

"O.M.G. Look at that, Ruby!" A young girl was paddleboarding out into the bay with a small dog on her board. It looked like a chihuahua. "Now that's something you don't see every day!" Olivia took out her camera and snapped a quick photo. "Soon that could be us!"

All of her family and friends would be looking for her Instagram story posts. As a teacher, she had to be careful what she posted on social media. She couldn't post any crazy photos of herself, so she kept it pretty tame. Even though most of her accounts were set to private mode, you could never be too careful. She'd learned her lesson the hard way.

Olivia remembered she needed to text her parents that she had arrived safely. It had taken much longer than anticipated because she decided to take a short detour to the Blackwater National Wildlife Refuge. She'd driven by it so many times when she was younger and always thought about stopping. Nothing was stopping her from doing what she wanted now!

Earlier that day, at the wildlife refuge, Olivia had driven slowly around the reserve looking and listening for birds. She hadn't been able to believe her eyes when she saw two bald eagles! She tried to zoom in with her phone to take a video, but it ended up being so blurry.

She turned on her Merlin bird app to try to identify birds on and off during the drive, holding her phone out of the car window. The app would listen to bird sounds, and you could also use a photo to identify what kind they were. Last year, her entire family had become obsessed with the bird app, and each of them were on a mission to have the most bird sightings in their "Life List," where the identified birds were archived in the app. Olivia had identified more than 100 birds.

At the refuge, her app identified a bunch of new birds: Caspian Tern, Least Tern, Virginia Rail, Willet, Marsh Wren, and Seaside Sparrow. She already had a Great Blue Heron and Cormorant, among other common birds in Maryland like the Red-Winged Blackbird, Eastern Kingbird, Blue Jay, Indigo Bunting, Common Yellowthroat, and Chipping Sparrow. She had taken a screenshot of the new birds and sent them to her family's group text message list.

When she left the refuge, she saw the Harriet Tubman Underground Railroad National Historical Park was right in front of her and pulled in to take a look. Since she had Ruby with her, she was only able to do a quick walk around the exhibits outside of the museum, but it was still very cool. She'd have to go back to see the museum exhibits another time.

As Olivia walked back to her place, she looked more closely at her neighbors' front porches, trying to get decorating ideas. She noticed there was someone walking into the house two doors down on the other side of Ray. An older woman who looked like she'd just gotten back from a trip to the grocery store. *That must be Andrea.* She would go and meet her later.

Unfortunately, the closest full-size grocery store was not on Fenwick Island—it was over on the mainland in West Ocean City. There was a grocery store further north in Ocean City, but it was twice as far away. Now that traffic wasn't so bad, it would be easy to run to the store, but during the summer, she'd have to plan more carefully and take the traffic patterns into consideration. It wasn't like at home where she could easily stop into Safeway every day if she wanted.

She took a quick selfie of her and Ruby with the bay in the background.

Olivia to Mom and Dad (with picture):
Made it downy oshun, hon! LOL

Next, she had to carry in all of her stuff. But first, she'd take some time to explore the house. When Olivia walked into her place, she couldn't help but smile. Her parents had renovated it right after they bought it, and it was sparkling. Her mom had asked the cleaner to get it ready for her that morning. There was even a vase with flowers on the counter! Her mom was always so extra. But it made Olivia feel loved.

The kitchen was all white cabinetry and countertop with light gray walls. It was on the small side, but all of the appliances had been updated to stainless steel. In the rental market, high end was necessary to bring in the big bucks. The floors were dark gray wood laminate. The kitchen table was too big for the space, trying to fit eight chairs, with four stools along the kitchen island.

The main sofa was a sleeper and looked like the perfect cozy place to take a nap after a long day at the beach. The three bedrooms upstairs were all good sized with beds to sleep 10, so 12 total with two and a half bathrooms. The primary bathroom had a jacuzzi tub crammed into it. Olivia had noticed all of the home television shows called it a "primary" bedroom now instead of the outdated "master" bedroom. It made sense.

From the outside, you would never know how nice the house was inside. She thought she'd try to rearrange one of the bedrooms to fit her desk and elliptical into it. She would move more of her things to the beach house later on. Most of her personal stuff was in a storage unit in D.C. that she shared with her ex. Obviously, she needed to get her own stuff out of there for safety purposes. After the initial separation, they had agreed that they would continue to share the storage unit since it was a mishmash of all their things. Neither one of them wanted to sort it out. For now, she was thrilled this place was fully furnished and move-in ready.

Olivia sat in the stuffed recliner chair in the family room and realized she'd need to find a place for Ruby's dog beds. She had one for the living room and one for the bedroom. She also had Ruby's bin of dog toys, and her water and food bowl. That would be the first box to bring in right away.

Her mom texted back a smiley face with sunglasses. She would be at work and probably too busy to talk until later tonight. Olivia sent a quick pic of the flowers.

Olivia to Mom (with picture):
Thank you!! ILUSM!!

Olivia decided to relax for a bit after the whirlwind of getting to this point. She closed her eyes for a quick cat nap. She fell asleep thinking about the three restaurants she'd emailed the night before, inquiring about summer job openings.

CHAPTER 7
Evan

The apartment tour was depressing. It was so small. Evan did not want to have to figure this out right now, but Ellie was ignoring him. More than half of the stuff in the apartment was his. His bed. His sofa. His TV. She should be the one moving out. What was she planning? She wouldn't respond to any of his texts. He didn't want to stay at his mom's house any longer than necessary, even with the cute kittens as an incentive.

His mom had a boyfriend, and Evan suspected that Vernon stayed over frequently. But this was not a conversation he wanted to have with his mom. They'd been together for a few years now, and Evan liked the guy, but he honestly didn't know him very well yet. The most time they'd spent together was at church—where his mom and Vernon had initially met each other—and during that time, they were sitting in the pew watching the sermon. Not exactly a great way to get to know somebody.

At the church pancake breakfasts, Evan was always put to work as a server while his mom was in charge of making the pancakes. Vernon would try to make small talk with Evan, but it always seemed forced. Evan knew he needed to make more of an effort to socialize with Vernon. But doing it over breakfast in his boxer shorts was not an appealing thought. So awkward!

Ever since Evan's dad died, his mom hadn't dated until she met Vernon. At least Evan wasn't aware of any relationships, but he'd been a kid so he may not have noticed. Vernon was about five years older than his mom, who was 55. He had one daughter, Diane, who was much older than Evan. She lived in Annapolis with her family and would normally visit a couple times each summer. Even when she did visit, Evan rarely saw her. He'd only met her two times, and both times were at his Uncle Jack's bar for the annual family crab feast.

Every September for Jack's birthday, which happened to be the same week as Evan's mom's birthday, he'd close down the bar for the day and they'd have an epic crab feast for family, friends, and workers at the bar to celebrate the end of the summer season.

As any Marylander knows, crab feasts are a big part of the summer ritual. Nothing's better than a steaming pile of blue crabs with some cold beer, corn on the cob, and maybe some hot dogs and burgers on the grill for those who were too impatient to sit and leisurely pick their crabs.

Jack's crab feasts were legendary, and if you were lucky enough to get an invitation, you would undoubtedly work your entire schedule around the event. Evan's relatives would come in from out of town, employees would have their families visit, and aside from Christmas, it was Evan's favorite day of the year.

Jack would take people out on his boat at sunrise for fishing. Evan would take the surfers of the group out to catch some waves. Brandon would take the kids to the Jolly Rogers Water Park in the morning. And Evan's mom would go on a trip to the outlets with the shoppers of the group.

This year, the following weekend after the crab feast was the inaugural Oceans Calling music festival. That meant some of their regular crew were going to stay for the week after the crab feast and then attend the concert. The festival was supposed to have kicked off the previous year, in 2022, but it had been canceled at the last minute due to the severe weather caused by Hurricane Ian.

Evan had three-day general admission tickets this year and was super pumped for the event, which would have acts going on at three stages. Organizers were planning to fence off the entire downtown area at the inlet parking lot and the end of the Boardwalk to be part of the festival grounds. The buzz around the event was sky high, and it was already sold out.

Evan was most looking forward to seeing O.A.R., Third Eye Blind, Gin Blossoms, The Lumineers, Weezer, and The Wallflowers. Uncle Jack was most excited to see the celebrity chef Robert Irvine. Along with the music, there would be tons of local food vendors and cooking demos emceed by actor Jason Biggs. *They'd probably be making pie,* Evan laughed to himself.

Back to the task at hand, Evan looked up Vernon on Facebook. They were not connected as friends, and Vernon rarely posted, but when he did, it was public for all to see. His last post had a photo of him with Evan's mom and a few other people in Annapolis on a sailboat, from two weeks ago. Vernon had not tagged his mom, or else Evan would have seen it.

"Ok. I was not expecting to see that," whispered Evan as he opened the photo to take a closer look. Actually, now that he looked at the caption, he recalled his mom texting she was going to Annapolis for Vernon's daughter Diane's 40th birthday party.

They were on that boat that was made famous from the movie *Wedding Crashers*. From the photo caption, it was called the Schooner Woodwind and was 74-feet long. Crabcakes. Football. It's just a Maryland thing. That movie was a classic local favorite.

Evan turned his focus to Ellie and spent some time researching this old boyfriend she had, and found that he still lived in Virginia Beach, Ellie's hometown. Maybe she would move back there. Her family still lived there—and maybe Evan could stay in the apartment?

He decided he would go over to the apartment. She wouldn't be there at this time—she had a spin class. He still had his key. He was paying his share of the rent. Nothing weird about going to your own apartment, right? He slipped on his flip-flops and sprinted out to his car to make the short drive.

Once inside the apartment, he dug his big suitcase out of their cluttered storage closet and started throwing in more of his clothes and shoes. The apartment looked the same as it always had. But he felt weird to be in there.

He grabbed a tote bag from the hanging hooks on the back of the bathroom door and tossed in some toiletries from the vanity. He stopped by the kitchen and grabbed his favorite coffee blend and YETI mug. He grabbed the Wüsthof knife set, the expensive set his Uncle Jack had given him when he got a new one for himself. Did he need this in his mom's house? No. But it was the principle of the matter. It was his, no debate. He didn't want Ellie using his knives to cut her expensive organic avocados.

Next, he went to the small cabinet under the coffee table. *His* prized collection of board games. He grabbed some classic staples and his current favorites, as many would fit into one bag—Trivial Pursuit, Settlers of Catan, Wits & Wagers, One Night Werewolf, Codenames, Exploding Kittens, Sushi Go! A couple decks of cards and his fancy case of poker chips that were his dad's. *Enough games for now*, he thought. Next, his records and CDs.

"I'll just take the most valuable ones," he said to himself as he carefully flipped through them.

He piled his stuff up on the kitchen table and scribbled a quick note for Ellie. *Got some of my stuff. We need to talk about next steps with the apartment. Please text me back. - EAM.*

He tried to collect everything, so he'd only have to make one trip down to the car, but one of the tote bags slipped and tumbled to the ground. Somehow—and he didn't know how this could have happened—but a knife slid out of the knife block and punctured the bag of coffee. Coffee grounds spilled all over the floor.

"F.M.L." Evan exclaimed, momentarily wondering why he was saying texting acronyms out loud. He put all his stuff back up on the counter, got a plastic container, and poured the remaining part of the coffee grounds into it. Then he swept up the remains on the floor. The smell of coffee was overpowering. Annoyed with himself, he grabbed the bag of perfectly ripe avocados and threw them into his bag too, mumbling to himself about his bad luck as he finally left and slammed the door shut behind him.

Evan was driving back to his mom's house and received a text from his surfer friend, D'andre: "Surfing at Hammerheads. Waves look great! U in?"

It didn't take much convincing. Ellie couldn't get annoyed with him, so he headed into Ocean City. Given his bad luck today, he'd probably get bitten by a shark.

Remember (Walking In The Sand) by Aerosmith was playing from his playlist. He had his surfboard strapped to the top of his car, a gray Subaru Forester. It was his mom's old car, but it wasn't *that* old. It was perfect for carting around his camera gear, his fishing gear, and his surfing gear, depending on where he was headed. He always had the surfboard on top. His wetsuit was always in the back, along with a cooler.

The way the surfing works during the summer in Ocean City is that it alternates two blocks each day, so vacationers aren't inconvenienced for more than one day at a time "in season," but that didn't start until Memorial Day. Also, you could surf anywhere you wanted before 10 a.m. and after 5:30 p.m. in the summer.

Today, Evan was heading to 10th Street. The way most people remembered where to go was not the street numbers but the main Boardwalk attraction at that block. In the summer, after surfing, he would head over to Hammerheads for happy hour. The popular restaurant/bar had recently expanded operations to take over the space next door.

It was a Monday in April, so not much on the Boardwalk would be open. He'd probably head to the Green Turtle, which was open year-round and was a hot spot for locals.

This would be Evan's first outing in many years when he didn't have a steady girlfriend. As he parked along the mostly empty roadway, he thought about what he would tell his surfing buddies about breaking up with Ellie. There was not much talking during surfing, so he'd have plenty of time to figure it out.

As he ran into the water with his board, he realized he was putting on a bit of a show for the minimal beachgoers. Part of the rush was having a crowd watching you surf! Evan paddled out to his friends who sat on their boards waiting for the right wave. They'd spend more time sitting on their boards than actually surfing, but that's the way it was in Maryland. The waves were okay for surfing, but small by West Coast standards. Evan had never been surfing in California or Hawaii, but it was a dream to do so at some point.

After about an hour of mediocre waves, they packed things up. When his friends asked him if he was heading home to have dinner with Ellie, he just deflected the question and said he'd join them at the Green Turtle.

There was a bit of a crowd at the restaurant. People turned to look when his crew entered—a group of young, fit, good-looking guys. Evan was used to getting attention. He was tall and muscular. Not bad looking. Not model handsome, but definitely above average. He considered his vibe to be more of a fun Chris Pratt than a sexy Chris Hemsworth.

He normally blocked out all attention from girls but now, he was single again. He would have to think about his next steps. Should he wait a few months to try to avoid a rebound relationship? Should he make a Bumble or Tinder profile? This was depressing to think about.

Many of his buddies were using artificial intelligence to help make their dating profiles, a scary thought to Evan. Hell, people used AI to produce everything nowadays—their text messages, emails, social posts. He wondered how it would eventually affect the content creation where he worked. And those fake AI-generated photos seemed so real. You really couldn't take anything at face value anymore.

Despite his boyish good looks, Evan was not a player. He was not great at dating, or flirting, or picking the right girl it seemed. Sure, he was a fairly good conversationalist at the beginning of a relationship. After the initial exchange of pertinent information, he was content to just sit in silence, which most women hated. He was a-ok with long silences and didn't try to fill them with random chit chat. He asked questions, but only if he really wanted to know the answer. Did that make him awkward? Maybe so.

He zoned out as he thought about how a few of his friends were recently engaged. At 25, he felt too young to be married, or even engaged. But he didn't want to be one of those old dads who couldn't even play a simple game of catch with his kids. He didn't understand why those old geezers in Hollywood were having kids up into their 70s or 80s. Sure they had plenty of money, but they were old enough to be great-grandparents!

After he ordered some food at the bar, a girl came up to him and patted him on the arm, interrupting his internal dialog. "Hi. Don't I know you? You're Evan, right? We were in high school together. I'm Casey. We're friends on Instagram."

"Oh. Yeah. Hi, Casey!" Evan said as he reached out to give her a friendly hug. "I hardly ever go on Instagram unless it's for work. I do marketing for local businesses. But, of course, I remember you!"

"Yeah. Your company just redesigned the website for my family's pizza restaurant," she said. "I was in the photo with my granddad, parents, and sister on the *About* web page. But you probably didn't connect it all. You and your boss met with my dad a couple times at the restaurant."

"Ooooh. Yeah. Sorry. I did not connect that at all from your last name or the photo. The Eastern Shore once again proves that it's a small world," Evan replied.

"Antonio's Pizzeria. Antonio is my granddad's name. Our place is always overshadowed and confused with Tony's Pizza on the Boardwalk," she shrugged. "Hopefully, your awesome website and social media plan will help clear that up! Our place isn't open tonight, and I'm able to have a guilt-free night out at the competition." Casey laughed, and it looked like she was blushing.

They both smiled at each other and took a long sip of their drinks. Maybe fate decided that Evan was ready to get back into the dating market after all.

CHAPTER 8
Ray

Ray just wrapped up her 8 a.m. meeting with her election security team and looked outside. The rain had stopped, at least momentarily, and she thought she'd be able to get in a quick walk with Charlie over to the beach.

She checked the radar on her weather app. She was obsessed with her weather app, much more so since moving to the beach. She actually had a few weather apps—the default Apple weather app, The Weather Channel, and Weather Underground. She liked to compare the forecasts to see which was closest to being accurate. Nerdy? Maybe, but Ray didn't care. She liked to be prepared. And the weather was frequently the first topic of discussion in any virtual meeting.

At her parent's house north of Baltimore, where she grew up, they had one of those weather stations where it would measure the wind and rain outside and transmit it to the base inside. Ray loved to look and see the humidity and the amount of rain they had each day or week or month. Each morning, she'd closely examine it before going to catch the bus. She always had her little *Chuck E. Cheese* umbrella in her backpack, just in case. The weather in Maryland was very unpredictable, to say the least. Her parents used to ask her for the weather forecast each morning and had encouraged her to study meteorology at college.

One of Ray's favorite things to do during storms was to go out on her second-floor balcony and watch the lightning out over the horizon. Ocean City was so flat that at times you could see multiple strikes at once. Deep down in the recesses of her mind, she had a persistent worry about flooding and hurricanes and tsunamis and whatever other potential natural disasters could hit the area. Would Ocean City be underwater in 10 or 20 years? Her complex was built up off of the ground about one foot on wooden stakes. Underneath the house was a disgustingly gross storage area. City officials had recently raised the height requirements for new construction.

Charlie was pacing around the house looking very anxious since he hadn't gotten his early morning walk due to the torrential downpour. They'd run outside for a super quick potty break first thing this morning. Charlie didn't mind the rain so much, but Ray hadn't wanted to get drenched before work. She had her big webinar presentation at noon, and they wouldn't get a chance for another walk until after work.

Charlie's walks were as much for Ray's mental and physical health as they were for exercising Charlie. Ray felt like she would hardly leave her house if she didn't have the excuse to take Charlie out. She had an indoor exercise regimen, but the musty beach house smell seemed to linger no matter how long she aired it out or used air purifiers and air fresheners. Getting out into the fresh air was a priority for Ray and for the dog, even if it meant she had to interact with people.

Ray was an introvert. Whenever she took the Myers–Briggs Type Indicator (MBTI) test, which she'd done a handful of times for school and work, she was as close to an introvert as you could get on the scale.

People liked using that personality assessment tool because it was easy to administer, and the results were fairly easy to understand. Ray liked it because it helped her understand how to work with people. She didn't necessarily know everyone else's MBTI, but sometimes, she would think about their behavior and try to guess their personality type. Knowing that everyone would perceive situations differently, she could pivot her behavior accordingly. She wouldn't deal with every single person the same way and expect to always get the same kind of outcome.

In the MBTI, there are sixteen different personality types based on Carl Jung's four psychological functions, which were judging functions (thinking and feeling) and perceiving functions (sensation and intuition). The tool evaluated these eight areas: extraversion (E) / introversion (I), sensing (S) / intuition (N), thinking (T) / feeling (F), and judging (J) / perceiving (P).

Each preference was on a scale, and Ray was only obviously an introvert, the rest of the preferences she was closer to the middle. Ray was an INTJ, which generally meant she was independent, strategic, logical, reserved, and insightful… or a "judgy and intuitive thinking introvert," if you wanted to be literal about it.

Ray also put some stock in birth order playing a role in her personality. As the oldest child, and a girl, she could relate to the phenomenon of "Eldest Daughter Syndrome." At times, she felt like she took on too many adult responsibilities before she was ready for them. She was habitually striving for perfection, even though her parents were not super strict about her grades or behavior. She put the pressure on herself. *If you're going to do something, do it right.*

On top of that, or maybe because of it, she was extremely anxious. She never knew a time when she wasn't worried about something. During the pandemic, her anxious energy changed into various kinds of worries. She was worried about getting COVID and giving COVID to someone else. Those thoughts were obviously warranted, though, especially with her grandparents' fate.

Ray was incredibly careful, following all of the recommended precautions from *reputable* sources—no drinking bleach for her! As a result, she had never gotten COVID, at least she didn't think so. She must have taken a hundred tests over the course of the pandemic. Always negative. She bought one of those gun thermometers. She had a fever one time but had tested negative every day after it for a week. The moment free COVID tests were available via the post-office website, she submitted her online form.

During the pandemic, Ray's anxiety made her self-conscious about being on video for virtual meetings. She felt like her voice sounded weird. Her hair was too short. She had a birthmark on her cheek that was way more obvious on video calls than in person. Everyone in her family had a lot of moles. Her grandmother had had a huge mole on the top of her nose. Ray didn't like going on camera, but her company had a camera-on policy. For the most part, she would hide her self-view video from the attendee grid.

She had never been a fan of wearing a lot of make-up, but she bought some face powder and a ring light. She had her hairbrush and a small mirror on her desk to check her looks before meetings, specifically her teeth. She was typically getting food stuck in her top front tooth. There was a weird indentation there, so she was self-conscious about smiling whenever she was eating out.

As she walked over to the beach with Charlie, Ray started going through her presentation slides in her mind. She didn't think she had a photographic memory, but she could usually visualize things pretty well. She only had to close her eyes and try to imagine the slide. A lot of people would totally wing it, but Ray lived by the mantra of *practice makes perfect*.

She had written out all of her talking points and wouldn't necessarily read them during the webinar, but she had memorized enough of it to be able to act like she was doing it all impromptu. Even some jokes... although it was hard to joke about election integrity.

They were using Zoom for the webinar and had a participant limit of 500. They cut registration at 600 because typically for free webinars, a lot of people were no-shows. If it proved super popular and more than 500 attendees tried to login, they would just have to apologize and send any attendees who were turned away the recorded webinar afterward.

This particular webinar was sold out, and Ray felt excited and nervous. If the webinar went well, it would be a feather in her cap at work, and she'd have some ammunition behind asking for a much-overdue raise. She had given a similar webinar a few times before to smaller audiences, but this was the big time! Election officials from all 50 states would be logging in to watch as part of their official election training for the state and local level primaries. In addition, they'd invited members of the media and academia.

Election integrity was an interesting topic because many Americans believed that "election fraud" was widespread and covered up by officials. But in reality, the American election voting system was secure.

After the 2020 election, losers lamented there were unprecedented instances of voter fraud including noncitizen voting, voter impersonation, and double voting. Many states enacted laws that were supposed to limit ways to *cheat the system* but would effectively reduce turnout and make it harder for Americans to cast their votes via mail and early voting.

Fraud claims were mostly propaganda, and actual evidence of election fraud was never found. In fact, the only thing that was not fake news was that Russia was indeed meddling in the election via social media, email, and text messages. Misinformation or disinformation or fake news— whatever you wanted to call it—was rampant in America and around the world. Social media had its benefits and disadvantages. Obviously, there were hundreds of millions of people using apps and the instantaneous connectivity with people you know and people you don't know was unprecedented. Ray, for one, did not want to reconnect with any of her classmates, from elementary school through college. She did love the ability to get breaking news updates before the news media even reported on them. Part of her job was to know what was happening in the world, so she was online *all the time.*

The hard part for Ray regarding this particular webinar on election integrity was to keep everything impartial and clinical and not let her personal opinions come through. She had to make her commentary quite generic. Also, the current state of the truth is always evolving. The best a person can do is work with the information available.

The webinar was about the facts and making sure election integrity was upheld. Showing officials what to look for and when to alert the authorities. The federal government had an election task force that monitored everything that had to do with elections, and part of what they had to do was promote that local municipalities should report anything out of the ordinary to the proper authorities through the proper avenues.

For the most part, Russian election meddling was centered upon spreading misinformation. Since that was a fact, Ray could talk about it. As an example, Ray would talk about Election Day news that may be pushed out saying the lines at the polls were an hours-long wait, or that the machines were broken. Or beforehand, news stories might say a candidate was a shoo-in to win, so no need to vote.

Fake news stories would appear about candidates on sketchy websites that had literally just popped up right before the election. It was Ray's job to collect all of this election information and compile it into various categories and send it up the line to the election officials. Sometimes scammers would target school districts since that's where most elections take place. Fake emails to local election officials and volunteers would try to create logistical chaos at the election sites.

Leading up to the election, it was a distinct set of threats. Thousands of fake social media accounts and bots would relentlessly diss candidates. Ray knew these election trolls were not all foreign or computer generated, though. Many of the people trolling were American citizens. They would spend hours a day commenting and pushing their various agendas. After the elections, the propaganda would turn to stories about election fraud. It was a never-ending cycle. For Ray, it was a never-ending fight against corruption.

It was so easy to fall for a cyber scam, and during the webinar, Ray would start with the most clichéd example about the infamous Nigerian Prince needing immediate monetary help with the promise of a huge cash reward. She would recount the true story when her mom received a text message that *her daughter* urgently needed help and to wire money ASAP. Her mom called her immediately after receiving the text. When Ray answered, her mom realized she was the target of a scammer and was embarrassed.

Ray had experienced this next example herself. She got a phishing email from an account that seemed to be her boss asking her to buy a gift card to give to a top client. She *almost* fell for it.

Ray looked at her watch and saw it was time to start back home. She took a deep breath and tried to clear her mind and stop mentally practicing her webinar talk track. She turned and slowly walked back onto the Boardwalk from the beach. She saw her new neighbor Olivia and dog Ruby coming toward her and put her head down. It was too late—Olivia waved. No use trying to hide. Ray didn't have time to talk, but she had to be friendly. She'd been trying to avoid her for the past few days. Dealing with new people made her anxious. She wished she didn't have an immediate reaction in her mind telling her to avoid all situations that made her anxious. How could she reprogram it? It was frustrating. Change was hard.

"Good morning!" Ray said and waved as they got closer. Olivia had her AirPods in so maybe this would be a quick fly-by greeting. Ray crossed her fingers behind her back. Olivia reached up to her ears and removed the AirPods and quickened her pace.

CHAPTER 9
Olivia

Olivia loved music. If she didn't think people were nearby, she'd be singing out loud, even though she was not a good singer by any means. She walked along to the beat of her new morning walk playlist. Right now, it was Britney Spears, *Hit Me Baby One More Time*. As she turned the corner to come onto the Boardwalk, she saw Ray and her dog approaching the stairs from the beach. Ray was reaching down to switch Charlie's leash to a shorter one. Perfect timing.

Little did Ray know that Olivia had timed this walk to try to meet up with her. She'd been trying to run into her for the past few days and had failed miserably. Today, she kept looking out the window until she saw Ray leave the house and knew this was her chance.

"Hey, Ray and Charlie!" Olivia waved as she quickened up her pace and took out her earbuds. "So glad that it stopped raining, and it seems to be shaping up to be a beautiful day!"

"The weather here at the beach is always so unpredictable," said Ray as Olivia came down the stairs to the sand and the dogs started sniffing each other.

"Hey, I know this is last minute," said Olivia, jumping right into her main reason for stalking Ray. "But I got a summer waitressing job that starts tomorrow night, and I want to check out the place tonight as a customer to get a feel for it. I don't know anyone else in town. I was wondering if you would like to come with me?"

"Umm. Tonight?" Ray asked, looking down at the dogs trying to buy some time to think of an excuse, Olivia suspected.

With Ray's continued silence, Olivia put her hands together in a praying gesture and gave her the trademark-winning-Olivia smile. "Pretty please. My treat?"

"Ok. Sure," said Ray after another five-second pause. "I mean I have nothing else planned so it would be good to get out of the house. And there is no need to treat me. We can split the bill, ok?"

"Perfect! I'm so excited! It's within walking distance, so let's plan to leave at around 6 p.m.?"

"Ok. Sure. That works. Sorry to run, but I need to get back. I'm presenting a webinar soon and I need to get all set up," said Ray as she tugged on the leash and tried to pull Charlie up the stairs from the beach.

"Oh, that's fun! You'll have to tell me all about it later. Oh, wait," said Olivia. "Let's exchange phone numbers first."

Olivia handed her phone to Ray and asked her to type in her contact info. "Thanks," Olivia said. "I'll text you now, so you have my details."

Ray took her phone back and yanked again on Charlie's leash. "Come on, Charlie. Let's go!" That dog was flat out in the sand and wasn't budging an inch.

Olivia said, "Come on, Charlie! Let's take a walk!"

Charlie dug his nose into the sand, still lying flat out. "Is something wrong with him?" Olivia asked.

"He's stubborn and has refused to leave the beach before, but never like this," Ray said, starting to get embarrassed and worried she'd be late getting set up for her webinar. She kneeled on the beach next to him and rubbed his back, trying to get him motivated to stand up. "Come on, Charlie Bear! Let's go back home and get a treat!"

Olivia estimated that Charlie must weigh at least 75 pounds. He was a huge and solid dog. Way too heavy to pick up and carry all the way back to the beach house. But both of them could probably lift him up the stairs to the Boardwalk, and that was a good start, at least.

"Let's both try to pick him up," Olivia said. "I'll just tie Ruby to this bench."

Ray lifted his front legs and Olivia got his behind. Charlie wiggled and rolled onto his back and they both lost their balance and dropped down to the sand. Ray's hat blew off in a huge gust of wind. Charlie took that chance to break free, running excitedly across the beach, following the floating hat as it skipped along with the wind into the breaking waves.

"Oh my God! Charlie—you come back here right now, you naughty dog!" Ray screamed. Ray started running after him, taking an instant to fling off her flip-flops.

Olivia grabbed Ruby and followed them down to the shoreline, trying to herd Charlie closer to Ray.

An older lady with a cane yelled out as Ray ran past, "If you can't control your dog, you shouldn't bring him to the beach!"

"Thanks for that *awesome* advice, *Karen*!" Olivia spat out as she ran by. Charlie looked like he was having the time of his life. It was funny, but Olivia was so winded *she* was panting and could not get in enough air to laugh. She was out of shape! She hoped Charlie would run out of energy soon and stop these crazy zoomies. Ruby sat there quietly looking at the chaotic scene.

Ray's Orioles hat floated in and out of the crashing waves. Ray was chasing Charlie in circles, literally. Or was Charlie chasing Ray? Who could tell? Olivia tried not to fall as she lunged at Charlie every time he ran by her.

After at least five minutes—probably closer to 10 minutes—a surfer came in on a wave. He rode it up to the beach and grabbed Olivia's hat in one hand and lifted his board up in the other. He quickly took in the scene and tried to help wrangle Charlie, using his surfboard to try to fence him in. Olivia could see Ray's embarrassment level climbing. Her face was flushed, but Olivia was more distracted by the surfer than the dog at this point.

Exasperated after the all-out chase, Ray walked over and took her hat from the surfer and whispered a quick, "Thanks!" Then she stood still for a moment and stared out at the ocean to catch her breath. An instant later, a couple of seagulls flew down and flapped their wings at the still-sprinting Charlie. Almost immediately, Charlie ran over and sat down next to Ray, just like the entire exhausting episode had never happened.

"Boys. So unpredictable!" Olivia laughed.

Ray quickly grabbed the leash. "Thank you both for helping out. That was so embarrassing! He's not normally that crazy, I assure you."

The surfer called out a friendly, "No problemo! My pleasure to assist." Then he ran back into the ocean. He tripped at the drop off but then followed it up with an impressive dive under a huge wave.

Ray, Olivia, and the dogs walked back up to the Boardwalk. Well, Ray was practically jogging.

When Ray reached the beach stairs, she turned back, waved, and shouted, "Thank you, Olivia! I've gotta run to my webinar!"

"See you tonight! I'm gonna stay out a bit longer." She might as well take Ruby for a longer walk, even though she didn't feel like it. She had to live up to her summer 2023 motto of *eat less, exercise more*. (Also, surfers just begged to be watched, right?)

Research said that people with best friends had happier lives with fewer health problems and indeed lived longer—all those inspirational graphics said so on social media. She sent up a quick silent prayer that she and Ray would become friends.

Olivia had a lot of what many people would consider superficial friendships, mostly kept up virtually. People who she'd gone to high school and college with and a few former colleagues. There wasn't a "best friend" and had never been one since high school. Definitely not since she met Luke in college. They had been inseparable. They had some mutual friends, but they were really more his friends than hers. She rarely heard from any of them since the separation. And their former neighbors? Crickets.

Most of her pre-Luke friends from high school were getting married and having babies. Nobody else was already divorced. Olivia had never in a million years pictured herself as a 27-year-old divorcee. It was embarrassing. But she really had no choice.

Olivia blinked a few times as the sun was brightly shining in her eyes. She tried to focus on the crashing waves. High tide. There were five surfers out there. She sat down directly on the sand as Ruby snuggled up next to her, and they peacefully watched them drift on their boards, waiting for the perfect wave.

It was still before noon, and with the earlier rain, there weren't too many people out on the beach. A couple of families with little ones playing in the sand nearby. A man and a boy were fishing down a couple blocks in the rough surf. Olivia picked up a few shells and examined them to check if they were up to her standards to add to her new collection, which she had just started keeping in a huge wineglass on the coffee table.

She stayed on the beach until her stomach started growling, then meandered home. Back at the beach house, she made a simple lunch consisting of a turkey sandwich and some yogurt. She wanted to save calories for drinks and dinner later.

Her stomach rumbled on and off in protest as the afternoon crawled by.

She decided to rewatch *Bridgerton* Season 2 before the new spinoff, *Queen Charlotte: A Bridgerton Story* came out next week. She'd read most of Julia Quinn's novels and was a huge fan of British historical romance.

Speaking of books, Olivia had just seen some news about additional bans on books in schools. Mostly books by and about people of color and LGBTQ+ individuals, including many award-winning classics. As a teacher, book bans were obviously related to her work, and she tried to keep up with the latest bans. She'd seen that some elementary schools were even banning picture books.

The latest article she read said that standard fare like *The Giving Tree* and *Hop on Pop* had been banned in some places. When Olivia read that, she thought to herself, *so they'd ban* Hop on Pop *for promoting violence but not ban semi-automatic weapons? What a bunch of freaking geniuses we have leading our country.*

And the book *Walter the Farting Dog: Banned from the Beach* was indeed banned from the bookshelves too... for using the word "fart" too much. It was illegal censorship as far as Olivia was concerned. She loved it when she saw articles promoting banned books, saying they were obviously worth reading if someone was going to the trouble of banning them. Celebrities handing out banned books. *Kudos.*

As the next episode loaded, Olivia looked at her phone alerts. From the NYT: "Man vs. Mouse: Ron DeSantis Finds Taking On Disney Is a Dicey Business." Olivia didn't get why so many politicians were so extreme nowadays. Were they only looking for the sound bite? Their 15 minutes of fame? Or was it just the corruption of money and demands from their funding sources? Did they actually believe what they were saying? The spirit of freedom in America was dying as fast as a drag queen's career in Florida. Olivia was worried about the future of America. She would look at the faces of her students and wonder what kind of life they would lead.

She repainted her toenails while she watched the show. Then, she got the idea that she would invite Ray over to her place for a drink before they walked to the restaurant. If they didn't go until 6 p.m., they'd miss the happy hour specials.

Olivia to Ray:
Hi! Hope your webinar went well!!

Want to come over early and grab a drink at my place before walking over?

What do you like to drink?

I have Pinot Grigio and Seacrets Spiced Rum in stock!

BTW, the restaurant is called JJ's Bayside Bar & Cafe. 20th Street, right next to Fish Tales.

Olivia had a habit of texting a bunch of texts in a row without waiting for a response. Luke always got annoyed with her texting style and prolific use of exclamation points and emojis.

Three dots appeared. Then they disappeared. It was only 4:30 p.m., so Ray was probably still working. Olivia turned back to watch the end of the episode. Kate had just ridden off in the rain and Anthony arrived in time to see her fall from the horse, unconscious on the ground. They were such an attractive couple. Olivia liked Season 2 so much more than Season 1.

Next up on her to-do list for today was more research on Ocean City. She'd started a Google Doc and had about two pages of information so far. She'd read through a bunch of web pages. Olivia knew the information on Wikipedia was not 100% validated, but it still gave her something as a reference.

Olivia read back over her notes, saying the facts out loud to try to get them to stick in her brain, like she was teaching a class. She thought about the questions she would ask the kids and the visual aids she would need for the history lesson.

History of Ocean City, Maryland

Ocean City is located on the Atlantic Ocean in Worcester County, Maryland, along the East Coast of the United States. It's part of the larger Fenwick Island, which is a barrier island with the communities of South Bethany and Fenwick Island in Delaware and Ocean City in Maryland. Ocean City is a 36-square-mile beach resort town, mostly consisting of water with less than five square miles of land. The beach is 10 miles long. The local population is less than 7,000, but nearly 10 million tourists visit annually. Sometimes it is confused with Ocean City, New Jersey, which is further north up the coast.

Ocean City is now one of the largest vacation areas on the East Coast. 146th Street is the last street in northern Ocean City before Delaware. To the north of Ocean City are these beach towns in Delaware: Fenwick, Lewes, Bethany, Dewey, and then Rehoboth, which has become more well known because it's where President Biden has his beach house.

The land was obtained from Native Americans by Thomas Fenwick and in 1869 Isaac Coffin built the first guest cottage on the beach. The first hotel, The Atlantic Hotel, opened in 1875, and it wasn't long before more hotels and boarding houses were built. In December of 1925, the great Ocean City fire destroyed three blocks of old downtown and the pier, including The Atlantic Hotel, which was rebuilt the following year, and is still in operation on the Boardwalk.

Back then, the area was not very accessible from the mainland and most visitors arrived via boat or stagecoach. Shortly after houses and hotels were built, a railroad opened. The Chesapeake–Potomac Hurricane of 1933, which would have been a Category 4 storm by today's standards, brought considerable destruction, wiped away the train tracks across the bay, and separated Ocean City from Assateague Island, creating what we now call the inlet, the southernmost point of town.

In response to the storm, the U.S. Army Corps of Engineers dredged—or dug out the sand from the bottom of the bay—to make the inlet permanent, which helped make Ocean City such a popular fishing port with easy access to the ocean.

In the late 1930s, a new channel on the bayside of Ocean City was dredged to give larger boats access to Sinepuxent Bay. The Chesapeake Bay Bridge opened in 1952 connecting Annapolis to the Eastern Shore, making Ocean City easily accessible to people in Baltimore and Washington, D.C., and further west. In 1964, the Chesapeake Bay Bridge-Tunnel opened in Virginia, making Ocean City more accessible to points south.

It was a good start, she thought. She needed to visit the Ocean City Life-Saving Station Museum, which was located at the start of the Boardwalk. It wasn't only about lifeguards, though. Apparently, it housed a bunch of other historical items and photos. Maybe she could talk Ray into going there with her when it opened back up. She opened up her summer checklist on her phone and added it.

CHAPTER 10
Evan

Evan and Casey had been casually texting back and forth since they reconnected a few days ago. Ellie had *finally* texted him back this morning, while Evan was at a meeting in Ocean City at the pizza place with Casey's dad. Right after the meeting, which conveniently ended around 11:15 a.m.—not too early for lunch—he'd gotten a couple slices of free pizza. Which meant he had time to do some surfing with his friends over his lunch break before heading back home for the afternoon work-from-home shift.

While he was riding the waves, he tried over and over to compose the perfect response to Ellie in his mind, but he still hadn't texted her back. He'd opened the text more times than he could count, careful not to click on the response field so she wouldn't think he was actively responding. He was supposed to meet his brother tonight. He would text her back after he got some feedback from his bro. Looked like Ellie wanted to give it another chance.

Back at home, Evan took a quick shower to rinse off the sand and finished his pitch slides right before his self-imposed deadline of 5 p.m. He was about to hit "send" on the email to his boss when his phone pinged. It was Casey. He hadn't seen her since their meeting on Monday night, but he'd texted her last night to ask what she was doing Saturday night. He assumed her dad told her about the website meeting. He half expected Casey to be at the pizza shop during the meeting.

Casey to Evan:
Hi Evan! I'm scheduled to work most of the day Saturday. Bummer! What about Saturday morning brunch or dinner Sunday night?

He responded right back. He didn't want to wait to text back. He wanted her to know he was excited to see her.

Evan to Casey:
Hey - sure - how about Sunday night? That will help me get out of dinner with my mom and her boyfriend. LOL

He hit send on his email and closed the laptop. He walked down the stairs and into the kitchen. His mom was sitting at the kitchen table at her laptop.

"Hey, Evan," she said. "I was thinking I could come with you and Brandon tonight to Uncle Jack's?"

Evan's eyes opened wide, and he took a deep breath, contemplating what to say.

His mother laughed and clapped her hands together. "Honey. I'm just teasing you. I know you want to have a brother's night out to discuss guy stuff."

"Ha. Ha," he said. "Yeah. Brandon and I haven't had any time together for I don't know how long. I feel bad thinking about how self-absorbed I've been lately."

His mom smiled, nodded, and looked into Evan's eyes. "You're growing up and figuring things out on your own. It takes time to realize what's really important."

Evan nodded as he went to the fridge to refill his water glass.

"You know, if I could give myself one piece of advice when I was 25," his mom continued, "it would be to slow down and enjoy the ride. The past few crazy years have made us better appreciate what we have. I feel like all I did for most of my life was rush to work, rush home, rush around taking you and Brandon to all of your activities. Then I'd sit in bed at night and worry about everything I had to do the next day."

Evan stood drinking his water and didn't say anything but nodded. His mom would just keep talking, he figured.

"Now with virtual work, you can have such a better work-life balance. Maybe not in my job since a lot of it has to do with the on-site dining logistics but look at you—working from home 100% of the time, at a fantastic job in your field! So lucky! Your dad would have been proud of you, Ev. Life is so different with virtual work. You can take care of chores around your apartment during lunch and breaks. Take a walk, go to the gym. The level of flexibility is unprecedented! I'm so happy for you, Evan. With all of the benefits, I know it also has its disadvantages. I bet you're meeting fewer people. You need to find different social outlets, so you don't get isolated and depressed. How will you find a new girlfriend?"

Evan groaned. It had been less than a week and his mom was already on him about meeting a new girlfriend?

"Anyways, hon, right now I'm working on the monthly church flier for May. I need to get it done by Saturday night so we can upload it to the website and then distribute it at the end of the Sunday service. Will you be joining us at church this week?"

Evan stifled his internal groan as he swallowed the last gulp of water. He was not religious. Was he an atheist? He didn't know. He knew that he basically zoned out during the sermons when his mom made him attend church.

His mom knew how Evan felt. How Brandon felt. He looked at church as a community-building activity, though. If his mom used church as a way to make friends, what was it to him? If she didn't have any discretionary money, that would be another story. She was living a comfortable life, and if she wanted to donate money to the church, so be it. Evan and Brandon could support themselves now.

"Not this week, Mom. I met a girl. Well, a girl I knew from high school. We're going out some time on Sunday. Timing T.B.D." he said, stretching the truth a bit.

"Oh. Wow! Why didn't you say so sooner? Who is she? Do I know her?"

Evan took a deep breath, looked at his mom, and spit out the details quickly, without taking another breath. "Her name is Casey Marconi. Her family owns Antonio's Pizza in OC. She played lacrosse in high school and ran indoor track in the winter. She went away to UNC for college and does technical writing virtually for a government contractor during the day and works at the pizza place to help out on evenings and weekends."

"Oh, yes. Antonio and his wife Melissa. I know them both from the arts council."

Evan's mom seemed to know everyone. Whenever they went out, anywhere on the Eastern Shore, she would see people she knew. At Walmart? It was a parade of people to talk with. Church people. Salisbury University staff, students, alumni. Berlin people. She often talked about running for office as a councilmember. He dearly loved his mom, but she had some old-fashioned views.

Many of Evan's friends were in the same boat as him… dealing with changing views on the environment, women's rights, and gun control. Climate change was real, and it was hard to deny that. Guns killed people. The mass shootings in America were out of control! Why not ban automatic weapons? What's the big deal? And no question that women should have the right to choose what happens with their own bodies, he thought.

Technically, Evan was Gen Z because he was born in 1998, but sometimes, he felt like his preferences were more in tune with the previous Millennial generation. In his marketing work, he dealt a lot with targeting different generations, so he knew all of the years inside out.

The oldest generation right now had people born between 1925-45, and they were called The Silent Generation. Evan thought that was funny because you basically never hear anyone talking about them… so *silent* made perfect sense!

Next was the Baby Boomer Generation, born between 1946-64. The fact the Boomers were entering their twilight years was a big business opportunity—more people with changing needs for retirement-focused products and services. That's why there were so many 55-plus retirement communities popping up everywhere.

Evan had a side hustle where he would help people (mostly older people) set up their technology: computers, Wi-Fi, televisions, Alexa-related devices, Ring video security cameras. Nowadays, almost everything had a YouTube tutorial video. And if Evan couldn't find one, he'd read up on the manuals and make a video tutorial himself and post it to YouTube. He got most of his tech setup work via word of mouth, mainly from his mom's friends at church.

Then there was Generation X, with people born between 1965-80. That was where Evan's mom fit. She was resourceful and independent—traits that partly stemmed from her latchkey childhood, with both parents working and little supervision.

Possibly the most studied generation, Gen Y, or Millennials, were people born between 1981-96. They are highly adaptable multi-taskers, valuing trust and freedom.

Since Evan was an early entry into Generation Z (1997-2012), he felt he could easily fit into either category. Gen Z, the first true digital natives, were thought to be highly collaborative, self-reliant, and pragmatic. They thought *online first* for all things: learning, working, shopping, dating, making friends. They were hit especially hard during the pandemic. Many of them missed critical formative childhood milestones and activities—entire years of school, prom, graduation, sports, and on and on. Their mental health took a huge hit.

Evan missed his own college graduation due to COVID restrictions. Finding a full-time job using the skills he learned had taken almost a year. In the meantime, he had tried to fill the gap as a DoorDash and Instacart delivery driver. He had his tech support side hustle. He was also a part-time dog walker, which he still did from time to time.

As far as the most recent generation, Generation Alpha, kids born after 2013, Evan had not done a lot of research since he hadn't been targeting children in his work. He knew they were basically described as the children of Millennials. Evan thought it would be very interesting to see how they evolved with at least three years of their early life heavily impacted by the pandemic.

Evan had zoned out over the last minute or so of the conversation with his mom.

"Ok, Mom. I need to get ready to head out," said Evan as he walked over and kissed her on the top of her head. He bent down to the floor, gave each kitten a quick pat, grabbed his Salisbury University baseball cap from the kitchen table, and walked out the door. One thing he didn't lack was Salisbury-themed swag. His mom had a boatload of hats, shirts, polos, cups, pens—20 years' worth of merch.

As Evan drove into Ocean City, he listened to Aerosmith, streaming from his phone playlist. *Rag Doll* was playing. Evan was going to D.C. in September for their concert with his uncle and brother. They would spend the night at his mom's sister's house just outside of D.C. in Hyattsville, Maryland.

Once in a blue moon, they would do an outing like that, but due to COVID, the last time they went to D.C. was in the summer of 2019. The Lonely Island (Akiva Schaffer, Andy Samberg, and Jorma Taccone) played The Anthem. It was a weird band to want to see, but his family always sang their song *I'm on a Boat* because they had a boat… and how could you not sing that song? Their songs were weird and crude, and his mom hated it. Evan, his brother, and Uncle Jack loved toilet humor.

Living on the Eastern Shore meant it was normally a couple hours' away to see a concert—having to drive into Baltimore or D.C. Yes, there were some acts that would come to Ocean City or the newer venue up in Delaware called the Freeman Arts Pavilion in Selbyville, but most of the tours only hit big cities. Last summer, Evan's entire family went to Freeman to see Bonnie Raitt because his mom was a huge country music fan.

Mom to Evan:
Honey, I forgot to ask you. What's Venmo? One of the church members said we should set up a church account. Is it safe? Don't answer now, I know you're driving. Love you. Have fun.

Evan's mom was literally the sweetest woman on earth. As a mom, she nagged, but Evan knew she meant well.

The elephant in the virtual family room for them was Brandon's sexuality. Brandon was gay. He hadn't come out to their mom yet. Evan suspected that his mom suspected that Brandon was homosexual. That was between his brother and her, and Evan stayed out of it. Brandon had a boyfriend named Raymond who worked at Uncle Jack's place as a bartender. Uncle Jack knew. That made it a complicated family situation.

Evan knew Brandon would already be at JJ's because Brandon was always early, and he lived close by. Fortunately, traffic into Ocean City was moving since it was still April. It would only take about 20 minutes to get up to 20th Street. Brandon lived with Raymond in Raymond's family's beach house. A few years ago, Raymond's parents retired to Florida, and they only occasionally came up north to visit.

Raymond was probably independently wealthy, but he liked to keep busy. Evan's mom didn't even know that Brandon had a roommate. Their mom thought Brandon was renting a condo as a bachelor pad. He worked remotely as a financial planner and made good money. Evan always wondered why his mom wasn't more curious about the situation, and why Brandon remained in the closet.

Evan arrived five minutes early, and didn't see Brandon at the bar, which was surprising. Evan made a beeline to the kitchen to greet his Uncle Jack. Everyone at the bar knew Evan, so he had free reign to roam around JJ's.

When Evan opened the door that read "Staff Only," he saw Brandon and Raymond having an animated conversation in low voices in the staff room, which was adjacent to the kitchen.

As Evan entered the staff room, they stopped talking, and Brandon approached him.

"Hey, Evan. Long time no see, bro," Brandon said as the brothers gave each other a quick embrace. At that moment, Uncle Jack walked into the staff room holding a plate of fried fish bites.

"Hey boys, wanna give the fish of the day a try? I put some different beer in the batter today and I need some feedback," said Jack.

CHAPTER 11
Ray

Ray signed out of Slack and smiled because she was getting some major kudos from her team regarding the webinar, which was a huge success! Ray had been so freaked out that she wouldn't get set up in time after the Charlie debacle at the beach. Then again, Ray normally overperformed in stressful situations.

The webinar attendance didn't dwindle during the 45-minute presentation, and there were a bunch of well thought out questions during the 15-minute Q&A session. They didn't even need to use pre-written stock questions to keep things moving.

She deserved to go out and celebrate! They would publish the recorded webinar in their gated members-only portal tomorrow, and she would post about it on LinkedIn. What a relief!

Ray to Olivia:
Hey - just finishing up work. I'll take Charlie out for a quick walk and then I'll be over. Probably in about 20 minutes. I like Pinot.

When Ray walked through Olivia's front door exactly 20 minutes later, she had a pep in her step and was still flying high from her successful webinar.

"Whoa! This place is totally updated! It's so modern and bright. I can't believe it's the same layout as my place… Well, the mirror layout. It's like night and day. Or more like the 1980s vs 2020s." Ray looked around trying to take it all in while Olivia unsuccessfully tried to keep an exuberant Ruby from jumping up on her.

"Yeah. My parents completely gutted it when they bought it and tried to make it look perfect for the VRBO listing pictures," said Olivia. "They're so extra! I feel like their need to fit as many people as possible kind of makes the place look cramped with so much furniture, though."

"Well, I think it looks amazing. The kitchen is so sleek. This is definitely giving me a kick in the butt to update my place. I'd be embarrassed to let you see it now."

Olivia had wine and glasses set out on the kitchen table along with some cheese and crackers. She even had some fresh flowers in a vase. Music was playing. Entertaining was not something Ray was used to doing. She had never had another person in her beach house in the past few years, except for her family members who had occasionally visited.

"Alexa, volume down!" Olivia called out authoritatively. Ray did not have an Alexa device because giving AI the ability to listen in 24/7 was her worst nightmare. She had a general idea of how they worked, and smirked. Ray considered herself to be tech savvy, but Olivia was leveraging way more technology in her everyday life than Ray did.

Ray sat down at the table while Olivia poured the wine and chatted about the kitchen design. The appliances and electronics were all hooked up to Wi-Fi. She had fancy crystal wine glasses that matched. They had cute little dog wine charms. One was brown like Ruby, for Olivia. One was black and white—the colors of Charlie, the mutt. Olivia paid attention to details, she thought.

Olivia was wearing cropped jeans and a sleeveless white blousy shirt with large earrings and brown short leather boots. She looked fashionable. Ray hadn't been sure what to wear. Her wardrobe was limited. She had on straight leg dark jeans with her black Hoka running shoes. She wore a plain gray knit shirt with a black Under Armour running jacket. She mostly wore dark neutral colors; it was the easiest.

"So, how was your webinar?" asked Olivia. "During COVID, I had to teach exclusively over Zoom, and if I never see my pasty, pudgy face on a webcam again, it will be too soon!"

Ray went on to explain the webinar topic and they chatted easily until they finished their wine. Olivia had volunteered at the elections in the past, she explained. Ray got the feeling there was more to that story given the wistful way she said it.

When it was time to go, Olivia went to the bathroom and Ray took a better look around the place. It was spotless. The only real personality came from Ruby's dog toys that were spread around the floor and a handful of books and magazines on the coffee table. The refrigerator had a notepad with a grocery list. The kitchen counter was empty of clutter and showcased a bowl of fruit, which seemed a little too well-presented to be random, that was more like a piece of artwork.

"Need a lint roller?" Olivia asked as she came out of the bathroom. "Ruby sheds like a polar bear on a melting iceberg, and I have to buy lint rollers in bulk!"

"Same here," laughed Ray. "Since Charlie is black and white, I have no safe color to wear that won't show the dog hair. I lint rolled before I walked over here."

On the way to the restaurant, it was a little windy. At the beach, it was always a little windy. Sometimes, gale force gusts and sustained winds would come up out of nowhere. Ray knew it would be much cooler after sunset. Olivia brought a puffy coat that she draped over her large brown leather Coach purse. And were those Gucci sunglasses? *Wow. So extra*, Ray thought.

Ray didn't even carry a purse around town. She had a card case with her iPhone containing her driver's license and two credit cards. She liked to keep it simple and safe.

After the 15-minute walk, they stopped at the outdoor podium of JJ's and waited to be seated. Ray hadn't been there since last fall when she reluctantly met one of her high school friends and her boyfriend.

JJ's had a huge, covered bar area with high tops surrounding it. There were at least 10 TV screens mounted at the top of the bar with various sports-related shows… mostly college stuff today. Heaters and large roll-up transparent plastic blinds were hung for when the weather wasn't great.

The view of the bay and sunset at JJ's was not as good as Fish Tales, which was one block over. At JJ's, it was more of a canal view. The outdoor dinner seating area was made up of about 25 picnic tables with a mishmash of drink logo umbrellas. They had a few palm trees that had been shipped up from Florida, which was something a bunch of the restaurants did each spring.

Most of the restauranteurs in town knew each other or at least *knew of* each other. It was an interesting set-up in the resort town. Three summer months were crazy profitable and busy. Three months were average. Six months were either super slow or some restaurants closed things up completely.

Some places didn't survive the pandemic restrictions. Some were able to pivot and create outdoor dining spaces and take-out and delivery options. Everyone was affected by the travel regulations. Typically, a huge part of the summer workforce included students from overseas. Many shops and restaurants struggled to find workers during the pandemic. They still did, even in 2023.

Phillips Seafood was an Ocean City landmark restaurant since 1956 that had been right across the street from JJ's. At the end of 2021 it was sold, after 66 years of successful operations. Ray used to get carryout from Phillips at least once a week during the season. They may have specialized in seafood, but their fried chicken was so delicious!

After a couple of minutes of waiting at the reception podium, a server came up, and Olivia asked for a table for two. They were seated along the edge of the outside dining area near the canal. Olivia took out a small leather Moleskine notebook and a sparkly purple pen.

"I'm going to take notes about the food and drinks," she said. "Do *not* judge me! When I work here, I want to be able to answer questions about the menu!" She laughed. Ray was beginning to think there was a lot more to Olivia than her fashionable and friendly exterior facade.

They ordered orange crushes and some fried calamari to start. "You know that the orange crush was invented in Ocean City?" Olivia asked. "Harborside Bar and Grill."

"Yes. I've heard that. All the bars around here serve it and claim to have the *original* recipe," Ray replied. The drink was a refreshing cocktail with OJ, orange vodka, triple sec, and lemon-lime soda. Some people preferred to have it with rum instead of vodka.

"Honestly, it seems so rando given you can't even grow oranges in Maryland, right?" Olivia asked.

The crushes came in branded plastic cups, SOLO-sized. Olivia took a note and asked Ray how she felt about the drink. To Ray, it seemed tasty, and the oranges were sweet and fresh. She gave it a 9/10. The calamari was good—crispy and tender, not too chewy. A $5 happy hour crush, half priced apps, and a water view? No wonder JJ's was so popular with the locals.

"JJ's hardly does anything on social media, and they could really easily ramp it up," said Olivia. "But the question is, do they actually want more people to come or are they already working at capacity? Increased demand is not always a good thing."

"I always got the feeling JJ's was more low-key and that they like it that way," said Ray.

Ray looked around and saw there was only one bartender—maybe in his early 30s and kind of nerdy with a bright neon green and white Hawaiian themed shirt. Two servers—women in their 20s—took turns greeting and seating.

One busser seemed like a tween. It was only April, though, so it wasn't terribly busy on a Thursday.

Olivia took some more notes and snapped some pictures of the menu as she looked around. "I met the owner Jack on Tuesday! I contacted him about working here this summer via email on the contact form on their website. It sounds like he lives nearby. We met at the Starbucks over there near the Boardwalk. He has a chef and bartender that come back each year but has to hire all the other positions newly each April. He's probably in his late 50s? Has a David Hasselhoff vibe to him. Super chill and cool guy. Sexy voice. I don't see him here now," she said, looking around.

Olivia took a few notes, and Ray squinted looking around at the water and the boats passing by, wishing she'd brought her baseball hat. The sun was shining directly into her eyes.

"You know they're planning to build a Margaritaville over on the Boardwalk on 13th-14th Streets?" Olivia asked. "It's been all over social and the local newspapers."

"Yeah," Ray said. "I've definitely heard about it. It seems like it's a main topic of conversation for all the locals. Personally, I'm not into big crowds and party scenes. But I feel like it makes sense to have one here because it will elevate the status of Ocean City."

"Exactly!" Olivia said. "There are only a couple dozen Margaritaville restaurants in the entire world! To have one right here in Ocean City would be a real feather in our cap, in my opinion! Well, and I absolutely love Jimmy Buffett, so I'm obviously biased. I can't even count the number of times I've seen him in concert with my family back home."

They sat in silence for a few minutes, and Olivia wrote down some additional notes and then picked up her phone and started tapping.

"You know what I hate with a passion?" Olivia asked, only waiting a nanosecond before continuing. "OC has like a zillion

Facebook groups, and instead of hyping up what they like, tourists just anonymously bash places the majority of the time. Like if it sucked so bad, why didn't you tell anyone at the actual restaurant when you were there? So dumb."

"Karens," said Ray, remembering the rude old lady at the beach earlier.

"It's like you can't win as a business owner around here. Obviously, everyone has different expectations," continued Olivia. "If you're looking at a beautiful sunset while you eat your dinner, it's going to cost more, right? Location. Location. Location!" Olivia looked around and continued. "Take JJ's here for instance. Their bayside view is okay, but not the best. The food is solid. Some dishes are better than others, but people are mostly here for the drinks and the beachy vacation vibe. Decent food is an added bonus."

"Well, the calamari is excellent," Ray said as she took a huge bite.

"Some people want fancy tropical drinks with crazy names, some people want a cheap draft beer. You get a $17 fish sandwich with chips, and you'll probably be happy. You get a $55 seafood sampler; chances are that you'll be disappointed with something on the plate. It's nearly impossible to meet varying expectations. If you don't get alcohol, you could reasonably spend less than $50 to eat here for two people. That's a bargain in my book! Or you could easily spend $100 if you get drinks and an appetizer," Olivia finally finished her rant.

"So, I totally get what you're saying. And I was just reading an article about online ratings," Ray said. "Anyway, the idea is that if you're looking for decent food as a top priority, you shouldn't obsess about the overall rating—like on Yelp or OpenTable or whatever—since so much of the rating is about service. People are more likely to complain about bad service than they are to rave about the food quality. The article said the best overall rating may be a '3.5/5.' Who knew?"

Olivia nodded like she wasn't really paying attention and picked up her phone. Ray took another sip of her drink and fidgeted in her seat a bit. Olivia held up her phone and took a photo of the bar area.

"You know, that's smart," Olivia said, looking Ray directly in the eyes. "I've read the reviews of JJ's—there are only a couple dozen. They're average at best. Service is normally hit-or-miss from one day to another," said Olivia. "To be honest, Americans are so freaking obsessed about customer service. I mean seriously, get a grip people, and chillax, am I right? My toxic trait is that I assume people have common sense." Olivia laughed and picked up her phone again. "Sorry. Let me text my parents these photos. They've been asking me about my new job."

Ray took her own phone out of her pocket and put it on the table. No notifications. She looked across the canal at the western horizon. The sun would be setting soon. The colors of the sky and clouds were swirling pink and orange.

Their server arrived with the food in what Olivia proclaimed to be an acceptable time frame, and everything was delivered as ordered. Olivia took more photos. They ate mostly in silence as Olivia looked around the place, taking it all in. Olivia was bopping her head back and forth to the music and nodding every once in a while. It looked like she was having a silent conversation with herself. Ray smiled and wondered what it would be like to be as carefree and living in the moment as Olivia seemed to be doing right now.

"First. This orange crush is totally giving me life right now. So good! Second. Do *not* turn around and look, but there are two super-hot guys at the bar, and one of them keeps looking over here at us," whispered Olivia.

"At *us*?" asked Ray, rolling her eyes. "At *you*, you mean. I'm not the kind of girl that guys notice at a bar. I blend in. And I like it that way." Ray shrugged her shoulders as she slurped up the last of her orange crush.

"What do you mean? You're so pretty and fit! And you have such a sophisticated vibe with your short dark hair and gorgeous big eyes and luscious lashes," said Olivia. "I have such a boring *girl next door* look."

Ray batted her eyes, "Thank you, queen of hype."

Ray was feeling the effects of the alcohol. She wasn't averse to drinking, she just never really socialized anymore. So, she rarely drank. Ray tried to nonchalantly look over to the bar area. The men in question were both tall and fit and had a similar look. She wondered if they were brothers. One of them had a crossbody fanny pack. Ray knew men had stuff to carry around, especially with the pandemic. They had masks, hand sanitizers, not to mention mobile phones and keys and what not. To her, that fanny pack trend seemed like it would be fleeting. Would a *murse* be better, she wondered? Or should men stick with a standard backpack? Ray guessed it wasn't fair that women could easily carry any kind of bag, and it wouldn't become a controversial topic of conversation.

"One of them is wearing denim shorts, though," Olivia said, groaning. "What a total fashion faux pas."

"I don't know why women can wear as much denim as they like, but men are immediately on the worst-dressed list for wearing jeans shorts?" Ray asked. "What a double standard." Ray's dad normally wore denim shorts or jeans. He had no other types of casual pants that weren't some variety of denim.

Right at that moment, Jack walked out of the kitchen, which was inside behind the bar, over to their table. "Well, well, look who we have here! Olivia. Checking out the place before you start?" Jack asked.

"Hi, Jack. Yes! And this is my beach house neighbor, Ray," she said as they shook hands. "The drinks and food have been excellent!"

Ray looked at Jack and her first thought was that he did look a bit like David Hasselhoff, maybe mixed with Zac Efron. Definitely a *Baywatch* vibe. He looked like he was happy and living his best life. Seemingly happy people really intrigued Ray. Was it real? Was it a front? The people who would smile at you and their smile would make you smile back. The aura of positive energy. People longed to be near them, to bask in their glory, Ray immediately felt that way too.

That old cliche, *Smile and the whole world smiles with you*. All of a sudden, that got Ray thinking about vampires and that TV show *What They Do in the Shadows*. Was she an energy vampire like the show character Colin Robinson? She smiled to herself as Olivia and Jack chatted comfortably.

Ray often considered herself to be a behavioral chameleon. She would quietly assess any situation and morph her personality and behavior to best fit it. Later on, when she was alone, she'd sit quietly in silence and meditate to get her equilibrium back in balance.

As the conversation turned from work to home life, Olivia described where she was living.

Jack looked over at Ray and said, "Well, wouldn't you know it... You're Ray *Anders*? I knew your dad growing up. We were both on the beach patrol, lifeguards. And your grandparents. Lovely people. I was so sorry to hear about their passing awhile back."

That comment brought Ray's good mood crashing down. "Um. Yes. Thank you," she stuttered. "I'm living in their place now and my parents moved to New York to be with my mom's parents."

"Well, you ever need anything at all, Ray, you just let me know," said Jack as he looked back at the kitchen. "Work calls, ladies! See you tomorrow, Olivia."

Ray watched Jack walk away. "You know, it makes sense that people around here would know my grandparents and my dad, but I've been holed up in my house for the past couple years and never really thought about it before," said Ray.

Olivia reached over and grabbed Ray's hand. "My grandpa always says this line from the *Rocky* movie. Basically, life's gonna hit you, but you've gotta keep getting up and pushing forward."

Ray wanted to move her hand away, but she sat still as stone for a moment, and then nodded her head slightly. She knew she needed to move forward. She was stuck in a monotonous routine. Ray didn't know where she wanted to go next... so how could she break the cycle?

CHAPTER 12
Evan

"Who are those girls that Jack's talking to over there?" Evan asked Raymond, who was working behind the bar. "They look somewhat familiar."

"I think it's the new server because I heard him say 'Olivia' when he greeted them," said Raymond as he went over to the other side of the bar with a couple of beers in hand. "She starts this weekend. The one with the lighter and longer hair."

"Interesting," said Brandon, who was sitting next to Evan at the bar. "A little older than the normal college-age summer help, I see. Do I detect an interest from you, Evy?"

"Right, oh! Perhaps, there is indeed, my dear brother," Evan said in his best British accent. "But first, I shall present you with the latest text message from Ellie, of the back-stabbing cheating-with-Bob acclaim," he said as he grabbed his phone from his pocket and handed it to Brandon.

Ellie to Evan:
Evan, I know that an apology from me won't be enough to make things right, but I'm so sorry. I swear that nothing physical happened with Bob. It was all just stupid virtual flirting.

Can we give it another chance? I'm so sorry! I blocked him. It's over!

Evan took a long drink of his beer, draining the glass. He leaned his head close to Brandon to be more discreet as he set the scene for the breakup. "Ellie texting this guy… I saw it in real time, as it was happening. I was standing behind her. I'd just gotten home. I tried to get her attention, but she was wearing her earbuds. It was unlike anything she had ever messaged me or said to me in person," explained Evan. "Like, how could I think she could ever care as much about me as this Bob guy? I don't think we can come back from that. She's just not that into me. And that makes me not into her."

"Looks like you already made up your mind, bro. So now the question is, do you ignore her or text her back? Assuming you still need to clear up the apartment situation, though?" Brandon asked.

"Yeah. Most of it is my stuff. Both of our names are on the lease. Ideally, she would just move out because she can't afford it on her own," said Evan. "She doesn't have anywhere to go, around here at least. Maybe she can move back down to Virginia Beach."

Their fish sandwiches arrived. Evan was having grouper and Brandon was having flounder with a side of fries and the smallest cup of slaw possible. Evan didn't understand how a place could get away with calling that tiny sauce cup a legit side dish. But the slaw was so good. Not too sweet. Not too vinegary.

The fries were Boardwalk style—cut kind of thick, unpeeled potatoes, fried in peanut oil. Not as good as the original Boardwalk fries from Thrasher's, but way better than most fries. JJ's had vinegar on the tables, along with ketchup, mustard, salt, pepper, Old Bay, and a roll of paper towels in a wooden box painted red. Red and black were the main brand colors of JJ's. There was a subtle *Jack of Diamonds* card theme going on.

They ate while Raymond gave them the download on the new hires for the season. "Olivia, the over there, is starting her teaching job at the elementary school this fall but wanted a summer job to kick off her newly single life. She just got divorced." Raymond wiggled his eyebrows in a creepy way that made both Brandon and Evan cringe.

"Dude. Don't ever do that again," said Evan. "You're giving off mad pedophile vibes. Especially with your little round tinted glasses, scraggly facial hair, and loud Hawaiian shirt. Total ick factor going on, dude."

Raymond was truly insulted. "Man, don't joke about that kind of stuff in public! I have a reputation as the best bartender on 20th Street that I do not want tarnished! No telling who around us right now could be doing a TikTok or an Insta story!"

Brandon laughed and then popped up from his stool and gave Raymond a quick kiss on the lips. "Sorry, love. My little brother is drowning his sorrows tonight, so give him a pass. He just broke up with Ellie. She was cheating on him."

"Whoa. Wait. Are you two public?" asked Evan, looking around to see who was watching. "I mean, do people know you're a couple?"

"Yep. Everyone here knows," said Raymond, with a pointed glance over to Brandon.

"Everyone knows?" Evan asked, incredulously, raising his eyebrows and tilting his head.

"Yep. Even Mom," Brandon replied cautiously, eyes averted and fiddling with the label on his bottle of beer.

"Wait. Hold on. You *came out* to Mom and didn't tell me?" Evan swiveled on the stool to turn his body to better see his brother and then pushed Brandon's shoulder back (with a little more force than necessary, he could admit).

"There wasn't anything to tell, bro," explained Brandon, grabbing his shoulder and rubbing it. "She already knew. Or at least thought I was somewhere on the LGBTQIA+ spectrum. Apparently, she's suspected it forever and was waiting for me to clue her in. I wish I'd told her a decade—or two—ago. That would have made my life so much easier. Hindsight is 20/20 as they say."

"Okay. It *has* been forever since you and I have talked just ourselves," said Evan. "Now Mom's comments from earlier today make so much more sense. She probably realized you were going to tell me she knew all along. Did she know that *I* knew?"

"Yeah. I told her that you and Uncle Jack already knew I was with Raymond and had known for a while," said Brandon as they looked over and saw Olivia and her friend coming up to the bar.

Evan dropped down his prescription sunglasses from the top of his head to take a closer look at the girls. *Yes, definitely familiar*, he thought. Where had he seen them before? He turned back to the bar and asked Raymond for a glass of water as the girls got closer.

CHAPTER 13
Olivia

"Hi, Raymond, isn't it?" Olivia asked with a huge smile on her face. Ray stood quietly behind Olivia. "I wanted to come over and introduce myself. I'm Olivia McNalley, and I'll be starting tomorrow afternoon as one of the summer servers here!"

As they bumped fists, initiated by Raymond, he smiled and said, "Great to meet you, Olivia! I'm kind of busy here with the bar crowd right now, but this over here is Evan. He's Jack's nephew. And this handsome young man right here is my husband, Brandon—Evan's brother."

With that bomb dropped, Raymond did a quick turn and practically skipped to the other side of the bar.

"Husband!?" Evan blurted out in an octave higher than his normal voice, making everyone nearby turn and take full notice. Evan started coughing on his drink and sputtered out, "Okay, I know it is *not* April 1st. Am I being pranked right now? I don't see any *Impractical Jokers* or Johnny Knoxville around."

Olivia jerked back as Evan's eyes swept around the place, clearly looking for hidden cameras. Brandon groaned and put his head into his hands and then ran his hands through his hair in despair.

"So, I guess congratulations are in order?" Olivia asked, as it was clear they were still part of the conversation since Evan was coughing up a storm and Brandon was looking right at her. "Recently married?"

Evan looked up at the sky as Brandon appeared to be about to say something.

"Look, this is much less dramatic than you think, Evan. We knew we wanted to be together, forever. We want to start a family and adopt children. We're not getting any younger. We went to the courthouse a few weeks ago, and right beforehand, we told Mom and Vernon. Simple story, bro," said Brandon.

Evan nodded and said, "Bet."

He sat there in a dazed state, eyes straight ahead, appearing to be studying a bin of fresh oranges. Olivia was feeling increasingly uncomfortable with each passing second. If her sibling got married without telling her, she would have been hysterical. She checked her phone out of habit and grabbed Ray's arm, pulling her aside.

"This is so dramatic!" Olivia whispered animatedly to Ray. They looked away but continued to eavesdrop on this juicy gossip.

"You and Ellie were away on that trip to Florida when it happened. We didn't want to make a big fuss," said Brandon. "Mom told us you'd be upset to miss it. She wanted you to know. It wasn't a wedding or anything fancy. We just filled out the paperwork and went to the courthouse. Mom and Uncle Jack came along as witnesses. Maybe we'll have a real wedding on the beach now that the weather is getting nicer though. Maybe an informal private reception here at JJ's. Raymond has been after me to tell you. So, there it is!" Brandon's arms flew into the air as he shook his head.

"O.M.G. Evan must be so mad," whispered Olivia to Ray. "And their mom must be a saint to not have spilled the beans by now. My mom would have texted me immediately." Ray stayed silent and nodded.

Olivia saw Evan give Brandon what could only be described as an evil glare as he slammed his hands on the bar and stood up, jarring his stool back with a screech. He turned abruptly and took about a dozen steps away from the bar area. Suddenly, Evan stopped mid-stride, and his shoulders rose and lowered as he took a few deep breaths. He stretched his neck from side to side and finally looked up to the sky. Olivia heard a loud and overly dramatic sigh. She locked eyes with Ray, and their mutual anticipation of what would happen next filled the thick air.

Evan turned and walked back to the bar, his eyes on Brandon. "So, *everyone* in the family knew but me? *Everyone* here at the restaurant knows?" Evan said as he looked around. Olivia noticed a few staffers turning their heads away, not wanting to be caught gawking. "Seriously. How could you do this to me? I'm sorry for my initial reaction, but bro… you've gotta admit that I totally got played," said Evan, shaking his head.

"Dude. Look at my hand. I've been wearing a wedding ring for weeks," Brandon said, holding up his hand. "I haven't seen you in almost *two months*. Is it really *my* fault? I tried to get together with you *numerous* times."

Olivia turned to get a better look at Evan. Two months! she thought. And they lived practically right next to each other. Olivia couldn't be too critical, though. She rarely saw her siblings.

At that moment, Jack came out of the kitchen door, wiping his hands on a dish towel as he took in the tense scene and walked behind the bar. "Everything good out here, boys?" he asked in a way that was not exactly a question, but more of a statement.

Evan stopped, nodded his head. His demeanor changed on a dime. He almost smiled. The air seemed immediately lighter. Olivia let out the breath she didn't realize she was holding.

"Ok. Fair. Fair. I'll take the *L* and do better," said Evan, looking at Brandon, who was now standing up by the bar. Evan held up his hands in surrender. "Water under the bridge."

Evan pulled Brandon into a hug and punched his back repeatedly, in classic bromance fashion. "I love you, Bro Bra. Congratulations. You know I love Raymond. You two will be great parents. And I'll get to be the cool Uncle Evan. Really, I can't wait!"

Olivia teared up. It was such a sweet scene. She could tell they were close. Olivia had never been particularly close to her siblings. They marched to the beat of a different drummer, her parents would always say.

"Hey, ladies," Evan said, turning around and trying to get their attention. "Sorry for that outburst. As you could probably tell, we had some important family business to discuss. But we're all cool now."

Evan looked at Ray. Ray looked at Evan. They both realized it at the same time, eyes widening in recognition. "Wait a minute," Evan said in that lightbulb moment kind of way. "Were you both on the beach a little before noon today with two crazy dogs and an Orioles hat setting sail?"

"Well, that would be *one* lunatic dog—hers—and one perfect angelic puppy—mine," laughed Olivia.

"Oh my gosh. That was you? With dry hair and no wetsuit, I didn't recognize you. Thanks again for your help with that. I'm still completely mortified," said Ray, covering her face with her hands in embarrassment. "Normally, Charlie is such a good obedient dog."

"The waves kind of sucked, so it was the highlight of the day. We all had a good laugh watching your hat blow down the beach while your dog was running circles around you," laughed Evan. "I decided to be the hero and ride one in and come to the rescue."

"Evan's *Baywatch* moment finally happens!" Brandon joked. "He saved a hat."

Everyone laughed, and Raymond saw the coast was clear and came back around the bar with a sheepish grin on his face. Evan went around the bar counter and gave him a big hug too. "Got any champagne around here, Brother Raymond? Or what about that new Prosecco Aperol Spritz drink you've got on the menu this year?"

Olivia looked over at Ray, grabbed her hand, and then said, "We're going to hit the lady's room. B.R.B."

Once they were out of range, Olivia said, "So, do you want to stick around here and hang out at the bar, or walk back home? Evan is super cute. Don't you think? Too bad his brother is off the market... well, not that he was ever in our particular market."

"I don't know. I'm not good at this kind of thing. Talking to strangers at bars," said Ray. "But if you want to stay, I'm up for it. I am trying to reinvent myself. You know... come out of my COVID hibernation and live my best life. And all that positive energy and manifestation crap."

"You know... and not that you need it because you're so naturally gorgeous," Olivia said, "but I could give you a makeover if you want?"

"Ahh. Maybe," said Ray as she looked at her reflection in the bathroom mirror. "When I was looking at myself on my webinar camera today, I was thinking that I should try to put in some more effort with my look." She sighed. "But I like the low-maintenance routine, you know what I mean? But I also want to be taken seriously because I'm up for a promotion at work."

"I know *exactly* what you mean," said Olivia as she washed her hands and then checked her hair in the tiny mirror. "Zoom is unforgiving, unless you have the perfect lighting and adjust your video settings to the glamor blurry look."

Ray laughed as she dried her hands on her pants. Jack really needed one of those new powerful Xlerator hand dryers. "I also need some new pants or shorts or skirts. I haven't bought any new clothes for my bottom half since before COVID."

"Let's go to the outlets together!" Olivia said. "We can do OC or Rehoboth?"

They chatted about the shopping plan as they walked back to the bar. Olivia wondered if there was a significant other in Ray's life, but she wouldn't come out and ask her—at least not yet. Olivia was surprised that Ray was even entertaining the idea of a makeover and shopping spree. Ray had gorgeous eyes, and Olivia knew just the perfect makeup she would recommend to brighten them up a bit.

Evan and Brandon were talking with Jack when they returned to the bar. Raymond was pouring at least a dozen glasses of sparkling white wine.

CHAPTER 14
Ray

Ray couldn't believe that after only a couple hours together, she and Olivia were already acting like lifelong friends. Olivia was obviously a major people person, but for Ray, this was a totally alien experience. She rarely let her guard down, and she was contemplating going shopping with Olivia and getting a makeover? Olivia was a little much, to say the least. Like the polar opposite of Ray. Actually, Olivia was the kind of person who Ray normally tried to avoid at all costs. But maybe that's exactly the kind of friend that Ray needed at this point in her life. To top it off, this Evan guy was so good-looking. She felt like it was *her* he was into and not Olivia. Could that be true? It didn't make any sense.

As they walked back to the bar, Evan and Brandon stood up and offered their seats to the girls since it was standing room only. Olivia chatted with them while Ray kind of zoned out for a moment. Evan slightly leaned forward, putting his arm on the bar behind her, casually touching her back. His head was so close to her face. Her unmasked face. Was that coughing fit he had earlier just from the drink? Was he sniffling? Were his eyes red? Or, God forbid, did he have COVID?

Ray's thoughts were suddenly spinning out of control. She was starting to sweat and get uncomfortable, but it wasn't even a little hot out. In fact, the sun was about to go down. She'd been a hermit for the past few years and now, being in the growing crowd, it was igniting her anxiety. With acknowledgement of that feeling, she started to flush and feel embarrassed, which made it worse. She grabbed her phone out of her pocket, stood up, and claimed she was getting a phone call she had to take. She stepped away and walked over a short distance past the tables to the side of the canal. If anyone had noticed her odd behavior, they didn't let on.

She held the phone to her ear and nodded, pretending to be on a call. She looked over to the sunset and took some deep cleansing breaths. She'd read that if she took one big deep breath in, followed by another short breath in right afterward, that it helped better fill the lungs. Then, exhale it all out in a long relaxing sigh.

It was cooler over here and the breeze was nice. She felt her heart rate decrease with each breath. She pretended to end the call and then stood looking at the sunset and took some photos with her phone. She felt like she could stand there watching for a few more minutes without attracting any undue attention. Watching sunsets in OC was basically considered a required behavior. Tonight, it had a breathtaking pinkish purple tint to it.

Next thing she knew, Olivia was beside her, her gaze at the horizon. "This is the first Ocean City sunset of my new life!" It had been too cloudy the past few days she was in town to see much of anything at sunset. "It's so gorgeous!" She turned and said, "Let's take a selfie!"

As Ray looked at their reflection on Olivia's phone, she thought to herself, *How am I almost 30 and this is my first sunset selfie?* Olivia took a few shots, touching the screen to change the focus and lighting. She made different faces, but Ray looked exactly the same in each photo, with what she considered to be a forced and awkward smile.

"Guess what, girl?" Olivia said as she kept taking photos and moving her arm around. "I just gave Evan your phone number! And… now… we have the winning photo!"

"Olivia. You did not," Ray said in a forceful, but hushed voice as she grabbed her arm. Ray's heart began to pound all the way up to her ears.

"He got a call and had to leave abruptly. He had asked me about your situation because he was obviously intrigued by your mystique," said Olivia. "I told him you were single and ready to mingle. That's true, right?"

It might have been true, but Ray felt like Evan was way out of her league, and he seemed younger. *Much younger.*

Ray had only ever been in one serious, long-term relationship. That was during college and for a couple years after. Four years total. She thought she would marry the guy— a nerdy computer scientist named Arnold. He ended it, right when she thought they might be getting engaged.

It was a blow to her self-esteem. He moved to Silicon Valley and had been working for tech firms, making it big—at least that's what he led people to believe via his Twitter and LinkedIn accounts. She wasn't "friends" with him on anything else.

"Yes. Okay. It's true, I do want to find love," said Ray, feeling like she was in a confessional as a contestant on *The Bachelor*, which she would never admit to watching.

Ray let out a huge sigh and closed her eyes. Olivia looked up as she hit send on the sunset photos to Ray's phone.

"Don't you worry one bit," said Olivia. "I'm here to reignite your love life. I'm a certified professional matchmaker! That's what all my friends out west in D.C. call me… along with 'Nosey Nellie.'" Olivia laughed. "We will work on your *Rizz*, girl."

She'd only had two drinks. Not much for most people, but Ray could tell Olivia was buzzed. "Um. Rizz?" Ray asked. "What the heck is that?"

"Your charisma. You know, charm. Cah-rizzzzz-ma," Olivia sounded it out and waved her hand in the air with a large flourish.

The next thing Ray saw was Olivia's phone flying through the air. It landed with a thump right near the edge of the dock. It bounced in what seemed to be slow motion across the wooden boards, end over end, closer and closer to falling in the water.

Olivia screeched, dropped her almost-empty orange crush drink, and took a dive onto the ground to try to save the phone—but it was too late. It fell into the canal with a short unassuming, *Plop.*

Olivia was splayed out flat on the ground on her stomach looking at the rings in the water where her phone disappeared, whispering, "No, no, no! Not my phone!"

"Hey, lady, you must have had airplane mode turned off!" yelled one smart aleck kid who was with a group of teens seated nearby. They all started laughing. Ray tried not to smile. *That was a good one!*

Ray bent down and helped Olivia up, embarrassed by the looks they were getting from everyone at the restaurant. Nobody walked over; they kept their distance. They were probably unsure what to do in the case of a phone overboard. It wasn't like it was a legitimate emergency.

Ray looked over the edge and into the water. It probably wasn't very deep, but she couldn't see the bottom. It was getting dark, and the water was murky, probably from when the phone hit the bottom. She thought they'd probably be able to find it if they jumped in and searched, but that was up to Olivia. She didn't know if the phone was water resistant or waterproof. But Ray wasn't going to offer to go in there on a recovery mission anyway.

CHAPTER 15
Evan

It had been an eventful few days for Evan. He was still annoyed with Brandon for keeping him in the dark about his marriage. Sure, he could pretend like everything was cool now, but would he ever truly forget what happened?

Evan abruptly left JJ's that night because his mom had texted both him and Brandon that someone shot a bullet through the living room wall. Evan immediately called his mom back, asking her for details, making sure she was ok.

By the time Evan arrived back home—with Brandon and Raymond close behind—the police were there, saying that they would take the bullet and do forensics on it, but their thought was that someone shot the gun from the huge, wooded lot across the road. It was hunting season for wild turkey. There was drywall dust all over the floor and an obvious hole in the siding on the outside of the house. His mom was shaken up, but she was nothing if not resilient.

After the police left, Evan's mom uncovered a homemade apple pie that smelled delicious. She cut it into four huge slices, inviting them all to sit down at the table and have a family talk. They talked about Brandon's marriage, and Evan's breakup with Ellie. Evan started to feel like it was an intervention. His mom said he hadn't been acting normally for quite a while. He was aloof and just uninterested in the things that usually gave him joy. At the end of the conversation, which lasted at least 30 minutes, Evan realized that breaking up with Ellie was probably a good decision. He would also do a better job of staying connected with his family.

Ellie had moved out of their shared apartment yesterday with way less drama than he expected. She was going back to stay with her parents, at least that's what she'd told him when he said he never wanted to see her again.

Evan was moving back into his apartment later that day. Not that he had too much to move, but he was glad to be out of his mom's house. His work set-up at the apartment was so much nicer. He had his standing desk and fancy ergonomic chair, his ring light, double monitors, speakers, docking station, and his $350 gaming headset, thanks to his annual at-home office allowance from work.

Even though it was Sunday, he wanted to do a bit more research on their new client WAFN before his dinner with Casey tonight. And to top it off, he'd been texting Ray, too. He realized right away that Ray was a different kind of girl. More mature, and not just because she was older than him. Sophisticated. Not a party girl. If he wanted to date her, he wouldn't be able to date Casey at the same time.

Brandon had been shocked that Evan was more attracted to Ray since Olivia fit his normal type to a "T." There was something about Ray that was so intriguing. Hopefully, he would be able to take her on a date soon and upgrade from their nightly texting pattern. He got the impression this would be a slow build.

Evan had gone to JJ's again yesterday for lunch and talked briefly with Olivia, who looked like she'd been working there for years with her command of the menu and mobile tablet ordering process. She was a dynamo for sure. No wonder she was an elementary school teacher—she was so frickin' friendly. Since she was just divorced, she had sworn off men for the entire summer, apparently, much to the dismay of the new bartender named Dan who was helping Raymond out for the summer.

As Evan hooked up his computer, he put his phone on the charging station as it pinged. A text from Ray. *Oh, yes*, he thought.

Ray to Evan:
Good afternoon! You know by now that I'm so bad with texting, so apologies on the late notice, but I wanted to check to see if you're free later today for drinks.

That new brewing company at the old Embers buffet location is open now - The Other One. Olivia says she knows the happy hour entertainment, a guitarist/singer. We're both going. No pressure. Just trying to be proactive and friendly.

Of course, this conflicts with the Casey date, Evan thought. He was supposed to meet her at 7 p.m. He could still go to happy hour too, right?

Evan to Ray:
Yes! What time? I have dinner plans but could do happy hour until 6:30

After Ray didn't respond immediately, he walked back to his desk. He pulled out his chair and sat down, and as he leaned to scoot the chair into place, he heard a sharp "ping" like something had snapped. In an instant, the backrest of the chair fell backward to the floor while the seat remained solid where it was. Evan's legs shot up into the air and hit the desk as his head fell backward with a loud thump.

"What the…" Evan shouted as he picked his head up off of the now sideways chair back, rubbing his elbow, which had rammed into the armrest on the way down. "She must have boobytrapped the place before she left," Evan said to himself as he looked warily around at the rest of the room.

Evan had assembled the chair and knew there was no way that could have happened without some kind of tampering. He was sure the chair wasn't all that Ellie had planned for him. *She is so immature*, he thought.

After he stood up, he looked more closely at his scraped knee, which was sure to get a bruise. He walked around the apartment and didn't notice anything else out of the ordinary. She probably wouldn't do anything too obvious that couldn't be blamed on coincidence. What was wrong with her? She was the one who was cheating on him. Why was *she* so mad?

After Evan had calmed down and fixed the chair, he started researching WAFN again. He was still perplexed by their news feeds, which seemed to have no rhyme or reason to the content. Was it legit news? And did that matter? They were being paid either way to do the website, whether it was legit or not.

The Onion was super popular, and it was fake news. Everyone knew that. Well, almost everyone; except for those few people who were always commenting: "This can't be real!" *Duh*. His mom was probably one of those naive people.

Evan had signed up to follow all the WAFN social media accounts and subscribed to their newsletters. The latest one had the subject "Biden trips and falls. Again. His body is deteriorating from atrial fibrillation." Atrial fibrillation is a common thing—irregular heartbeat. But some people may have thought it was something more serious by the way it was worded. Not exactly fake news, but a dramatization and an irrelevant connection to his tripping. Evan went onto LinkedIn and found the WAFN company page. It had about a dozen employees listed, and he sent connection requests to the three people he recognized talking with during their initial video calls. Their profiles seemed a little light on information, but not everyone was as obsessed with LinkedIn as he was. He had a 95% complete profile, of which he was quite proud! For only being 25, having 300 connections wasn't bad. He only connected with people who he actually knew—classmates and teachers from high school and college, colleagues and clients at work, family friends, church friends. He had a large network. He looked at his notifications. Nothing major.

Evan thought for a moment and realized he didn't know Ray's last name. Not that he wanted to be a creepy stalker… and he *could* wait to ask her tonight. But she was a cybersecurity analyst, so surely she had a profile on LinkedIn.

He typed in "ray ocean city maryland" and then clicked on the people tab. There were 29 results. The benefit of living in a small town comes through for once! Many of the results didn't have photos, and none sounded like her. *Maybe Ray is short for something*, he thought.

He typed "girl names with ray" into the Google search bar. There was an actual blog post titled, *70 Girl Names Starting with Ray. Unbelievable*, Evan thought. They were all weird names except for Raychel. Or maybe her name was Rachel.

One more search on LinkedIn. Bingo. "Rachel Anders."

She had her profile view settings limited to non-connections, and he couldn't see much information. It was most definitely her. Now that he had her name, he'd do some other searches. After going down the Google rabbit hole for about 30 minutes, he knew a bit more about Ray, but given her profession, she kept a superficial online presence. And all her social media accounts were private.

She had a short profile on her company website and a couple of webinars on YouTube. He read her profile. "Whaaaaat?" Evan said aloud in surprise. "She went to frickin' MIT? And has a master's degree? Okay. So, she's super smart. Ray slays!"

She had lived around Baltimore or D.C. for most of her life, but her parents—likely named John and Gloria—sold the house a few years ago. And siblings—he saw just one at the home address, Brenda, younger. Ray's predicted age was 29. And the Ocean City townhouse was in her dad's name.

He was done being a creeper. He'd have to shower and get ready for his dates now. Only one week out of his long-term relationship, and two women!

When he got in the shower, he cautiously turned on the water and then smelled the shampoo to make sure it wasn't something like hair remover or bleach. Maybe that was Ellie's plan, to make him paranoid.

CHAPTER 16
Ray

Olivia to Ray:
I finally got my new phone!!! Yaaaaaaaayyyyy!!

TY for emailing your phone number.

Per email question: Your OOTD should be the new slim dark denim cropped jeans with white flowy shirt and lavender tank. And the three-tier gold necklace.

You can wear your sneakers since you have to walk. But if I were you, I'd wear those cute new navy sandals or Crocs but be sure to paint your toenails!!!!

Ray thumbs-upped the message and went to Google to search what the heck "OOTD" meant. "Okay," she whispered. "Outfit of the Day. Okay. That makes sense."

She was not painting her toenails, and she'd wear her sneakers. Olivia had coerced her into buying a pair of Crocs at the outlets. Ray had to admit they were much more comfortable than she expected, but there was no way she would ever wear them anywhere aside from the beach or to take Charlie out. They were mint green, and Olivia had added *Hello Kitty* shoe charms she called "Jibbitz." Apparently, when you taught elementary school, you had an entirely different perspective on fashion.

Olivia was still at work and was going to stop at the brewery on her way back after her shift at JJ's, which was done early today. Ray would go over and let out Ruby before she left.

Ray couldn't believe they'd exchanged keys in case of emergency. Mostly, it was for Ray to take Ruby on a walk if Olivia was stuck at work longer than anticipated. It made rational sense. When Ray had her quarterly work meetings, maybe Olivia could watch Charlie.

Ray had not been on a date since long before COVID. Not that she was sure Evan would consider it a date. There was a man involved who she was attracted to, and she was wearing her new clothes and makeup—so at least by her standards, it was a date.

She put on bigger earrings in place of her daily diamond studs. They were swirly blue and white, round with a sterling silver base. They looked like ocean waves. She'd never even worn them yet. With her short hair, she was generally self-conscious when she wore bigger earrings. She'd picked them up at Sunfest last fall.

Typically, she would stay away from touristy events like Springfest and Sunfest, but her mom had been visiting and wanted to go. They'd gotten matching earrings, and she'd insisted on buying a sun-themed metal art piece that they had hung on the front porch of the beach house.

Springfest was next weekend. That meant the summer season was ramping up. More people, more traffic. More things open, more options for dining, entertainment, and shopping.

Before leaving her bedroom, she looked into her floor-length mirror. She looked good enough. She took a deep breath and then started making circles in the air with her nose to loosen the tension in her neck. She rolled 10 rotations to the right and 10 to the left. She could hear her neck cracking as she did it. Then she rolled her shoulders forward 10 times, and back 10 times. More cracking, but she instantly felt more relaxed.

She walked downstairs and grabbed Charlie's leash. They stopped to get Ruby, and then all three walked around the corner of the building to the grassy area. Ray felt weird being in this different type of outfit. It wasn't dressy by any standards, but it was just not *her*. She felt uncomfortable. The shirt was blowing around. It looked like a tent. Her eyes felt weird wearing the mascara Olivia insisted she use on her already-long eyelashes.

After she put the dogs back, Ray ran up to her bedroom and grabbed her denim jacket and slid into it as she went out the door to walk over to the brewery. Just a few blocks away, going south.

"Why a very good evening to you, my dear! Where are you off to all dressed up, Ray?" It was Ray's neighbor on the other side, Andrea.

"I'm meeting Olivia after she finishes up work. We're going to that new brewery in the Embers complex," answered Ray. "Have you met Olivia yet?"

"Oh, yes, hon. Olivia is such a lovely girl. She invited me over for tea last week after she moved in," said Andrea. "She made fresh blueberry scones! I was extremely impressed."

At this rate, Olivia would know more people in Ocean City in one week than Ray knew during her entire life coming to the beach!

"I'm so glad you girls can be friends, dear. I worry about you getting lonely working from home every day," continued Andrea. "You need a social life, Ray! You know I go up to the Senior Center on 41st Street a few times a week to meet my girlfriends. I do the ceramics classes, the garden club, and bingo. There's even a man there who I have my eye on. You know, you're never too old to find love, Ray!"

"I know, Andrea. I'll keep my eyes open. Well, I better get going or I'll be late," Ray said as she looked at her watch, knowing she had more than enough time to walk there and still be five minutes early.

As Ray walked, she focused on her breathing. Deep breaths. In. Hold. 1-2-3. Out. 1-2-3. Shoulders back. Chest out. Nose up. Jaw and hands unclenched.

She opened the door. The place was packed. Thank God Evan was already there and had gotten a table in the corner. He waved her over. Ray didn't like beer, but she could stand drinking it to be sociable when necessary. He stood and gave her a quick hug and kiss on the cheek.

"Hey. You're looking fantastic," said Evan. "I love those earrings! My mom has a pair just like them!"

"Moms," Ray laughed. "My mom has the same pair too. From Sunfest last fall."

They both laughed. Evan said, "So this place is totally rocking for it being their opening weekend! Want a beer? Looks like quite a wait, though. I'll go up and get them. What'll you have?"

"I'm easy to please—just get me whatever you're having," said Ray nervously. Now she'd have to sit here in the noisy crowd by herself for who knows how long. That's the major benefit of having a mobile phone, she thought as she tapped it open. She contemplated putting on the mask she had in her jacket pocket. Crowds still made her anxious. So many germs. At least they were by the door for better airflow, she thought.

Olivia to Ray:
OMW

Ray to Olivia:
It's packed. Evan is getting drinks at the bar and I'm crammed into a table in the back corner. Hurry and save me from the awkwardness!

Olivia texted a Bitmoji of her avatar saying, "You got this, girl!" Ray texted an eye rolling face back at her.

Earlier, Ray had done a light background check on Evan. Evan Andrew Michaels. Born: January 29, 1998. Current Age: 25.

Evan had an apartment in nearby Berlin and worked at a small marketing agency. His social media was low-key. His Instagram was private. His profile picture was of him on the beach with a surfboard. Ray didn't have TikTok on her personal phone for obvious reasons—it's a foreign spying app. But she had a work phone with an account for research purposes. If Evan had TikTok, he wasn't using his real name.

It looked like he had a girlfriend at some point recently named Ellie because they were tagged in a Facebook post about an event at a brewery in Berlin a couple months ago. Ellie was currently listed as single. She had likely cleared her accounts of any mentions of them together. She was cute. In the one picture of them together, they looked more like brother and sister. No romantic vibes whatsoever.

His mom attended a non-denominational Christian church and worked at Salisbury University. Ray easily could have done a legit full-blown background search, which she would do if things progressed. She did that kind of in-depth research all the time in her cyber work.

She looked over at Evan, who was finally ordering. He glanced over his shoulder and gave her a thumbs up—and was that a wink?

Evan had a typical surfer-dude look with his dark blonde hair, a little long and messy. It probably had sand in it. He was so tall, but his body seemed a little out of proportion. His legs were long and muscular, which made his torso seem a bit too small, comparatively. He was wearing a light blue Vineyard Vines long-sleeved t-shirt that had a whale on the back with tan shorts and navy flip-flops. He'd left his Salisbury University cap on their table. Dating at the beach was a casual endeavor, Ray realized, even though this was her first date in Ocean City.

Ray felt her cheeks starting to flush as she smiled and looked down to scroll through her Slack messages from work. There was a cyber breach in Florida that she'd need to look into first thing tomorrow morning. Still waiting for the related files to be uploaded to the secure environment.

As Evan made his way through the crowd a bit of beer sloshed out on his arm and shirt. "Damn, this place is lit today," he said as he put the glasses down on the table. It was so loud that Ray could barely hear him. And the entertainment was about to start. A 30ish-looking guy was tuning his guitar, barely visible through the crowd.

"Olivia will be here soon, and apparently, she knows the singer… so let's hang here for a bit and then maybe we can go out into the courtyard where it's not so loud?" The new courtyard area had a bunch of high-top tables for the BLU restaurant, but that wasn't open tonight.

Evan grabbed a game off the shelf beside them—one of those tabletop ring-on-a-string toss games where you tried to get the ring on the hook. They laughed as they finally got the *swing* of it, and Ray scored first. She was super competitive—in a friendly way—and it seemed like Evan was too.

CHAPTER 17
Olivia

Well, well, well. Olivia smiled and nodded as she made her way through the crowd and over to the corner table where Ray and Evan were laughing and playing a game. "I predict another Matchmaker Olivia success story!" She took her new phone out and snapped a picture of them. *They would thank her for that in the future!*

She slid into the bench seat next to Ray and said, "It is a very happy hour indeed, my friends!"

Ray smiled and Evan said, "Hey, Olivia! You made it! Ray tells me you know the singer?"

"Yes, well, 'know' may be a strong word for it. We met next door at Jay's Cafe last Friday. I've been stopping there each day on my way to JJ's to pick up coffee," she explained. "He had fliers and gave me one. We talked for about three minutes while I was waiting for my drink."

"You already know so many people. We are such opposites," said Ray, shaking her head.

Olivia laughed and quipped, "It's not what you know, it's who you know, they always say!"

"Want a beer, Olivia?" Evan asked, pointing with his thumb to the packed bar area. "Ray? Another?"

"Don't mind if I do, Evan!" Olivia laughed.

"No, thanks. I'm good," Ray said.

Olivia snapped a quick picture and video of the singer, whose name she couldn't remember. She would check later and tag him on her Insta story. Then she turned to Ray and said, "So give me the download! How's it going so far?"

"It's going too well, and I'm suspicious," said Ray. "Why does he seem to be into me? It doesn't make sense."

"Ray, you're a queen. You've got that thang! The *it factor*," she continued. "Like you're hiding secrets. It's intriguing! Downright fascinating!"

"Olivia, could you *be* a better hype person? I think not," Ray said in her best Chandler Bing impression. "And you haven't even had a beer yet."

"Oh, girl, I had two green tea shots with the crew at JJ's before I left there," Olivia laughed. "Ok, so more importantly, should I scoot and leave you two alone after I finish my beer?"

Olivia was bone tired. She wasn't used to being on her feet for hours at a time, and the clientele at JJ's was so diverse.

Families with crying toddlers to groups of rowdy teens. It was pure chaos. She was dreaming of her bed, and the sun hadn't even set. But she never let that side show. She was always the picture of positivity in public.

Ray said, "Evan can only stay about 30 minutes longer anyway, so wait and we can walk back together?"

"Ok. Cool. After I get my beer, I'm going to walk over near the singer and get some close-up pics," she said.

Olivia didn't want to get into it here with Ray, but she'd run into her ex-husband's sister (well, his stepsister) and her family at JJ's this afternoon. Her ex-niece and nephew were so cute. Was she still even "Auntie Olivia" to them? To say it was awkward was an extreme understatement.

They had no idea Olivia had moved to Ocean City and was working as a server at JJ's. In fact, they didn't even know she and Luke were divorced! Olivia immediately switched tables with another server, but she didn't completely ignore them. She gave the kids quick hugs and wished them a fun time at the beach. Her former sister-in-law texted her from the table, saying she was sorry for the awkwardness of the situation.

Evan brought back Olivia's glass of beer and Olivia stood up to get it. "Hey, let's take a quick group picture and then I'm going to make my way up to the singer."

Olivia had to reset most of her passwords because she couldn't remember them as she logged into the apps on her new phone earlier that day. And many of her frequently used passwords included Luke's name, and that was obviously unacceptable now. For some reason, her account information hadn't successfully transferred to her new phone from the cloud.

As she was posting the picture to her Instagram story, her phone pinged. She swiped down to check the text. It was Luke's number. Was she psychic? She had literally just thought of his name when he texted her.

She hadn't had a chance to sync up her contacts yet in her new phone, or block Luke. Of course, his sister would have told him she saw her at the restaurant. Unbelievable!

Luke to Olivia:
Hey, my stepsister said she ran into you waitressing at a place in Ocean City today. And she gave me hell for not telling her about the divorce! Could you please refrain from mentioning my name to anyone? My life is not any of her business – or yours at this point.

Are you short on money? You seem a little old to take on a summer job like that?

Olivia closed out of it straight away and took a close-up video of the guy singing *Hotel California…* he had changed up the lyrics in a super corny way saying, "Welcome to the beach in OCMD."

Olivia dropped her phone into her purse and took a deep breath. *Do not respond.* That's what her therapist would have told her to do.

For a minute, she wondered if she should dump her plan to stay away from men until 2024. It looked like it might be an extraordinarily long and lonely six months; especially if she lost her new best friend to a budding romance.

Olivia looked over at Evan and Ray, still playing that silly game with such intensity! Honestly, though, they were so cute together. *Le sigh.*

She checked her watch and sang along, swaying to the music and drinking her beer. She loved live music. She would try to get Ray to go with her to one of the top night spots like the newly opened Marlin's Point or old staples like Purple Moose, Seacrets, and Fagers Island this summer to check out the live music scene. She had a favorite local band she loved that would be in OC a few times this summer.

Olivia began to sing very loudly with full vigor when he started playing *Sweet Caroline* and tried to forget about her ex-husband problems. After Evan left, she'd tell Ray all about the Luke situation.

CHAPTER 18
Evan

Evan didn't want to leave Ray to go and meet Casey, but he would because he was not the kind of guy who would stand someone up or cancel at the last minute. Also, it was always better to leave on a high note than to wait until it became too awkward. He wouldn't have tried to give her a kiss, anyway. This was barely a date, in his opinion. It was too short, too crowded, and no food was involved. He would jump up and say a quick farewell.

He'd already finished his one beer. "So, I wish I didn't already have dinner plans for tonight, but I've gotta get going or I'll be late. Maybe we can meet for dinner sometime during the week or next weekend? Some place that isn't so loud?"

Ray nodded and said, "Sure. Maybe sometime this week? I'm on call for work next weekend. You know, in case there are any huge cyber threats that might take down the entire U.S. infrastructure and end humanity as we now know it."

Evan smiled. "Ok, sure, I'll check my calendar and text you. Say goodbye to Olivia for me? Looks like she is busy singing and dancing! See you soon. It was fun!"

He stood up and waved and walked out the door, hitting his shoulder into the door frame, and then his foot knocked over the *Grand Opening* poster that was up on an easel outside the door. He was able to grab the poster before it hit the ground.

He always felt so uncomfortable in his own skin, except when he was surfing. He had zero game with women. He was such a big dorky giant. Hopefully, she hadn't been watching. He set the sign back on its stand and then rubbed his elbow.

Of course, it was the same elbow he crashed into the chair earlier today.

His phone vibrated, and he saw that Casey had texted him saying she was running about 10 minutes late. He went and sat in his car.

The Embers mini golf across the parking lot was packed. He watched the volcano do its timed eruption. He hadn't played there in a while, but throughout his entire life he'd played every single mini golf course in town. There were more than a dozen. As a child, he thought there must be more mini golf courses in OC than anywhere in the world. He'd recently read an article that Myrtle Beach, South Carolina, boasted the most mini golf courses in the world, at around 50. He'd been there a few times and could attest there were a lot of them.

A couple walked in front of him with a collie. He chuckled and said to himself, "Gonna go and save Timmy from the well, Lassie?" The dog pranced down the sidewalk as if she were the star of her own pet parade.

Evan loved animals. When he was younger, though, his dad had been allergic to pets, so they hadn't ever owned anything other than a few goldfish in a bowl. Once his dad had died, it was too expensive to consider getting a pet. Ellie had talked about wanting to get a dog. She always had pets growing up, but pets were a big commitment. And now his mom had two kittens? Life was impossible to predict.

Walk This Way on his Aerosmith playlist automatically started as he turned on the car. It would only take him five minutes to get to where he was meeting Casey, so he continued to sit there. After a few minutes, he saw Ray and Olivia walking up the street. That's weird, he thought. He could have sworn they lived in the other direction.

As a pair, Olivia was by far more conventionally attractive. She was tall and shapely, and approachable. Her makeup and hair were always perfect. Ray was more striking with her chiseled body and short hair. She had such a sexy vibe, like she was unapologetically herself no matter what anyone else thought about her. A cool confidence. It was intense and alluring. Not Evan's usual type. And she was a few years older. He barely knew her, but there was a spark he couldn't ignore and had to explore.

He pulled out of the parking lot and passed them as they walked on the sidewalk. He got to the restaurant, was seated, and began to munch on some tortilla chips and salsa and ordered ice water. Casey had texted again right as he sat down that she was still enroute. Evan mindlessly swiped through Instagram stories until she arrived.

When she arrived, he stood to give her a hug, oblivious to the fact Ray and Olivia had just walked into that same restaurant.

CHAPTER 19
Ray

After Olivia told Ray about her ex-husband drama, she'd suggested they go and grab some dinner at the new Mexican restaurant down Coastal Highway called Papi's Tacos.

When they walked in, Ray immediately noticed Evan directly across from the front door. There was only one table visible in front of her, past the bar. He was just sitting down with a girl. "What the hell," she whispered to Olivia. "Look over there. It's Evan and some rando girl. We have got to leave."

"Oh, come on, Ray," said Olivia. "You never know—maybe it's just his sister?"

Olivia grabbed Ray's hand and struggled to pull her over to Evan's table. Evan had seen them at this point, so there was no point in trying to ignore him.

"Hey, Evan! You left your baseball hat at the brewery just now. We followed you all the way here to return it," laughed Olivia. "Seriously, though, it is such a coincidence that we're all here now, right?"

Evan reluctantly grabbed his hat, which Olivia had taken out of her bag where she had put it at the brewery for safekeeping. Olivia looked directly at the woman—who seemed very confused at this point in the conversation—and held out her hand. "Hi! I'm Olivia, and this is Ray."

Evan finally gathered himself together, and said, "Yeah, sorry. This is Casey. She and I went to the same high school."

Evan was noticeably embarrassed, and Ray's heart was beating into overdrive as she felt beads of sweat gathering on her upper lip. Ray stayed back. Honestly, she was still not comfortable shaking hands. She had hoped it would never come back into fashion.

Olivia just kept up with her chipper charade and said, "Oh, that's great. Old friends catching up? Fun. Well, we'll leave you to it! See you soon, Evan!"

Olivia grabbed Ray's arm, and they went over to the bar. The far side of the bar. Ray had been rendered mute.

"Ray, you don't need to be embarrassed," said Olivia. "You knew he had dinner plans, but he still wanted to see you beforehand. This Casey girl is obviously a friend. He is so into you!"

Ray knew she had no right to be jealous. She had literally just asked him to happy hour a few hours ago. And he came. Even so, she felt her eyes welling up a bit.

"I'm heading to the bathroom, be right back." Ray did her best to look away as she darted past the front door and into the restroom.

When she got back to the bar, Olivia had ordered loaded nachos and margaritas for them. Ray had not had this much to drink during one week since she'd been in college. Even the nerd herd at MIT could party it up. She took a sip of the margarita. The lime was fresh, the ice was perfectly crushed.

The fact that Evan seemed embarrassed was positive. It meant that he liked Ray, right? She turned her attention to Olivia who was staring at her new phone with a very irritated look, which quickly turned into a smile when she noticed Ray was looking at her. Fortunately, Evan's table was completely blocked from their view by the bar.

"What's wrong?" Ray asked as she pointed to Olivia's phone. I saw your face just now and you did not look happy."

"My ex-husband is such a total freak," she replied. "Now that he knows where I am, he won't stop texting me, so I blocked his number… again." Ray nodded, unsure of how to respond. "And now I'm posting some pics of our happy hour to my story," she said. "Look at this cute one of you, me, and Evan."

"You're like a Kardashian or a Jenner, capturing every single minute of your life on camera! I've never even looked at an Instagram story before," said Ray.

"What's your username? Let's connect," said Olivia.

"I'd rather not, but I know you will keep pestering me about it," laughed Ray. "It's a weird handle. It's CharlieRay1029384756…"

"Ok," Olivia interrupted. "Found it. You have no followers. No posts. And you're not following anyone? No wonder you've never seen an Insta story before, girl. Give me your phone. Now. We must fix this." Olivia took Ray's phone and uploaded the sunset pic of them as Ray's profile picture. "Thank goodness I texted those sunset pictures to you before I dropped my phone in the bay! Otherwise, they wouldn't have been backed up to my cloud and would have been lost forever," said Olivia.

"Yeah, thank goodness for that," Ray said in a very sarcastic tone.

Olivia ignored her and continued her tapping as Ray sipped her drink. She followed her own account and then started following all the mainstream accounts she was following on Ray's account.

"What kind of music do you like?" Olivia asked.

"Don't laugh, but I like older stuff. Well, old for us," Ray answered. "Like the 80s and 90s."

"I'm an expert on all types of music," said Olivia. "So, I approve. A bunch of the older pop stars don't do their own Insta, so they have sorta lame posts."

After a few minutes of speedy tapping, she said, "This may seem very random, but I love Brian May's Insta. You know— the guitarist from Queen? And obviously Adam Lambert. So good."

If this was the kind of distraction both Olivia and Ray needed to feel better, Ray was all for it. She was fairly certain that having a legit Instagram account would not put her in any kind of risk of cyber threat. She was keeping it private. And only had one follower in Olivia.

"I watched that Queen documentary on Netflix the other night. *The Show Must Go On* or something like that," said Olivia as she continued her furious phone tapping. "It was so good. I cried. You know, I saw Adam Lambert and Queen at a concert a few years ago. Totally epic."

Ray thought she could easily just sit there quietly and not say another word while Olivia chattered away, mindlessly lost in Instagram.

Living alone in Ocean City for the past couple years, Ray had almost given up on finding love. Even if this thing with Evan didn't progress, Ray realized that although she felt completely comfortable in her life as a hermit, she needed to give some hard thought to what she wanted out of life. She was almost 30 years old. She had an excellent job making good money. But what else did she want out of life? A husband and children, she thought. She didn't *need* a family to be happy, but it would surely help.

This is why she didn't drink alcohol frequently. She was a quiet contemplative drunk and always ended up pondering life's big questions after she had more than a couple of drinks.

CHAPTER 20
Evan

After the fastest dinner date on record, Evan said goodbye to Casey outside in the parking lot with a casual hug and then sat in his car until she drove away. He then walked back inside the restaurant and straight to the bar where Olivia and Ray were still seated.

Olivia was staring at her phone, and Ray was watching the ball game on the big screen on the wall across from the bar. The Os were winning, playing the Detroit Tigers.

The seat next to Ray was open, and Evan inconspicuously slid into it. She hadn't noticed him yet since her body was turned toward Olivia. He had to play this exactly right or he was doomed.

He watched the game, and the Orioles had a base hit. He clapped and shouted, "Let's go, Os!"

Ray turned, and the look in her eyes told him all he needed to know. She was into him too. She smiled... such a beautiful smile that lit up her entire face.

He smiled back and let out the breath he didn't realize he was holding. He reached out and grabbed her hand and pulled it up to his lips and gave it a quick kiss. "Need a ride home, my lady? I'm at your service."

"Evan! What's going on here?" Olivia said as she finally noticed he was there. "Of course, we'll take a ride home! We're totally wasted! But wait. Where's your *lady friend?* And are *you* okay to drive us?"

"We're just friends. Nothing romantic at all. Yeah. I only had one beer earlier and drank water here before I was able to escape that disaster of a dinner," Evan replied.

When Casey had finally arrived at the restaurant, Evan immediately got the vibe that her mind was a million miles away and she was not interested in being at dinner with him.

After their awkward greeting, Evan's stomach dropped the moment he noticed Ray and Olivia walking to his table. He was literally without words when Olivia handed him his baseball hat.

Casey was not oblivious, and realized the connection between Ray and Evan. After they left the table, she told Evan that she'd been hanging out with a guy she really liked right beforehand, but she didn't want to cancel on Evan. Both relieved, they made it through the rest of dinner reminiscing about high school friends and teachers. Wondering if they'd attend their 10-year reunion. Their fifth hadn't happened due to COVID. Casey had kept in touch with way more high school friends than Evan did, so she had a lot of interesting stories to tell. But Evan could hardly concentrate on what she was saying.

Once the girls settled their bar tab, Evan walked them out to his car and asked where they lived. It was a short drive. Aerosmith's *Dream On* was playing. Olivia started singing… or more like screaming from the back seat. Ray had closed her eyes, and her head was swaying to the beat. He turned it up louder. He started singing. He opened the windows. Olivia was playing the air guitar now during the gratuitous guitar solo.

By the end of the song, they pulled into the parking lot. "This is as close as you can get," said Ray. "We'll just have to walk down along the pier from here."

Evan put the car in park and said, "Want me to help you walk back with Olivia?"

Ray said no and thanked him for the ride as she got out of the car and opened the back door to collect Olivia.

"Come on, dreamer, and let's get you to bed," said Ray. She gave a quick wave to Evan as she put her arm around Olivia and led her down the wooden walkway next to the canal. He stood by his car feeling like he should be helping, but Ray said no, and he would honor her wishes. Evan called out, "I'll text you about going to dinner later this week, ok?"

Evan kept watching until they entered the townhouse, and then he got back into his car. He grabbed his phone out of his pocket and checked for any notifications. Brandon texted him asking about his two-date night. Ever since the big bomb dropped at JJ's, he'd been texting his brother a few times a day and it felt good to be more connected with him.

Evan looked up and saw Ray walking two dogs around the far side of the complex. He opened the car door and started walking over to the grassy area where he could see her struggling to hold both dogs while she tried to open a plastic poop bag.

He walked up behind her. There were a number of streetlights, so it was bright enough but he didn't want to startle her as she finished the poop pickup. Suddenly, Ray turned around and bam! She literally ran right into Evan. "Dude! Stalk much! You scared the crap out of me!"

"I was waiting to make sure you got into your place okay. Then I saw you walking back here with the dogs and I thought maybe I'd try to grab you for a proper good night without Olivia witnessing it."

Evan leaned down to pet the dogs and said, "Finally! I'm getting an intro to this hyper hat-chasing beach-zoomie dog!"

Ray laughed. "Crazy Charlie here is my dog, and this one is Ruby, Olivia's dog."

The dogs were both very friendly and were pushing their bodies up against Evan, tails wagging for attention. When

Evan stood straight and turned his attention back to Ray, the dog leashes started wrapping around Ray and Evan, pulling them closer together. Ray tried unsuccessfully to sort it out, but Charlie jumped up. The next thing Evan knew, he lost his balance and he was falling down backward and took Ray with him.

They hit the grass with a thud, both dogs and Ray all on top of him. A pile of arms and legs and furry bodies. The dogs squirmed to stand up first and then started licking Ray and Evan's faces, thinking it was playtime.

"Ok. That was not the kind of kiss I was expecting," Evan laughed as he tried to cover his face with his hands and sit up at the same time. "Ray, are you ok?"

She mumbled something incomprehensible as she tried to untangle herself from the leashes. She looked unscathed. A little annoyed, maybe?

They stood up and got the dogs situated. "Should we try that again?" Evan asked.

Ray shook her head, and she seemed flushed. Evan wondered if she was embarrassed or was giving him a signal she wasn't interested in him. "Why don't you come and help me get the dogs back inside and I'll make sure Olivia is settled in?" Ray asked as she started pulling the dogs back to the complex.

Evan followed her around the building, and she handed him Charlie's leash. "Maybe just take Charlie back to my place and I'll be back momentarily. Over there, right next door."

Was she inviting him back to her place? That was unexpected. A dozen thoughts crept into his mind. He didn't have any condoms on him. But no. He would not sleep with her on the first date anyway. He was not that kind of guy, no matter how attracted he was to Ray. And she was not that kind of girl, right?

Different scenarios were going through his mind. He could stand inside her front door, which seemed creepy. Or maybe he'd go outside to the front step and sit there. Her place seemed cozy, uncluttered, and clean. The decor was definitely dated. It didn't go with the modern and sophisticated vibe he got from Ray.

As he opened the door to go back outside, she was coming up the front steps.

"Hey," she said.

"Hiya," Evan said as he took a step down to her level. "So, I was thinking that since I made a mess of this day, why don't we have a do-over on Tuesday night? Taco Tuesday?"

"Actually, I thought today was perfect," said Ray as she walked a step higher to be more even with his height. She leaned in. "Do you want to give a good night kiss another shot and try not to knock us both over this time?"

Yes. Yes. Yes, thought Evan. He locked eyes with her and leaned his head down and pulled her body into his with one swift motion. He took an extra few seconds to really look into her eyes and touched his nose to hers. She moved in and started the kiss, gently touching her lips to his before putting her hand on the back of his head and pulling him down closer to deepen the kiss.

It started slowly, but quickly escalated into something inappropriate for the outdoors as the neighbors were bustling about, closing up their doors and windows for the night.

Evan pulled away, reluctantly, with a huge smile on his face. "I'm going to wish you a very good night with sweet dreams and take my leave now," he said as he nervously backed down the rest of the steps. He waved and said, "Tuesday, we start where we just left off?"

Ray smiled and looked down at her hands, which were tightly gripping the railing by the front steps. "Yes. Sounds great. Thanks so much for the ride back home," said Ray quietly as she glanced over at her front window.

Charlie was looking at Evan through the window with a quizzical look on his furry face. Evan waved again. To the dog? He needed to turn away and stop with the cheesy waving.

Ray watched him walk down the path. He could feel her eyes on him and didn't hear her door open and close. A couple seagulls stood on the top of his car's hood, creepily staring at him as he approached. They flew off when his car door slammed shut. He got into his car and started the engine and let out a quick, "Oh yeah!" and tapped his hands on the steering wheel with the beat of the music. *Back in the Saddle* was playing. Was his life story an Aerosmith musical?

Now that was a legit kiss. At that moment, he felt like all his previous kisses had been so immature. Was this the kind of fireworks moment people talked about in the movies? If you know, you know?

It was still kind of early to be calling it a night for his normal routine, but it had been a long day, so he started the drive back to his apartment. He still needed to finish the laundry and get some fresh sheets on the bed and clean towels in the bathroom. He'd kept the fancy bamboo towels his mom had gotten them last Christmas. Small victories were sweet.

As he drove, he wondered how he ended up falling flat on his back twice in one day. He mentally started counting how many bruises he'd probably see on his body tomorrow.

Once he got home, he walked straight to the dryer to get out a load of laundry. He had a definite spring in his step and was whistling a little tune his dad used to always whistle. Evan hadn't known much about the ditty except that it was in *The Parent Trap* movie, which his parents loved, and they watched over and over again when he was little. The original Hayley Mills version and also the Lindsay Lohan re-make. Later on, he had looked it up and found that it was officially called "Colonel

Bogey March," which was also in the old-time movie *The Bridge on the River Kwai*. It was a British military march. *Props to the internet, once again, for the win*, he thought.

"What in the bloody hell?" Evan said as he opened the dryer. The laundry was all completely discolored; it looked like it all had been tie-dyed pink. "What did she do? Put actual red paint in there?" He angrily threw everything into his laundry basket, shaking his head back and forth in disbelief. He would have to be more resilient with checking for booby traps from now on, he figured.

After he put the stained sheets on the bed, he was exhausted and was asleep within 30 minutes. His alarm went off what seemed like only moments later. He opened his eyes. It was still pitch-black outside. "What in the actual hell? That's not my normal alarm sound." He sat up and tried to track the sound. It came from the closet. He stumbled across the room and turned on the light and opened the closet door.

"So frickin' childish, Ellie. A hidden alarm clock?"

Monday, May 1, 2023
A few hours later.

CHAPTER 21
Luke Lewis

It was well after midnight, but Luke hardly ever went to bed before 2 a.m. Now that he wasn't married, there was nobody nagging him to get off the computer and come to bed. Also, his friends were most active online from 10 p.m. to 2 a.m., after the rest of their families went to sleep. As for his overseas connections, it was early morning or middle of the day. He only had to roll out of bed at 8:30 a.m. to log in to work now that he was a full-time remote worker as a financial analyst.

Right now, however, he scrolled through Olivia's Instagram story for the fifth time, and he was fuming mad. She had blocked him on all his legitimate accounts long ago, but he'd made accounts in the name of their mutual college friend Nate Smith. A generic name and a good-looking guy. Nate didn't use social media. He'd moved away to the U.K. after graduation and didn't keep in touch with anyone. The farce was unlikely to be detected by Olivia, or anyone in their friend circle.

Luke never posted anything from that account; he was just a social media voyeur. The most anyone could tell was that he was active online, but so far nobody had ever DMd Nate. He'd followed about 50 other accounts to make it seem more legit and had accepted anyone who wanted to follow him. Olivia had followed back. He would only be considered a catfish if he engaged in conversation, right?

This was how he tracked Olivia. She was prolific on Instagram. Posting stories almost every single day. She was religiously active on TikTok too. She would buy fancy coffee drinks or matcha tea and post photos, barely taking five sips of the drink in total. Back when they were together, the various cups would sit on the kitchen island for entire days. The liquids slowly separated into disgusting layers, visible like a chemistry experiment in the clear plastic cup. That particular habit always irked him to no end. Wasting money like that.

He knew Olivia went to Ocean City last week and that she was likely to be staying in the beach house her parents bought a few years ago. She tried to get him to go there several times, but he hated the beach. He hated vacations in general. Or maybe he hadn't ever had a good vacation? Or the kind of vacation he would enjoy? Or maybe it was that he didn't have the right person to go on a vacation with.

Luke's family was not the vacationing type when he was growing up. The most they would do was travel to visit relatives… and that was never much fun. Same old routine every time. They'd put together puzzles and play the same board games. Eat at the same restaurants. His grandma would cook the same boring dinners. Hell, they'd even tell the exact same stories!

Now might be the perfect time to make his first trip to the Eastern Shore, Luke thought as he contemplatively tapped his index fingers together. He'd try to find out who this loser beach bum was in half of her 20 Instagram story clips today— well, yesterday at this point.

Talk about a random coincidence, but he heard from his do-gooder stepsister that Olivia was working at some ridiculous-looking dive bar called JJ's. At least his so-called sister was good for something. He'd been shocked to see a DM from her on his legit Instagram. She had never messaged him before. He hadn't seen her in years. She didn't even have his mobile phone number. Luke knew Olivia was in touch with his family prior to the split. She would always comment on their social posts and act like a doting auntie.

Afterward, he texted Olivia and was surprised his text went through since she had previously blocked his number. She didn't respond, and she hadn't texted him a Happy Birthday wish either. His birthday was a couple days ago. In fact, not a single person acknowledged it was his birthday. Sure, he got a dozen marketing texts and emails from lame companies trying to lure him in with miniscule discounts or a free appetizer, but no personal wishes. Not a single one. Not even on Facebook, and he had over one thousand friends on there!

He spent his birthday evening in the basement gym of his condo complex. He'd been pumping iron for the past few months, and his weight was below his pre-pandemic numbers. He listened to the *Conservative Review* podcast while he worked out. He was not really into music, and he relished the quiet in the condo now that Olivia was gone. She was always playing music, and it was so distracting.

Luke's mom had been dead for more than a few years now. His dad had a fancy new life with his new wife and her two grown children. He never figured his dad, a lifelong conservative, would marry someone who was an atheist and a vocal supporter of pro-choice and gun control issues. And to top it off, she was rich. Not that she made the money herself. Her first husband died and left her rolling in it. It's always the undeserving ones who luck out like that, Luke thought.

Luke had been invited to his dad's wedding in 2021. It was a small ceremony due to the pandemic. Luke claimed he had COVID at the last minute and couldn't attend it. That bitch Olivia had still gone without him! Olivia knew he was lying and that she hadn't been exposed. She told his family she hadn't been near Luke and had tested negative. Trying to make him look bad, no doubt. After that, she had made all of their mutual friends think *he* was the reason why they had split up. She was such a lying bitch. He would get his revenge. He just had to wait for the right time and keep planning. She had ruined his life. He would do his best to ruin hers, even more so than he'd done already.

His computer beeped. It was an email on his new secure email provider that he used for his *special projects*. Anyone on the Dark Web could find out names, emails, mobile phone numbers, usernames, and passwords. Even social security numbers! And most people were so clueless. They used ridiculously easy passwords or the exact same password in every single account. When accounts were compromised, they may have been prompted to change that particular password, but the same compromised password they used in all of their other accounts? Never changed it.

Up until today, Luke was able to log into Olivia's personal Gmail account. He monitored it somewhat regularly, and it was beyond boring. She communicated almost exclusively via text and social media DMs. Her inbox was a dump of promotional emails, except for when she was applying for new jobs a few months ago. Luke knew Olivia had gotten the job offer as a teacher in Ocean City before she knew herself. The email came in around 6:30 a.m., and he'd read it immediately and then marked it as unread. He'd considered replying and saying, "No, thank you," and then deleting it before she could read it.

Olivia must have just changed her password. It used to be his name and her name and their anniversary year. Now he couldn't guess what it was. He'd tried the dog's name and all the usual combinations. *Nothing.*

As far as the dog went, Luke didn't miss Ruby. *At all.* Having a dog was a hassle. It was expensive. Ruby loved Olivia best, and Luke was a distant second. The dog would look out the window and bark at people walking by on the street. Luke was embarrassed by what the neighbors must have thought of them. Oh, he claimed to be *so put out* that she wanted to take the dog, though. Luke had to play up his disappointment, so she'd feel guilty.

Luke opened Google Maps, and in another tab, he Googled "Hotels in Ocean City Maryland" and started planning his first trip to the Eastern Shore.

PART 2
Friday, June 9, 2023
More than a month later.

CHAPTER 22
Olivia

Olivia had settled into a comfortable yet chaotic routine, and each week was flying by. She couldn't believe it had been more than a month since she'd packed up and moved to the beach to start over. She'd taken a few days off from work to go with her mom, sister, and a couple friends to see Taylor Swift's *Eras Tour* in Philadelphia. They'd had the tickets since last August and had witnessed firsthand the online ticket sale debacle.

When Olivia started working at JJ's, she'd told him that she would need to have off the weekend of May 12-14. She drove to her parents' house that Friday, and then they all drove up to Philly on Saturday for the concert. It was only about a two-hour drive from Baltimore, so they came back home afterward. As far as concerts went, it was as amazing as she anticipated. Taylor's from Philly, so Olivia assumed the hometown concert was probably way better than others, right? Taylor sang more than 40 songs, and it lasted more than three hours. Olivia was going with the same crew to the Beyoncé concert in Washington, D.C., in August. It was a Girl Power summer. A Barbie Dream summer. And it was also #RatGirlSummer—that trend from TikTok about being a little selfish and doing what you like to do, with no regrets. Scurrying around town, going to places you shouldn't, and nibbling on junk food.

Now that summer was right around the corner, Olivia worked six days a week. JJ's was open every day, but she was able to take off every Monday or Tuesday, and her counterpart would take off Wednesdays or Thursdays. She had varied hours on the other days, mostly depending on the weather. The more hours, the better! She was saving up for her dream vacation to Europe, which she hoped to take early next summer. Maybe she could get Ray to go with her?

Ray and Evan were still seeing each other, but nothing serious yet, at least as far as Olivia knew. Evan had been super busy with a work project. He would come to JJ's whenever he was done surfing with his buddies, and then Ray would walk over with both dogs. Jack had no written policy on whether dogs were allowed, but since the tables were outside and the dogs were well behaved, nobody had said anything to Olivia yet.

They had become the three musketeers. Olivia smiled at the thought. They were almost always together. Jack had a boat, and they ended up going out on the bay almost every Wednesday to watch the sunset. Sometimes, they would ride over to Assateague Island and watch the wild ponies wander through the swampy bayside marsh. Olivia would look for birds. Sometimes, they'd have a picnic dinner, or else they'd dock at Macky's or de Lazy Lizard for a late meal.

Olivia initially thought she should back off as the third wheel, but Ray assured her they both wanted her to be there. Olivia was *fun* and having her around always made people *relaxed*, so Ray told her. Sometimes Evan's surfing buddies would join them, it was fluid. Olivia could have sworn Evan was trying to fix her up with his friends, but she just wasn't ready to date yet. Or maybe it was just that his friends seemed so immature?

Today, the weather was perfect, and Olivia was about to head over to the beach for about an hour until 10:15 a.m., which was when she had to get ready to go to work. Now that it was summer and dogs were not allowed on the beach, she was solo with her book and phone.

Mom to Olivia:
Good morning! How's everything going? Dad and I are thinking we might want to come down the weekend before July 4th. Ok with you?

Olivia to Mom:
Sure!! I'd love to see you both – I've met a lot of people but it's been lonely! Is Paula coming too?

Paula was on summer break from college, but she hadn't answered any of Olivia's recent texts. Olivia had no idea what her summer plans were.

Mom to Olivia:
I got today's Wordle in three guesses. Also, there's another game from NYT called Connections in beta. It's super fun!

Let's talk later and I'll give you the latest on Paula! Gotta run to class now. Have a fun day!!

Olivia tapped back to the OfferUp app. She had put in a bid on a bicycle that was a few miles away in West Ocean City, over by Assateague Island.

"Yay! I got it," she said to herself, pumping her fist in the air. She typed the seller and arranged a time to meet up to collect it. Like a lot of the bikes in town, it was simple and cheap and a purple pastel color with a cute little white basket on the front. No need to have something fancy and tempt a thief. The island was completely flat, so it wasn't like she would need a lot of gears anyway.

As Olivia opened her beach chair, she snagged her fingernail. She sat down and examined her fingernails more closely. She'd gotten acrylic nails at the salon for the first time as part of her Taylor Swift concert weekend festivities. She'd never had them before, and as far as she was concerned, she'd never get them again! They were super uncomfortable, and it was nearly impossible to type or put any of her jewelry on. Her jarred creams and make-up all had little stab marks in them as she tried to scoop out a bit. A couple nails kept getting caught in her hair when she washed it or tried to put it up in a ponytail. She'd heard that they would fall off on their own at some point, but right now they were just getting too long, and she couldn't stop obsessing about that annoying growth gap where her nails were naked.

She'd gotten the ombre French tip style, which did look amazing. Typically, she liked to use those popular stick-on Color Street nails, sold by the Avon ladies of the 2020s, her mom would always tell her. They were economical, looked great, and lasted for a few weeks. Being a server, she had to make sure her nails were on point. And she did have to admit she'd gotten endless compliments on the acrylics. Maybe she shouldn't say never again? She had a pair of Tokyo Lights from Color Street ready to go. Olivia liked the glittery ones best because it was harder to see the imperfections. She was now a total pro at applying them and had it down to a science, zooming through the process in half the time it took her when she first tried them out.

Olivia looked up over the water as a huge roar sounded. The planes were already practicing. It was so loud! The air show practice had made the beach much more crowded than usual for this early time of the day. Also, it was senior week and there were about four groups of recent grads setting up their beach camps nearby. There were a bunch of high-rise hotels around here at the end of the Boardwalk. This stretch was typically busier than other sections of the beach.

Olivia took a video of a plane flying by and a selfie with her book, donut, and iced coffee. Then, she posted them to TikTok and Instagram with all of the appropriate hashtags: #BookTok #Bookstagram #Summer #OCMD #AirShow #FracturedPrune #CoffeeBreak.

Olivia was trying to achieve success with the TikTok algorithm and accumulate more than 1,000 views straight away. Typically, all her posts would get around 230 views and wouldn't be shown on the "For You Page" by TikTok for longer than 30 minutes. Gradually, they would accumulate more views through the hashtags over time. She'd read that if she was able to get 500 views in 30 minutes with most of her viewers watching more than three seconds, that was the golden ticket. So far, the best videos she had were from the Taylor Swift concert. Taylor's stage dive was totally epic! Olivia posted something every single day. She had thousands of random videos on her phone, and it was easy to keep up with the content.

She switched apps and saw three posts on Facebook about graduations and said to herself, "How on earth can my little cousin Zoey be graduating?"

Then, Olivia realized she was "graduating" from *middle school.* As a teacher, she understood the importance of celebrating milestones, but all these inconsequential so-called graduation ceremonies were just plain ridiculous.

"Kiddo, if you can't graduate from middle school, you're in serious trouble in this world!" Olivia liked the post but didn't comment. She put her phone down and grabbed her book.

Different groups of teens had competing music playing on the beach. One was the local independent radio station—Ocean 98.1 WOCM, that broadcasted live from the Seacrets complex up the road. Back before streaming, pretty much everyone played that local beach station. Lately, however, most people brought Bluetooth speakers and played a variety of music, and more times than not the music was not appropriate for little ears. The loud music with offensive lyrics was one thing that Olivia could do without. Not that she minded the bad language so much, but to think that little kids were also hearing it, that got her fired up.

She couldn't concentrate on her book, and she put in her earbuds to try to block out the noise. She'd recently read a research article saying that when you were listening to music that you knew, it was easy to concentrate on other things. If you didn't know the music, it ended up being distracting because you couldn't easily tune it out.

Olivia had talked Ray and Evan into joining her for some live music this weekend. She'd seen three of the local cover bands performing this weekend in the past and loved them all. Her friend from high school was the drummer in a local Maryland band called Chesapeake High Tides, so she hoped they'd pick that one to go to. She followed them all on social media. She was excited to get back into her passion of live music after the pandemic drought. Brandon and Raymond might be joining them too, which would make things even more fun.

Olivia saw a few kids pointing out to the ocean excitedly and noticed a pod of dolphins not far behind where the waves were breaking. She took out her phone and took a few photos, trying to capture them when they came above the surface. After a few unsuccessful photo attempts, she switched to video. She took some vertical and some horizontal and made sure to wipe off her phone's camera lens, so the photo was crisp. There were some pelicans flying over too, diving into the water. *There must be a school of fish there too*, she thought.

Out further into the ocean she saw a boat pulling a parasailer. She was afraid of heights, but she also longed to try it. If she was going to be a local, she would have to do it, right? She wanted to go on the boat with the Maryland flag themed parasail. She did her best to get a video of the dolphins, pelicans, and parasailers all together. She would post it to Insta and TikTok.

An older man walked slowly, alone by the water, wearing a Ravens shirt and an Orioles hat. He looked over to her and

Olivia waved to him. Olivia loved the Ravens and the Orioles. As much as she didn't like the Patriots and the Steelers and the Yankees, she understood that people who lived in those areas should like those teams. What she didn't understand was how you could be a lifelong Baltimorean and not like the Ravens and Orioles. Why were some people just so contrary? It was fun to cheer on the home team! Olivia was not a fair-weather fan.

She had a list on her phone of all the activities she wanted to do—not necessarily all this summer, though. Parasail, fishing at the pier, renting a jet ski or wave runner, sunset tiki boat, go karts, Ferris wheel, mini golf, Ripley's Believe it or Not, Jolly Roger's water park, mirror maze, and those carnival games like whack-a-mole and spraying the water gun into the hole to make the balloon pop. She wanted to win a large stuffed animal. Obviously, it would be more exciting if a guy won it for her.

One thing that was not on her to-do list was the slingshot ride where you were flung high up into the air. *No, thank you,* she thought. That ride looked terrifying. She conscientiously added new things to the list every day.

She couldn't believe that she hadn't played mini golf yet! It was her favorite childhood summer vacation activity. Olivia had seen on Instagram that Tiger Woods had designed some totally epic mini golf courses that were now at a few locations in the U.S. Not around there, but Ocean City had so many courses! Some were better than others.

When she was little, her dream was to own a mini golf course. Olivia always loved playing with her family, even though she would rarely win. She knew her mom would throw the game to make the kids feel better, but her dad was always too competitive and would do his best to beat them all.

Her little sister Paula would almost always get frustrated and give up halfway through the course, throwing her always-pink golf ball into the water trap. If there wasn't a pink ball, Paula wouldn't want to play. It got to a point where her mom would secretly carry a pink golf ball with her on vacation to try to avoid the meltdowns.

Each person in the family had their assigned colors. Olivia's was purple, her mom's was yellow, her dad's was red, and her brother's was blue. A few times her mom won the free game at the end of the course, and she would always laugh and say that she must have gotten lucky. Afterward, they would walk to get ice cream or a funnel cake.

Olivia smiled at the thought of a funnel cake and brought herself back to her present situation on the beach. She checked the time on her phone. She would stay out on the beach for about 30 minutes more. She put her empty plastic iced coffee cup into her tote bag. She still had trouble getting her head around the fact that Ocean City didn't collect recycling separately from trash like most places in Maryland and D.C.

She'd done some research and found that residents could drop off recycling over in Berlin near Walmart. Olivia kept a big bin for recycling in her house, but honestly, carrying around recycling was not always practical. The inconvenience bugged her.

As she sat there looking out at the ocean, she started to think about Luke. She wondered what he was doing right now, still feeling annoyed he had never wanted to come to the beach with her. She could have been enjoying this gorgeous view for years now! If they had been staying in Ocean City during the pandemic, would things have turned out differently?

At the end of their relationship, she'd taken a deep dive into anything she could find out about his radical change in behavior. She *wanted* to save their marriage. The problem was that you couldn't try to be rational with someone who was irrational.

That mob mentality could easily brainwash normally good people into doing terrible things, Olivia thought. Not that Luke was ever really what Olivia would consider to be a genuinely good person on all counts. She didn't think he was a bad person who would intentionally hurt people. She would never have married someone like that. She wasn't that naive. Was he a narcissist? Maybe. She was no psychiatrist and wouldn't label him. He was a troubled soul, though, no doubt.

Luke wasn't romantic or even what she would consider gentlemanly. He didn't open the door for her or offer to help carry heavy things. He was normally oblivious to most things happening around him. He wasn't very observant, but was that on purpose or an avoidance behavior? In Olivia's experience, people conveniently "forgot" things all the time—not responding to a text or forgetting to take out the trash.

Over the pandemic, she felt like all his negative qualities got exponentially worse. He didn't help around the house at all, and Olivia felt like she was his live-in servant more than his wife. They were both working full-time, but Luke never helped with dinner or cleaning. He claimed he didn't know how to run the washing machine or dryer. He took out the trash and would walk Ruby for her last outing of the night. He would complain about what she wanted to watch on TV—calling it trashy—but make her suffer through his mindless shows without ever once asking her what she wanted to watch.

During that depressing period, Olivia's thoughts often spiraled, and she wondered what exactly she did like about Luke because the "con" list had gotten quite long. Luke had always been very self-centered, but why had he become so judgmental and downright cruel?

Her parents always encouraged her to try to put herself in the shoes of others. Every single person has a different point of view in any given situation. Nobody sees things exactly the same way. People naturally thought the things they liked were better—sports teams, musicians, TV shows, actors, states, colleges, churches, restaurants, food, books, etc… Some people were short-sighted and honestly didn't recognize that everyone had different likes and dislikes. People ended up mixing with people who were like them, so their beliefs got reinforced. They were unlikely to seek out opposing opinions. They only wanted confirmation that their opinions were valid.

People who liked the same things typically liked each other, and many times, they didn't get exposed to a bunch of different perspectives. They consumed news they agreed with. Most people avoided confrontation. Sure, they were opinionated and gossipy in their thoughts and to their loved ones. Being PC had a different meaning than it used to. Political correctness was almost a joke nowadays given that few politicians were polite. Spewing crude language and lies in public was the norm. To Olivia, so much of today's political posturing was just plain cringey.

Olivia's family always had deep conversations on tough topics like this. They were indeed *woke*. Olivia wasn't embarrassed by it. She was proud of it… being aware of and actively attentive to vital facts and current issues, especially news of racial and social justice. How could that be wrong?

She missed her family's intellectual exchanges, being all alone at the beach. Back when she was first married, she and Luke were always debating all kinds of hard-hitting topics, but that stopped during the pandemic.

The conversation she had with her parents at dinner the night before she left for Ocean City was about diversity, mostly because they worked at a university and the abolishment of affirmative action was on the docket at the Supreme Court.

Her parents believed the principles America was founded on were gradually being broken down. Not just over the past few years, but over many years basic rights and opportunities were diminishing.

Diversity was key for innovation, her parents always said to her and her siblings. Different perspectives helped build the best teams with the best ideas. America had so much diversity, but as a country people generally lacked acceptance and understanding. People were afraid of what they didn't understand, and who could blame them, Olivia thought. It wasn't that people were becoming more diverse over time; they were just more comfortable opening up about it. Well, they *were* more comfortable, Olivia thought. Who knew how much longer there would be a safe space.

When Olivia sat on the beach, she tried to keep her phone out of sight and relax. When she watched and listened to the waves, her mind always wandered, jumping from memories to questions to analyzing realities.

Olivia often thought about how many people must have been living secret lives in the past, repressing their true feelings, trying to fit into uncomfortable accepted roles. Olivia had read recently that Gallup estimated that 7.2% of the U.S. adult population was lesbian, gay, bisexual, transgender, or something other than heterosexual. Olivia often thought about inequities… really, she was absolutely obsessed with fairness. She tried to control her anger over recent monstrosities—the multitudes of them—because if she was 100% positive about anything, it was that life wasn't fair. Nothing was fair. And lately, *fair* was somehow subjective. Facts and science be damned, why don't you? Olivia shut her eyes tightly and took a deep breath.

"You can't solve the world's problems right now, Olivia. It's almost time to leave the beach," she said to herself—but she couldn't stop her mind from racing.

Many people were blissfully ignorant. Floating through life on the path of least resistance. Few sought out the truth, they jumped on a popular bandwagon without trying to educate themselves on the issues.

As a teacher, cultural appropriation was a hot topic. Confederates? Nazis? Slavery? Christopher Columbus? Olivia thought it was a little late for this to become a topic of concern for politicians and business leaders. After years of criticism of the "Washington Redskins" football team's name, they temporarily changed it in 2020 to the Washington Football Team, then to the Washington Commanders in 2022. The talk was that with the new owners in 2023 that the name might change again. Olivia had read an article saying it was as early as the 1960s when the team's name initially drew criticism from Native Americans. Progress takes time, folks. *That's why it's important to start now*, Olivia thought.

She remembered other recent changes that Luke had called, "woke liberal garbage." In 2021, the "Aunt Jemima" brand name was rebranded to "Pearl Milling Company," among a handful of other name changes that were way past due, in Olivia's mind. And taking down statues celebrating Confederate leaders and slave owners? *Yes, please,* Olivia thought. More reparations for Native Americans and start reparations for descendants of enslaved African American Black people, if you please.

She wondered when Harriet Tubman's image would grace the $20 bill. They did have the women's quarters series, though, which came out in 2022. The coins featured Maya Angelou, Dr. Sally Ride, Wilma Mankiller, Nina Otero-Warren, and Anna May Wong. Olivia had bought a set of the quarters to show her class during their module on currency.

Regarding affirmative action, it was something that most people didn't fully understand. Nobody was getting into a university if they didn't meet the qualifications. The bottom line was that most universities and colleges were less diverse than the general U.S. population.

The student profile varied each year in all levels of schools as you would expect it to. During the pandemic with the travel restrictions (and before that with the previous administration's extreme student visa policy), there were fewer international students coming to the U.S. for college.

Olivia didn't want to think about the tragic overturning of Roe v. Wade almost a year ago. That was by far the biggest blow to not just women's rights, but fundamental human rights in America. What a huge step backward! Her mom had become so distraught, she ended up taking a week off work. She had been on video calls non-stop with her like-minded friends, trying to decide what steps they could take next.

Olivia felt fortunate she lived in a progressive state like Maryland. She felt sorry for the people who lived in states where legislators tried to use abortion as a lever to show their support of the extreme right wing. Olivia saw a stat saying 85% of Americans believe abortion should be legal, in at least some fashion. How could laws pass that were so restrictive? A lot of it probably came down to religious organizations that paid huge amounts of money to influence their radical missions. Was freedom the foundation of America or was it greed?

Olivia was an idealist, but truth be told, she knew that nothing was ever going to be ideal. She'd been working her entire life to accept that life wasn't fair. She would graciously deal with whatever circumstances were thrown at her the best she could. She wasn't great at reciting famous quotes or lines from movies, but she always remembered the gist of this particular saying, something like, *"2% of life is what happens to you, and 98% is how you react to it."* In the heat of the moment, that thought always helped calm her down.

She tried to be agile and positive and take the good with the bad. She had faith that it would all work out for the best in the long run. Every day was a new adventure, and she was done trying to crush down her zeal for life to fit into a box that she didn't belong in anymore. She only had one life, and she wanted to live it her way with no more regrets. *Smile, and the whole world smiles with you.*

She saw a family walk by with a cup of fries that they were feeding to the seagulls, the kids screaming in excitement as dozens dove down to grab them in a chaotic scramble. Some called seagulls flying rats, scavenging for whatever food they could find. Instead of calling out tourists for feeding seagulls unhealthy food, Olivia had done some research which said that potatoes are not exactly bad for birds, it was actually the salt and oil they were fried in that was bad for them. That kind of food isn't healthy for any living being.

It reminded her of when she was a little girl and had brought a piece of stale bread to the small stormwater pond in her neighborhood to feed the ducks. A grumpy old man who was sitting on a bench had yelled at her, asking if she wanted the duck's stomach to explode. Olivia ran home crying, the slice of bread flattened in her clenched fist. Her mom consoled her and said that bread might not be healthy for birds, but it would not kill them. If that episode had happened today, her mom probably would have run down to the pond and taken a photo of the grumpy man in question and posted it with a cringey message blasting his behavior on the neighborhood community Facebook group.

That traumatic experience stayed with her, and when Olivia was older she looked up what to feed ducks on Google and it said things like frozen peas and sliced grapes. Not exactly a handy kind of thing that was easily carried to the park, she thought. Getting rid of old bread was one thing, but buying food just for wild ducks was another altogether.

Her mind wandered with the smell of fries and Olivia thought if she had to pick between a plate of fries and a funnel cake sitting in front of her, she would pick the funnel cake nine times out of 10. The only time she wouldn't pick the funnel cake was if it were really windy and she was wearing black clothes. To each their own!

Olivia stood up and walked down to the shoreline to dip her toes in and check the water temperature. She let out a small yelp as she jumped back—the water was frigid. She picked up a small white shell and examined it. It was perfect to add to her growing collection. She sat back in her chair and put the shell in her beach bag pocket.

She'd go and pick up her new bike tomorrow morning. She added the appointment to her phone calendar. She'd stop by Walmart to pick up a helmet on the way back... and at Dumser's to get her favorite summertime drink, a black raspberry milkshake. Her mouth was watering just thinking about it.

She had to pack up. She'd gotten lost in her thoughts. She was always thinking about something. She couldn't turn off her mind. It was always churning through past conversations and contemplating future ones. Overthinking and analyzing and picking up her phone to look things up. She always considered her curiosity her best and worst quality. Ray had told her to try out yoga to help calm her mind. Maybe she would give it a go. She stopped to add a yoga mat to her shopping list.

She slid on her flip-flops, stood up, and turned around to fold up her chair. Just as she picked it up and started shaking the sand off of it, she heard someone yell, "Heads up!"

She turned her head to the voice and saw a soccer ball heading straight for her head.

"Look out!" the teenage boy said as he ran to try to get to the ball before it hit her.

She dropped the chair and reached up in an attempt to grab the ball, but it was coming too hard and fast. Her hat was blocking her view. She tried to duck and cover her face, but the ball hit her right on the side of her head and the corner of her sunglasses, pushing them into her nose with a stabbing motion.

"Oh, my God. I'm so sorry, lady!" the boy said as he picked up the ball. "Are you ok?"

Olivia picked up her sunglasses from the sand and looked at them, longingly. They were a gift from her mom for her for her 25th birthday. Her family had taken bets on how long she'd be able to keep them, without losing or breaking them. It had been more than two years now, and she'd outlasted all the bets. They seemed intact but seriously skewed like a parallelogram.

She rubbed her nose, which was aching. She might have a bruise there later and it felt like a headache was coming on right away.

Olivia was not the type to ruin this kid's day and ask him to pay for her sunglasses or ream him out for playing ball on the beach during the day, which was against the beach rules.

She bit her tongue and said, "Be more careful. You could have hit one of these little kids running around."

"Bruh, so sorry," he said again as he put his hands in a prayer gesture, nodded his head, and backed up to his group of friends. "Definitely. Yes. We'll be more careful."

As she packed up, Olivia couldn't get Luke out of her mind. Was he still obsessively promoting conspiracy theories and trolling people on social media... had he changed?

Olivia looked up at the sky and recited her personal affirmation she'd seen on Instagram and had been trying to recite daily since moving to Ocean City: "I am enough. I have enough. I am in the right place at the right time, doing the right thing. I am kind to myself and to others. I believe in myself. I do my best, and my best is good enough."

CHAPTER 23
Luke

It couldn't have been easier to track down Olivia. Luke had checked into an oceanfront room at the Hilton last night. He knew where her parents' beach house was—this same block, bayside. Olivia had just posted something on her Instagram story, and he walked out onto his balcony with his binoculars. He saw this very hotel off to the left in the background of her selfie, and she was in a purple chair. Of course, it was purple. She was obsessed with purple and the Baltimore Ravens. She was like a walking advertisement for all things Maryland.

Bingo. He found her through the binoculars. It took less than one minute. Maybe he should be a private investigator? *God, this was too easy*, Luke thought. She was tapping on her phone and had on a huge hat. He needed to take this slowly and do his research before any accidental confrontations. He knew she'd be going to work at 11 a.m. He had reserved a boat rental for later that day to try to watch her work from the water. He hadn't realized there was an air show, and all the boats were booked through early afternoon. He'd gotten lucky and was able to reserve this hotel room after a last-minute cancellation, he was told.

He took off work today and Monday, so he'd have a few days to check things out and relax. Maybe he'd watch the air show from his balcony. He was curious about his ex-wife. *Nothing illegal about taking a vacation to the beach*, he thought.

He walked back into the hotel room and put his hat on. It was not *that red hat*. He hadn't worn that hat in more than a year, although he still had it in his car trunk, just in case he needed it. Wearing that hat in public was asking for it, especially in Maryland or D.C. Damn coastal elite snobs. The Eastern Shore was a little more blue-collar redneck, from what he'd heard.

Previously, Luke had much longer hair and a trimmed beard. That pandemic look so many men were still rocking. Now, Luke was cleanly shaved, face and head.

He was trying to be inconspicuous. His hat was solid navy blue. His shirt was plain gray, his swim trunks, sea blue. He wore very dark sunglasses and some new black sneakers. He didn't have any flip-flops or sandals. He'd have to buy a pair. He grabbed his backpack and slid the binoculars in there along with an umbrella.

Luke made his way out of the hotel room and decided to walk along the Boardwalk. Once he stepped out onto the ocean side deck, he realized that his hotel was not quite on the Boardwalk, so he'd have to walk through a stretch of beach or else go inland a bit and walk through an alleyway to get to the end of the Boardwalk.

He decided to walk along the sand pathway, which was a much shorter distance, but he immediately regretted his decision when sand started going into his socks and sneakers.

Once he got to 27th Street, he hit his shoes against the curb to try to get some of the sand out. He was standing next to the dunes that were built up between the beach and the hotels and it looked like there was a peach tree growing there, right on the sand dune. Or a nectarine tree? *So odd*, he thought.

At the end of the Boardwalk, along with the tram stop there was a huge bike rental area set up and a few police officers were on bikes too, talking amongst themselves. A family was renting one of those four-person trolleys with a red and white striped canopy. The kids were jumping around, unable to contain their excitement. If things had gone his way, he'd already have had a kid or two with Olivia. But she wanted to wait. She was so selfish. If they'd had kids, he knew things would have turned out differently.

As Luke walked, he casually glanced over to where Olivia was sitting on the beach. She wasn't looking, and he went over to a bench that was facing the ocean and sat down. He was about 25 yards away. He zoomed in with his phone camera and took a few quick photos of the back of her chair.

He looked at the photos on his phone, trying to pick out details of her beach set-up. The Maryland flag print tote bag she had hanging on the back of the chair was very familiar. He recalled when she bought it at the Downtown Christmas Market in Penn Quarter a few years ago, before COVID. It was a very cold evening in D.C.—below freezing—and Olivia insisted they wait in line for more than 30 minutes to get hot chocolate. She got hers with little marshmallows, a huge tower of whip cream, and peppermint sprinkles on top. She took at least a dozen photos of it before she even took a sip. At that point, the whip cream was starting to slide down the side of the paper cup, making a huge mess.

Afterward, they froze their butts off, sitting in cold metal chairs to watch a lame jazz band play a few holiday songs. As they walked through the lineup of vendors, Olivia started up a conversation with an old lady who was selling various crafts with locally themed fabrics. D.C., Virginia, and Maryland sports teams and state colors. Olivia paid more than $60 for the tote bag. Way overpriced. Luke had to leave the tent he was so annoyed.

After she made the purchase and stowed her normal purse inside the large tote bag, she insisted they walk over to the U.S. Capitol to see the National Christmas Tree before heading back home. She must have taken 100 photos and videos from all different angles. The sun was setting behind the Washington Monument, so Luke didn't complain too much because he had to admit that it was a cool view.

Luke allowed only a few selfies with both of them in front of the tree. Their noses were so red from the cold, they looked like Rudolph. Olivia had thought it was funny, but Luke was cold to the bone and wanted to get back home to warm up.

He looked up from his phone and she was still sitting in the chair. A middle-aged man sat on the far side of his bench. Luke waited a few seconds and stood up and walked a couple blocks over and went into The Grand hotel coffee shop. He got a bottle of Diet Coke and a breakfast sandwich. It was only a few blocks south on the Boardwalk and then a few blocks west to get to the dump where his ex-wife worked. He wanted to scope out JJ's before it opened for lunch.

As he walked, the family in the trolley whizzed past him. The toddlers were in the front basket seat laughing and waving energetically at everyone they passed. He wondered how long that would last. He'd bet they'd be crying to stop in less than 10 minutes after jostling around with so much wind.

He ate his sandwich in a few quick bites, wiped his mouth with a napkin, and tossed it into the trash can. Then he started walking more briskly as he opened the bottle of soda. Next up he needed to get some beach shoes. Fortunately, there were dozens of beach shops along the Boardwalk. Along with a pair of flip-flops, he got some sunblock and a beach towel that said "Ocean City" on it. It was the cheapest towel in the shop. He put it into his backpack and continued down the Boardwalk, mentally planning out the rest of his busy day of gathering intel.

As he walked, he heard his burner phone ping and got excited. He slid his main phone into his left shorts pocket and quickly swung his backpack off his shoulders as he kept walking. He unzipped the main compartment and took out the other phone to check the notification. *Perfect timing. The girl accepted his offer.*

CHAPTER 24
Ray

Ray to Evan:
> Good morning! Which band are you more interested in seeing this weekend? I looked at all of their websites and videos. I'm voting we

go to Marlin's Point. Either tonight or tomorrow night. Also, you know one of the bartenders there, right?

Ray knew she shouldn't text Evan until after 10 a.m. due to his morning routine and meeting schedule. He wasn't an early morning kind of guy. Typically, she would text him the first text of the day around 10:05 a.m. Did he realize she did that? She had no idea.

She knew that at any minute Olivia would be texting both of them to ask what band they wanted to see this weekend. If it was up to Ray, they would have decided the plan days ago, but she was learning to go with the flow. Being spontaneous did have its advantages.

Evan to Ray:
TGIF! Looks good to me. I like all music, you know that! Can't wait to hang with you later! This week has been a drag. I didn't get to surf at all!

And more importantly I didn't get to see you nearly enough! Damn work. Xo

She and Evan didn't text that often during the day. They were both remote workers but were busy nonstop, so their schedules were not that flexible. Ray knew that working remotely, she put in way more hours than when she worked in the office.

She was taking things slowly with Evan because she knew no other way. Ray made rational decisions—although, deep down, she had this voice in her head begging her to be more spontaneous. *Don't let life pass by you*, the voice would whisper to her when she was overanalyzing a topic. Sometimes, Ray thought the voice was her grandmother's. Grammy—her dad's mom—was always the loudest in the room, with a larger-than-life personality, the one who made the family gatherings fun.

Ray overanalyzed everything. She was overly methodical with her decisions. Why couldn't she be more effervescent like Grammy? Her ex-boyfriend was always harping on her to chill out. Was she too uptight to be in a normal relationship? Ray was not a kid anymore. She was almost 30 years old. She needed to figure out what was next in her life.

She looked at her phone. Evan had written "xo" at the end of his text message. That had to be a good sign. Ray still couldn't believe she initiated the first kiss with Evan. It was so out of character for her. It had felt like such a boss move, and it made her smile thinking about the courage it took her to do it.

Evan had just broken up with his long-term girlfriend right before they met. Was Ray a rebound? Also, apparently, Evan had told Olivia that Ray wasn't his normal type. She wondered what that meant.

Ray was multi-racial, and that frequently made her uncomfortable. Honestly, she didn't know exactly *what* to call herself. What box to check. Sometimes there weren't enough options.

Many Puerto Ricans identified as "White." Ray looked more White than Latinx. Her mom was of Puerto Rican heritage but born in NYC. Her dad was American, born in Maryland, as were his parents. Ray's younger sister had a darker complexion, more like their mom.

Ray often wondered why checking one distinct box was so important to Americans. Why was everyone so obsessed with rigid classifications? Ethnicity, religion, politics, sexuality or even diet and exercise. Everyone was unique, at various places on an ever-changing continuum. No spot was better or worse than another. Why force a person into a box to conform to preconceived—and often misunderstood—norms? What was wrong with uncertainty? How could Ray figure out who she was if there wasn't even a relevant box to check?

Ray had learned that the best answer to any subjective question was: "It depends." Her accounting professor frequently drilled that into their heads, along with debits left, credits right.

Ray was a scientist at heart and knew for a fact that different situations yielded different results. Everything was variable, even in the lab. Standard error and standard deviation factored into any situation.

People's behavior changed under different circumstances. Ray hated thinking in absolutes… always, never. It just didn't make practical sense. Once a cheater, always a cheater? Nope. Once a criminal, always a criminal? Nope. Behavior was normally situational. A pinch of personality, pint of peer pressure, and a pound of privilege (or lack thereof).

Most people never encountered an alluring opportunity to test their resolve, Ray figured. What if… an A-list actor showed up at the front door with an indecent proposal? You found a sack of money in the back seat of your car? A bag of drugs showed up in your gym locker? Your daughter was raped and became pregnant? Your nephew was killed in a mass shooting at elementary school? Your dad got caught up in the impromptu march to the U.S. Capitol to *Stop the steal*? What would you do? It really does depend.

Ray had sent a sample off to 23&Me a few years ago, which classified Ray's ancestry composition as about half "Northwestern European" (French/German, British/Irish) and half "Indigenous Caribbean," which was a new classification that reflected a multiethnic genetic mix of Indigenous Taíno, African, and Spanish heritage.

Ray's mom's parents were born in Puerto Rico. Ray and her mom were bilingual but had no discernable accents, aside from a faint Baltimore "O." Ray found it beyond frustrating that if you didn't look White enough, some people didn't think you were American. It was always, "No, I mean where are you from originally?" or "What is your ethnicity?"

And what was more frustrating was that Puerto Ricans were indeed U.S. citizens. Puerto Rico became a U.S. territory in 1917—more than 100 years ago! After the devastation from Hurricane Maria in 2017, and the infamous presidential paper towel throwing incident, at least more people acknowledged the existence of the beautiful tropical island territory.

Ray had been to Puerto Rico only four times in her life but was hoping to visit again with her family sometime soon. They still had relatives living there. It was all dependent on her parents and whether they would feel comfortable traveling post-pandemic. They still wore masks and tried to avoid large crowds. They hadn't flown anywhere since 2019.

Mom to Ray, as if right on queue:
Good Morning Ray Ray! How's the smoke down there? The air in NYC is as thick as orange juice! I guess I never realized how close we are to Canada. Those wildfires are crazy!

In the photo from her mom, she could hardly even see the sun. So creepy! She could tell the air was a little hazy here. The newscasters were predicting low air quality for this weekend. Which was a pity because it was the annual air show weekend.

Mom to Ray:
It's the air show this weekend, right? Be safe and stay inside if it's too smokey, or else wear your KN-95 mask outdoors!

Ray to Mom:
Good morning! The Air Quality Index doesn't say it's unhealthy yet. I can see a haze but I'm not sure if it's the typical morning fog or smoke.

BTW, I'm thinking about giving a new coat of paint to the inside of the beach house. Are you and dad ok with that?

Next, Ray texted Olivia to be proactive. Olivia had just walked back through her front door.

Ray to Olivia:
Happy Friday! Evan and I are thinking Chesapeake High Tide Band either tonight or tomorrow night at Marlin's Point. Sound good?

Olivia texted back immediately:
Yaaaaaaas Girl! Was hoping you'd pick that. I'm friends with their drummer!

This air show is crazy loud! Ruby is so far cool with the planes flying over during the practice flights, but if she starts barking can you bring her over to your house? TY! ILU!

Also, I'm dropping off a French toast donut for you on my way to work. You're welcome. I thought I wanted two donuts. But thought better of it when I looked at my double chin in my beach selfie.

Olivia was so nice. She had needed that bright light in her life. This was the most social Ray had been in years. She didn't want to admit she was happy and jinx it. Ray knocked on her wooden desk at the thought of being *too* happy with her new friendship.

Her teammate at work was on vacation this week and her workload was different than usual. Aside from monitoring election fraud incidents, she would have to review the never-ending submission list of lower-priority phishing scams.

Phishing was the fraudulent practice of sending emails or text messages pretending to be reputable companies, trying to get people to reveal personal information—like passwords and credit card numbers. For the most part, the monitoring would be to make sure their current clients didn't have any data breaches from phishing attempts.

At lunchtime, Ray decided to take a walk to pick up lunch. She placed an online order at the Happy Jack Pancake House, which was about a 10-minute walk. She'd been going there with her family since she was a child and loved the food and the staff. She was getting cinnamon bun pancakes, trying not to think about the donut she'd just eaten.

As she started to cross the road, Ray almost slammed right into the back of a guy who stopped abruptly in the middle of the road, distracted and looking down at his phone. Ray hated people like that—more interested in their phones than the world around them. He was walking with a bit of a limp. As Ray glanced over his shoulder, she did a double-take. This guy was looking at Olivia's Instagram story! Ray had just seen the very same beach picture herself before walking out the door.

The guy was muttering to himself and said something like, "Oh. Damn. That bitch got me."

After the initial shock, Ray took her phone from her pocket and with shaky hands opened her camera app. The crosswalk timer read 10 seconds. She took a few quick steps to catch up with him and tried to covertly snap some photos. She hit the camera button at least five times. He stepped up on the curb and kept walking straight. Should she follow him? No. She stopped at the corner and pretended to tie her shoe, then stood up and looked at the photos. *All blurry.*

Ray to Olivia:
This rando was looking at your Instagram story! Do you know him? Saw him by Happy Jack just now.

No response. She must be slammed. OC was packed for the weekend. As Ray was walking back with her food, a flurry of texts came in.

Olivia to Ray:
This guy has no style!

His flip-flops are gross and he has a sock tan. Have his legs ever seen the sun before?

His swimsuit looks like it's from the bargain bin at Walmart. The hem is not even and it's fraying.

My Insta fans have more taste than that! LOL.

Seriously, though. I can't really tell. It's way too blurry.

Ray to Olivia:
Well, he was acting angry when he saw the photo, and it sounded like he called you a b*tch. It kind of freaked me out.

Olivia to Ray:
I'll check to see who viewed my story later today when I have time so we can narrow it down. #UnsolvedMysteries

CHAPTER 25
Evan

Evan opened his apartment door and grabbed his delivered lunch order off the small bench outside his front door. He'd gotten an Italian sub, BBQ chips, and a Coke. He hadn't shopped for about a week and he had zero food in the house. Ellie had always been the grocery shopper, keeping the house stocked with food that Evan considered to be way too healthy and way too expensive.

He'd been working on the new WAFM website for the past few weeks, and they wanted to get it launched by July 1. The wireframe and universal navigation had been approved, but he was still waiting on the second wave of lower-level content so he could start to fill in the blank placeholder pages.

His spidey sense was on high alert because the content was being provided by some foreign freelance team and the English was atrocious. He had asked his boss more than once if he should edit it, but she said that she'd ask the project manager if he wanted to pay a higher fee for editing services.

The way it was, he wouldn't put this website on his resume. He would take liberties with the headlines and featured text on the main navigational pages, but the blog was such a mess. It wasn't even good keyword SEO. It was just repetitive gibberish.

After he ate his sub, he picked up his phone.

Evan to Ray:
Hey - how about we do the band tomorrow night? Traffic into town is always jammed on Friday nights and it'll be even worse with the air show.

He ate the rest of his chips and then added another text to the stream:
Also… do you have plans to watch the air show tomorrow? I could come over early and we can have a proper beach day?

Ray to Evan:
Sure - that would be fun! I think the show starts at 11:30. I can pack a picnic lunch for us? Also, you'll need my extra parking pass so you can use my lot.

You can shower and change at my place before dinner.

BTW, it's a 70% chance of rain at 3PM so keep that in mind.

Evan gave that text a thumbs up.

He had been taking things slow with Ray. So far, they'd mostly met and hung out at JJ's with Olivia and his brother. There hadn't been a lot of one-on-one time, aside from a few walks on the Boardwalk. They shared a funnel cake one time and got milkshakes from Dumser's another time. With the summer crowd, that could hardly be considered quality alone time. Although, they did text at least a dozen times each day.

Maybe this weekend was time to take their relationship to the next level? He wasn't dating anyone else, and he was 99% sure she wasn't either. He would ask her if she wanted to be exclusive.

He was all in on Ray. He would wait for her to make the first move, but he'd bring everything he needed for an overnight stay, just in case.

His phone dinged with a group text alert from his mom asking what kinds of Bath & Body Works shower gel he and Brandon liked best because she had a deal where she could get buy three and get three free. Leave it to his mom to not just get six of her own favorite scents, she'd probably be buying lotions, gels, and soaps for the entire family forever. And don't forget about Black Friday deals—she always went crazy buying a dozen discounted candles!

Phone in hand, Evan mindlessly scrolled through Instagram and noticed he had a notification with a friend request. He hardly ever posted on Instagram, and he didn't know why someone he didn't know would want to be friends with him. A guy called Nate Smith. He was also friends with Olivia. Evan accepted the connection. Looked like a normal dude, who also didn't post anything.

Evan clicked back into his email. He had no idea what kind of spam list he'd gotten added to, but his inbox was out of control with so much junk over the past month. He could hardly find his legitimate emails. And why weren't the emails being caught by his spam filter? It was almost as if someone had subscribed to all this crap using his email address.

Also, he kept getting so many spammy calls on his phone. He didn't answer them, though, and they never left voicemail. He wondered if it was Ellie or her boy toy Bob behind it.

He looked down at his pinkish socks, and for a moment, wished he was the type of guy to pull a few pranks on Ellie—but that wasn't his style. He opened his spreadsheet and got back to work. Only a few more hours until he could call it a day and sign off of his computer.

CHAPTER 26
Olivia

Olivia had a break and went to today's Instagram story to see who had viewed it so far. She had almost 3,000 followers, and her friends from college were regularly active. She had nearly 150 views of her story so far today. Stories stayed up for 24 hours, and she wanted to try to ID the dude Ray saw now before the number got too much higher.

She was confused because the photo Ray sent of the guy's back, which included a small bit of the side of his face didn't look like any of her followers, who were mostly women. It was not her brother or anyone in her family. Not Evan, or any of the guys at JJ's. Her old college friend Nate, who now lived in England, was viewing all her Instagram posts lately, which was a little odd. Olivia thought he despised social media. It was not him because he was Black.

She went through and counted the guys who had viewed the story—only 30. It seemed like Ray was blowing this way out of proportion. It was probably someone connected to JJ's. Maybe it was a friend of one of the staff members. It could have been any one of the 150 people who viewed it or maybe someone who was using one of their phones.

Ray was such a super sleuth, though, and she'd want the details on each viewer, so Olivia did a series of screenshots and texted them all to Ray.

Ray to Olivia:
On it. That guy creeped me out. Seriously bad vibes.

BTW, Evan wants to do Marlin's Point tomorrow night.

But we could hang tonight? LMK

Olivia was only momentarily bummed once she realized Ray could still do something tonight. Olivia knew she needed to find a few more friends around town, aside from Ray and the crew at JJ's. She also knew that once she started teaching, she'd be part of a tight group of fellow educators.

Normally, at the end of her weekend day shifts, Olivia was tired to the bone, but life was more than work. She wanted to get out and explore Ocean City this weekend now that the weather was nice and everything was open.

Olivia loved the energy from crowds, but Ray was more of an introvert. The good news was that Ray was also trying to get outside of her comfort zone, so that made Olivia feel like it was her job to show Ray a fun time.

Olivia switched over to Facebook. She had started following about a dozen Ocean City related accounts and her feed was getting bombarded with people posting questions about restaurants (the same kinds of questions, over and over and over again). Didn't these people know how to scroll down to read previous posts or do a simple Google search?

The one account that she really liked was *The Dispatch*, a news site. They'd also post historical photos, which she loved to dive into. They also had a paper newspaper version which had advertisements for the popular local shops and restaurants, along with a comic strip that frequently featured seagulls in funny situations around town. She had a Note on her iPhone where she kept track of Ocean City history that she could use in her class.

This was interesting:

Resort officials this week agreed to install 28 new digital message signs on the Boardwalk, but not before a lengthy discussion on visual clutter. On Monday, the Mayor and Council had before them a request from the town's tourism department to purchase and install 14 double-sided, or 28, variable message signs (VMS)...

The rest of the posts had to do with crime... Olivia wondered if crime was indeed getting worse, or it only appeared to be worse since it was so easy to publicize it to the masses on social media. People were always saying how bad the crime was getting in Baltimore, but it was actually worse in the 1990s. She'd read an in-depth story about crime trends from NPR. She wasn't an expert on it, but at least she was informed.

Olivia continued to scroll through her feeds and read a few *Ted Lasso* appreciation posts. She was initially resistant to watching the show thinking it was just about soccer, but once she started she was hooked and zoomed through all of the seasons earlier this year. She wondered—along with the rest of the world—was it over? Would Ted return to Richmond? It was a cruel mystery!

Olivia texted Ray:
Jamie Tartt or Roy Kent? Don't overthink it. Which one?!
Me = Roy Kent
He's every-f***ing-where

Then, she couldn't get the Jamie Tartt *Baby Shark* parody chant out of her mind. Her break was almost over. The air was thick—the Canadian wildfire smoke wasn't as bad as it looked in NYC, but there was an obvious haze when she looked out over the canal and into the bay. The sun had a *Star Wars* look to it—a fuzzy orange orb. She'd brought her favorite Maryland flag patterned mask with her today, just in case it got too bad.

Ray to Olivia:
Jamie. Initially, I'd have picked Roy, but now Jamie.

TBH, I'll take Sam Obisanya over both of them.

IRL, let's move onto a Pedro Pascal convo though
#Zaddy #LastOfUs #TheMandalorian

Olivia was not a potty mouth. It wasn't part of her DNA. When she was growing up cursing wasn't as prolific as it was nowadays. And initially, even watching shows that had so much bad language offended her sensitive ears. Now, cursing was a given in all of the streaming shows. She still didn't curse, even to herself while she was all alone in her house. She had her list of preferred exclamations. *Crap* was her favorite. Her ex-husband was always cursing. Another reason they were not compatible.

A group of jets flew by for the air show, and she took a video. It looked like the Blue Angels. Olivia was not an expert on planes, by any measure. Living in Maryland, the Blue Angels were just a well-known entity. The Naval Academy was in Annapolis. She also knew that the U.S. Air Force Thunderbirds had a similar formation.

She took one last look at the text from Ray before she put her phone back into her locker. Her break was over. The guy in the photo seemed somewhat familiar, but she couldn't pinpoint the connection. He didn't look like any of the 30 men who had viewed her Instagram story.

She walked back to the bar and did a little twirl with her hands together in a triangle up above her head—to the left, to the right—as Jimmy Buffett played on the sound system.

CHAPTER 27
Luke

Luke was sitting on the balcony of his hotel room watching the planes fly by with his binoculars. He could see the pilots as they zoomed by. *Pretty cool.*

He wiggled his bare feet, uncomfortable from the Band-Aids he just applied to the blisters in between his toes. Stupid flip-flops. How could anyone stand wearing those uncomfortable devices of torture. He'd gotten blisters almost immediately after only walking a few blocks.

JJ's was not as much of a dump as he had predicted, as far as he could tell from his quick walk around the place earlier today. The picnic tables were freshly painted. The bar was huge with comfortable-looking stools. Could have been much worse. There was a guy raking up trash from the sand around the picnic tables. Luke kept his surveillance low-key and took a few photos of the set-up, while pretending to take selfies.

Luke started to assemble his fishing rod for the boat trip. He didn't necessarily want or need to catch a fish, but he wanted to look like a legitimate fisherman. He'd be taking out his rental boat from Fish Tales, which was right next to JJ's. He'd have to go out into the bay first, for at least a little bit, or else he'd look too suspicious hanging out in the shallow canal the entire time.

Before his surveillance, though, he had *work* to do. His secret squad had fun terms for it like viral sloganeering, leak forgery, evidence collaging, and keyword squatting. There were all sorts of underground networks for political groups to connect to devise their plans, but it wasn't as organized as you'd think. It was kind of haphazard and if you didn't keep up with the messages, you could miss something important.

Luke was tuned into the conversation 24/7. He had a text group with his local contacts on a burner phone and sometimes they would meet in person. Obviously, the main goal was the 2024 Election, but there were dozens of smaller tasks to complete along the way.

He opened his most recent anonymous Twitter account and started the process of commenting on all those idiotic woke threads. He had to make new accounts every couple weeks because he would eventually get blocked. Thank God the rules were so lax now.

Luke had a new GIF of the President tripping on the steps up to Air Force One. It may have seemed trivial to a casual viewer, but this was the kind of stuff that his network compiled and distributed to make people question the appropriateness of voting for a senile, physically failing ancient grandpa.

Sure, these people might not ever vote for a conservative, but at least if they got some less popular candidate for the opposing nomination or a third-party candidate, it would be easier to secure the win. Getting fewer people to vote was a key priority in their mission. Creating confusion. Spreading misinformation. Chaos. Luke was smart enough to know how the grand plan worked.

He knew that most Americans were just plain dumb, though. Easy to brainwash or persuade. People lied all the time. Luke never took anything at face value. Everyone was trying to work an angle and get ahead. In his work, there was power in numbers, and you had to take what you could get. People were happy to jump on any bandwagon that came their way. Voters didn't know what was best for America and until recently, before the great divide, they didn't even care much who was President.

Luke looked at his watch. He'd still have about two hours to go online and post some comments. It was not great timing for his personal vacation because of the just-filed federal indictment for mishandling classified documents.

Luke had procured a few different pieces of content to post as commentary to all the mainstream news story posts about it. Mostly the usual: how it's a witch-hunt, and many others have had classified documents in their possession on private property.

It was a basic deflection strategy. Deny, deny, deny. Lie, lie, lie. Create chaos and uncertainty. Nobody on either side of politics was straight up. The mainstream media made it seem like only conservatives leveraged sensationalized news, but he knew that liberals did the same thing.

Luke had mentally blocked out his part in the sordid events of January 6, 2021. In hindsight, he realized he was lucky to not have been identified as part of the group that walked over to the Capitol building. Many of those people—people he personally knew and they knew him—were in jail right now.

That day, it was not well organized, and he didn't know what was happening. He got swept up into the crowd, and the next thing he knew, he was dodging cops and helping people climb over the security wall. Fortunately, he'd been using a burner phone for all those text communications.

Now, Luke made sure that his political efforts were completely virtual and anonymous. Sure, he met up with some of those people every now and then, but he didn't ever use his real name or talk about any details of his personal or professional life.

He had also been doing some undercover comms with Olivia's new *friend* Evan Michaels. Luke messaged him on LinkedIn from a fake account asking about working on a website project. Luke's fake LinkedIn account was of a middle-aged woman who was CEO of a media company.

All in all, Luke had about a dozen fake accounts. He kept a Google Sheet with all of the details—name, email address, work history, his communication history using their profile, etc.

He didn't regularly monitor all the accounts, especially not on his phone. That would have been too confusing. Every once in a while, he screwed up and sent an email or posted something from the wrong account, but typically, he caught it in time or was able to explain it. He had to be very systematic about it all. One misstep and it could all come crashing down.

Luke glanced out at the kids playing in the ocean. Every so often their screams of excitement—or maybe it was fear—would float up to his balcony over the steady sound of the waves crashing. The older kids were riding boogie boards or body surfing. The little ones were holding their parents' hands and jumping waves. There were a bunch of sandcastles in various stages of development.

Back behind the umbrellas, the older kids were throwing footballs and frisbees. The distant bass beat of music came from one of the groups of teen girls who were all lying in a row on multi-colored beach towels. They had a big Bluetooth speaker set up under their umbrella. They were all directly in the sun, hats covering their heads, and bikini-clad bodies slick with lotion.

It was low tide and Luke wondered if he should go down to the beach and dip his toes into the water. The water would still be cold so early in the summer. He had never even put his toes in the Atlantic Ocean. That was kind of crazy seeing how he'd lived on the East Coast for his entire life.

The only beach he'd been to before this was Cancun with Olivia for their honeymoon. He'd gotten a horrible sunburn and was miserable for most of the trip. After that, he'd sworn off beaches and vacations. But maybe tomorrow he'd walk on the beach, he thought. Why pay astronomical oceanfront prices to be so close to the beach and never step foot on it?

His gaze quickly returned to his laptop and Luke zoned out and got lost in the Twitterverse, and when he looked at the time, he realized he was running late to pick up the boat. He quickly checked Olivia's Instagram story again. She had posted a few more videos of the air show from the restaurant. He grabbed his stuff and went down to his car. It was a short distance away, but he didn't want to walk that far with all of his gear.

Fish Tales was crazy busy. He knew enough about Ocean City from his research to learn this was one of the most popular bayside restaurants. People were everywhere, lounging on yellow and red Adirondack chairs at the dock and playing cornhole. He lucked out finding a parking spot when someone pulled out in front of him. He'd rented a 16' skiff with a motor from Bahia Marina and would have it for four hours. That would take him through sunset if he wanted to stay out that long.

Once out in the boat, his first time piloting a boat by himself, he was anxious. Anxious about spying on Olivia and maneuvering the boat. There were so many other boats and jet skis out today. He safely made it out of the canal repeating the mantra "Red, Right, Returning" he'd learned in his high school boating safety class. The expression served as a reminder that red buoys were kept to the starboard/right side when proceeding from the open sea into port, or upstream. The green buoys were kept to the port/left side.

He decided to cast a few times to see if anything was biting. He had been fishing plenty of times before while growing up, so at least he knew what he was doing on that front. He'd watched a few YouTube videos, just as a refresher. A quick Google search earlier today told him that in Assawoman Bay in the summer he should be able to catch flounder, croaker, spot, striped bass, Spanish mackerel, bluefish, and speckled trout.

A crab got caught in his line, and he used his beach towel that he'd been sitting on to cover his hand as he tried to remove it. He grabbed his phone again and checked Instagram. Olivia was wearing a tight red JJ's tank top with denim shorts. Probably the same outfit as all of the other servers.

Her hair was up in a ponytail, and she wore a white baseball cap with the restaurant logo. She had put on some weight since he'd last seen her. Not that she looked bad, though. Her weight was always fluctuating, and that's how he could tell what year it was when he looked back at their photos. Fat Olivia or skinny Olivia. He would always get on her for eating so much junk food.

Luke got out his binoculars and looked around. He couldn't see JJ's from where he was, but he could still see Fish Tales. He'd motor back into the canal now. It was all out in the open around here. No trees or bushes to hide behind, so he knew he would look suspicious using his binoculars closer to land.

As he motored down the canal past the line of docked boats to JJ's, he was easily able to pick out Olivia from the crowd. She was carrying a tray of fruity looking cocktails. *Yuck*, he thought. America was full of overweight gluttons. He tried not to stare at her and put his phone up to his ear, pretending to have a conversation.

Olivia went over and sat down next to a woman. Luke held up his phone, turned on the camera and tried to zoom in on them. It was that foreign-looking woman with the short black hair who was in all of Olivia's posts. Olivia gave her a side hug and then jumped back up. Luke snapped a few photos and a short video of the interaction.

The other woman was reading something on a tablet and also had a newspaper spread out on the table. She sat alone with what looked like a can of those disgusting hard seltzers that were so trendy now with women. Olivia used to buy them all the time. He'd rather have water. He could not understand the iced coffee or hard seltzer crazes. Both types of drinks tasted disgusting to him.

Luke had been hoping to catch Olivia with that guy Evan, but after watching her for more than an hour, nothing had happened except that she was feverishly working the happy hour and dinner crowd. She did seem to be acting quite flirty with the bartender, but Luke would bet his life the dude was gay.

Luke had put on sunblock before he left his hotel, but the back of his neck was burning up. He leaned forward to grab his beach towel from his bag so he could put it around his neck to help block the sun. It was just out of reach. He set down his fishing rod and crouched to try to reach his bag. His right foot slipped on the wet surface, and he lost his balance, his knee slamming down to the bottom of the boat.

The boat started rocking back and forth as he tried to gain his balance, his arms flailing. Just as he was about to steady the boat, his fishing rod dropped into the water. *Dammit!* Luke knelt back down, both knees on the bottom of the boat. He reached into the water, trying to save the rod before it slipped completely away. As he bent over the side of the boat and reached into the water, his sunglasses fell from his face. *You have got to be kidding me.*

He returned the boat to the marina, his fishing rod and sunglasses at the bottom of the bay. To top it off, he hit another boat as he was trying to motor into the slip and some asshole on the dock was recording it with his phone. Luke was super pissed off.

He stormed back to his car, which was steaming hot inside. His next step was to check out Olivia's beach house. After that, he'd get a drink, or two—or three.

Saturday, June 10, 2023
The next day.

CHAPTER 28
Ray

Charlie's wet nose woke Ray up earlier than she would have liked after a late-night binge session of Season 4 of *Never Have I Ever* on Netflix with Olivia. They still had three episodes left to find out where Devi would be going to college. And would she end up with Ben or Paxton or the bad boy Ethan? Or someone new?

Olivia liked Ben best, and Ray thought Devi should go to college as a single girl. Ray couldn't get over how old Paxton was in real life and that made her feel like he was a creeper on the show. Also, Ben wasn't actually dorky at all, he was a good-looking guy. To top it off, if his family was really so rich, why was he in a public school in the first place?

They'd gotten carryout for dinner, the legendary 28-inch pizza from Ripieno's, which was just a few blocks north. It was one of Ray's favorite pizza places in town—brick oven, fresh ingredients. Ray also loved pizza at Grotto and Ledo. It was hard to pick an absolute favorite, in her opinion.

To drink, Olivia had gotten a three-liter pouch of Hoop Tea, which was a locally made spiked iced tea that was *Born on the Boardwalk*. Ray and Olivia had gotten a free sample when they were at the Rum Shack on the Boardwalk last week. It was good and supporting local businesses was important to both of them.

For dessert, Olivia apparently always had to have a fresh half gallon of Dumser's black raspberry ice cream in her freezer. She also had a tub of Fisher's popcorn with caramel and peanuts. It was an indulgent dinner and Ray's stomach was feeling the aftereffects.

Ray yawned and sat up, rubbing her gurgling stomach. She would take Charlie out and then do a quick yoga session. First, though, she looked around her room trying to see it from an outsider's perspective. She rolled her eyes and let out a deep sigh as she frantically started picking up random clutter and throwing it into drawers. Tonight, could be the night Evan would finally see her bedroom for the first time! Her out-of-date grandma-looking room.

For a quick moment, panic swept through her body, and she tried to take some deep breaths to calm down. *Chill out, Ray! Come on. You've got this,* she thought. *You are not a virgin. Sex is a natural progression of a relationship.*

In anticipation of this day, she'd gone online and ordered a new dark blue comforter with sheets and curtains to match. Along with a new bathroom rug and matching towels. And a cute little sky-blue nightie with a matching robe. It was comfortable and she would wear it all the time. *Nothing weird about purchasing that*, Ray thought.

For their picnic lunch today, Ray had picked up chicken salad, bakery rolls, and some carrots, celery, and hummus for a snack along with two Berger cookies and a bag of Utz Old Bay flavored potato chips. Those snacks were Olivia's idea to get that Maryland flare into the picnic basket. She also had three bottles of wine, a six-pack of Coronas, and cheese and crackers for happy hour.

Ray opened Instagram and saw that Olivia had already posted a picture from sunrise this morning… around 5:30 a.m. How did she manage that kind of sleep schedule? They'd been up until after 1 a.m. watching TV.

Olivia to Ray:
Hey girl! It's the big day! Want to walk down the Boardwalk to burn off those dinner calories from last night? Let's touch the spot!

Ray and Olivia had this new routine where they would walk the 2.9-mile Boardwalk end to end at least three times a week. There was a sign with a big yellow dot at both ends of the Boardwalk that literally said, "Touch the Spot."

They would also make a game of guesstimating how many steps they got in each day. Walking the entire boardwalk would give them more than 10,000 steps, which was a lofty daily goal. Ray also went running a few times a week, so the walking she did with Olivia was a piece of cake.

Ray knew that Olivia was on Instagram and TikTok constantly. Ray had this theory that Olivia would see when Ray was active each morning on Insta and then text her, knowing she was awake. Not that this text proved it, but it was adding fuel to the fire.

Evan was not on Instagram nearly as often and Ray could see that he hadn't been on it yet this morning. Not that she was obsessively checking it for that sole purpose.

Ray to Olivia:
GM! Sorry. Not today. I'm on a strict schedule and I need to do yoga first!

Olivia to Ray:
NP. Figured as much.

So I can't help but think that they didn't explain very well where Manish has been in NHIE but he was obviously busy filming Ghosts!!

Utkarsh Ambudkar = Kamala's BF

Ray to Olivia:
Yeah totally! I love Ghosts too. So freaking funny! Huzzah!

Olivia to Ray:

Do you have any pink clothes? If not, order something online! We need to dress in pink when we go and see The Barbie Movie next month.

If you want to see Oppenheimer too, we can do the #barbenheimer double feature?

Ray to Olivia:
I have no idea what you're talking about!? Fill me in later. LOL

Ray ate some yogurt and a banana for breakfast. After the virtual yoga session, she showered and put on her bathing suit… which was also new. It was a two-piece tankini. It was sapphire blue, and the bottom was short-shorts style. The top was mostly backless, except for a thin crisscross to hold it all together in the back. The front was low-cut, but very secure.

Ray liked it because it looked stylish, but she could also jump some waves or go boogie boarding and she didn't have to worry about it riding up her butt or having a wardrobe malfunction and flashing the people on the beach. So many women's bathing suit styles were only made for lounging. And one-piece suits? They were ridiculous—going to the bathroom in a wet one-piece was a total nightmare. At least there were a bunch of options to choose from by shopping online, not like when she was younger and it was either a boring one-piece, a granny skirt style, or a skimpy bikini.

Most of Ray's clothes were black, so she was trying to branch out into blue. She thought of it like Picasso's blue period. She had her yellow sun-patterned coverup, which was obviously a present from her mom. That would add a fun vibe to her look.

As she started making the sandwiches, her watch vibrated, indicating a text message.

Evan to Ray:

Good morning sunshine! Checked traffic and its jammed. leaving now

Hopefully be there <60m

Ray to Evan:
Drive safely and see you soon!

The weather was shaping up to be surprisingly good, aside from the smoky haze from the Canadian wildfires. Ray gathered up her beach umbrella and chairs and sat them on the front porch. As she walked out, she noticed Andrea was watering her plants. She waved.

"Good morning, Ray," Andrea said. "You know there was a young man here last night looking for Olivia. He knocked on her door a few times and I heard Ruby barking, so I peeked out from my bedroom window to see what was going on."

That was odd, thought Ray, quietly contemplating the stranger's identity as Andrea picked a few dead leaves off of her plants. She had never seen anyone at Olivia's place before and Olivia would have surely told her about any potential guests.

"That's weird," said Ray. "I was over with Olivia at JJ's until closing time and then we were at my place watching TV after that. She didn't mention she was expecting to see anyone this weekend. What did he look like?"

"Oh, he was tall and thin and had super short hair. He was walking with a bit of a limp," said Andrea.

Very interesting, thought Ray. *Was it the Instagram guy?* Ray's mind went into detective mode as Andrea rearranged some of the flowerpots.

"Oh, I almost forgot, hon," said Andrea. "I snapped a photo of him through the window just in case he was a stalker or a murderer. You know you can't be too careful nowadays.

Us single ladies, we must stick together! So much crime around here!"

Ray tried not to laugh. Ocean City did have some crime, but compared to a big city, it was not much at all. One incident would happen, and the news media would obsess about it 24/7.

She walked over to Andrea's porch and looked at the photo. Her eyes grew big, and she tried to control her reaction so Andrea wouldn't get spooked. It was most definitely the guy from the crosswalk. But now, they had this blurry picture of his face to help with the identification!

"Let me check my Ring doorbell camera footage to see if it caught this guy sneaking around," Ray said as she tapped on her phone to open the app. "Hmm. Nope. Nothing suspicious in my Ring history. If only Olivia had a door camera, we would be in business! The only doorbell movement notification I have from this week is that rowdy group of teens renting that end unit, doing that dumb 'ding dong ditch' social media fad. Driving Charlie crazy, no doubt."

"They did that to me too, but I surprised them because I saw them at your house and was at the door and flung it open right when they rang it," laughed Andrea.

"You did not! They must have freaked out," Ray said. "Hey, can you text that picture to me?"

"Oh dear, can you do it for me? I'm not very technical," said Andrea, handing her phone over.

Ray texted it to herself. She would forward it to Olivia, who she had seen through the window walking away about 15 minutes ago.

Ray handed back the phone to Andrea as a text came in and the phone started playing the *Golden Girls* theme song. "Oh dear, I'm getting in some details about this sex party I'm hosting later today."

Ray nearly choked on her own saliva. "Um. Excuse me? A sex party! I think that's a little too much information for me, Andrea!"

"Oh no, hon. You know what I mean," said Andrea, laughing. "My granddaughter is pregnant and we're having a party here at the house to find out the sex of the baby. They have one of those balloons filled with either pink or blue confetti."

"Oh. You mean a *gender reveal* party," said Ray, relieved as she grabbed Andrea's arm. Andrea laughed such a loud laugh like she was about to choke. Her eyes were watering.

Ray joined in the laughter, saying, "I don't think I've laughed that hard in a long time! I have to go, but have fun at your *sex* party!"

As Ray walked over to her front stairs, Evan came around the corner. He was carrying a duffle bag in one hand and a bouquet of flowers in the other. Goodness. He was so handsome, Ray thought. And he was her boyfriend! Well, at least her date for today. She didn't want to get ahead of herself.

Andrea waved at Evan as she opened up her front door and looked over at Ray and whispered with a wink, "Have fun at *your* sex party too, dear." Ray missed a step and stumbled as she turned around to face Evan, blushing with embarrassment.

"Hey, you made it right on time," said Ray as Evan walked up the stairs to meet her.

He locked eyes with her, dropped his duffle bag, and wrapped one of his arms around her waist as he pulled her into a hug. Ray had completely forgotten about texting the photo of the mystery man to Olivia.

CHAPTER 29
Evan

Evan wouldn't admit to Ray that it was Olivia who suggested he bring her flowers. Seeing Ray's eyes light up at the sight of the flowers was well worth the inconvenience of stopping to pick them up on the way, and the cost. He had never really been a flower-purchasing kind of guy, but he could change if it made Ray happy.

He wasn't sure if he should try to kiss Ray hello or keep it simple with the hug. After the hug went on a little too long, he decided to give her a quick kiss on the cheek. If the neighbor was still keeping tabs on them, he wouldn't want to embarrass Ray with too much PDA.

He stepped back and handed her the flowers, which she immediately put up to her nose to smell the roses. It was a mixed bouquet, with a pink and purple theme. Not too small, not too big, just enough to look impressive, Evan thought.

"You shouldn't have, but they're beautiful. Let's go inside and I'll put them in water," said Ray. As they went inside, Charlie ran over to greet Evan. He kneeled on the floor and rubbed his belly affectionately.

"It's very interesting that Charlie likes you so much," said Ray. "I adopted him and was warned his previous owner abused him and he was scared of men. I haven't ever had any men over here, so I didn't know if it was true or not. I guess not!"

"How long have you had him?" Evan asked, realizing Ray was basically admitting she hadn't had a man at her place in a long time.

"I moved here in 2021, so only about two years. He was older when I got him, and I have no idea how old he is now," explained Ray.

"Well, you're a happy boy now, aren't you, Crazy Charlie?" Evan said as he threw his ball across the room. "Dogs always like me. And I like them. Even though I've never had my own dog."

"Really? I've had dogs since I was young," said Ray. "You know, we should probably head over to the beach right away. It will be super crowded already, I bet."

"Sounds good. I'm already in my swim trunks, but I need to use the bathroom before we go. It was a long drive over and it was a two Keurig pod morning," said Evan. Ray pointed to the door down the hall and he walked away, feeling a little awkward being alone with her in the house.

"Ok. Man up! You got this, Evan!" he said quietly as he slapped his face a few times with his wet hands as he looked into the mirror over the bathroom sink. "Stop being so awkward! You're a cool guy. She likes you. You like her. Don't overcomplicate it."

Ray was putting on a straw hat when he came back out. "Hey, can you grab that insulated picnic basket on your way by the kitchen?"

He grabbed it, but then sat it down on the sofa. He walked a few steps over to her as she closed the closet door and turned right into his chest. She hesitated for a moment, tilted her head up and brought her hands to rest on his shoulders.

"I forgot to tell you that you look exquisitely beautiful today. And I also forgot to do this," he said as he brought his head down and gently touched his lips to hers. He ran his hands down the sides of her body and then brought them to rest, nestled together on her lower back.

Ray's hat slid off the back of her head as she wrapped her arms further around Evan's neck and leaned into him as the kiss deepened. She let out a soft sigh, and the next thing Evan knew, he was lifting her up and pushing her back into the closet door as her legs wrapped around his waist.

He had not planned on ravishing Ray within five minutes of arriving today, but he would go with the flow. Did they need to see the air show? He'd let her take the lead. Whether right now or later tonight, Evan would definitely be taking things to the next level with Ray.

Ray

Ray had expected today would be the day, but not like this. She had it all planned out in her mind. Her sexy after-beach outfit and the happy hour drinks and the romantic playlist she'd put together last night with Olivia.

Options were racing through her mind. But the hot kisses were blurring all efforts toward rational thought.

Should she abandon her plans and see this through now rather than break the spell? So what if they missed the start of the air show, and so what if their first time was technically morning sex since it was still before noon. Was that a bad thing? Wouldn't doing it now, first thing, help the rest of the day go more smoothly? Or would it make the day more awkward? If they did the deed now, they would most assuredly do it again later in the day, right? All of the options were swirling around chaotically in her mind.

Ray felt her anxiety go into high gear and she mentally detached from the passion of the kiss. Evan moved his lips from hers and then nuzzled her neck for a few seconds. When Ray's arms loosened their grip around his neck, he moved his head back and looked into her eyes.

"Hey, are you okay with this?" Evan asked as he brushed his finger across her cheek. "You suddenly seemed to freeze up? I don't want to rush you into anything."

Ray shook her head and closed her eyes for a moment. "No. Sorry. It's just that I had this vision of how today would go, and falling into bed first thing wasn't part of it. So, I freaked out for a minute," she explained.

"Ok. So, what do you want to do? Head out to the beach? Stay here for a bit longer? I am a-ok with whatever you decide, Ray," Evan said softly, rubbing his hands down her side in comforting circles.

Ray looked into Evan's eyes; their bodies still pressed together up against the closet. Ray slid her hands over his chest, pushing him away a bit. Then she reached down and grabbed the bottom of her coverup. She pulled it up over her head in one swift motion.

"I say we throw caution to the wind." Ray took the untied strings from Evan's bathing suit, pulling him over to the stairs. "Right this way."

They both scrambled up the stairs, Evan took off his shirt and kicked off his flip-flops along the way. Charlie started barking with excitement in anticipation of playtime. Ray had to push him out of the bedroom and closed the door, shooing his nose back. She hoped he wouldn't keep barking!

Evan

Evan was not a man-whore, but he'd been around the block. He'd had plenty of good sex, plenty of mediocre sex, and his share of bad sex. And now, he'd finally experienced exceptional sex. It's all relative, so how was he to know that it could be that good? Maybe he'd just needed to be with an older woman who was more mature?

Ray was in the bathroom, and he finally had a chance to look around the bedroom. Opposite the bathroom, which was at the back of the house, there was a small balcony with a set of French doors that overlooked the canal.

The bedroom furniture seemed old but well cared for. The bed was a little wobbly and squeaky. He could probably tighten up the frame to fix that. There were a few nicknacks here and there on the dresser and bedside tables. Way less than most girls' rooms Evan had seen.

The bed comforter was super soft, Evan thought, as he ran his hand along it. There was a large painting of a sunrise at the beach over the bed. Probably a piece from the Boardwalk's Ocean Gallery. A floor length mirror was on the back of what he presumed was a closet door. It was very tidy. Much more organized than his own bedroom, which had piles of clothes in the corners. One corner for the dirty, another corner for the clean.

For a moment there when he had first kissed Ray earlier, he thought that maybe he'd been reading the situation completely wrong when Ray froze up. If there was one thing he knew, it was that he tended to overthink everything and it seemed like Ray did, too.

They would only be able to make this work if they had open lines of communication. Having them both second guess every little thing that happened would be disastrous. Nothing good ever came from such idle speculation. He learned with Ellie that everyone had different perspectives and perceptions of the exact same situation.

Ray came out of the bathroom, dressed back into her smoking hot bright blue bathing suit. She came out sooner than Evan would have had expected. Caught off-guard, he realized he should have put his clothes back on while she was away.

She walked around to his side of the bed, sat down on the edge, leaned over his still naked body, and gave him a short and soft kiss on the lips. "That was very fun," she said, then gave him another kiss. "You are so…" another kiss. "Very…" another kiss. "Sexy."

Evan put his arm around her and pulled her on top of him, her legs straddling him. "You're the sexy one, Ray. Look at you in this bathing suit. So fit, babe," he said, running his hands down her back and onto her butt.

Ray leaned down and kissed him on the tip of his nose. A jet flew by, and the entire house shook, windows rattling, and Charlie started barking. "Ready for takeoff, Captain?" Ray asked.

CHAPTER 30
Olivia

Olivia finally had a chance to take a quick break at 2 p.m. JJ's was the busiest she'd ever seen during lunch. The guests were watching the air show, and the table turnover was much slower than usual. She grabbed a fish sandwich and fries from the kitchen and walked to the staff break table in the back room. As she ate, she took out her phone and scrolled through her texts. She had a bunch from Ray, which was unusual.

Ray to Olivia, almost three hours earlier:
!!!!!!!

You won't believe this... it happened already, right after he got here!

I'm in the bathroom now and he's in my bed

All of the romantic plans we made went out the window. LOL

The next text, 30 minutes later. Ray to Olivia:
And... AGAIN!!!!!!

Now we're finally going to the beach

The next text was a picture:
My first beach selfie. Are you proud?

Olivia added a heart response to the picture.
Olivia to Ray:

OMG!!!! YAAAAAY!!! You two look so cute in the pic!!

Olivia clicked on the photo again and zoomed in. She hadn't ever seen Ray smile like that before! Even when they were watching both of the *Glass Onion* movies the other night, which were super funny!

Olivia to Ray:
That boy has got some fine looking abs!!! I'm having all the feels. #ThirstTrap

I'm on a quick break now. JJ's is so crowded and I'm exhausted.

But don't worry, I'll still be ready to dance the night away.

I'm going to pop over to Starbucks and get another iced coffee on my next break.

Olivia tapped over to TikTok and mindlessly watched some videos as she finished her lunch. She opened Instagram. Nate Smith had liked her story? That was weird because he'd never actually interacted with her stories before, even though she could see that he'd been looking at them regularly.

She clicked to see his profile. He had zero posts. "Oooooh. Interesting! He's active now!" Olivia decided to DM him a quick message.

Olivia to Nate:
Hey, Nate, my Mate! How are things in cheery ole England? I'm hoping to take a trip to Europe next summer!! Maybe we can meet up? I could definitely use some travel tips.

No response.

Anyway, I'm at work now so I'll TTYL!!

She looked at the photo Ray had texted her again. She was happy Ray and Evan were together, but undoubtedly, things would change now that Ray had a boyfriend.

She sighed as she stood up and tossed her paper plate into the trash bin. She put her phone back into her tote bag and plugged it into the portable charger, which was in her assigned staff cubby. Since she worked the late, late shift last night, she would take off after dinner tonight. That would give her time to relax a bit before they went out dancing. The band didn't start playing until 10 p.m. Maybe she would take a short nap. Olivia was not normally a napping kind of girl, but being outside in the heat all day was so exhausting.

Olivia grabbed her sunblock out of her cubby and reapplied liberally. Her skin was not the kind that burned too easily, and she was already getting quite a good tan, and it was only the beginning of June! This summer she would certainly be the most tan she'd ever been in her entire life.

She had a choice of what to wear at work—either a branded tank top, polo, or a t-shirt—and normally she picked the tank so she wouldn't get a weird tan where her sleeves were. Growing up, Olivia was always embarrassed of her dad's perpetual "farmer's tan" he got each summer from wearing his t-shirt around the yard and not applying sunblock. When they went to the beach, his torso was always very white, and his arms were so tan. All of the shirts and hats at work were Under Armour. The Under Armour company founder went to the University of Maryland and Marylanders loved their Under Armour, just like people in Oregon loved their Nike, and New Englanders loved their Vineyard Vines.

Olivia was also getting an annoying watch tan but if she took it off, she'd lose track of her daily steps! She figured if she took some time to tan on the beach in a strapless suit it would help balance the tan. She had ordered two new bathing suits that should be coming in the next couple days.

Olivia walked over to the bar where Raymond was keeping busy. When people were on vacation, they tended to drink all day long. JJ's wasn't open for breakfast, but on the weekends, they had brunch specials from 11 a.m. to 2 p.m.— seafood omelet and avocado toast sprinkled with crab meat. Bloody Marys with some crab meat piled on top were all the rage for people to post on social media.

The blue crab was a staple of Ocean City dining, and it was normally one of the most expensive things on the menu. Over the past couple of years, prices had skyrocketed higher than expected. Of course, all food prices were up with inflation, but they say that the crab population was declining due to overfishing… the laws of supply and demand entered the equation. A bushel of steamed crabs was about twice the cost as it was prior to the pandemic.

Olivia had done some research on the topic because she wanted to do a lesson on it for her class. The blue crab was found in the Chesapeake Bay and also in the Gulf of Mexico. The color came from blue-green pigments in the shell that broke down during cooking, when it turned orange-red. There were a bunch of complicated names for the pigments, but Olivia couldn't recall what they were without looking at her notes.

A lot of people would ask about ordering Alaskan or Red King crab legs, which always boggled her mind. Maryland was as far to the other side of America as you could get from Alaska. And lobster or lobster rolls? Much further up the East Coast, people! You could find those foods in Ocean City, but for Olivia having locally caught fresh seafood should be the priority when you're at the beach! A lot of places imported seafood, and it was one of those hush-hush practices that nobody wanted to discuss in public.

Another thing that irked Olivia was when tourists would seek out chain restaurants while on vacation. Olivia couldn't understand it. There were dozens if not hundreds of local options that had fresher and better tasting food. She knew that some people found comfort in the known routine of eating at their favorite restaurants, but she always preferred a culinary adventure. Some people were creatures of habit and that was probably why new restaurants had such a low success rate. Dozens of restaurants were opening and closing in Ocean City every season.

Olivia had a list of about 20 restaurants she wanted to try out and was hoping to get through the list this summer. Eating out was expensive, and she allotted money in her budget to eat dinner out twice a week. Olivia's budget was much tighter than Ray's and she had been spending a bit more on food and drinks over the past few weeks than she'd planned. The good news was that her tip money was much more than she'd been expecting, so she hoped it would even out.

In resort towns, she knew that restaurant prices would be higher for several reasons: they were not open year-round, and they needed to make their money in the summer months. They had high rental or ownership costs for prime waterfront locations, sourcing the food and ingredients—aside from the fresh seafood—was not as easy as it was further inland. Some restaurants cooked everything from scratch and some offered pre-made meals or a combination of both.

At JJ's, they mostly bought bulk frozen food: fries, burgers, chicken breasts, chicken nuggets for the kids. Some of the fish filets were frozen, some were fresh. They made the slaw fresh each day. JJ's was never meant to be a fancy dining experience.

A lot of newer restaurants in Ocean City advertised that they were "farm to table" with "locally sourced" ingredients. Olivia had to admit that their food was fantastic! You could really taste the difference. But sometimes people just wanted something quick, easy, and cheaper and that was JJ's niche. Better than fast food, not as fancy as a Wagyu beef burger.

As she went to take the order of a just-seated table she absentmindedly rubbed her eye as a bug got caught in her eyelashes.

"Oh, shoot!" Olivia said as she got sunblock in her eye. It started stinging and watering. "Great timing," she thought as she stopped mid-stride and turned around to get a napkin from the bar to soak up her tears.

As she was walking back from the bar area with only one functioning eye, she literally ran into a customer.

"I'm so sorry, excuse me! I'm so very sorry," said Olivia as she stepped back and blinked her eyes, trying to bring everything into focus. "I have something in my eye. I couldn't see where I was going properly."

"Olivia, is that you?" It was her high school friend Bam Bam… the drummer from tonight's band she was planning to see. He was there with the rest of the band for happy hour.

"Oh, my goodness! Yes," said Olivia, still wiping her stinging eye. "Bam Bam, it's so great to see you and the rest of the band! I'm actually planning to come and watch y'all tonight!" Olivia grabbed him into a quick hug and stepped back to say, "Hi" to the rest of the group.

"Dude, you know everyone around here," said the lead singer. Olivia couldn't recall their names. "You're like the fifth person we've seen around here that Bam Bam knows."

Bam Bam and Olivia were in the same class at Ellicott City High School. They didn't go to elementary or middle school together but were in classes together throughout high school. Bam Bam ended up going to the Peabody Institute at Johns Hopkins University in Baltimore on a scholarship because he was basically a musical prodigy. He played drums for his band, Chesapeake High Tides, but he also played so many other instruments—guitar, piano, sax, violin—and those were just the ones that Olivia knew about. He gave private lessons and also had a huge YouTube following with his instructional videos.

"How's Luke doing? I thought I saw him on the Boardwalk last night. In Candy Kitchen? But I don't know him very well, so I wasn't sure," said Bam Bam.

"What? Oh no, he's still in D.C. He hates the beach. And he doesn't like candy either. We're actually divorced now," said Olivia. "I kind of kept that on the down-low on social media because I didn't want to make a big deal about it."

"Yeah, got it. Totally understandable. You're coming to the show tonight?"

"You know it! I'm coming with my new neighbor Ray and her boyfriend, Evan," explained Olivia. She pointed to the bar and added, "Raymond, the bartender here, may be coming too with his husband."

"Cool. Cool. I'll save a dance for you during one of our breaks," said Bam Bam, nodding his head. "Looking forward to it, Olivia," he added as he leaned in and gave her cheek a kiss that seemed to linger a little too long to consider it completely casual. "Later," he waved as he walked over to the table his bandmates were sitting… not in Olivia's section.

Olivia gave her head a quick shake and squeezed her eyes shut to try to quell the stinging pain. She pivoted and walked over to her new table to get the drink order. Bam Bam was always in a world of his own in high school. He seemed more mature than everyone else, but also completely uninterested in anything aside from music. Now he seemed quite handsome and intriguing. Was he always that good looking? "My heavens," whispered Olivia. "Calm down, girl!"

Pre-pandemic, she'd gone to about half a dozen of his band's shows. She took Luke to two of them, and he seemed miserable, so she went to a few other gigs with two of her BFFs from high school.

Luke. Would she ever be able to get him out of her mind? Olivia knew she needed to take time to figure out what *her* dreams were, short term and long term. She had to be intentional about her next relationship and not jump into something as a rebound. But oh, how she longed for a new man in her life!

CHAPTER 31
Luke

Luke watched the air show from his hotel balcony. He'd brought out his laptop and he kept busy on that and would look up when the planes flew over. He'd checked out the performer schedule online, so he'd know what the planes were. Many of them, he'd never heard of before.

The entire line-up would take a few hours: U.S. Air Force Thunderbirds, F-35 Lightning II Demo Team, F-18 Rhino Demo Team, A-10 Thunderbolt IIS, Red Bull Air Force, Coast Guard SAR Demo, E-2C Hawkeye, L-39 Cold War Era Jet Demo, and the KC-135 Stratotanker.

Luke had to admit that the air show was much more entertaining than he'd anticipated. The planes were literally right in front of him over the ocean and with his view from the balcony, many were straight out and level with his altitude. There were people as far as the eye could see—umbrellas upon umbrellas all the way from the shoreline and back to the Boardwalk. He had a perfect view.

He drank a sip of his Diet Coke and munched on some of the chocolate fudge from the Candy Kitchen.

Last night, he decided to drive down to the inlet at the Boardwalk to look around. It was about a three-mile walk, but his feet were still sore from his new flip-flops, so he didn't want to walk more than necessary. He didn't stay as long as he would have liked because once he got there, he realized that he'd left his phone in his hotel room.

The parking lot had those self-pay stations where you could use a credit card or pay via an app. But par for the course of his continued bad luck, the kiosk wasn't reading credit cards. A bunch of people were lined up trying to pay, but none of the stations were functional. Without his phone, it was impossible for him to pay. He walked around the Boardwalk for about 30 minutes and left. He hoped he wouldn't get a ticket since he stayed under half an hour, and it was free parking for up to 30 minutes.

While walking, he had noticed a local cover band that Olivia liked was playing at Marlin's Point this weekend. He had peeked in the front door, but they hadn't started their first set yet. It seemed packed. He had checked Olivia's Instagram. She hadn't posted anything about it. Luke figured she wouldn't miss seeing Bam Bam's band, so she would probably go on Saturday night.

After looking into the club, he'd stopped at the Candy Kitchen because he'd read an article about the shop in the free magazine he got at the hotel—family-owned, founded in 1937, all hand-made in Ocean City. Luke didn't really have a sweet tooth, but he wanted some snacks in his room. He got a prepackaged bag of gummy bears.

When he paid, the cashier got all flustered and said that his receipt had a red star on it, and he'd won a free pound of fudge. He tried to be excited because the staff was going crazy congratulating him. But honestly, he was wary of all the attention from the other customers in the store. He was trying to be incognito this weekend. But hey, he wouldn't pass up something for free! He'd gotten some plain chocolate, chocolate peanut butter, and maple walnut.

Sitting on the balcony, he watched another plane fly by. Then he saw something run through the dunes out of the corner of his eye. It looked like a fox?

He picked up his phone and did a quick search. "Yep," he said, reading out loud. "Ocean City has been home to red foxes for decades. Interesting."

Next, he checked the Chesapeake High Tides Instagram account. He saw that Olivia had posted a comment a little bit ago saying she was excited to see them tonight. Jackpot.

It was confirmed. Tonight, he'd go to Marlin's Point. He had a disguise and a plan to shake things up. He'd created a fake account on a dating app a couple weeks ago and had been exchanging messages with a local girl. She seemed like a total spaz. It had been so easy to catfish her. Luke would ask her to meet with him for after-dinner drinks down at the Boardwalk later tonight. He had two crisp $100 bills in his wallet as an incentive for her to be his accomplice in a plan he'd been hatching to shake things up and add a little bit of *excitement* to Olivia's pitiful life. He'd watch it go down, and he was 100% sure she'd never suspect he had anything to do with it.

Olivia had ruined his life… his family and friend relationships… his reputation… his financial security. She'd completely decimated his entire life plan. He was supposed to be having kids by now. Moving out to the suburbs into a single-family home. And now he had to start all over? *Damn you, Olivia.* She was so selfish. He was lucky to be rid of her. But that didn't mean she didn't deserve payback.

Luke was frustrated and felt like he was stuck. He touched the mousepad on his laptop and his monitor flickered on. The only place he really felt like he belonged was in this virtual community with others like him… the people trying to make the world a better place again… at least that gave Luke a purpose in life.

He looked out at the ocean as a boat with a huge screen showing ads drifted by while he ate the fudge, which he reluctantly admitted was incredibly good. He took a deep breath. The air felt refreshing in his lungs, and it smelled so clean and fresh. He thought to himself that the beach was not that bad. Why had he never given it a chance in the past?

Luke's burner phone pinged. *How many times is she going to text me?*

CHAPTER 32
Ray

Ray hadn't been to a club since long before the pandemic. She rarely went out to see live music or go dancing after she'd graduated from MIT with her master's degree. Before she moved to the beach, she'd been living in D.C., which had no shortage of clubs, but living the nightlife hadn't ever been her scene. Ray was not one to overindulge. In fact, she'd never even been drunk before, but she loved wine. Pairing it with the perfect meal used to be one of her secret hobbies. She'd love to go to France or Spain or Italy and tour wineries. She'd settle for keeping it domestic and visiting Napa Valley.

Ray had a small circle of friends who'd been at MIT with her and also lived in D.C. They had a text group and would meet up on the first Sunday of every other month for a long and leisurely late brunch—and they'd drink wine. No mimosas or Bloody Marys for them.

Ray missed the companionship and easy conversation, even though she was hardly friendly with them outside of the regular meetups. It had been forever since they'd gotten together since the brunches had died down during the pandemic. They'd tried to become part of each other's quarantine pods, but after one or the other of them would come down with COVID, Ray decided to skip them altogether, afraid she'd catch it. The text group was basically dead except for a random "Happy Holidays" message, or a birthday wish.

Living in D.C. did have its advantages. Ray loved to walk around the National Mall area and wander in and out of the museums. Her favorite was the National Gallery of Art. The *Ginevra de' Benci* was the only painting by Leonardo da Vinci in the Americas. Ray longed to go to the Louvre in Paris to see the famed *Mona Lisa*. Some day she would.

Looking around Marlin's Point, it hadn't gotten too crowded yet, but it was still about 30 minutes until the band got started with their first set. They were setting up now. Bam Bam had given a quick wave to Olivia when he walked out on the stage. Ray swore that he also gave her a wink, and Olivia blushed as she waved back. The place was new, and it was located at the end of the Boardwalk behind Harrison's Harbor Watch restaurant. They'd renovated that entire area over the past couple years, and it finally was open for this season.

Marlin's Point could be completely enclosed in dangerous weather. The main building had sliding glass doors around the entire area, except for the back wall where the kitchen and restrooms were located. Outside the sliding doors, it was surrounded by a huge, covered deck with picnic style tables.

The stage was inside and seemed really small, in Ray's opinion. But she wasn't an expert on stage set up. The dance floor seemed pretty large. There was a spinning disco ball that had been making her dizzy with the lights rotating on the floor. It had black lighting and everything white was glowing in the dark.

It was not as intense outside on the deck, and there were varying sizes of palm trees sitting around in colorful mosaic pots. Twinkle lights were strung around the trees and the roof overhang. Ray would have preferred to sit outside and watch the waves in the inlet. There were spotlights on the water and seagulls flying back and forth, trying to catch fish.

The DJ played some heavily mixed dance music, which for the most part Ray didn't recognize. She bopped her head around and sipped from her bottle of Angry Orchard. They didn't have much of a wine selection here. Evan was over at the bar talking to one of his high school friends. Ray and Olivia had grabbed a table by the dance floor with an unobstructed view of the stage. It was so loud that they didn't even try to talk.

Suddenly, Ray remembered she'd forgotten to show Olivia the picture from Andrea, with all of her *sex party* excitement.

She tapped Olivia's arm and felt like she was screaming. "Hey. I totally forgot. Andrea said a guy was at your house last night knocking on your door. She took a picture of him. Look," Ray said, handing over her phone. "Does he look like any of your friends on Instagram? He also looks like that mystery dude I saw on the street."

Olivia held the phone close to her face and kind of squinted to see the photo since it was so blurry. "This is going to sound weird, but it kind of looks like my ex, but not exactly. My ex has longer hair and a beard and is not as thin. This is so sus, though," she said, handing the phone back. "Why would this stranger be at my house? This is totally giving me the creeps!" She took a deep breath. "What do you think, Ray? Did you have a chance to look at my male Instagram followers? ID any creepers?"

"I started to look through them, and none of them looked like the guy I saw who was scrolling through your Insta story," said Ray. "Who also looks like the one in Andrea's picture. Tall, thin, and it seemed like he was bald with no facial hair. I didn't have time to do any actual background research on the names, though."

"You're totally glowing," said Olivia, abruptly changing the topic. "Cheers to a new romance!" Olivia lifted her rum and Coke to clink it against Ray's bottle.

"I'm going to text my former neighbor to check in and see if she's seen Luke around the condo complex," said Olivia, returning to the earlier topic.

Ray leaned in and looked down at Olivia's phone as she typed, thinking she would never randomly text any of her former neighbors. She barely knew their names, let alone their phone numbers.

Olivia to Neighbor:
Hi Tina! How's it going? I've been trying to get in touch with Luke for a few days, but no response. Have you seen him around this weekend? TY! Take care.

Neighbor to Olivia:
Hi! So great to hear from you. I hope all is well. We miss you around here! It's not the same without your smiling face. We haven't seen Luke lately. His car has been gone for a couple days. Hope everything is ok?

Olivia to Neighbor:
Thanks for the quick response! Nothing urgent, just wondering why no response.

He's probably out of town and unplugging. I'll give you a shout out tomorrow to check in. It's getting late today. Sweet dreams!

Ray sat back in her stool and looked at Olivia, wondering if this guy was her ex-husband. It wouldn't be so far-fetched—exes are always the primary suspects in crimes.

"So. Luke has been away for a few days, according to the neighbor!" Olivia shouted directly into Ray's ear. "Very interesting. It could very well be him. Bam Bam said he thought he saw Luke on the Boardwalk, but I dismissed it as totally unlikely. Now, I'm not so sure?" Olivia looked very worried, which was a look Ray had not yet witnessed.

"Enter paranoia," said Ray, looking around the club. "Assuming things were not amicable between you all? Is he a physical threat?"

"No. I mean, I don't think so? Look, he went a little bonkers over the pandemic, but who didn't? I don't think he would ever actually hurt me physically?"

"Go on," said Ray, leaning forward, closer to Olivia.

"He blames me for turning our friends and family members against him. He doesn't realize that his own erratic extremist behavior did it. Most of our mutual friends drifted away over the past years. But they did message me asking what was up with Luke's crazy behavior," said Olivia.

Ray looked over and saw Evan coming over. "Ok, well, let's continue this chat later, for sure!"

"Ladies. How's it going?" Evan said in a booming voice. "Ready to get your groove on? By the way, is that guy really named Bam Bam? I mean that would be totally iconic as a drummer?"

"His name is Bahram Bahmadi... so Bam Bam for short," said Olivia.

"That is so lit. Love it," said Evan. "Are you going to introduce us to him?"

"Of course! I'm sure he'll come over between sets," said Olivia.

"Oh yeah, we're with the band," joked Evan as he sat down next to Ray. "If they need a guest guitarist, I'm available."

It was almost time for the band to start. Brandon and Raymond came over to the table to take their seats. After some quick hugs, they all settled around the table as the band started playing its first song. Straight into some hard rock, *You Really Got Me* by Van Halen.

The band exceeded Ray's expectations, which granted, were low. The vocals were strong, the musicians were talented. No keyboardist, which was somewhat disappointing to Ray. Only guitars and drums. It was so loud! She knew her ears would be ringing tomorrow morning. Ray could tell that Olivia and Raymond wanted to run out on the dance floor from the way they were dancing in their chairs.

As if reading her mind, suddenly, Raymond grabbed Olivia by the hand and led her to the dance floor. Olivia was wearing super high heels and had insisted on driving around the block twice to find the closest parking spot next to the club. Ray watched them move so fluidly together, almost like they had a practiced routine. She was glad it wasn't her out there with everyone watching. *How did Olivia even balance on those shoes?*

Ray was a solid dancer but hated to be the center of attention. The rest of them were happy to sit on the sidelines and just watch. There were about a dozen other people on the dance floor at this point. Two bachelorette parties, with twerking brides-to-be dancing with creepy older guys, who were clearly taking advantage of the situation.

The band went on, and Ray was surprised that she knew every song so far. She sang along quietly, enjoying herself more than she anticipated. It was a good mix of rock and pop from different decades. Right at the end of the first set, a young girl tapped on Evan's shoulder to get his attention, just as Olivia and Raymond walked back over.

"Evan!" she said in a startlingly loud voice given the relative silence before the DJ started the music back up. "Are you ghosting me? Why haven't you responded to any of my texts?"

"Excuse me? Do I know you?" Evan asked. He seemed confused. He'd only had one beer, and Ray knew he wasn't drunk. Ray looked on at the scene with wide eyes and anxious hands, a white-knuckle grip on her drink bottle, her body tense and back, straight as a board.

"I mean, seriously! I would hope you remember me after we spent the night together last week?"

"Whoa. Slow your roll, lady. I've never even seen you before," Evan said, holding his hands up, quizzically looking at her face and shaking his head.

"So, you didn't send me this photo last week? In your underwear?" She held up a photo that was clearly Evan's face. She swung it around so everyone else at the table could see it, stopping right in front of Olivia.

"What the hell! That is my face, but it is definitely *not* my body," he said. "What are you trying to do here?" Evan grabbed the phone and looked at the photo more closely. Ray leaned in to see the phone. "That's my head from my Instagram profile pic."

"Look, Evan, deny it all you want, but it's not cool for you to have your way with me and then ghost me like that. I thought it was love at first sight! You know I'm not the kind of girl who has sex with a stranger," she said dramatically, taking her phone back in disgust. Ray felt her heart start to race as she took in the dramatic scene unfolding.

"Come on. Seriously? I don't know what kind of girl you are. I've never even seen you before in my life. I would obviously remember if we'd had sex! What's your angle here?"

The girl stood there, staring at Evan directly in the eyes. Then, she closed her eyes and covered her face with her hands and appeared to be sobbing. It was hard for Ray to tell if there were real tears or if she was faking it. Ray looked over at Brandon, questioningly. He was the oldest one of the group and seemed to be the most level-headed, Ray gathered. Ray was getting a horrible pain in the pit of her stomach. Was Evan a player? She started to feel anxious, light-headed, and flushed.

"Miss," Brandon said, suddenly and authoritatively. "We're going to have to ask you to leave our table. My brother says he doesn't know you, and this is all very confusing and inappropriate." Everyone looked at the girl, who remained there, sobbing and causing a scene.

Ray looked down at her clenched hands that were resting on her lap with wide eyes, trying to control her embarrassment and shock at the allegations being thrown at her new *boyfriend*. Yes, he was her boyfriend now. It was official—at least it had been official for less than 12 hours.

CHAPTER 33
Olivia

Olivia walked around the table and touched the girl's arm and said, "Hey, sweetie, let's go into the bathroom and get you fixed up." *Always kill them with kindness*, Olivia thought.

Everyone at the table looked on, wondering if this was a practical joke. Evan seemed beside himself with anger, or confusion, or fear. Olivia couldn't tell, but she would try to get the girl to stop her dramatics and see what she could find out.

Once in the bathroom, which was super crowded, Olivia pulled the girl over into the corner by the hand dryers. "Do you think he bought it?" the girl asked with a huge smile on her face. She'd done a complete 180 and was totally relaxed and smiling.

"What the heck are you talking about?" Olivia said, anger growing. "Do you even know Evan?"

"No. This guy I just met here in the bar on a blind date gave me $200 to pretend like he had his way with me last week and then ghosted me," she said.

"Are you even serious right now? Did he say why? This is completely crazy," Olivia said, shaking her head in disbelief. "Evan is a stand-up guy. I don't see him as a player, at all."

"Honestly, I low-key enjoyed it. I knew I should have been an actress," she said, with an air of confidence that was chillingly evil.

"Listen to me, Missy, you're going to go out there right now and apologize to Evan," said Olivia, pointing her finger at the girl's face in true schoolteacher fashion. "That was a cruel joke. And you're going to show me the creep who gave you the money."

"Look, lady, I don't have to do anything you tell me. So what? He got played, and I'm sure he deserved it," the girl said as she sashayed into a stall that was just vacated and closed the door.

Olivia was so angry she was shaking. She looked at her reflection in the mirror and pressed her hands to her flushed cheeks. Her makeup was fading, and her hair was a damp mess. All of that dancing in the humidity had taken its toll on her cool band groupie vibe.

She would wait until the girl came out, even if it took all night. She wanted to confront the beast who set up this cruel prank.

Olivia to Ray:
It was all a joke. She says some creep paid her $200 to do it. He's somewhere in the bar. Now she's hiding in a stall and won't come out. FML.

No answer. Olivia began mindlessly tapping through notifications on her phone. Texts. Email. TikTok. Instagram. Facebook. LinkedIn. She was trying to preserve her phone battery, and she'd put it on airplane mode while she was dancing.

She realized she hadn't wished anyone a happy birthday today. After more than a decade of doing it daily, it had started to feel like a chore. Aside from the annual birthday wish, she hardly ever communicated with most of the people she was *friends* with on social media. It seemed like many people were abandoning the need to wish everyone from family members to distant acquaintances an HBD, or a happy mother's or father's day.

The girl was *still* in the bathroom stall. "Look, girl, you better come out because you *are* going to show me the guy who paid you off!" Olivia yelled at the closed door.

Olivia leaned against the wall to try to take some weight off her aching feet. She was a prisoner of fashion. Her high-heeled black sandals were on a great sale at the Kate Spade outlet. A parade of scantily dressed, sweaty, drunk young ladies bumped into her as they moved around the bathroom. They were practically screaming at each other as they refreshed their makeup and tapped on their phones.

It had been almost 10 minutes. Olivia clicked on a news article that said that breathing in wildfire smoke for one day was comparable to smoking somewhere between three to 11 cigarettes. *No thank you*, she thought. She had asthma when she was a child, and it sometimes got worse with bad air quality and seasonal allergies. She couldn't even stand being near a campfire for too long.

Olivia walked outside of the bathroom door, hoping the girl would finally come out. She opened the covert photo she'd taken of the girl at the table before they came into the restroom. It was blurry and the stage lights had totally washed out her face, but it was better than nothing. Also, she'd taken a number of photos and videos during the first set. She'd review them and try to see the people at the bar to see if any of them looked suspicious.

Ocean City was an interesting place—all kinds of people were out and about and apparently liked watching live music. The age range was from the minimum of 21 all the way up to 70s maybe? So different from the dance clubs in D.C.

As she watched the videos, there were two creepy older guys trying to dance with the bachelorette party girls. She hadn't noticed them while she was dancing. *So cringeworthy.* One older couple was super cute on the dance floor. The woman was a great dancer, and the man was barely keeping the beat. They were singing along to the songs, knowing every word. Olivia hoped she would have a special someone when she was old, retired, and without a care. When the video got to the spot where she could see the people at the bar, she stopped it.

"Oh. Yaaaaaas! Our little actress is talking with a guy at the bar and looking over at the dance floor." He was barely visible, but you could tell he had on a dark baseball hat and long blonde hair. He was wearing a blue t-shirt with something written on it. That must be the guy. Olivia took a screenshot.

Olivia to Ray:
This must be the guy. Reviewing my videos from earlier.

Do you see him? The girl is still in the bathroom.

Olivia zoomed in on the guy in the video and got a notification that her college friend Nate had finally messaged her back. *He's a night owl,* Olivia thought, mentally trying to calculate the current time in England.

She read the message from Nate. She switched back to the screenshot of the guy in the club. It all started clicking. *He was behind it all. That bastard.*

CHAPTER 34
Evan

Evan was embarrassed for sure, but he knew he had never seen that girl before. But who would try to sabotage him like that in front of his new girlfriend, his brother, and their friends? It was beyond hateful. He racked his brain trying to figure out who could be behind it.

He and Brandon had walked outside the main building and were standing along the railing, looking at the waves in the inlet with hundreds of birds flying in the floodlights, diving into the choppy water. Ray had stayed inside with Raymond and Brandon to save the table. She had looked like a deer with headlights in her eyes. Evan needed to get some fresh air to clear his head. It was so loud in there!

"So, you really have no idea who that girl was, right?" Brandon asked. "She seemed unhinged."

"You know I'm not like that. And I never get drunk," said Evan. "Well, except for that one time when Ellie broke up with me. That was a rare occasion. I hope Ray didn't believe it."

"I know. I know," said Brandon. "Not a good look, for sure!"

Both brothers had a serious aversion to alcohol, well in excess. They drank socially, but one was their limit. Their dad had been killed in a drunk driving accident not far from where they were standing. He was sober, but the car that ran into him was full of underage drinkers, who all also perished in the horrific accident. Ever since then, they had been overzealous about making sure nobody was driving under the influence.

"By the way, Ray seems so nice," said Brandon, breaking the silence. "I really like her and you together, bro. You seem much more relaxed and like your normal self when you're with her. With Ellie, it always seemed forced and fake, to be honest."

Just then, Ray came up behind them. Evan reached out to grab her hand and looked into her eyes. Ray was smiling! He felt so relieved and looked on with great anticipation to what she would say next. Two seagulls landed on the railing next to him and he stepped away, closer to Ray.

"Hey. So, Olivia texted from the bathroom and said that the girl was paid off to deliver that crock of crap story."

Simultaneously, both Evan and Ray's phones buzzed. "From Olivia," Evan said as he held up his phone. They all took a close look at the photo and then turned around to check out who was nearby.

"What the hell, is that him? Wait. Don't look. At 9 o'clock," Evan said, turning back to the water. Ray held up her phone and turned the camera into selfie mode and zoomed in on the guy. They all looked at her phone.

"It's gotta be him. What are the chances that there are two guys with bleach blonde hair wearing a navy baseball cap? Hair like that? It's a weird look," said Ray.

"I'm going to walk over there. If he gets spooked, we'll know it's him. If not, I'll strike up a friendly conversation," said Brandon. "Evan, you go over to the exit in case he tries to make a run for it."

The exact moment Brandon turned and started walking over, the guy hightailed it to the exit. Brandon and Evan took off after him as Ray was initially startled and left in the dust.

"Oh my God," Ray said. "Be careful!" Then, she started off in a sprint after them.

The guy was running down the wooden stairs to the ground level. Evan was about 20 yards behind him and closing in fast. Brandon hated running and was falling back. Ray easily passed him with her smooth and speedy pace. A huge gust of wind blew off the guy's hat… and his hair? "W.T.F. That was a wig!?" she heard Evan shout as he closed in on him.

"Dude. Slow down!" yelled Evan as he sprinted faster. "Who the hell are you? Why did you pay that girl to go off on me?"

There was a lot of traffic, and the guy was dodging in and out of cars as he tried to cross the street, heading east toward the Oceanic Fishing Pier. Evan almost caught up to him and lunged forward to grab his arm. "Hey. Come on, I'm not going to hurt you. I just want to know what's going on!" said Evan.

The guy stopped and was panting, trying to catch his breath, bouncing from foot to foot. "Don't mess with my wife again and we won't have a problem," he threatened.

"Your wife? Who? Ray? She hasn't been married before, has she?" Evan asked as a dozen questions popped into his head.

"Olivia. You're dating Olivia, right?"

"No. Olivia is friends with my girlfriend, Ray," said Evan, shaking his head.

The next thing he knew, the guy bolted and was running up the road with a definite limp in his gait. He looked back and slowed down when he saw they weren't after him. He took his phone from his pocket, looked at it, and then crossed over the road back to the Boardwalk. Suddenly, he tripped and fell. A car turned right into him, probably never even realizing he was on the ground.

"Oh, snap," said Evan, covering his mouth with his hand. "Look," he pointed, as Ray caught up with him. "I think he just got hit by that SUV!"

"Oh my God!" Ray exclaimed. "It looks like the car that hit him is driving off!" Brandon fast-walked up to them, looking down the street. Traffic was suddenly stopped, and a crowd was gathering. They all turned and started jogging down to the scene of the accident.

"Are you both ok? Who was he?" Brandon half-panted as he tried to keep up with Ray and Evan.

"I have no idea. I think maybe he's Olivia's husband. Or ex-husband? He seemed to think that I was having an affair with his *wife*. Then he ran off when I said I was dating Ray and not Olivia," said Evan, with a huge sigh.

"You know. He does look like the guy I saw earlier this week who was stalking Olivia's Instagram and potentially snooping around her house. Tall, thin, extra creepy vibe," said Ray.

"Wait, what? Stalking?" Evan asked. As they reached the scene of the accident, two police officers on bikes had stopped and were assessing the situation, telling people to back away. The guy was sitting up on the curb and seemed ok.

Ray explained in a loud whisper what was going on with the mysterious Instagram stalker. "Hold on while I pull up the photo of the guy that was snooping around the house," said Ray.

Ray found the photo from Andrea and showed it to the brothers. "It looks like the same guy to me," said Evan.

Ray said, "Cover me while I take some pics," Evan stood sideways as she snapped some photos with her phone.

"This is definitely the guy I saw near my place looking at Olivia's Instagram story," she whispered. "He doesn't look like any of Olivia's male Instagram followers. He must have a fake account."

Ray texted a photo of the accident scene to Olivia and got her up to date, asking if the guy was indeed her ex-husband. Ray told her to leave the bathroom stakeout and join them. Olivia got there about 10 minutes later, just as the ambulance was pulling away.

"Hey, I got here as fast as I could," she said, clearly out of breath, barefoot, face flushed, holding her shoes in her hand.

"The guy in the pic looks like he could be my ex-husband. But, honestly, it's not the way he normally looks. He has—or had—longish black wavy hair and a full beard and is not as thin. It's hard to be 100% from the photos. And he is definitely not following me on Instagram. I blocked him."

"Why would he be out for revenge?" Evan asked.

"It's a long story, but bottom line, he is definitely cray-cray," said Olivia. "He blames me for all of the problems in his life. That's why I wanted to move away. Far away from him."

Evan could tell that Olivia seemed a little zoned out. How could she not recognize her own husband, or ex-husband, Evan wondered.

Suddenly, Olivia dropped her knees to the ground and let out a huge sob. "Why can't he just leave me alone!" she wailed. Then, she looked up and said, "How badly was he hurt?"

"He seemed okay, but he couldn't stand up. Maybe a broken leg?" Brandon said as he walked back to the group. "I talked with the police officers, and they said that it was standard procedure to take him to the hospital for observation. They also asked if we had seen what happened. I said that from our vantage point a few blocks away, it looked like a light-colored SUV hit him and then fled the scene. It was hard to tell if it hit him or not, right?"

"It looked like it hit him," Evan said, "But yeah, it would be impossible to tell from our perspective, behind the car."

Olivia continued to sit on the ground, tears running down her cheeks, causing a bit of a scene herself.

"Let's walk over and sit on the Boardwalk," said Ray. Brandon reached for Olivia's arm to help her up and kept his arm around her to keep her steady.

It was late, but many of the shops were still open since it was Saturday night. Brandon and Olivia veered off to a lemonade stand. Evan put his arm around Ray and pulled her towards his side. "I'm so sorry this was such a dramatic evening after our super sexy day," he whispered into her ear. He kissed her head and squeezed her tighter. "Believe me. There is nobody but you!" Ray relaxed into Evan's embrace, and he hoped she believed him. Olivia and Brandon were about 20 feet away from them.

"If this dude is really Olivia's ex-husband, it seems like there's way more to the story than she's telling us, right? Like why on earth is he out for revenge? This is all so suspicious, Ray," Evan said, concerned.

"Yeah. I just don't know what's going on. She is acting so detached right now. Is she even comprehending that her ex-husband just got hit by a car and is being taken to the hospital?" whispered Ray. "I did some simple Google searches on Olivia when she first moved in next door, and she seemed squeaky clean—elementary school teachers have to be vigilant about their reputations!"

Evan and Ray sat along the beach barrier wall that bordered the Boardwalk. It was late enough that there shouldn't be any kids running down the wall, like they did during the day. They looked out into the dark ocean, Evan's arm still around Ray.

Olivia and Brandon walked over with four bottles of water and two funnel cakes precariously stacked on top of each other, powdered sugar floating off, cloudy white in the breeze.

"If anyone's wondering, Raymond is still dancing at the club for the second set, and I'm going to head back there when we're done with this debrief," said Brandon as he blew on a chunk of steaming hot funnel cake.

"There's nothing better than a just-made funnel cake," said Olivia. "Not too thick and doughy, not too thin and crunchy. Just the right consistency. Absolute heaven." Olivia closed her eyes and chewed, taking a deep breath of the warm sugary scent.

"So. Olivia. Do you want to explain what you think is going on with your ex?" Evan asked the question everyone was thinking.

CHAPTER 35
Luke

The ambulance traveled with its lights on, but no siren. *It didn't seem to be going that fast*, Luke thought. He was stable and alive, which was a blessing. As the ambulance hit a huge bump on the road, he clenched his muscles as the pain swept through his body. The initial indication from the paramedic was that something was wrong with his ankle and potentially some broken ribs, and maybe whiplash and a concussion.

Luke didn't think he was actively bleeding, but he felt like his entire right side was bruised. And when he initially tripped and fell before the collision, he'd scraped up the knee and hand on his left side. If his ankle was broken, how would he get back home to D.C.?

What bothered him more than the accident was that Olivia knew that he was in Ocean City. There was the issue of the restraining order. Well, in D.C., it was officially called a civil protection order (CPO). They'd texted a few times, but did that really count? But evidence of him stalking her would obviously be a problem.

This little diversion wasn't part of his original plan. He'd gotten too cocky and messed up, he thought. He didn't have the right intel, and he never should have contacted that girl to mess with Evan. Was Olivia seeing someone? If she wasn't, why was he even in Ocean City right now? What a damn mess.

Saturday, June 11, 2023
After midnight.

CHAPTER 36
Olivia

Brandon left the group to go back to the club after finishing the funnel cake. Olivia finally got up enough courage to tell Ray and Evan about Luke. She took a deep breath and began.

"Look, I've never told anyone the full story about why Luke and I split up—not my family or even my virtual therapist. So, bear with me as I try to verbalize this, keeping in mind that I'm mentally and physically exhausted," Olivia tried to laugh, but it came out more like a somber grunt.

"Since you never know who's lurking around listening, I'm going to keep some of the things vague for our own safety," Olivia said as she looked around, more paranoid than ever.

She continued after taking another bit of funnel cake. "I've been trying to analyze Luke's behavior for many years. I don't know if he's technically a narcissist, a sociopath, or an extremist. He definitely has no empathy for others, he ignores right and wrong, he tells lies to take advantage of others. He's not respectful and has a sense of superiority. And more recently, he's entered the world of criminal behavior."

Olivia paused to take a sip of water. Ray and Evan looked on patiently, seated next to each other on a bench, Evan's arm around Ray's shoulders. Olivia sat on top of the sand barrier, bouncing her legs nervously against the concrete wall.

Olivia continued, "Being locked up in our house during the pandemic, he did not deal with the isolation very well. He's not super outgoing like me, but we had a lot of friends, and he was buddies with his work colleagues. We were always out and about in town doing stuff. During the lockdown, he changed.

It's like he was out to get me—somehow, I ruined his life? I had to get a restraining order against him last year after we separated."

"Whoa. A restraining order? That is very serious! What did he do?" Evan asked.

"Let me go back and give some foundational details to explain how it all started going downhill leading up to the lockdown. Luke had always been completely apathetic regarding politics or other social issues. He never even wanted to vote! He would go with me because I pressured him into it; although he did care about the Second Amendment because he liked to go hunting—that's the only thing he really took a stand on," Olivia described with a glassy faraway look in her eyes.

"I don't know if he fell in with the wrong crowd at work or college or high school friends. Or if it was all virtual brainwashing and manipulation? But before the 2020 election he began trolling strangers and elected officials online, posting all types of delusional propaganda. At first, he did it from his personal accounts, which was so embarrassing! Then after his friends started ignoring him, he created several fake accounts. He didn't hide that from me—it was like he was proud of his part in helping to make America great. With our friends and family members, he'd make negative comments on posts they made on social media that he didn't agree with. It was so embarrassing!

"After Election Day in 2020, Luke went off about how the election was rigged. He broke our TV and punched a hole in our wall. I ended up driving to my parents' house to get away from him. He literally drove to my parents' house every single day with flowers trying to get me to come back. He said he was going to stop posting so much on social media. After a week, I agreed to give it another try, and we spent the holidays together and things really did seem better. Like we could salvage our marriage."

Olivia took a deep breath. "Then came the infamous January 6th insurrection. He was all worked up, and obviously, I had no idea the extent of what was about to happen. Luke left the house early that morning and I tracked his phone. I know he was there at the Capitol. I never told anyone about it, even him. When he got back home, I pretended to be feeling sick and kept away from him. It seemed like he had gotten scared by the rioting and arrests. I thought—hoped—that maybe he was better?"

"That must have been so scary to be trapped in such a toxic environment like that," said Ray, patting Olivia's leg.

"I blocked it all out and we basically went along living our separate lives for more than a year, into 2022. We did a few months' worth of sessions of online couples counseling. I stayed because everything was so uncertain with the pandemic. I loved living in D.C. I thought we could live our separate lives and save money on living arrangements, right?"

She took another sip of water. "Looking back, they say hindsight is 20/20. I thought things were getting better, but I was turning a blind eye to his increasingly obsessive behavior. But then we reached the final straw when he called me and my family a bunch of '*baby-killing libtards*'," Olivia winced as she said that out loud.

"Yikes! No coming back from that," said Ray, covering her face with her hands.

"Last May, before Roe v. Wade was officially overturned by the Supreme Court, I was making posters for the Women's Rights March. My family and I were attending the protest in D.C. I joined marches in D.C. all the time—I was living right there, and I had no excuse not to support the causes I believed in, right?

"Anyway, Luke was livid that I was going to attend the march as a pro-choicer. I'd gone to women's marches before, but as I said, he'd recently gotten more fanatical. He decided he would also go and promote pro-life. He grabbed a piece of my posterboard and some markers and stomped off to his home office to make his own sign," Olivia explained.

"Talk about irreconcilable differences, right? It gets worse. The morning of the march, he must have gotten up super early—he was sleeping in the guest room, because I'd locked our bedroom door. He took my purse (with my wallet and car keys) and every single one of my pairs of shoes suitable for walking—which I kept in a rack in our hall closet. Like how on earth did he think of something like that? All I had left were pairs of dressy heels I kept in my bedroom closet. I ended up having to wear my most comfortable pair of dress shoes. I walked a few blocks to the pharmacy and got a pair of cheap slides with a $10 bill I found in my jacket pocket."

"Wow. That's some legit crazy ass behavior," said Evan. "So, what happened next? Did you go to the march? What did your family say?"

"Well, fortunately, he didn't take my phone," said Olivia. "And thinking back I probably could have used Apple Pay to get some better shoes, but I didn't think about that at the time. I texted my parents and they told me to pack up a bag and that they would take me home to their house after the march. They were relieved that I was finally going to leave Luke. They were worried about me and had been for some time. They drove by the house, picked me up with my luggage, and then we went to a nearby parking garage.

"But, during the march, I forgot Luke could track me via my phone. I hadn't changed my location preferences. My dad saw him first… with a huge sign that said, 'Equality Begins in the Womb.' He was staring at me with such an evil look. It gave me literal chills and goosebumps. We turned away and quickly walked into a nearby store. When we came back out, we didn't see him again," she said. "It was eerie, though. I was completely paranoid."

Olivia paused, wondering how much of the story she should share. "Luke is so freaking two-faced because when we were first dating, he had told me his girlfriend before he met me had an abortion and he wasn't ready to have kids yet. He seemed completely neutral about it all. I mean, it's a fact that a quarter of all women have had an abortion. I just saw a poll that said more than half of Americans now identify as pro-choice."

Ray said, "I don't even want to think about the current state of women's rights." After a minute of silent contemplation, Ray said, "Ok. It's getting late. Olivia, do you have more on Luke's story?"

"Yes. Just a little bit more, for now at least. Anyway, I was so mad at Luke for being hypocritical! When I saw him at the march I took a picture of him with his stupid sign through the shop window. Later that night when I was at my parents' house, I posted it on Facebook and tagged him with the caption, 'HYPOCRITE' and a side-eye emoji."

"Oh my God," said Ray, covering her mouth with her hand. "So how did *that* turn out?"

"Ha!" Blurted out Olivia. "The next morning, I blocked him on all of my social channels, which effectively untagged him from that post. He had commented on it… multiple times. Things I can't even repeat right now. I took a screenshot of it all and then I deleted the post," she added with a sigh.

"He sent me dozens of threatening texts. I took screenshots and then blocked him on my phone. My parents knew a divorce lawyer and they set up a meeting for me. And here we are now more than a year later with him apparently *still* stalking me and trying to destroy your lives, too," Olivia sighed in desperation and stood up. The conversation was clearly over.

After that, Ray and Evan went back to Evan's car after walking with Olivia to the club. Olivia would watch the last set of the night and load up on water. Then, she'd drive back home by herself. Her car was parked a few blocks away on a side street. She'd abandoned her shoes by this point, so the walk would be tolerable.

CHAPTER 37
Ray

Ray had been exhausted by the time they got back home, well after midnight. She wasn't used to staying up so late. She was a morning person and liked to be in bed by 10 p.m. It was the way she was programmed. She invited Evan to stay over, and he accepted. They were both so tired, they collapsed in her bed and fell asleep after only a few minutes of innocent cuddling.

She and Charlie woke up early. She took him out and then settled down at her computer in her office to see what she could find out about the accident last night. Also, she'd never thought about doing a complete background check on Olivia before, but maybe there was something she was hiding too? It was all so mysterious. She and Evan had talked more about it on their drive home last night. Olivia was acting weirder than usual.

Finding out about Olivia was a snap via a simple Google Search. There was no other Olivia McNalley in Maryland or D.C. Her married name was Lewis, so next, Ray looked up "Luke Lewis," which was a much more common name.

Luke worked for a company in D.C. Olivia had worked for a private school in D.C. Interesting, thought Ray, because it looked like she left that job late last year and not this spring at the end of the school year like Ray had assumed. Ray wondered what she'd been doing for the past few months before moving down to the ocean.

Ray scrolled back through Olivia's Facebook and Instagram pages, looking at older posts which she hadn't checked out before. Nothing out of the ordinary. Lots of photos of her family and Ruby.

Olivia had taken a few domestic vacations with her parents, it appeared. It looked like the family had a cabin by a lake in upstate New York. One trip to Disney World and one to NYC. She attended a taping of *The Late Show with Stephen Colbert*. Ray had never been to Disney. It was expensive and if her family had had money to spare, they would have gone back to Puerto Rico to visit family.

Ray was normally asleep before the late-night talk shows aired, but she longed to see *SNL* live, though. It was almost impossible to get tickets to that. Every August she would enter the ticket lottery, which was basically emailing NBC and saying why you deserved to get tickets. She'd been doing it for at least five years now (not counting COVID years) and had never received any response. This year, with the SAG writer's strike, she'd stopped obsessively checking her email for a notification since they hadn't been airing any new shows in the spring.

She kept looking and found some posts with Olivia's wedding photos by friends, and even her profile on The Knot wedding website. They looked like a happy couple.

As far as the accident was concerned, nothing had been posted anywhere in the local news about a pedestrian hit and run. *There is something more to this*, Ray thought. She tried to rewind her brain and recall what kind of car hit Luke. *A white SUV*.

She got an alert on her phone. It was time to "Be Real." Olivia had added the app to her phone on Friday night and told her how it worked. She was only friends with Olivia and only Olivia would see the photos, which were supposed to capture her in real time, not a curated look. She snapped a photo looking outside the window and smiled at the camera, then silently questioned her sanity for letting Olivia add all these social media apps to her phone.

Ray logged into her identity monitoring service. After a vulnerability, companies typically offered customers access to free security monitoring for two years. Many didn't take advantage of it, but Ray was a proponent of as much monitoring as you could get. She had four recent compromises of her email address through her doctor's office, her retirement fund, her phone company, and her fitness app. Fortunately, her social security number had not been found on the Dark Web.

In the past, she'd had a stranger sign up for a credit card in her name, but with a different address. That was a mess to clear up and the perpetrator's address was still listed in her "previous addresses" in the credit system. There was no way to remove it! The fake address was in Maryland and she'd driven by the place in Snow Hill, which was an abandoned house.

Something caught Ray's eye in her phone's newsfeed about the show *Jury Duty*. She and Evan had watched it a few weekends ago, and it turned into an unexpected binge; it was so clever and funny.

She clicked on the link to a short story about James Marsden, who she mostly remembered as Prince Edward from the Disney movie *Enchanted*, which was one of her favorite childhood movies. She remembered seeing it in the theaters for her thirteenth birthday with a few of her friends. They'd all gotten kid packs with a tiny bag of popcorn and an Icee. Ray had gotten her own pack of ROLOs, chocolatey caramel deliciousness.

Ray hadn't gone to a movie theater since long before the pandemic. She hadn't experienced those fancy theater recliner seats that everyone raved about. She was a child of RedBox, and she still gravitated to DVDs, rather than subscribing to a dozen different streaming services.

There were two RedBox kiosks within walking distance from her beach house. Her grandparents had accumulated a massive collection of DVDs, if she wanted to go old school and watch some classics. They also had dozens of board games and puzzles. She'd have to see if Evan was a puzzle kind of guy, or not.

Ray picked up a lint roller from her desk and absentmindedly rolled off the accumulated dog hair on her shorts and shirt as she kept browsing and lost track of time.

Ray got a notification that Olivia had posted on Be Real. It was a photo of her bedroom ceiling to the front, and Ruby to the back. Ray laughed. It was still early, and Evan was still asleep. She had plenty of time to dig deeper into Luke Lewis.

After about 30 minutes of relatively simple searches on the Dark Web, Ray found about a dozen aliases that she could track to "Luke Lewis" of Washington, D.C. Almost all of his activity was politically charged commentary—mostly on websites published by a pseudo-news organization called WAFN with ties to Russia. They would spin up fake news stories to try to influence the election and other timely controversial topics.

"What!" Ray whispered to herself as her eyes moved down the GOP donor list and she mentally added numbers up in her head. Luke Lewis donated a combined total of exactly $27,550 over the past three years! "Wowza!" she said in disbelief. "Olivia could not have been happy about that. Yikes!"

CHAPTER 38
Olivia

Olivia had been awake for at least an hour, flopping around in bed, trying to get comfortable and clear her mind so she could go back to sleep. She didn't feel guilty about not telling Evan and Ray the entire truth about Luke and why she had to hold her cards close to the chest. Wasn't she complicit in not telling the FBI what she knew about Luke's questionable activities? Once she'd seen the chaos on the news that day, she immediately looked up where Luke was and took screenshots of his location. But more than that, she headed to the National Mall area herself.

January 6, 2021

Olivia was on winter break from school and had just finished eating lunch when her phone started pinging with breaking news alerts that the U.S. Capitol was under siege. She turned on the TV and was shocked to see an angry mob climbing over fences and barriers trying to enter the Capitol while security guards linked arms to hold them back. She switched around to different channels, and it seemed like nobody knew exactly what was happening.

Luke had left the house a few hours ago, saying he had a work meeting, but now Olivia was not so sure that's where he went. She picked up her phone and opened the Find My iPhone app.

Her heart raced and the locator icon spun and spun and spun in circles, trying to locate Luke's phone. Finally, it reset and said Luke was three miles away. Olivia zoomed in on the map and saw that he was indeed outside of the Capitol building. Olivia's heart dropped, and she became angry and worried, simultaneously.

Mom to Olivia:
Honey, are you ok? Have you seen the news??? There's an attempted coup happening right now at Congress!!!! Stay safe! Xoxo

They—researchers, doctors, those who know best?—say everyone has a fight versus flight instinct and Olivia was always running to dangerous situations, much to her parents' chagrin. She wanted to be in the know. She was innately curious.

Olivia wrote a quick response to her mom as she grabbed her purse and put on sneakers. She would ride the Metro as far as she could, but she might end up having to walk quite a bit. Once she got downtown, however, she second-guessed her plan. How dangerous was it, she wondered?

In her mind, she had underestimated the seriousness of the situation. It was total chaos. Thousands of people were in the area surrounding the National Mall. Television crews were whizzing around. Police sirens were blaring. Olivia rushed past people who were screaming. Most were running the other way. Some were bleeding. Many were crying. It was like a scene out of an apocalyptic movie.

Luke must have turned off his phone because she couldn't locate him on her app. The cellular network was overloaded, and her phone was struggling to connect. From across the street, she scanned the people on the Capitol steps for about 15 minutes and was about to give up when she finally spotted him. She almost didn't recognize him, but he was wearing the hat her mom had knitted him, pulled down very low on his head. She zoomed in on her phone camera to take some photos and videos. He was standing there on the steps with a hoard of people. Some were just standing there like Luke was doing. Some were angrily chanting. The guy next to him had a huge banner that said, "Stop the Steal." After about five minutes, she lost him in the crowd and realized she needed to get out of there as soon as possible. Things were not getting under control; it was getting worse.

Later on the news, she would learn that the police had used flashbang grenades and tear gas to help clear the crowd.

That's when she left the scene, when she heard loud bangs and saw smoke.

She wondered if she should leave D.C. Should she call her parents? They would still be at work, and she could take the Metro up to College Park. Was the Metro safe? How serious was this? So many unknowns and possibilities floated through her head. Would there be a coup? Would people be killed? Would government officials be assassinated? Olivia walked back in a few phases, stopping at cafes and shops along the way to see if Luke turned his phone back on and to check the news coverage of the unfolding situation.

Back at her apartment, she kept her eyes glued to the news coverage. Luke arrived home about an hour later and walked straight to his home office. He closed the door and locked it, never saying one word to Olivia. From there, about 30 minutes later, he texted her saying he had a lot of work to do, and he wasn't hungry, so she could eat dinner on her own.

Olivia never replied. Overwhelmed with relief she wouldn't have to face Luke, she finally let the tears come that had been threatening her all day. Her walls were up, and nothing would ever be the same in their relationship. She had to start planning her next steps. But it was the middle of a global pandemic, and next steps were hard to take with the incredible uncertainty of the times.

June 11, 2023

Since that ominous day, Olivia kept her distance from Luke but also tried to keep track of his fake social media accounts and online activity. If he was out of the room, she'd take photos of his monitors and look at them later. His laptop had a password, but she never tried to login, even when she knew he was away. Knowing him, he'd have some kind of booby trap set up to catch her trying to spy on him.

As Olivia stood in the bathroom, waiting for the girl to come out of the stall last night, it all started coming together. Bam Bam thinking he saw Luke on the Boardwalk. The random Instagram stalker. Realizing that Luke could realistically be in Ocean City, Olivia logged into her long-abandoned *Finsta*—anonymous Instagram account.

They'd blocked each other long ago, but Luke had quickly accepted the invite from her fake account last year. Olivia's fake account was of a fictional girl who went to his high school, a few years behind him. With girls getting married and changing last names, it was always hard to recall if you knew them or not, Olivia figured. She had looked it up online and "Emily" was the most popular girl name of 1996, so that's what she picked: "Emily Johnson." The photo was of a random woman… a beautiful woman who was listed as single.

Olivia frantically swiped through her feed. Luke had posted an Instagram story with a video from the air show on Saturday morning. Olivia stood outside the bathroom and watched it five times to study the scenery. He was staying at the beachfront hotel directly across the island from her house!

Her blood was boiling—and just at that moment, her phone vibrated with a message from her college friend Nate. After not getting a response from him on Instagram, she'd messaged him on LinkedIn. He seemed surprised and said he had no idea what she was talking about regarding the Instagram account. It was not him. He was not on Instagram. Olivia took a screenshot of the account and sent it to him, and he was angry, to say the least.

If Luke was trying to spy on her, Olivia had no idea why he would make posts about being in Ocean City and give away his location, but he slipped up. *Rookie mistake*, she thought.

Not only was Luke catfishing *her* on Instagram, but he was also the one behind the real-life attack on Evan.

The hat and wig he wore last night didn't help disguise Luke after Olivia realized he was in town. The hat had the logo of his D.C. gym on it. Right as Luke was running away from Evan, Ray, and Brandon, Olivia stormed out of the club and went to her car. She was planning to drive to Luke's hotel and confront him in private when he returned. This crazy game of chicken had to stop. While at a stop sign, Olivia unblocked Luke and texted the photo of him at the bar to his phone number and typed: "Stalker." She hit send just as she was about to merge onto the main road.

Some people may call it destiny, or fate, or serendipity, or just plain bad luck or good luck, depending on their perspective. Olivia was looking to the left as she waited to turn right onto the main road. As she was turning, Luke was running across the middle of the road, dodging cars, and looking down at his phone. He turned his head to the right, noticed her car turning behind him and tripped. If he hadn't tripped, he surely would have made it across the road in time. Given the circumstances, though, Olivia could not have avoided hitting him, even if she had time to swerve or stop. But did she really try? She couldn't remember.

It was like she had an out-of-body experience and lost control of her movements. One minute she was looking at his face, and the next, it was gone from her line of sight. It was like he disappeared into thin air.

She looked to the side of the road to see if he was there and then heard a thump as she drove forward. She kept driving. There were people walking around, but had anyone seen what happened? Were there cameras in the area? Did Luke see her? Or know it was her car? She drove a couple blocks and pulled over onto a side road to catch her breath. If it was anyone aside from her ex-husband, she would have stopped immediately.

Olivia sat there in stunned silence with eyes wide and hands shaking. Her phone pinged, and she was startled by the incoming text from Ray asking her to come to the scene of the accident. Olivia waved her arms wildly and screamed to try to bring her mind back to the present. She drove back and parked on the same road where she was originally parked. She took a few deep breaths and walked back to the scene of the accident, but only once she saw the ambulance pulling away.

Now as she lay in bed the next morning, she could hardly believe all that happened last night. She had a bad headache, and her throat was so dry. Her stomach was in knots. She was shocked she was able to sleep. Thinking more about it, though, she remembered from her psych class that the brain needed extra rest to repair and recover after a traumatic event. That was probably what was going on.

She looked at her phone and posted a few more pictures and videos of the band from last night. It would help with her alibi, if it came to that.

She checked all of Luke's accounts—real and fake. Nothing new since the air show post yesterday morning.

She pulled her pillow over her head to block out the light. What had she done, she thought. This was not the way her new life was supposed to start out.

Ruby was sitting patiently in her bed on the floor next to Olivia's bed. Ruby could tell that something was not right, so she just sat there, looking at Olivia and she let out a little whine every few minutes.

Olivia threw the pillow from her face and stood up in one swift motion. She ran into the bathroom and threw up. She still couldn't be sure that she actually hit Luke. Maybe it was his backpack? Was it really a bump that she felt in the car? It could have been a pothole. It all happened so fast.

She got into the shower and stood there for what was probably close to half an hour. After she washed her hair, she closed her eyes and let the water continue to pour over her.

She rested her head on her arms and balanced, leaning against the side of the tiled shower.

The water started getting cold, so she turned it off. She had a normal shower routine, but it was thrown out the window this morning. She lost track of whether or not she'd used conditioner. Did she shave her legs? She put on her robe and knew that she'd need to take Ruby outside.

Olivia never left the house without getting fully dressed, but today was the exception. She walked outside in her bathrobe with her hair wet, her face bare of makeup. A lot of people wore beach robes, so maybe she wouldn't stand out. She could have just come back from a swim. Nobody else would know that she was naked under the robe.

Andrea looked over at her, waving from her front steps. She was replanting some bright new flowers in her pots. Olivia looked at Ray's house. All seemed quiet. She wondered if Evan was still there. She had seen his car in the lot when she got back last night.

Ray to Olivia:
Hey, I see you out there. Want to stop over for breakfast? Are you feeling ok? I have donuts. Your favorite!

Olivia to Ray:
Hey I'm spent. I need to chill before work or I may not make it through my shift.

Did you get any intel on my ex's condition?

Ray to Olivia:
Yes. That's what I wanted to talk about.

Olivia to Ray:
K. I'll stop by in a few.

Is Evan still there?

Ray to Olivia:
No, he left to go surfing.

Olivia was normally an open book—unafraid to be emotional, always giving too much information. As she slowly walked to Ray's house, she stopped on the stairs and closed her eyes, trying to clear her face of all expressions.

CHAPTER 39
Evan

This was turning out to be a very eventful weekend, Evan thought as he sat on his board facing the ocean and watching the incoming waves. On the positive side, he officially had a new girlfriend who was the most amazing girl he'd ever met. On the bad side, he was the target of a crazy ass prank gone wrong. And he witnessed a hit and run accident.

At Ray's house that morning, she was on her computer trying to find news about the accident. Evan's uncle had connections everywhere, so he had texted him to see if he'd heard anything about it. He had. Jack had a friend who worked at the hospital where Olivia's ex was taken.

Obviously, it was all confidential, but it seemed like the dude was okay aside from bruising and a badly sprained ankle. Word was that he wanted to get discharged as soon as possible. No charges, no investigation. He had told the police that it was his fault for jaywalking, not looking where he was going. And after all, he had tripped so it wasn't the driver's fault if they hadn't seen him.

Given what had transpired before the accident, it was no wonder the dude wanted to get the hell out of Dodge. What was the real story? Their divorce was finalized, so why Olivia's ex spying on her? Trying to get revenge? There had to be more to it than trying to stop her from dating a new guy. Maybe that's why she had sworn off men for the summer?

Olivia's explanation last night had seemed legit, but maybe not completely comprehensive. There had to be some missing parts to give the guy a reason to get back at her. Evan had been around the block enough to know that every couple's story had three perspectives: person one, person two, and the truth.

No use trying to speculate about it, he figured; a great wave was forming. Evan spun around and got ready to catch it. As he rode it in, he saw a dolphin jump out of the water behind him. Now that was not something you saw every day. Sure, there were plenty of dolphins around this area, but right next to a surfer? Not very often. Mostly, he saw pelicans and seagulls. He'd never seen a shark while surfing, but he'd seen plenty while out on the boat fishing.

He wondered if anyone happened to be recording him and the dolphin from the beach. So cool, he thought, wishing he had a GoPro and then he switched his concentration back to the wave. It was fizzling out and he cut back to try to get some more momentum.

The ocean water was clean in Ocean City, but it was not the crystal-clear blue like it was further south down the east coast in Florida and the Caribbean. Evan would consider the water in the Mid-Atlantic to be a sea green color, depending on the light and the angle you looked at it from. Further out from the beach, it was the typical dark blue of the deep sea.

Evan had looked this up when he was younger and found that the greenish color was from the presence of algae and plant life churning around in the surf. It contained chlorophyll that was green, absorbing red and blue light. It made perfect sense. Evan often wondered how climate change would affect the ocean water here.

It already seemed warmer for this time of the year than normal, to him. He'd heard that further south in Myrtle Beach they'd been experiencing unusually clear blue waters this summer, mostly due to the lack of storms that typically stirred up the sediment.

Later next month, when it was warmer, the jellyfish would come to Maryland. Evan was not a fan of that time of the summer. In his wetsuit, he would be able to avoid their stings on most of his body, except for his head, hands, and feet. And to all those people who thought peeing on a jellyfish sting would help? Nope. A total myth made up by a wiseacre as his dad used to say. The urine could make it sting even worse.

After about another hour out in the ocean, he and his friends called it quits. They stood on the beach and took off their wet suits and sat in the sun to dry off a bit. It was an enjoyable day, and the air show was about to start for the final day. The beach was really crowded.

Evan and his buddies decided to go up to Brass Balls Saloon on the Boardwalk for brunch. It would undoubtedly be crowded, but they weren't in a rush. They were on beach time today. The best thing about eating breakfast there had to be the huge biscuits. They made the largest breakfast biscuits that Evan had ever seen in his entire life. And they were so frickin' good. He could use a heavy dose of carb loading after the last 24 hours.

Evan to Ray:
Hey babe. I miss you already. Did you talk to Olivia yet? Xoxoxo

CHAPTER 40
Ray

Ray was waiting for Olivia to come over after putting Ruby back at her place. She would tell her all about what Evan had heard from his uncle. But first, she wanted to try to pry some more information out of Olivia about herself. Hopefully, some mimosas and donuts would do the trick.

"I know it's early, but it's never too early for a mimosa. It's five o'clock somewhere, right?" Ray asked Olivia as she took a seat on the sofa.

"Ray. Girl. Don't even try to tempt me with alcohol. I'm done drinking for the rest of my life," said Olivia, putting her head into her hands and rubbing her temples. She'd changed out of her robe and had put on some short black running shorts and a red tank top that said, "Maryland" on it.

Olivia sat there quietly for about a minute and then reached out to grab a donut. Olivia not saying anything was a bit of a shock to Ray. She would have to pivot her plan.

"Ok. So. I got some intel on your ex. Well, Evan did. From his uncle." Ray went on to explain what they had found out, while Olivia sat there and nodded, not saying anything.

"He was literally hit by a car, but doesn't want to find out who did it? That doesn't make any sense," said Olivia. "Do you think he's just trying to get out of the hospital because he knows I figured out what he did to Evan?"

"Maybe?" Ray said. "Truthfully, it's all a little sketchy to me, Olivia. Why did he do that to Evan in the first place? Just because he thought you were going out with him? It really doesn't make any sense. You're divorced!"

"I know. It's so weird," said Olivia. "I mean it's not like it's the first time he's stalked me, though. It's the first time he's done something so elaborate. He's always throwing shade at me at every chance he gets. On social. In person. He gets his kicks from putting me down. He's the founder of gaslighting. He mansplains every little thing like I'm so freaking stupid."

Olivia grabbed one of the mimosas. "Since you went to the trouble, I might as well drink it," she said, smiling.

Ray grabbed her drink and a donut from the box... *Blueberry Hill* flavored.

"So, be real with me so I can try to help you. Ok? What else is going on with your ex? It's time to spill the proverbial tea," Ray said.

"It's just so convoluted! It was so dumb," Olivia said. "Can't a girl just have some fun without worrying about the consequences? *Seriously.* Everyone makes mistakes, right?" She crammed the last quarter of her donut into her mouth. "He has a video of me from when we had our honeymoon in Mexico. It was basically a girls-gone-wild drunken moment he captured on his phone. Honestly, I didn't even remember it existed until we got separated," she continued.

"Okay. That's definitely not good. But how has he threatened you with it?" Ray asked.

"Luke has been holding it over me because obviously as a teacher, a video like that—with nudity—could ruin my career. It *has*," said Olivia looking blankly out the window. "I thought if I came out here and got away from him that he would finally leave me alone. Will I ever be able to live my life without fear of that stupid video? I feel like I'm Kim Kardashian, but without the monetary resources to fight back."

"I don't get it, though, because you have the whole insurrection scoop on him," Ray said. "Doesn't it even out? I mean if you provide that to the authorities, he could potentially get arrested, right? Can't you come to a truce? Not that I condone bribery," Ray added.

"He doesn't know that I have insurrection evidence, though! I never said anything to him about it. I have no idea why he showed up here and did that to Evan," Olivia said. "Maybe he's just completely jealous that I'm going to move on and be happy without him? But also, the fact I haven't turned over any of the insurrection evidence so far might put me in danger too—covering up the conspiracy, right?"

"Hmm. Maybe," answered Ray, contemplating the facts. If Luke had donated so much of their money to a cause that

Olivia was morally opposed to, Olivia should be the one wanting revenge.

People normally think they're more clever than others, Ray thought. Overestimating their own abilities and underestimating others' abilities. Ray could tell the game of chess Olivia was playing with her ex was getting to the endgame. If Luke was going to bring Evan into their sick drama, then Ray was going to do her best to get to the bottom of it once and for all.

Olivia reached into the pocket of her shorts and took something out, saying, "I found this last night at the scene of the accident," she said. "But I can't get into it."

CHAPTER 41
Luke

Luke sat in his hospital bed, flipping through the stations on the TV. He felt lucky to be alive. As time passed, he started to remember more about what had happened before, during, and right after the accident.

As he was crossing the road—jaywalking, he could admit it—he didn't realize a car was turning onto the road from the side street. He was jogging, and beyond distracted, looking at his phone. The driver must not have seen him darting across the road because he or she was looking left at the oncoming traffic and waiting for a clear spot to make the turn.

Luke had been almost across the road when the car started turning. Then, he tripped and lost his balance. His backpack slipped off his shoulder and he bent down to pick it up, and the car hit him.

His backpack and everything in it was crushed, but fortunately, the way he fell when he tripped, he was only knocked by the car and not actually run over by the tires. The fact the driver didn't stop was somewhat surprising to him in hindsight, but maybe they didn't realize they bumped into him, given the circumstances.

Luke had a badly sprained ankle. He would need crutches, at least for the short term. Fortunately, it was his left ankle, so he'd still be able to drive. Luckily, there were no broken bones, only a bunch of bruises and lacerations on his legs and arms from where he hit the road.

He'd be able to check out of the hospital today. He was just waiting to be released. He would call a rideshare to take him back to the hotel. He still had it booked through the next day, but he would have to decide what his next step was since his plans to blow up Olivia's love life were thrown out the window.

His phone screen was cracked, but still usable. He had a charger cord in his backpack and thank God the phone hadn't been crushed, and he was able to charge it last night. The only thing he couldn't find was his burner phone. It might still be at the scene since it wasn't with the rest of his stuff. It must have flown out of his pocket when he hit the ground. It could have ended up anywhere. Someone may have picked it up… and hopefully, it wasn't the police.

There wasn't anything on the phone to tie it to him. No personally identifiable information. The recent text messages would obviously make sense to Olivia or Evan, and they'd probably be able to put the pieces together. Olivia was no tech genius, though, so there was no way she'd be able to hack into it. The latest texts were with Evan's ex-girlfriend and that ridiculous girl Luke had coerced into helping him last night. She was a total ditz, but he'd have to give her credit for her acting skills. She seemed pretty believable.

Luke had no idea how Olivia had realized he was in the bar last night. His disguise was on point, and it just seemed unimaginable to him she would have any idea he was in Ocean City. He hated the beach! When she texted him that photo as he was crossing the street, he was in total shock… and that's when he tripped and fell. As Luke was face first—half on the curb, half off of it—people began to gather around him. Someone bent down to see if he was still alive, their hand gently pressed on his neck looking for a pulse. He heard another person on the phone with 9-1-1.

"That person who hit him just drove away!" Luke heard someone say.

"I couldn't tell if he just tripped or got hit by the car. It happened so fast," said another person.

"That car clipped him, for sure. He seems ok, at least. Nothing critical."

Luke was conscious the entire time. He hadn't done anything illegal… he was just crossing the street. *Well, jaywalking was technically a misdemeanor*, he thought to himself. Going off in the ambulance was probably a good idea since his ankle could be broken or he could have gotten some kind of internal damage.

While Luke waited on the curb, he noticed that off to the side, back behind the others, stood Evan, his actual girlfriend Ray, and some other guy who had been dancing with Olivia at the club. No sign of Olivia, though. He swore he saw Ray take a photo of him with her phone.

Now all he could think about was getting discharged and back to his hotel. The gig was most definitely up. Olivia knew he was following her. Would she confront him? How would he explain it to her?

All of a sudden, he noticed a local news story come up about "another pedestrian accident" in Ocean City last night. "You're welcome for the news content, lady," Luke groaned.

CHAPTER 42
Olivia

When Olivia finally left the club last night—for the second time—it was closing time, around 2 a.m. The Boardwalk still had some people loitering about. Mostly groups of teens. It was chilly with the breeze coming from the ocean. Bam Bam had walked her out to her car. He'd tried to give her a goodnight kiss, but she dodged him and gave him a hug instead.

When she got into her car, she drove on the same path as she had been earlier that evening. She stopped at the scene of the accident and pulled into a nearby parking spot on the street. She decided to get out and take some photos of the scene because she documented everything in her life. As she was walking around the area, looking for skid marks or anything out of the ordinary, she spotted a phone in the bushes.

"Are you even serious right now?" she whispered to herself, trying not to get too excited. "This has got to be Luke's phone!" *Well, one of his many phones*, she thought. It was a cheap burner phone.

It was still charged, and Olivia could see the notifications on the locked home screen. Four notifications were visible. One message from before midnight around the time of the accident said it was from "Kristina." Three more after that, about every half hour, said they were from "Ellie."

Now, as Olivia sat in Ray's house on the sofa eating a donut and drinking a mimosa, she handed the phone to Ray. "I think it's Luke's burner phone."

"Burner phone?" Ray asked. "That screams suspicious activity!"

Ray looked at the phone while Olivia looked at Ray. "Oh. My. God. Olivia. These texts last night are from a girl named *Ellie*?" Ray showed the phone to Olivia.

"Ellie is the name of Evan's ex-girlfriend!"

"What? How would this Ellie girl know *my* ex? I'm shook. This is getting more ridiculous by the minute!" Olivia screeched, throwing her head back against the sofa pillow, loud enough to make Charlie let out a boisterous whine. "We need to get Evan over here too and get everything out in the open to see if we can solve this mystery," Ray said. "I'll check out the specs on this phone and see if I can figure out a way to access it. At least there's no way that your ex will know we have it, right? Or wait. Do you think he has tracking on it?" She nervously looked at the phone in her hand. "Can you track this kind of phone? I don't know."

Olivia followed Ray up to her home office. Ray typed in, "Can you track burner phones" along with the phone brand into Google. After clicking on a few different results, they found that since that particular phone didn't have GPS on it, it wasn't trackable like a normal smartphone, but law enforcement could track it down using cell tower data.

Olivia to Evan:
Hey. What's up? Again, so sorry about last night!! It was such a cluster.

Ray and I have new intel that's sending me into orbit!!

Can you come to her place at some point before 1 so we can chat before I have to go to work?

Evan to Olivia:
Be there in like 30 – just finishing up brunch with the boys

"Look, Olivia, people are not as innocent and naive as you think they are," Ray said as she entered some searches about the phone type. "People are out there Googling up a storm every single day. There is so much info out there about every single one of us just waiting to be accessed. Addresses, how much our house costs along with a complete virtual tour if it's been sold lately, public court records… So much freaking personal data. Evan didn't tell me about his ex-girlfriend being named Ellie. I found out because I looked him up and did the research. They were tagged together in old social media photos."

"Wow. Okay. I guess you're right," said Olivia, rolling her eyes. Did Ray not realize that Olivia was the queen of Google research?

Charlie started whining and Ray got up from her desk chair. "I'm going to run Charlie out. Be back in a sec," said Ray as she locked her computer screen.

CHAPTER 43
Evan

After finishing brunch, Evan pulled into Ray's complex, he saw her and Charlie out in the dog area. It was always interesting to look at someone when they didn't know you were checking them out, thought Evan. Ray didn't normally appear to be an impatient type—not one of those people who seemed to be put out to be walking their dog, always so anxious to finish it up and get back inside. Like they had something better to be doing. Evan knew Ray was worried about Olivia. How did she always appear to be so outwardly calm?

Ray was wearing black spandex biker shorts and an oversized MIT t-shirt. She was casually standing there like she didn't have a care in the world. She was looking at her phone as Charlie sniffed around and found the perfect spot.

Evan to Ray:
How did I know that you would look super sexy even picking up dog poop?

Ray looked over to the parking lot, smiled, and waved. She started walking over to him as he got a shirt out of his trunk. It was so humid. He needed to change his shirt for the second time today. He tossed the sweaty one into a plastic bag in the back of the car. He kept a pile of clean shirts handy for just this very reason. He pulled on a Night's Watch t-shirt—one of his many *Game of Thrones* fan shirts.

When Ray reached him, he bent down and gave her a quick kiss on the cheek. "So, we're going to play detective?" Evan asked.

"Yes indeedy. We need to pull all our intel together to crack this case," said Ray, looking up and smiling as she held up her hand to shade her eyes from the bright sun. She did a double take as she looked across the parking lot. Evan turned his head to follow her glance.

"Wait a minute. Olivia's SUV. It has one of those Maryland flag crab stickers on the back window," she said, and then stopped, clearly contemplating her next sentence. "It's white. Evan. Don't you see what this could mean?" Ray said, pointing to it. "Doesn't her car look like the one that hit Luke last night? I clearly remember seeing a crab sticker on the back car window. At the time, I didn't really think much about it because like half of Marylanders have that same sticker," Ray said as she started pacing back and forth behind Evan's car, Charlie tugging on the leash to stay closer to Evan.

Evan reached down to pat Charlie, trying to recollect the sequence of events last night.

"Think back," she continued. "Olivia was acting super weird when she ran up to us last night. She came to the scene after I texted her, but only after Luke left in the ambulance. We know she was in the bathroom when we left the club."

"How would she have known where Luke was walking or that it was him in the first place?" Evan asked as he rubbed his hand across the unshaven bristle on his chin. "I didn't really look too closely at the car; except that it was light colored and an SUV. I was focusing on the dude." He paused for a moment, and when Ray didn't say anything, he continued, "I know that white Honda CRVs are super popular. Those crab stickers are also popular. My mom even has one of them. But the timing? Could it be a coincidence?"

"There's actually a lot of research on coincidences," said Ray. "Not to get too sciency on you, but the mind automatically searches for structure—trying to find connections so you notice things that are similar and try to find a coincidence. Specifically, the year you're born in or your birthday. And just FYI, you and Olivia have the same birthday. Not the year, but you're both January 29."

"Awe, babe, you remember my birthday?" he said, putting his hands to his heart, feigning bashfulness. "Ok. I admit it, I remember yours too. July 22," he laughed.

"This is serious, Evan. I'd bet my last Fractured Prune donut that this same car situation is not a coincidence. That could have been Olivia hitting Luke last night," Ray said, pushing her index finger into Evan's chest, repeatedly. "Fortunately, he is not seriously injured, but if we're going to sort out this mess, she needs to come clean. Is she in danger? Is she putting us in danger?"

Evan grabbed Ray's hand, the one that didn't have Charlie's leash, and they started walking to her place. When they got there, Olivia was nowhere in sight.

CHAPTER 44
Ray

"Olivia! I'm back. Evan is here, too," said Ray in a louder-than-usual voice as Charlie ran to his water bowl and started barking when he saw it was empty.

Ray took his bowl to the kitchen sink and started filling it up as Evan went upstairs.

"She's not up here either!" he shouted as he sprinted back down the stairs.

Ray to Olivia:
Hey. Evan is here. Where did you go?

"Just texted her," said Ray as she put Charlie's bowl back down on the floor. Evan entered the kitchen area. He grabbed a donut from the box and leaned against the counter.

"No immediate response," Ray said to Evan. "Another mystery on our hands!"

"She probably went back to her place to get something," said Evan as he pulled Ray closer to him and gave her a kiss. "Or she wanted to give us some alone time?"

Ray smiled up at Evan and said, "Maybe, but doubtful. I think she's up to something!"

"Wait a minute," Evan said, looking out the front window. "I swear I just saw her ride by on a bike…"

They separated and walked over to the front screen door just in time to see Olivia pedaling around the corner into the parking lot.

"Olivia! Where are you going?" Evan yelled as he sprinted down the front porch steps. "Hold up!"

Ray thought Olivia likely heard Evan, but she appeared to ignore him and went merrily on her way to who knows where.

"Ok. That was strange," said Evan. "Where was she going in such a rush?"

"That girl is such an enigma to me!" Ray said. "Ok, well, let me fill you in on what we know so far about her ex." Ray brought Evan up to her office and showed him the burner phone.

"You see these last few text message notifications from last night? One of them is from someone named Ellie. Does that number look familiar to you?" Ray asked Evan.

"Oh my God," exclaimed Evan as he brought the phone closer to his face to be sure of the number he was seeing on the screen. "Ellie. That's my ex-girlfriend!" Evan shook his head in disbelief. "How in the unholy hell did *he* get hooked up with *her*!?"

Evan reached into his pocket to grab his own phone. "I'm calling Ellie right now," he muttered as he spun around on his heel and stormed into the hallway. "I'm going to get to the bottom of her role in this damn circus!"

Ellie did not answer her phone, any of the four times in a row that Evan called her, so he was relegated to sending her a text.

Evan to Ellie:
Hey. You must be busy… ignoring my calls. Do you know someone named Luke Lewis? Please call me ASAP to discuss. It's urgent.

After Evan hadn't heard back in a few minutes, he sent another text.

Evan to Ellie:
He was hit by a car and is in the hospital.

Evan's phone started ringing almost immediately.

"Hey, so I know this looks really bad," Ellie said quickly, "but this guy—Luke—contacted me on Facebook a few weeks ago and said that my boyfriend was having an affair with his wife. Long story short, he said he had a plan to shake things up and asked if I wanted to witness the event unfold in person. I said we had broken up and asked him to stop texting me! Well, I never thought more about it, and then last night, he texted me a photo of you and Brandon in a club. I texted back asking what he was doing, but no response. Are you ok? Is he ok? What happened to him?"

As Ellie was talking, Evan was pacing up and down the stairs. "I'm ok. He's ok. He's just got a sprained ankle when he was hit by a car. Look, sorry that you got mixed up in this drama but please let me know if someone threatens me in the future, ok? Have some common decency."

"Sorry. I know I should have said something, but…" Ellie just stopped talking mid-sentence.

"Whatever. Have a nice life," he said as he tapped his phone to end the call.

Evan walked back into Ray's home office and recounted his conversation with Ellie as he sat on the bed that was next to her desk.

"I feel like we need one of those detective boards with pins and string to try to connect all of this together," said Ray looking at her computer. "I just found some records that Olivia and Luke have restraining orders against each other. There must be something beyond the normal bad divorce drama. Like was there domestic abuse or sexual assault?" Ray did a quick search. "So, this says restraining orders against stalking or harassment helps prevent abuse, threatening behavior, or bothering you or your family members. Attempts to enter your home, workplace, school, or other location. And ability to communicate or attempt to communicate with you."

"I had a cousin who got a restraining order against her ex-boyfriend, but he was actually assaulting her. She would show up to family gatherings with unexplained black eyes and broken bones," said Evan. "It was so sad. She ended up going to live with my grandma in Virginia to escape him. He kept harassing her online and on her phone. She kept changing her number, and we think that another relative was a mole and feeding info to her ex."

"Ugh. That is so sad! They say cyberbullying and catfishing are commonly done by someone you know. Look at that show *Catfish* on MTV. So many times, it's a spurned lover or even a best friend," said Ray.

"I had a friend who was catfished a few years ago on a dating app," said Evan. "It ended up being his frickin' brother! His brother was upset, he'd taken *his* crush to the prom years ago. So juvenile! Some people just can't move on and insist on ruminating on the past. You can't control what happens to you, but you can control how you respond. If people stopped taking things so personally, life would be so much more enjoyable."

"Okay," said Ray, abruptly getting back to business. "So now we know Luke has a girls-gone-wild kind of video of Olivia. And Olivia has proof Luke was at the Capitol on January 6th. But is that all there is to the story?" Ray asked. "It all seems so dramatic!"

"No cap," said Evan.

"What? No 'cap?' I am truly robbing the cradle. Talk in plain English!" laughed Ray.

Evan laughed and grabbed Ray around the waist. "I'll be sure to offer running commentary to bring you up to date on the current slang, bae. No cap means 'no lies, for real,'" explained Evan as he squeezed Ray into a tighter hug.

Ray brought up the document with the research she'd been doing on Olivia and Luke and moved away so Evan could read it.

What we know:
- Luke's thinks Olivia ruined his life.
- Luke at Capitol on 1/6/21. Olivia has evidence.
- Luke has incriminating video of Olivia that he's threatened to use maliciously.
- Mutual restraining orders.
- Luke donated $27,550 of their savings to the GOP without her knowledge.

- Luke catfished a girl and then bribed her to do an IRL attack on Evan. Contacted ex-Ellie to be part of the sabotage.
- Luke has burner phones and dozens of fake accounts.
- Stalks Olivia and posts fake news on social media. Works with "WAFN."
- Olivia made a post on Facebook about Luke pretending to being pro-life (deleted it).
- Olivia may have run over Luke with her car.

"Wait. What?" Evan exclaimed. "WAFN. That's our new client at work! How the hell is Luke involved with them? This is getting fishier and fishier by the minute."

CHAPTER 45
Luke

Luke's rideshare had dropped him off right next to the hotel entrance, which was fortunate since he was hobbling along trying to get used to his walking boot. When he went into the lobby, he tried to remember where the elevator was to judge the distance he'd have to walk. He spotted it and realized there were a bunch of wet kids jumping around waiting, and he'd happily take his time walking over there.

Just as he reached for his wallet to get his key card, he felt the presence of somebody walking up beside him.

"Fancy meeting you here, stranger."

Luke's heart rate jumped and he whipped his head to his right at the voice. "Olivia," he said like a kid whose mom caught him with his hand in the cookie jar.

He never in a million years would have thought that she could have tracked him directly to this hotel. She looked like a psychopath. Her face was flushed, and her hair was windblown. He could feel the anger radiating from her, but she had a huge fake smile plastered on her face. But Luke knew better. If they hadn't been standing in the middle of a hotel lobby, she would have been throwing a huge hissy fit right now.

Luke was awkwardly balanced, trying to put his weight on his good leg. He had his wallet in his hand and his backpack on his back.

"Looks like you've been having quite an eventful 24 hours, huh?" Olivia replied. "Are you ok?" she asked as she looked him up and down.

"Yeah. I sprained my ankle and am bruised up," said Luke, hobbling a few paces back, trying to regain his balance. "Assuming your friends told you about the little accident I had last night?"

"Yeah. I arrived on the scene right as the ambulance was taking you away," said Olivia.

Luke hobbled over to the sofa in the lobby near the front desk and sat down, stretching out his bad leg. It would be a safer spot for whatever this conversation turned out to be, with hotel staff nearby, he thought.

"Well, look. I guess that by now you know I had a part in the drama last night with that guy Evan. It was a mistake. I admit it," said Luke. "I got carried away, and Lord knows I have no idea why I'm here right now. It was all a big mistake."

"What about getting me *fired* from my teaching job in D.C. last fall? How do you feel about *that*, Luke? Was *that* a big mistake too?" Olivia hissed. "You're trying to ruin my life! Can't you just leave me and my friends alone?"

"Olivia. You're one to talk! *You* are the one ruining lives. I have no friends. No money. My family members don't trust me. I'm the one suffering because of *you!*" proclaimed Luke, pointing angrily at her and drawing the attention of the crew at the front registration desk.

"That was all you, Luke. You didn't need any help from me to trash every single one of your relationships. You did that all on your own," protested Olivia, lowering her voice. "And you have the nerve to blame *me* for the money situation when *you* just threw it all away? You are unbelievable! How did trying to make things *great* go for you? Did you feel so *proud* in the end?"

"You self-righteous bitch! You're the problem with this country. You and all the people like you. So woke, and high, and mighty. Thinking you know what's best for everyone!" Luke exclaimed. "You have no clue what an average person in middle America wants. You're a spoiled coastal elite living in your fancy beach house that your mommy and daddy gave you. They probably pay for all the utilities, insurance, and cleaning. Do they even give you a weekly allowance for groceries?"

Luke was disgusted by Olivia's entitlement. She had no idea how easy she had it with her fancy family and her fancy friends, living it up at the beach all year. She was so out of touch with reality.

"If there is one thing I've learned in my therapy sessions, it's that it's impossible to try to have a rational conversation with someone who is behaving irrationally. I know that you won't listen to logic. You project, you deflect, you reject everything I say. Luke, I can only hope that someday you will think back on this time in your life and realize I wasn't against you. Your friends and family weren't against you. You were working against *yourself*. You did this to *yourself*."

Olivia turned and walked away, leaving Luke sitting on the sofa. Luke looked up at the ceiling and put his head back against the wall and closed his eyes. His ankle was throbbing. *She doesn't understand*, he thought. *She* was the one who would look back and realize she was wrong about him. Wrong about everything. She was the one with the problem. She just couldn't see it because she was so obsessed with blaming him for all of her problems.

He looked out the window as Olivia shot like a bullet out of the hotel. "What a bitch!" Luke said under his breath. Then, he looked over into the parking lot and suddenly remembered his car was still parked at the end of the Boardwalk.

He punched his fisted hand onto the sofa. He'd be getting a huge parking ticket, and possibly the car was already towed. "Dammit to Hell!" Luke growled as he tried to stand up.

CHAPTER 46
Olivia

As Olivia exited the hotel, she felt so angry that she was channeling the Incredible Hulk stomping so hard it seemed like she'd crack the walkway with each step. She made her way over to where she'd left her bike on the sidewalk, locked to a street sign. She stood there for a moment and then decided to leave her bike and walk over to Candy Kitchen, which was across the street. She needed chocolate.

She paused and took a few deep breaths. As she walked, she started humming the lyrics to Taylor Swift's *Anti-Hero* song.

If Olivia had harbored any thoughts that Luke was getting better, they'd all flown out the window. She couldn't trust him. She wouldn't trust him. How could she get that video back from him or be sure he wouldn't keep using it against her?

Last fall was when the feud escalated. He'd posted the video—which was only about 30 seconds long—on a fake, public YouTube account he'd created in her likeness. He then went on to create a fake email address for one of the parents at the school where she worked. Next, Luke sent an email to the principal with a link to the video claiming that along with the video, Olivia had been overheard talking with some friends at a local cafe about her work at a strip club on the weekends.

When Olivia was called into the principal's office before school started the next day, needless to say, she was surprised at the last-minute meeting request. She thought it had to do with her work on the fall fundraiser, which was a read-a-thon that had taken place the previous week. It had been an enormous success and had brought in much more money than the holiday gift wrapping paper sale from the year before.

When Olivia walked into the principal's office, she knew something was wrong immediately. The principal was clearly nervous. She didn't make eye contact and was a bundle of nerves and couldn't keep her fidgeting hands still. She was twirling a pen so aggressively that it flung into the air and landed with a thud on the ground. She left it there and took a deep breath. Her face seemed overheated and flushed.

The principal clearly had a speech planned out—talking points printed on a paper in front of her. She said they had a policy that prohibited teachers from posting inappropriate content on social media. Olivia had signed it as part of her onboarding paperwork. And that if a teacher's public social media profile contained inappropriate content, they could be subject to disciplinary action, including termination.

Hearing this planned speech, Olivia withered down into her seat, immediately realizing that her crazy video from Mexico may have somehow gotten out. Well, she knew exactly who did it. But how did he do it? Why did he do it? Why now?

The principal turned her monitor around so Olivia could see the YouTube channel profile page. Olivia didn't have a YouTube channel, so she knew it was fake. The video of her on the beach, clearly drunk, topless, and dancing around like a maniac was not fake. She knew her excuses wouldn't help, but she gave them anyway. She told the principal that it was not her YouTube account—she didn't even post on YouTube— and that her ex-husband had been threatening her with making the video public ever since their separation. It was taken years ago during their honeymoon to Mexico. The only fortunate part of this entire drama was that YouTube doesn't allow nudity, so there was a black bar across her chest. Looking just like a contestant in an episode of *Bachelor in Paradise*.

To say Olivia was mortified was an understatement. The school had arranged for a substitute teacher to take over her class that same day and she was immediately escorted out of the building in tears. They told her that she'd be able to clean out her classroom closet and desk after school hours later in the week.

Her two closest teacher friends started texting her at lunch time as gossip ran rampant through the teachers' lounge. She hadn't responded to any of them. After she had gotten into her car, too stunned to even start it up at first, she had decided to drive downtown to the National Mall, her happy place. She had walked around a bit and then went into the National Gallery of Art and sat there, staring at the artwork. She moved into different rooms every 15 minutes or so. She spent the most time looking at one of her favorites, *The Boating Party*, an 1893 oil painting by American artist Mary Cassatt. She never took one photo. It was that bad.

Olivia had contemplated what to tell her family. Should she tell them the truth? Could she sue Luke? Was she even sure it was him? She'd have to confront him. They already had restraining orders against each other. She had so many questions. Everyone made mistakes. Her family would understand… and at least the video was edited. Technically, the video was Luke's because he was the one who recorded it on his phone, and it would be hard to sue for invasion of privacy. *It was defamation, for sure*, she had thought to herself.

Later that week, her teacher friend had texted her the parent in question denied having sent the email and said it was not her email address. But it was too late. The video did exist, and it was online. Olivia had contemplated her next steps and decided that the damage was done, and she would move on. The school ended up making accommodations to give her a reference without mentioning the incident since they believed her story, and the parent corroborated it.

After a few threatening texts to Luke about suing him for defamation, the entire YouTube channel disappeared.

PART 3
Friday, July 21, 2023
More than a month later.

CHAPTER 47
Luke

After Luke returned to D.C. from the beach last month, he was completely exhausted. His ankle hurt and his entire body was bruised. Fortunately, he was completely self-sufficient at home by himself. He didn't need to leave his house. It was like COVID lock-down part two. He typically ordered DoorDash for lunch and would make his own dinners with items he got from the Instacart grocery delivery. He could cook if he had to—it was so simple to follow recipes on YouTube. He hated cooking. It seemed like a monumental waste of time since he could just order something or have a frozen meal for less money. He ordered everything else he needed from Amazon or Walmart.

During the past month, he'd only left his house for two doctors' appointments. The condo was a huge mess. He'd been bad about taking the trash out. It smelled. It was cluttered beyond belief. The kitchen sink was a disaster zone. The pile of dirty laundry in his bedroom was a mile high. He'd ended up ordering new underwear online. He couldn't easily carry the laundry basket with his bum ankle. He'd bought one of those knee scooters and could roll around the condo to most places.

He felt like all people were all a little depressed sometimes and didn't put any stock in all that mental health mumbo jumbo. Everyone had highs and lows. He was not depressed. It was only a bad spell, and things would be looking up as soon as his damn ankle was back in business. It was all Olivia's fault. She wanted to ruin him.

He tried to get comfortable in his office chair and prop up his leg on a box under his desk. He opened his calendar for the day. A meeting with the HR lady at his company had popped up on his calendar for this morning, out of the blue. Now anyone with a job knows that an unplanned meeting with the HR folks is almost never a good thing. Luke immediately wondered if he was getting fired. It was no secret he made a mistake the previous week and his boss had been upset. It was a minor typo. Anyone could have done it.

He joined the HR meeting, and it was pleasant enough at first, with some friendly exchanges about the weather and summer vacations.

"Luke, I have to admit, I'm concerned about you. Some of your teammates contacted me, saying you're looking sickly, and being forgetful, and that you've been dozing off in meetings," she said. "How *are* you doing?"

"Ah. No need to worry, Janice. I'm just trying to get my ankle back in service and it's been a little challenging keeping up with things around the house," said Luke, dismissively. "I'm having trouble sleeping, but it will all work out in due time."

"About the situation last week. You undoubtedly know it was a costly mistake. And not just the money. But more importantly, it's about our reputation with the client," Janice said. "I know you're talking with them later today, and I do hope it goes well."

"Yes. Not a big deal. I'm sure that we can clear it all up," said Luke, with a fake smile plastered on his face.

"Well, from the senior leadership's point of view, it actually was a big deal. The purpose of this discussion right now is to let you know that if anything like that happens again, we won't be able to overlook it. This will serve as a first, but also a final warning," Janice added. "We have to put our clients first. You must understand that."

Luke said, "Yes." They ended the call. He leaned back into his office chair and slid down so he could lean his head on the backrest, closed his eyes, *just for a minute*, he thought, and nodded off.

He missed the start of his next meeting, even though his computer dinged with a reminder notification 10 minutes prior to the start. This meeting was the follow-up to his "mistake" last week, with his boss and two reps from the client. He was supposed to profusely apologize and promise that it wouldn't happen again. Luke was startled awake by the much louder ringing sound of an incoming Zoom call through his computer. It was his boss. The meeting was 15 minutes underway.

"Dammit! I am *cooked*," Luke whispered aloud, closing his eyes in alarm and slamming his hands down on his desk in frustration. He opened his eyes again and pressed "Accept."

"Hey, Mike. So sorry. I was having internet issues and had to reboot," stammered Luke. "I'll join the meeting right away."

"Luke. No. Don't bother. It's over. You had this one chance to try to redeem yourself and you blew it. I'll ask Janice to give you a call with the next steps. I have no other choice. Thank you for your service, but I'm going to have to let you go. Effective immediately," said Mike.

"Wait. Mike. I can explain," said Luke, realizing that begging would probably not work, but he had to give it a shot. "I just took too many pain killers for my ankle. I'll cut back, though. I swear. I'm almost healed."

"I'm really sorry it didn't work out, Luke, but this is the end of the road for us. Goodbye," said Mike, and he clicked to disconnect the call.

Luke turned in his chair and threw the closest thing he could find, his coffee mug, against the wall. Stale coffee splattered across the pale gray wall and onto the white curtains. Olivia had decorated the office (well, it was the third bedroom) when they first moved into the place. Chunks of white ceramic scattered across the floor in a wet mess. It was a stupid mug anyway. Something that Olivia had given him for his birthday a few years ago. It said "Pretty Fly for a Jedi" on it.

Who held important meetings so late on a Friday afternoon anyway? He thought to himself. Obviously, he was tired. It had been a long and stressful week. His computer pinged. Janice sent him an email saying his accounts would be locked out momentarily and she would email him the next steps to his personal email address she had on file. Luke yelled out a few choice words about Janice and tried to think if there was anything personal on his work storage drives or in email he should try to save or delete. He couldn't think straight. He was a ball of pent-up adrenaline. Luke feverishly clicked from window to window and then in what seemed like an instant, but was probably more like 15 minutes, he was locked out of all the company systems.

Luke didn't have an updated resume. He hadn't been networking since before the pandemic. And he knew that the only reason he ever went out to functions previously was because Olivia made him go with her. Luke had no idea what he would do next. He didn't particularly like his job, but he didn't have experience doing anything except being a financial analyst. Fortunately, he had a personal laptop he could use in the meantime. But his savings was limited. Extremely limited; especially since the divorce. He had no nest-egg. Nothing saved up for a rainy day. He'd depleted it all. Sure, the donations were for a very good cause, and he wouldn't regret it. He was supporting his country and the survival of democracy!

Luke picked up his phone. He had nobody to call. Nobody to text. Nobody would care that he was just fired. He opened Twitter, which was about to officially changeover to be called "X," and went to town commenting on any and all posts he found that had anything positive to say about the current administration. After that, he started responding about the latest indictments being an evil and heinous abuse of power.

As he slammed his fingers down on his keyboard, angrily posting one comment after another, he drank directly from a bottle of tequila. The hours seemed to speed by in a dazed angry haze. His online behavior and actions became increasingly more erratic. He was spiraling down, fast.

Right before Luke's head collapsed onto his desk, he had hit "Submit" on an online order for a prank candle. He'd found this article in a simple Google search: "The Complete List of All the Stuff You Can Anonymously Ship Your Enemies." The description said that it was labeled "Apple Pie," but it actually turned into a "Dirty Fart" smell. Luke was laughing uncontrollably as he placed the order. Olivia loved candles, and she would waste no time lighting it up. He would send one to Janice too. Hell, he should order an entire case, he thought as his eyes closed and he passed out.

CHAPTER 48
Ray

Ray was driving back to Ocean City from her quarterly meeting, which had been held in an airport hotel near the Thurgood Marshall Baltimore-Washington International Airport, or BWI for short. To celebrate the last day of the meeting, they held a happy hour at the Guinness Open Gate Brewery. Although Ray was not a huge beer drinker, there were some beers that she liked—normally the darker, sweeter ones. She was not a fan of hoppy IPAs. In any event, they also had a nice food selection. She'd only had one beer because she had a long drive back home.

Her company had arranged a group tour of the brewery that would lead into a happy hour with heavy appetizers in a private room. Many of the staff members continued the party outside in the huge courtyard after the official gathering was over.

Since it was a Friday, Ray wanted to delay her drive back to the beach as late as possible to avoid traffic. Under normal circumstances, the *Old Ray* would have bolted at the first opportunity to leave the gathering. She would have sat alone in her car in the parking lot until her app said the traffic had cleared up. However, the *New Ray* ended up spending a pleasant few hours with some of her teammates who were flying out the next morning. After only interacting with many of them over Zoom for the past two years, it was almost surreal to meet them all in person. In real life, the majority of them were not at all what she expected. Some were much taller or shorter. Some looked so much younger, and some looked so much older in person!

One of her colleagues told her she was much more friendly in person than they expected her to be. A backhanded compliment, for sure. Ray vowed to work on her virtual meeting persona and be more approachable.

Around 8:30 p.m. she checked her map app and decided it was time to head out so she would arrive home before midnight. Evan was staying at her house tonight with Charlie and she knew that he'd be at his uncle's bar before getting home right around the same time. Ray was looking forward to a quiet weekend after being around people all week. She was exhausted.

During the afternoon session, they had split up into small groups for a team-building exercise where they needed to accomplish certain goals to survive being stranded in the wilderness. The strategy part of it reminded Ray of the Marshmallow Challenge she'd had to do in graduate school, which was supposed to teach lessons in collaboration and product development. Small teams had to build the tallest free-standing structure from spaghetti sticks, tape, and string, and place one whole marshmallow on the top. The team with the highest marshmallow won. Many teams couldn't get their marshmallow on top without the entire thing collapsing. Ray's team won at 20 inches.

Ray to Evan:
The happy hour was fun but draining talking to so many people! Getting ready to head out now! Looks like I might be passing through a storm in Cambridge.

Can't wait to see you! Xoxo

Evan to Ray (with a photo of Charlie):
Drive safely. I missed you so much! And so did Charlie

Ray queued up the *SmartLess* podcast with Greta Gerwig to stream on the drive. Olivia had texted her a few days ago begging her to listen to it before they went to see *The Barbie Movie* next week. Olivia had arranged a Barbie watch-party for the late afternoon on her day off. Olivia and Evan had even agreed to take off work a little early so they could do the Barbie and *Oppenheimer* double feature.

This kind of fanatical behavior was not something Ray was used to… Sure, she loved Harry Potter and enjoyed Marvel movies, but she'd never been the type who needed to go on opening weekend.

Olivia's *kenergy* about Barbie was so hyped up that it would be impossible for Ray to get out of seeing the movie, though. The one thing Ray didn't have trouble saying no to, though, was being in a Barbie-related TikTok. Olivia wanted Ray to go to the beach with her to film an "I'm Just Ken" TikTok. Going to the movie wearing pink was more than *kenough* for Ray. Evan could record her video, that was his area of expertise!

After the podcast was over, Ray pulled into Royal Farms, got gas, went to the bathroom, and bought a lottery ticket. The Mega Millions jackpot was $720 million. Ray was not a gambler, but her mom had texted her earlier saying that she should get a ticket. Her parents regularly bought lottery tickets whenever the jackpot got big. They had loved to fantasize about winning a huge jackpot growing up.

Ray got back in her car and switched the audio source to the local radio station and started daydreaming about what she'd do if she won the lottery. Given her single status and her rent-free living arrangements, she'd been able to save up quite a bit of money. The tech industry was fickle, and Ray was always worried about losing her job or some kind of family emergency coming up. She never felt secure in her financial situation.

If she did win the lottery, she would surely help her parents and sister pay off their debt as a first step. Helping her extended family in Puerto Rico would also be a priority. She was not exactly a car person, but she'd love to get an electric vehicle. She couldn't imagine not working. Maybe she'd go back to school and get her PhD? Or set up a philanthropic foundation?

She and Olivia had talked about trying to manifest things that they wanted to accomplish, calling it the 369-method, which she got from TikTok. It involved writing down what you'd like to manifest three times in the morning, six times during the day, and nine times in the evening. They'd also talked quite a bit about positive affirmations. Sayings like, "I am enough, I am complete," and "I define my worth and I am worthy," and "I trust myself completely."

The hard part for Ray was trying to figure out what she wanted to manifest. Happiness? Success? Health? Love? Olivia told Ray she always wished the exact same wish, but she wouldn't say what it was because it was bad luck, of course.

Olivia's parents had visited the beach house a few weeks ago for July 4th and Ray could have easily picked Olivia's mom out of a crowd. Olivia and Mariana were like two peas in a pod as far as looks and personality. Their styles were different, but each was dressing age appropriate. Olivia was more fashion-forward, wearing sporty and somewhat skimpy clothes (as far as Ray was concerned, at least), whereas Mariana was more boho—long, flowing, flowery shirts and dresses. Olivia's dad, Danny, had a typical professor vibe—scholarly and contemplative. He didn't say much, but when he did talk it was normally a clever joke or something so insightful that everyone had to take a moment to digest it. He wore collared shirts and tan shorts. At the beach, both stayed under the umbrella with big hats to block the sun. They read books on their Kindles for hours on end.

Olivia had taken some time off, but since it was a holiday week, she had to work most days. While she was at work on the Fourth of July holiday, Ray and Evan took Olivia's parents and a few others out fishing on Jack's boat. The bay was packed with jet skiers and boaters. The worst part was that many of them were not used to boating and didn't know the rules of the water, so Evan had to be extra careful in the captain's seat.

Ray's phone started ringing through the car sound system, interrupting her thoughts. It was Olivia. She was practically screaming over the noise at the bar. "Hey, girl! I'm on a short break. The bar is hopping tonight! How's the drive home?"

"Traffic is high-volume, but things are moving. There are so many police cars along the way slowing things down," replied Ray.

"Say 'hi' to Evan! He's helping out behind the bar because Brandon and Raymond are out at dinner for Raymond's birthday," said Olivia.

"Hey, babe! Can't wait to see you," said Evan, clearly busy beyond belief. The sound of the bar was deafening.

"Anyway, we were wondering… Can you stop by the bar on your way back and drive us home?" asked Olivia.

"Sure. I should be there by around 11:15 p.m. if all goes as planned," said Ray, and then they hung up. *That was a little mysterious*, she thought.

Olivia was unpredictable, and although that was at constant odds with Ray's scientific mindset, she was trying not to overanalyze Olivia's odd behavior. But Olivia's reactions regarding her ex seemed so immature. There had to be more to the story.

Ray figured Luke would remain obsessed with Olivia until he found a new girlfriend to torment or got too scared about potential retaliation. Over the past few weeks, Ray and Olivia had been meticulously scheming. While Ray was closer to D.C. this past week, part two of their plan, nicknamed *Laserbrain*, was put into motion.

Part one of the plan was simple and happened last Sunday. They'd spent the entire day organizing things and then submitted all of Olivia's photos and videos from January 6, 2021, to the FBI Capitol Violence website. The FBI was seeking the public's assistance to identify the individuals who made unlawful entry into the U.S. Capitol building. Along with the footage, they identified Luke. They still weren't sure if he'd gone into the building or not. They figured he would likely have valuable intel about who the others were there that day.

On the FBI website, dozens if not hundreds of defendants charged in federal court related to the Capitol breach existed. All of the associated documents were online and available to the general public. Ray spent a few days reading through them in the evenings after work.

Criminal complaints for many of the defendants were consistent: knowingly entering and remaining in any restricted building or grounds without lawful authority, violent entry, and disorderly conduct on Capitol grounds, knowingly engaging in disorderly or disruptive conduct in a restricted building.

Through search warrants, investigators gained access to phone records that in some cases were able to show "maps display radius" that were under 100 feet, which would have encompassed an area that was entirely within the U.S. Capitol Building. They were also able to use driver's license photos to run image searches in the available footage. Ray couldn't believe that Luke hadn't been identified yet, thinking he must not have entered the building.

There were still five insurrection suspects who had not been caught, and their wanted posters were on the FBI website. Ray was surprised that she hadn't spent more time perusing the FBI website in the past. It was fascinating! She'd often wondered if she should have pursued law school instead of sticking with cybersecurity for her master's degree. She loved research, and if it helped solve a mystery, all the better.

Part two of their *Laserbrain* plan happened Monday evening. Ray was staying in a hotel near the airport for her quarterly meeting but didn't have plans after the workday ended. Olivia had the day off and had driven over to meet her. Then, they'd driven to Olivia's storage unit in D.C. that she had with Luke. Ray rented another unit under her name, and they moved everything over that was Olivia's, aside from the things that Olivia wanted to bring back with her to the beach, including five huge boxes of Christmas decorations.

The unit was being paid automatically to Luke's credit card. For the most part, it was a bunch of old junk. There were probably some collectables—old sports memorabilia and records. Not a big payoff for anyone in *Storage Wars*, for sure. They didn't find anything too interesting or incriminating. However, they did leave something there they hoped would be *very* incriminating.

CHAPTER 49
Olivia

"Look, I know that she'll be tired," Olivia said with a dismissing attitude. "The entire party will only last about an hour, right? Just until we can make a toast at midnight when it's officially her birthday. She'll love it! She's turning 30, and we can't let that go by without a celebration!"

"*You* love parties, Olivia. But does *Ray* love parties? She's such an introvert," replied Evan, his eyes squinting with worry.

"Come on. *Try* to be positive, Evan! If she doesn't like it, it's my fault. If she loves it, you can take *all* the credit," beamed Olivia with her million-megawatt smile.

Evan laughed as he handed Olivia an order of 10 orange crushes and 10 green tea shots for a table of aging women having a rowdy bachelorette party. Tons of soon-to-be-newlyweds came to the beach to celebrate their bachelor and bachelorette parties. Many were in their 20s, but with so many people getting married later in life, or remarried, it was interesting to see how off-the-hook some of the parties got. These older folks had a lot of money to spend and many times they partied much harder than the younger folks.

Olivia often wondered if she'd remarry, and if she did, would she do all the customary events like a bridal shower and a bachelorette party? She desperately wanted to find her soulmate. Her forever love. She knew he was out there somewhere! Hopefully, he lived or vacationed in Ocean City.

The crowd was thinning out, and Olivia wanted to start to set up the birthday table decorations. Everything was ready to go back in the staff room and the kitchen, she just needed to push together some tables and bring it all out. Ray should be arriving in about 30 minutes if all went as planned with her trip.

Olivia brought out her box with party supplies—a generic *30th Birthday* set she'd ordered online with a pink and purple color theme that included a plastic tablecloth, plates, napkins. She had a huge bouquet of flowers and a bundle of balloons. No surprise that it was windy, and the balloons were blowing around and she had trouble getting the tablecloth to stay on the table.

Brandon and Raymond had arrived back from their dinner just in time to take over the bar duties. Evan would help her set things up for the party.

As Olivia was coming back out of the kitchen, she saw Andrea walking over from the parking lot with a much younger—and unbelievably handsome—man. Olivia quickly shouted, "Howdy, neighbor!" She couldn't wave because her hands were full of the cake and a gift bag with some small, but meaningful presents she'd carefully curated. The cake was nothing extravagant—a chocolate sheet cake with white icing and purple flowers. She'd made some cookies and brownies herself and placed everything strategically around the table to hold down the tablecloth.

JJ's had some Edison bulb lights strung across the outside area, but Olivia set out some little LED battery powered strands on the table to make it look more festive. Olivia didn't have the budget to go all out, but she knew that Ray would appreciate it, no matter what Evan thought.

Andrea and her handsome companion made their way over to the party table. Olivia was initially surprised that Andrea had accepted the invitation to such a late-night party and had doubted that she would show up. Olivia needed to move the balloons because they kept blowing around and hitting into the cake and pummeling the purple flowers.

"Hi, hon! This is my grandson, Harry," said Andrea, sitting down at the party table. "I took a long nap this evening after dinner. Then I had an iced coffee, so I'm awake and ready to party with you young folks tonight!"

"I'm so glad you could make it, and nice to meet you, Harry," Olivia said as she untied the balloons from the chair of honor. A huge gust came and swept two of the balloons out of the bunch. Of course, it was the balloons in the shape of the "three" and the "zero." Fortunately, they got caught up in a palm tree, which was right next to the table. "Oh, shoot!" Olivia cried as she tried to reach the dangling strings.

Harry came over and offered a hand. "Here, let me try to get them." He could almost grab the string, but not quite. "I'll stand up on this chair," he said, pulling it out a bit from the table right as the wind picked up again. "Can you steady it?"

Olivia grabbed hold of the chair with one hand and tried to hold the other balloons further out to stop them from bashing around as Harry jumped up on the chair.

He had some nice legs. And a *very* nice butt, Olivia thought, as her head was literally less than five inches away from his backside. She turned her face away, wide eyed and blushing. *Oh, my heavens.* She squeezed her eyes tight. *Forget a snack. This guy is putting me in a food coma.*

Another big gust of wind came, and Harry was able to grab the balloon strings right in time and stepped down off of the chair. The sand beneath the chair was uneven and he stumbled a bit and grabbed out to the chair to gain his balance. His hand landed right next to Olivia's hand. She jerked hers away in an unconscious reflex and as she did so, her elbow hit the vase of flowers, which started to fall over right next to the cake.

"Oh no!" she screamed as Harry deftly reached over to lift up the vase with his free hand almost as soon as it fell vertical, with only a quick splash of water escaping.

"No worries! I think I got it before it could do much damage, right?" Harry said, straightening the vase and wiping his wet hand on his shorts.

"Thank you so much! You saved the day twice in less than two minutes," laughed Olivia.

"Glad I could be of service!" Harry said as he grabbed the other balloons from Olivia's hand, taking a little longer than necessary to pull away. "Where do you want these tied up?"

"How about on that light post over there so they won't hit anyone at the table?" Olivia said, pointing.

Next, Olivia walked over to Andrea's chair and gave her a friendly side hug. "I'm so happy you could come, Andrea! I know Ray will be so glad you could make it. And an even bigger thank you for bringing your very dashing grandson!"

"Wouldn't think of missing it, dearie! I'm glad Harry was in town to escort me," said Andrea, grabbing a brownie from the serving dish. "Ray and Harry go way back, you know. She's only a few years older, but Ray used to babysit Harry back when both families happened to be here on summer vacation at the same time. He was more than happy to accompany me to the birthday party, weren't you Harry, darling?"

"Yes, Gran. I am indeed very happy I escorted you here tonight," Harry said, as he sat down on the other side of his grandmother. "I've heard a lot about you, Olivia. Thanks to both you and Ray for keeping an eye on Gran," said Harry, with a big smile as he grabbed a brownie from the platter.

"Are you just here visiting for a summer vacation?" Olivia asked as she tried to straighten up the table decorations. She shooed away two seagulls who were eyeing the cake a little too closely.

"I'm here for the next week or so, at least. I just got laid off from my job in a tech startup, so I'm basically rethinking my entire existence," he replied, laughing nervously.

"Oh no. I'm so sorry about that! So many people are losing their jobs lately. My LinkedIn is full of posts about companies that are downsizing," Olivia said.

"To be honest, I wasn't really happy there anyway, so this is good timing," said Harry. "And Gran was kind enough to let me come and stay with her while I contemplate my next move."

"Aw. You can stay as long as you want, my darling boy," said Andrea, patting his arm. "Even with my friendly neighbors, it can get lonely for an old lady like me in a young beach town like this!"

Olivia smiled but was starting to feel stressed about the party timeline as she looked at her watch. "I've got a few more things to do to get ready. Can we catch up later? I need to change before Ray gets here. Evan is over there behind the bar, and he can get you set up with some drinks," Olivia said, backing away from the table.

Olivia had brought a change of clothes for the party. Fortunately, the breeze had picked up this evening after sunset and things were finally cooling down a bit. She'd brought a simple flowy purple dress with a white flower pattern. She also brought a dress for Ray, along with some shorts and a shirt if she didn't want to wear a dress.

At the end of her shift, Olivia always felt disgusting. It had been a very humid summer, and she found herself changing shirts and fixing her makeup a few times a shift. She'd wear workout clothes to work as she rode her bike. Then, she'd change into her work outfit once she arrived. In her locker she had extra bras, underwear, shorts, shirts, and jackets. It was crammed full of things she may need, due to sweat or spills. Many times, she would take a shower and change during her breaks in the staff bathroom. If she didn't have time to shower, she'd apply extra deodorant and body spray. She felt like her entire day was made up of never-ending assessments of her perspiration situation. Tonight, it was Sweat Level 9, bordering on 10. The gusts of wind may have been wreaking havoc on her decorations, but they were simmering down her body temperature, at least.

As she freshened up, she thought about her initial meeting with Harry. He was attractive. A 10. Olivia had looked like a total mess! Figured! He was probably late 20s. He was a little taller than she was, and he was bald. Or his hair was shaved off? He had a five o'clock shadow that was too perfect to be natural. He had a gorgeous smile, and his eyes seemed to sparkle in the twinkling lights. He was wearing a black Ravens polo shirt with dark cargo shorts and sneakers. He was a Ravens fan and was not wearing denim shorts. *Another two checks.*

Olivia finished and then walked back into the kitchen to count the number of restaurant staff members that would be attending the party. Since Evan and Ray spent so much time at JJ's, Olivia had asked all of them to stay on for the party. It looked like there would be 12 people in total, including Jack. This also helped make it seem more festive since Ray didn't have any other friends in town.

Last week, Olivia had covertly contacted Ray's mom over Facebook to tell her about the party, but really, she wanted to make sure her mom was doing something for Ray's big 3-0 birthday. She'd found out that Ray's parents and maternal grandparents from Brooklyn were coming down to Ocean City tomorrow to surprise her. They would all be staying at the beach house and had been in touch with Evan to organize it all.

This worked out perfectly as far as Olivia was concerned. Ray could celebrate with her friends tonight and her family tomorrow night. Ray had no idea any of this was happening. There would be a string of surprises, and Olivia loved nothing more than a surprise party!

CHAPTER 50
Evan

Evan hooked up his phone to the bar's Bluetooth speaker system. He made a 30th birthday playlist for Ray with songs from 1993, the year she was born. It started playing *Amazing* by Aerosmith. He also brought his guitar so he could play while they sang *Happy Birthday* to her.

He brought over drinks for Andrea and her grandson—an orange crush and a summer shandy. He got together some glasses of water and placed them around the table along with a full pitcher. He also put some wine glasses out and bottles of wine.

Evan was exhausted. After work yesterday, he'd cleaned Ray's place top to bottom, went to the store and filled the fridge, and had a huge bouquet of flowers on the kitchen table. He also made reservations at Ruth's Chris Steak House for her family birthday dinner. Ray had told him in the past that her grandparents were not big seafood eaters and steak seemed like a better option. Her grandparents spoke English but mostly communicated with each other in Spanish around the house. Evan had taken Spanish in high school and college, but he was rusty. This would be a good test of his fluency.

He worried a bit that maybe it was too soon to meet the family, but hopefully Ray was okay with it all. If she didn't feel comfortable, he didn't need to go to dinner with her family. However, Evan had a gift certificate for the restaurant, and he figured he'd pay for the dinner. So many what-ifs. He held his eyes closed with a silent prayer that it would all go smoothly, and that Ray wouldn't be too overwhelmed.

Evan walked into the kitchen to grab some more pitchers of water. Jack was in there wiping down the counters.

"Hey, Unc, need any help in here?" Evan asked as he walked to the shelf where the pitchers were stacked up.

"Thanks for offering, Evan. But I've got it covered," said Jack as he gathered up the dish clothes and tossed them into the washing machine.

"You know I never really understood your obsession with cleaning the kitchen each night until I started watching *The Bear*. And now, I finally get it," said Evan as his phone buzzed.

Ray to Evan:
Hey! I'm just over the bridge and in OC. Should be there in about 10 minutes. Xoxo

"She'll be here soon! So, let's get this party started!" Evan said as he walked to the kitchen door.

"You know, Evan, it's been a long time since I've seen you this happy. Ever since your dad died, it seemed like a little piece of you was missing. But now, that perpetual sadness deep in your eyes, it's fading," said Jack as he walked closer to Evan, standing right in front of him. "Ray is good for you. I can tell she makes you happy. And it sure looks like you make her happy, too. I'm proud of the man you've become, Ev. Your dad would have been proud, too. You've got to know how much he loved you and Brandon. And, of course, your mom, too."

"Yes. I do know, Uncle Jack," said Evan, tearing up. He bent his head down and touched his thumb and index finger to the corners of his eyes to try to stop the emotion from taking over. "Thank you for everything you've done for me. For all of us. Without you, we couldn't have survived the loss."

Jack reached out and pulled Evan into a hug. Uncle Jack was not a touchy-feeling kind of guy, so that just made the gesture even more meaningful.

"I love you like you're my own, you know that kiddo," Jack said, ending the hug and taking a step back. "Now go out there and surprise your girl."

"Yes, Chef!" Evan said as he patted Jack on the arm and turned to the door, giving him a quick salute and a huge smile.

Evan looked at his phone and sent a thumbs up to the message. "Ray should be here in about five minutes! Everyone pick a palm tree to hide behind," Evan shouted out. "When she comes, we all yell, 'Surprise!'"

Olivia had a handful of sparklers ready to light when Ray pulled into the parking lot. Evan thought that was a little overboard, but that was on her to sort out. Evan had *Whoomp! (There It Is)* ready to go on the sound system.

The bachelorette party hadn't left yet. Jack had let them know about the birthday party, and they'd agreed to join in the "Surprise" part of it if they could stay a little longer and finish their drinks. One of the ladies offered to buy a couple bottles of sparkling wine for the occasion.

"I'm so obsessed with these sparklers!" Olivia said as she passed them out, lighting them, and twirling them around in circles like a circus performer.

CHAPTER 51
Ray

Ray to Evan and Olivia:
Here. Ready to leave? FYI, there's a chance of rain in 30 minutes.

After not getting an immediate response, Ray yawned and turned off the car. She would need to walk around the back of the building to get to the bar area.

"What's that playing on the sound system?" Ray wondered. It sounded like *Knockin' da Boots* by H-Town. "What in the world! Not the normal JJ's playlist," Ray laughed to herself.

As she walked around the corner, she got a whiff of smoke and was shocked by the sight of flames. It looked like one of the palm tree branches was on fire.

"Oh my God! What's going on?" Ray said mostly to herself because nobody else was looking over at her. She saw Jack running with a bucket of water from the bay over to the burning palm tree. Fortunately, it looked like it was only one frond on fire. Olivia was holding sparklers. And why on Earth was Andrea sitting at a table? Was that her grandson, Harry, with her? Ray hadn't seen him in years! *My, my*, she thought. Harry—of the dorky and skinny all arms and legs teen years— had grown up into a fine-looking man. Evan was messing with his phone and suddenly the song changed.

Ray stopped in her tracks, taking in the full sight. A decorated table with balloons that read 3-0. Flowers and a cake. It was a birthday surprise! For her. She let out the breath she didn't realize she was holding. The fire was out and thankfully, the only damage was part of one branch.

"Surprise, Ray! Happy Birthday!" Evan said as he ran over to give her a big hug and kiss. "Are you surprised?"

"I can honestly say I'm more surprised than I've ever been in my life," laughed Ray as others started coming over to give her hugs.

"Oh, my heavens," said Olivia, giving Ray a hug. "I have no idea how that fire happened! I thought I was being so careful lighting the sparklers! Well, at least your 30s are coming in with a bang!"

"Thanks, guys," said Ray, a little teary. "I really didn't have any idea! Truly, this is a huge surprise. You didn't have to go to so much trouble!"

"It's our pleasure, Ray! I have some outfit options in the staff room if you want to freshen up?" Olivia asked. "Or no pressure—you obviously look great in your company polo shirt!"

"Ok. Yes. Thanks. I do want to go to the bathroom, at least," said Ray. She turned to everyone else and said she'd be back in a few minutes to get the party started.

As Ray followed Olivia into the staff room, she still couldn't believe that this party was for her. It was the first surprise party she'd ever been thrown. If anyone had asked her if she wanted a surprise party, she surely would have said no, never. But somehow, she was not feeling embarrassed or worried or even especially self-conscious. She was out of her comfort zone. Somehow, it felt good. She was changing. She was changing for the better! Her professors had always said that change was the only constant. *Yes. This change felt very good.*

Olivia handed her a tote bag with some clothes and a make-up bag. "Go in and freshen up and I'll wait here for you."

Ray looked at the dress. It was brand new. She tried it on. She was normally hyper-critical of her looks. She turned from side to side and checked out all the angles in the mirror. This dress looked good. It was simple. A dark blue halter top style with a flowing skirt. And brown sandals. There was even a headband—woven brown leather. She sniffled, looked up to the ceiling, and tried to control the tears that were coming on. She finally had a best girlfriend. And a boyfriend. She wasn't alone anymore.

She opened the door and looked over at Olivia, who was looking at her phone.

"Ray. Oh, my stars in heaven," said Olivia, standing up and opening her arms up. "Come here. I'm having all the feels. Ray, you totally slay in that outfit!"

"Thanks, Olivia," said Ray, coming over to give her a hug. "You're such a good friend. Thank you so much. Really, you've gone overboard with all this."

"Evan helped plan the party! But he said if you didn't like it, it was my idea," Olivia laughed.

Olivia pulled out her phone and said, "You know what we must do now, don't you, birthday girl?"

Ray laughed and said, "Go ahead. Let's take my very first birthday selfie." Ray smiled into the camera and tilted her head back and forth. They even made duck faces as Olivia kept tapping on the phone, taking photos from every angle.

When the mini photoshoot was over, Olivia put her phone back in her pocket and sang out, "Come on, Barbie. Let's party!"

Ray laughed as Olivia grabbed her hand. Ray paused for a moment, trying to think of the right words for the situation. "Thank you. Thank you for all of this, Olivia. I really appreciate it. Thank you for being such a good friend."

As they walked outside to the party, applause broke out. Ray held her head high and smiled until her cheeks started hurting. *Thirty looks good on me.*

CHAPTER 52
Olivia

As they walked out to the party table, Olivia's phone pinged.

Unknown to Olivia:
Having a fun party tonight? Trying to set the place on fire, huh?

Olivia to Unknown:
Who is this?

Unknown to Olivia:
I know what you did

What the heck, Olivia thought. If somebody was out there watching her right now, it had to be Luke. Who else would it be? She couldn't ruin Ray's party! She turned off her phone and slid it into her dress pocket. *Ignore. Ignore. Ignore.*

She went over to the table, put a smile on her face, and started serving the wine. She kept looking beyond the rope fence, wondering if Luke was out there watching, spying, trying to ruin her life. Everyone around her was having so much fun, and she felt hopeless.

"Are you okay, Liv?" Evan whispered. "You look spooked."

"Something weird is going on, but I'll fill you in later. I don't want to disrupt the party, ok? It's nothing big," she said, muttering, "I hope," to herself after he turned away.

Olivia sat down next to Harry and Andrea since they didn't know many of the other people. It turned out that along with being an IT developer, Harry was an amateur filmmaker. He was planning to work on a short film for the Ocean City Film Festival. He showed her his various social media accounts and Olivia followed him on all of them. She kept her physical distance from him though. She didn't want to flirt too much in case Luke was out there watching. Olivia offered to help him out during her non-working hours over the next week.

Right at midnight, Olivia lit the candles on the cake, amidst about a dozen fire jokes and attempts to grab the lighter from her hands.

Evan tapped his fork on his glass and then raised it. "Everyone, thank you all for coming. This party is *truly lit!* Let's raise our glasses in a toast to Ray! Olivia may have set the expensive palm tree on fire, but Ray, you set my heart on fire when I first officially met you over there on that very bar stool back in April. Happy 30th birthday, babe. Cheers!"

As everyone clinked their glasses together, Ray stood up. Olivia knew that this was likely the time of the party that Ray had been dreading, and she grabbed her hand in support.

"Thank you, everyone," Ray said. "Thank you so much. I was so surprised! I feel like moving to Ocean City and having you all as part of my beach family has been the best decision

I've ever made. Olivia and Evan—thank you so much for this party. For everything you do! Nothing can *extinguish* my love for you both," Ray laughed. Olivia and Evan leaned into hug Ray.

Olivia was openly crying now. As was Ray. It was the wine. Evan walked over to the bar and started fiddling around with the TV and his phone.

"Enough sappiness for now, people!" Evan yelled over at the table. "Can you all please head over here to the bar area so I can present one of my gifts for Ray?"

People started getting up and heading over to the TV, wondering what was up.

"So, I know a lot of people wonder if vampires are real," said Evan. "And honestly, I don't think they are unless you Count Dracula."

"Dude. That was weak sauce," laughed Raymond, punching Evan on the arm.

"Ok. So, this may be a present that only Ray Ray will appreciate, but I decided to show it to all of you."

Olivia put her arm around Ray's waist and leaned into her. "Ohhh, a special personalized gift for the birthday girl!"

Evan hit play on his phone.

"I was relentless. I would just never relent," a guy with long hair was saying in the video that Evan was playing. "Unfortunately, my human familiar and my fellow vampires of Staten Island could not join me for these festivities early this morning as they are out, shall we say, looking for a midnight snack. Evan—not Evan Almighty as you might be thinking— but Evan Michaels... quite frankly a boring name if you ask me... has asked me to wish Ray Ray—a very peculiar name that as a vampire I am hesitant to say out loud given the visions of sunlight it is evoking—but nevertheless, a Cameo fee has been paid, so I am wishing Ray Ray a very happy birthday. Zee beeeg three zero. I, myself, am over 700 years old. So, Ray Ray, you are practically a baby compared to me…"

Olivia looked around. She had no idea who the vampire guy was, but half of the other people at the party were speechless with excitement, faces all a grin.

"Evan! I'm in shock! My low-key favorite TV vampire. Really. Mind blown." Ray jumped up and gave Evan a huge hug and he swung her around.

"Super cool, bro. Play it again!" Brandon said. "Amazing present for zee beeeg three zero."

Olivia's mom had gotten her dad (Olivia's grandfather) a Cameo video Beaver Cleaver, a few years ago because their family had loved watching reruns of *Leave it to Beaver* with her grandparents. At first, Olivia's grandpa had no idea what was happening as he watched the iPad, wondering how the heck Jerry Mathers knew who he was. After that, Olivia had done a deep dive through almost all the stars on Cameo. She decided to get her sister a Cameo from American Idol runner-up and "Little Sweet," Justin Guarini, because her sister was addicted to Diet Dr Pepper! It was so freaking funny!

Olivia yawned. She covered her mouth and realized it was nearly 1 a.m. Everyone started standing up and carrying things to the trash or back to the kitchen. Ray left her car there and Olivia put her bike in the back of Evan's car. Evan was driving them back home since he hadn't been drinking. Harry had left with Andrea about 20 minutes ago because Andrea was having trouble staying awake.

As they drove home, Olivia smiled thinking that Ray was still completely unaware that her family was coming tomorrow—or rather later today! She would be even more surprised by that!

"Hey, just remembered! The *Dueling Pianos* show is at Shenanigans on Sunday night! You ladies up for that? It doesn't start until late," Evan said.

"Oh, I love, love, love piano bars!" Olivia sang out from the back seat but kept her sleepy eyes closed.

"They have different pianists each time. They're always super funny. They take cash for requests, and you can also Venmo them," Evan added. "It's basically a huge sing-along and everyone always has a fun time. It's an Irish pub slash restaurant slash music venue."

"I've never been to anything like that before, but it sounds entertaining," said Ray. "I've eaten there before—they have a huge variety. I'm definitely up for it. I took piano lessons as a child. It didn't stick, but I enjoy watching others play."

"Is there dancing?" Olivia asked as another yawn escaped her mouth, quite loudly at that. She tried to remember how many glasses of wine she had. She started holding her fingers up as she counted to herself. *One.* During the party set-up. *Two.* Right before the fire. *Three.* Right after the fire. *Four.* With the cake.

"There's normally some drunk lady who gets up and dances," laughed Evan.

"Perfect! That will be me," Olivia laughed as she lost count of her drinks. "And Ray has a beautiful singing voice! I sometimes hear you singing through the open windows, girlie."

"What? You do not! Oh my God, I'm so embarrassed," said Ray, sinking into her seat.

"Why? If you were bad, I'd understand, but you're so good," Olivia replied.

"Ok. I'll be the judge of Ray's singing quality," said Evan turning up the volume on his car stereo. *Livin' on the Edge* by Aerosmith was playing. They all started singing and Olivia had deja vu from the last time they were riding in Evan's car.

"Dude. You were the bomb. You're good, dawg!" Evan said. "Ray Anders, you're going to Hollywood!" They all laughed and clapped, like audience members on *American Idol.*

Olivia opened her eyes, all of a sudden remembering the mysterious text messages. She powered her phone up and saw a few more texts from the unknown number.

Unknown to Olivia:
You can ignore me. But I won't go away.

Sweet dreams. I'll be watching you again tomorrow.

"What the freaking heck!" Olivia screeched, interrupting the singing. It must be Luke and either the FBI had contacted him, or he'd been to the storage unit.

"What's wrong?" Ray asked, turning to look at Olivia in the back seat, clearly concerned.

"Nothing. Sorry. I'll fill you in later. Just some family drama via text," said Olivia, turning to look out the window.

Olivia took a screenshot of the convo and texted it to Evan so he would know what was going on in case anything suspicious happened tomorrow.

Olivia wouldn't ruin Ray's birthday with this drama. Even if it killed her.

CHAPTER 53
Luke

Luke woke up earlier than he would have anticipated given he was up until after midnight watching Olivia and her crew of weirdo friends. At around 12:30 a.m., he couldn't keep his eyes open and went back to his rental and crashed. He'd booked a last-minute vacation rental and was able to check-in the same day. It was located right next to Olivia's beach house, so he'd be able to keep track of her more easily than he had at the hotel last month.

Luke had not been planning to come to Ocean City this weekend, but yesterday afternoon, while he was still at home in D.C. and had just woken up from a short nap, he decided to take a walk—or in his case, it was more of a hobble—to try to clear his head. He wasn't wearing the huge boot, but he still had a Velcro brace on his ankle. He was supposed to use crutches. It had been a while since he'd left home, and he was so frustrated with everything in his life. How had he gotten to this point? He stopped at the corner cafe and got a Diet Coke and a sandwich.

When he got back to the lobby of his apartment building about 30 minutes later, the building concierge, Benji, gave him a heads-up there were two FBI agents headed up to his apartment right at that very moment. He tried to recall the conversation again to see if he missed anything.

All Benji had said was the agents had some questions they needed to ask him. They showed their badges, and he had buzzed them up. He said he had no choice. Fortunately, Benji had not been at the front desk when Luke walked out earlier. A string of happy coincidences for a change.

Luke had put three $20 bills—all he had in his wallet—on the counter and told Benji that as far as he was concerned, he hadn't seen Luke all week. Luke then walked directly to the door of the parking garage. He got in his car and drove to the ATM and took out the max possible, $200. If the FBI was at his house, they were probably already checking his accounts and would be tracking him. He booked three cheap vacation rentals—one in Ocean City—on his credit card to keep them guessing. If he used a credit card, he knew he would be leaving a data trail.

Next, he went to his storage unit. He knew he had at least some clothes in there—mostly old shirts and workout clothes from college. Maybe he'd find some other stuff that would be useful. When he opened the unit, he took a step back and realized at least half of the stuff was gone. "What the…" he said, looking around and clenching his teeth in frustration. "Olivia has been here and didn't even tell me? I guess I shouldn't be surprised."

He kicked a shoebox across the floor as he looked to find his clothes bin without much effort and grabbed a handful of shirts, shorts, and some old sneakers.

"Holy hell," he said, picking up a phone from the top of a cardboard box laying there in plain sight. It was his burner phone he'd lost at the scene of the accident. "You have got to be kidding me right now. Did she *plant* that in here? That bitch. I'm going to have to teach her *another* lesson not to mess with me anymore." He kicked the box, and it fell over, and a pile of his old college textbooks tumbled out on the floor.

Last night, before Luke went to check in on Olivia at JJ's, he stopped by her car in the parking lot and put a tiny magnetic GPS vehicle tracker on it. He'd ordered a multi-pack online for less than $30 each a few weeks ago just to have them on hand. It came with an app. Luke knew that Olivia hardly ever drove her car at the beach. Maybe he'd also try to put one on her bike, but the chances were good that she'd spot it, even though it was very small. He'd also put a tracker on his car.

As he thought about all that had happened over the past 24 hours, Luke rubbed his eyes and felt the soft mattress and sheets surrounding him. This place was nice, he was disappointed he had to check out that morning. He would drive to the cabin tonight and stay there as long as he could. He'd stopped and bought a new phone on the way to the beach and that's what he'd used to text Olivia last night. He had not used his main phone or turned on the burner phone he found in the storage unit.

Luke had no idea if the FBI had searched his house or storage unit, but if they had, they would undoubtedly have found some incriminating evidence related to his political campaigning. He had his next step planned, but what would he do after that? *This entire thing is Olivia's fault*, he thought. *Why doesn't she have any common sense?*

Forcing himself out of the comfortable bed, Luke took a shower, watched a little TV, packed up, and at exactly 11 a.m., he walked out the front door of his rental. He went over to his car and took his time putting his duffle bag into the trunk, casually checking his phone and looking around to see if anyone else was out and about. He could see Olivia's house in the distance. She would have already left for work by now, but Ruby would be inside. He checked the GPS tracker app, and her car was still in the parking lot.

He had some dog treats in his pocket. As a disguise, he wore a baseball hat and his new sunglasses. He wanted to blend in and not look too sketchy. His outfit was a simple bathing suit with a zipper pocket, flip-flops, and a water shirt. He carried a cheap plain blue boogie board.

When he'd checked out the scene at her place last night, he noticed Olivia had left the back window open a few inches. It was behind some trees, so nobody would have noticed unless they made their way back there through the brush. He hoped it was not secured today. There were trees and bushes lining the road and Luke thought he'd be able to jump into the window without being seen from the road. If not, he'd have to abandon the plan.

He lucked out. The window was not locked, and he was able to pull off the screen and lift himself up into the window. It was a tight fit and he landed with a thump—that made his ankle throb. He was on the floor in the downstairs bathroom and heard Ruby start barking almost immediately. She ran to him, her tail started wagging and she seemed happy to see him.

"Hi, Ruby Scooby Doo. Yes, you're a good quiet girl, aren't you?" Luke rubbed her belly.

Luke knew Olivia was gone for the day, but he still wanted to be quick and quiet about it. First, the keys. Normally, she would keep her keys on a hook by the front door at their house. *Bingo.* There they were—a series of small hooks in the kitchen, by the refrigerator. He grabbed the car keys and all of the other keys on the hooks, sweeping them into his bathing suit pocket. His hope was that one of the keys was for her family's cabin in the Adirondacks near Blue Mountain Lake in upstate New York. She always used to carry it with her other keys and would sometimes remark it seemed dumb to carry a key around she would never use. Sure, he could have broken into the cabin, but a key would make his visit more legit.

The cabin was originally bought by Olivia's grandparents long ago and nobody in the family ever used it anymore, as far as Luke knew. He'd been there only one time back when he and Olivia were first dating—a secret rendezvous. They'd felt so grown-up sneaking away to the cabin for a long weekend.

Now that the first order of priority of finding the cabin keys was taken care of, Luke headed up the stairs to Olivia's bedroom. He was looking for cash. He opened her top dresser drawer and found her passport and random travel documents in a little box. He took the passport and stuffed it into his pocket. He sifted through her extra purses and picked up about $30 and a credit card that had not expired. He went into the room she was using as her office and looked around for her checkbook. Ruby followed him around without a sound. He scored $20 more. He went back downstairs and looked at the pile of mail on the kitchen counter and threw it at the bottom of the trash can, just for fun.

"Dammit, Ruby. It seems like your mama doesn't keep much spare cash around here," Luke said. He opened the fridge. He took out a can of Diet Coke. He ate a donut from a box on the counter as he looked around the place. *It is really nice*, he thought. His former mother-in-law always had a sophisticated way of decorating. Too bad he hadn't decided to come here with Olivia back when they were married.

Luke debated whether he could go out the front door or if he should head back out the bathroom window. He looked out the front window and saw a neighbor by the dock and figured he needed to play it safe and walked to the bathroom. He knew his ankle would hurt when he landed, so he was reluctant to jump out, but he had no choice. He shut the door to the bathroom so Ruby wouldn't bark or try to follow him out the window.

He dropped from the window and when he landed, he tried to hold back a yelp of pain and then fell back into the house with a loud thump. He winced as he grabbed the board and peeked out from behind the shrubs. There was a steady stream of cars. He waited a couple minutes until the coast was clear. He walked over to the parking lot and straight to Olivia's car and didn't see anyone else in the lot.

He hit the trunk button on the key fob so he could throw in the boogie board. As it opened, he saw there was a bunch of random crap in the trunk area. A beach chair, an umbrella, some tote bags, water bottles, sunblock, bug spray, and baseball caps. He tossed it all around, trying to see if anything would be useful.

He got into the car and set about adjusting the seat and mirrors. She had a full tank of gas. Perfect. Next, he would drive back to his car and pick up his stuff, then it was north to NY. He'd find an ATM and get a cash advance using her credit card. She probably still used the same PIN she always had.

CHAPTER 54
Evan

Although they had an extremely late night, Evan knew today would likely be even busier than yesterday. Ray wanted to get up bright and early to watch the sunrise on the beach to start the first day of the third decade of her life off right. They'd sat on a beach blanket as the sun rose, and it was a dazzling display of orangish pink clouds along the horizon. Evan would have preferred to be in bed, but watching sunrises and sunsets were Ray's favorite pastimes.

Now, it was almost 11:30 a.m., and Ray was doing a virtual yoga session. Evan was also doing a balancing act, but on the roof of Ray's townhouse. For her birthday, Evan had gotten Ray the most complicated weather station he could find. He'd just finished mounting it up on top of the roof when he heard an odd rumbling coming from the back of the house. He walked over and it looked like there was a person walking around down there, rustling around in the brush.

Evan got off the roof and came inside the second-floor balcony.

"Hey, Ray! Did you hear anything weird out back just now?" Evan asked, his mind immediately going to Luke, and the text Olivia sent him last night.

"Yeah. I heard some kind of thumping sound like something was hitting the back wall, maybe? I thought it was you?"

"It looked like someone was walking around the back in the trees. Quick, let's go check it out."

Ray was dressed in her yoga outfit, with bare feet. She ran over to the closet and grabbed one of her grandfather's canes. "Here. Take this as a weapon," she said as she handed it to Evan, who looked at her quizzically.

"A cane? Um. Ok?" Evan took the cane, slid on his flip-flops, and grabbed his phone from the kitchen counter where it had been charging. Ray slid on her new Crocs and clipped Charlie's leash, and all three ran out the front door and around to the back of the complex. They didn't see anyone in the brush by the back of the house.

"Evan. Look. Isn't that Olivia's car? Oh my God," whispered Ray, grabbing Evan's arm and ducking behind a tree. "Is that Luke getting in?"

"Oh shit! You call 9-1-1 and I'll run over and confront him."

Evan had no idea if this was a good idea or what he would say when he got there, but he had no choice, right? This dude was stealing Olivia's car. And by this point, he was probably a wanted fugitive with the FBI!

Luke started to reverse the car right as Evan reached the driver's side window from the back. Evan banged on the car window with his free hand and Luke was startled. He immediately floored the gas, and the wheels spun. The car fishtailed, nearly hitting two other parked cars as he put it in drive and sped away. Evan started running after the car, but Luke was booking it. Evan kept running at full speed and Ray and Charlie were close behind him at this point. He heard Ray yell she was still on the phone with the 9-1-1 operator.

It was just before noon on Saturday, and traffic on the main road was completely stopped with people leaving at hotel checkout time. Evan could see Luke in the distance, at a complete stop with nowhere to go but back. The car door opened, and Luke jumped out and looked back at Evan running toward him. He turned and took off, weaving through the cars, crossing the street mid-block.

"What the hell are you thinking, dude?" Evan said to himself. "There is no way you can escape me on foot!"

Evan shouted back to Ray. "You stay with Olivia's car and wait for the police and let them know he's headed over to the Boardwalk! I'll try to catch up with him. Maybe conference me into your 9-1-1 call so I can keep you posted?"

Evan was making good time, even in his flip-flops. When he got to the main road, he heard sirens in the distance and hoped that help was on the way. He ran north to the traffic light, which was fortunately red, and he could easily cross the crosswalk. He saw Luke ahead of him, about a block and a half, almost to the Boardwalk. Evan accepted the call from Ray on his phone, put it on speaker, and slid his phone back into the zippered pocket of his shorts.

"I still have him in sight!" yelled Evan as he ran east. "He's almost to the Boardwalk at 27th Street."

When Evan made it to the Boardwalk he stopped for a hot second, looked around, and it was immediately obvious that there was a chaotic scene at the tram stop. An older man was laying on the Boardwalk holding his arm. The Boardwalk tram (a Jeep pulling the open-air trolley cars) was speeding away, so fast that the back car was teetering back and forth.

"Are you frickin' serious, bruh?" Evan said. He raised his voice and yelled to his phone, "Plot twist! He hijacked a Boardwalk tram! Pushed the driver onto the ground—may need medical assistance. I'm running after the tram now!"

Evan started off after the tram. There were only a handful of people riding it, but the attendant—an older lady—who was sitting on the back seat was about to fall off. Right as she lost her grip, Evan was able to swoop in and catch her before she hit the ground.

"Don't worry! I've got you… Grab onto my neck!" Evan set the lady down on the Boardwalk and then ran to catch up with the tram again. He hooked the top of the cane around the side rail and pulled himself up into the last row.

He yelled to his phone: "I'm on the back of the tram. There are three groups of people riding it. We're just passing 23rd Street."

Luke was beeping the horn non-stop, trying to get people out of the way as he barreled down the Boardwalk. Bubbles were floating through the air, and kites were flying overhead in the brisk breeze. One couple seated in the middle of the tram edged over and were about to jump off.

Evan tried to catch his breath and figure out his next step. He heard sirens. Then, he heard a loud thumping coming from behind the tram. He looked back and saw two officers on horseback galloping and closing in the distance.

Suddenly, Evan spotted someone running up next to the back of the tram. It was Harry. Andrea's grandson. What were the chances of that happening! *Miniscule, for sure*, he thought.

"Evan! What the hell is going on here, dude?" Harry yelled as he jumped on the tram right in front of Evan. He had a GoPro camera hooked onto the hat on his head and was carrying a big backpack. Evan surely hoped it was recording this crazy scene!

"It's Olivia's ex. Long story, bro, but he's wanted by the FBI," said Evan, as he ditched the cane and started hopping over some seats, making his way to the front.

"It looks like the police should be able to càtch up with us soon," said Harry. "But what will they do? A horse is no match for a Jeep."

"Let's try to unlatch the rest of the tram from the Jeep since there are still a few people on here and at least get them safe," said Evan. "But that will make the Jeep more agile. So, it's a risk."

"Be careful, Evan! I love you," Ray's muffled voice came from his pocket. "Don't let that asshole get away!"

Evan and Harry quickly climbed their way over the bench seats of the tram as it sped down the Boardwalk. They unhooked the last trolley with ease. A young couple with two toddlers were on board and thankfully, now safe. Behind, the horses were losing steam and falling back.

Evan did a double take as he noticed an older man dressed as Santa sitting in the first seat of the first tram.

"Ho-ho-hold on tight, Santa, it's going to be a bumpy landing!" Evan yelled.

"Don't worry, sonny," he laughed. "I'm used to those!"

Harry tried to release the front car's hitch from the Jeep, but there were multiple safety chains and latches. Up ahead, it looked like the police had put up a barricade of black SUVs, police cars and motorcycles across the entire Boardwalk. The crowd had been cleared off, inside the various stores and restaurants.

A handful of officers on bicycles were speeding straight toward them, head on. A couple seagulls flew down and started dive-bombing directly at Luke's head. Evan jumped into the back of the open Jeep, thinking he a very bad feeling about this.

Harry was finally able to release the final hitch latch and detach it from the Jeep. The hitch fell and scraped against the walkway, causing the trolley car to screech to an abrupt halt. Harry was flung forward and landed on his hands and knees on the cement. Santa had braced himself in the trolley seat and was unhurt.

The Jeep accelerated, out of control, and Luke swerved a hard turn to the left. The Jeep flew through the air, off of the elevated Boardwalk and smashed into a huge religious sandcastle of Jesus. The Jeep's wheels spun as Luke tried to gain traction to keep up the chase. Evan was thrown from the Jeep but fortunately hit the sand about 10 feet away without incident.

He landed right next to the sand carving that read, *Romans 12:21—Do not be overcome by evil but overcome evil with good.*

The Jeep was immediately surrounded by armed agents and police officers. The Coast Guard helicopter appeared overhead, the chop-chop-chop sound was pounding through the air and sand was swirling.

"Luke Lewis! Exit the vehicle slowly with your hands raised above your head," one of them said into a megaphone. "Everyone else, stay where you are with your hands in the air."

Luke opened the car door, raised his hands, and fell to his knees on the beach. Two agents sped over to him, cuffed his hands behind his back. He was half-carried and thrust into a black SUV.

Harry ran over and offered a hand to Evan to help him stand up. They stood off to the side looking in disbelief. Another officer approached them and asked them to come to the local police station to give their account of the events. They got into the squad car and sat in silence.

Evan to Ray:
Are you ok? I'm ok. Luke was arrested. On way to the police station for a debrief. In the cop car now with Harry. Will text you when I'm headed back. Xoxox

Ray to Evan:

OMG. I'm so glad you're ok and he was captured! It was hard to hear what was happening. I was so worried! xoxoxoxoxo

Evan to Ray:
BTW, Happy Birthday!!!! It's turning out to be one for the memory books! LMAO

Ray to Evan:
The police officer here let me take Olivia's car. Just back to the parking lot.

They found a tracking device on it!

I texted Olivia and called and left a message but haven't heard anything back yet.

Evan to Ray's Mom:
Hi Gloria! Just a heads-up that I may not be there when you arrive at the beach house. Ray is there with Charlie. Everything is AOK but we have a crazy story to tell you! Safe travels. - Evan

Ray's Mom to Evan:
Very interesting! Can't wait to hear it! Take care and looking forward to meeting you! We should be there by 2pm. Do you mind if we stay in for dinner? We're bringing the ingredients to make Ray's favorite meal.

Evan to Ray's Mom:
Fantastic idea! She'll love that.

This was Evan's first time in a cop car. He looked around the back seat to take it in, feeling glad he was not the one who was arrested. The back windows had a weird film on them, and there was a cage separating the front and back seats. There was a video camera. There were padded panels on the bottom of the doors. It seemed small, claustrophobic.

Evan's elbow was bleeding and so was his knee. The cops had given him some bandages at the scene, but they were too small to do too much good. He looked down at his feet. They were scraped up with a few blisters forming. No active bleeding, though. *Always wear the appropriate shoes for the activity at hand,* he thought to himself, thinking of his father's mantra from when he was younger.

"I'm just texting with Gran about the tram chase," said Harry, breaking the tense silence. "She saw that dude trying to steal Olivia's car and you and Ray running after him. She texted me straight away. So, when I saw the tram speed by, I was already on high alert that crazy stuff was going down. Dude. I could hardly believe my eyes. Hijacking the Boardwalk tram? Like where was he gonna go? And there you were like Indiana Jones in hot pursuit. Seriously swaggin' it up, bro!"

Evan laughed and fist bumped Harry. "I know, right? Thanks for jumping on to help me, man! *Mind blown.* Seriously. What even happened there? Did you get it all on video?"

"I think so. Fingers crossed," replied Harry as he was messing with the camera trying to get it to the right spot in the footage. "Damn. This footage is better than I expected!" he said as they pulled into the police station headquarters.

CHAPTER 55
Olivia

Olivia looked out the car window and wished she had changed her shirt before being carted off by the police to give her official statement regarding Luke. *Sweat level: a zillion!*

Her legs were sticking to the car seat and the disgusting smell of hundreds or thousands of criminals was emanating from the upholstery, making her gag and feel sick to her stomach. The officer who was driving cleared her throat to get Olivia's attention.

"As I was saying, we just arrested Luke Lewis. The FBI has some follow-up questions regarding your submission on the Capitol Breach tip line, and Luke had your passport in his pocket."

"What! My passport? That's at home in my bedroom. You're sure it's mine?" Olivia said as she sunk down into her seat, closing her eyes in disbelief.

"We'll go over everything with you when we get to the station," the officer replied, sternly. *Why is she being so rude?* Olivia wondered.

"So, will I have to actually see Luke right now? Or is this just a statement that I give to agents? Do I need a lawyer? This is so confusing," Olivia mumbled to herself. The officer was pretending not to listen. *Rude.*

Olivia pulled her phone out of her backpack, which she'd quickly grabbed from her locker as the police escorted her away from work. Now *that* had been quite the scene! How embarrassing! Jack was beside himself, insisting he wanted to come with Olivia to the police station, but they wouldn't allow it.

Olivia to Ray:
OMG!!!!!!! Just seeing your text from earlier. I AM IN A POLICE CAR NOW!

They're taking me in for questioning.

When they got to the station, Olivia saw Evan sitting on a chair in the hallway and walked over to him. His shirt was torn, and his left knee and left elbow were both bandaged up. "Oh my gosh, Evan. What's going on? Are you ok?"

"I'm fine, Liv. Don't worry. Luke was arrested and everything is a-ok," said Evan, pulling her into a hug. "Ray drove your car back to the beach house."

"Wait. What? My car?" Olivia was so confused.

"I'm sure the agent will explain everything. Luke stole your car and that's how this entire chase started," Evan said as Olivia was pulled away and directed down the hall.

Harry walked out of another room as Olivia passed by. "Harry! You're involved in this, too? What in the world?" Harry had huge bandages on both of his knees and around his wrists.

"Don't worry, Olivia," Harry said, raising his hands in the air. "Everyone's fine. No biggie. Just some superficial cuts and scrapes. And I got it all recorded," he laughed, pointing to his GoPro. "They just finished downloading all of the video files. His ass is grass!"

Olivia shook her head, unable to put all the pieces together. When she got into the interrogation room, an assistant offered her a bottle of water. Two agents—who seemed quite nice, compared to her driver, at least—started questioning her about her relationship with Luke, starting at the very beginning.

She told them absolutely everything and didn't leave out a single embarrassing fact, even the things that made her look bad. She was no criminal. Maybe she'd been vindictive, but she'd done nothing illegal. Well, the one thing Olivia did not mention was the hit and run incident—Luke was okay, after all. And who was to say she actually hit him? He had clearly tripped. It was all circumstantial evidence, right?

Olivia was in the room for almost two hours. She was allowed one bathroom break. When she came out, Evan and Harry were long gone. An officer said she would take Olivia home and they could also check the house since it seemed likely that Luke had broken in to get the passport, credit card, and keys.

Once back at her beach house with an officer, she noticed immediately that all of her keys were gone from the key hooks. Things looked a little off, like they were moved from their normal places. Olivia kept things orderly, items sitting in varying states of 90-degree angles, perpendicular on the counter. The donut box was sitting at a thirty-degree angle from the edge. The mail was gone from its pile. As she walked around, she noticed the bathroom door was closed. When she saw the window wide open, she realized that was how Luke had gained access to the house.

"Oh my gosh. I'm so dumb! I left the window open and unlocked," she said to the officer, putting her hands up to cover her face in embarrassment.

Upstairs, it was even more of a mess. Things in her bedroom were amiss, and her office desktop was cluttered. Why had Luke wanted her car? Did he think that trying to outrun the FBI was a good idea? He was just making things far worse for himself.

The officer left without any pomp and circumstance, and Olivia was left alone in the quiet house. She stood there, pondering the state of her life, in disbelief over the crazy events of the afternoon. Ruby whined to break the silence, and Olivia went to pick up her leash for a quick potty break. Back in the house in record time—no dillydallying today, Olivia turned on the local news. They were showing some amateur footage that looked like it was taken from a vertical TikTok video.

Luke was speeding down the Boardwalk, driving the tram, honking nonstop. "Is that the Boardwalk Santa on there?" Olivia shouted out in confusion, but also trying not to laugh. It was just so ridiculous!

Evan and Harry were jumping over the seats, making their way to the Jeep. The person filming made a short attempt to run and keep up with the tram, but it eventually faded into the distance.

The newscasters interviewed some bystanders on the Boardwalk about what they'd seen, with the tram's Jeep still buried in the sand in the background with yellow "crime scene" tape surrounding it.

"Oh! I didn't realize it was that bad! Poor Evan and Harry. They're heroes!" Olivia started crying and buried her face in Ruby's furry neck.

Olivia's phone rang with the *Mamma Mia* ringtone. "Mom! You won't believe what happened," Olivia cried.

"Honey. Are you ok? Dad and I are watching the news right now and we just saw Luke get arrested in Ocean City on the Boardwalk. He hijacked the Boardwalk tram? What on earth is going on?"

"Mom! You really won't believe it. I just got back from the police station. Luke was part of the January 6th insurrection at the Capitol in D.C. I submitted evidence that he was there to the FBI."

"Honey, it will all be okay. He's detained now! We'll start driving to the beach right now. We'll be there in less than three hours. Dad can make sure everything is sealed up tight with the case against him."

"Mom, you don't have to do that. But thank you. It would be amazing if you could come here and be with me," Olivia said.

Olivia to Jack:
Hi Jack. I'm back from the police station, but I can't come back to work today. So sorry! Can I also take tomorrow off? My parents are coming to help sort things out.

Jack to Olivia:
Are you ok? You and Evan are the talk of the town... and Harry. Everyone's watching the Boardwalk chase scene play out on the bar TVs!

Don't worry – Brandon is here and says he can fill in for you

Harry to Olivia:

Hi Olivia! Are you ok? Got your number from my gran. It's Harry.

The news coverage is crazy! I feel like I was giving off a Michael B. Jordan vibe on that tram chase, right? LOL

Apparently, it is NATIONAL NEWS! My parents texted me and said they saw the tram chase on CNN's social media!!! LMAO!!!!!

Olivia to Harry:
OMG! My parents just texted me too and said they saw it. I was just watching it on the local news. I can come over and give you and Andrea all the tea! And we can monitor the news together.

Harry to Olivia:
Yes! Can you bring drinks? Gran does not have anything alcoholic in the house - but we do have a splendid selection of cheese and crackers.

Olivia to Ray:
I'm finally back home!! OMG. I can't even believe all that's happened! My parents said they would drive down tonight. And I'm heading over to talk with Andrea and Harry now. xoxo

Evan to Olivia:
Hey, hey, hey! Holding up ok?

FYI, Change of plans – you're invited to another birthday dinner! Her mom is making dinner (a surprise)

Can you also invite Andrea and Harry? Ray just told me you're heading over there now. Dinner time is 7:30. We can eat on the picnic tables by the dock and then watch the sunset? Your parents can come too if they've arrived by then?

Olivia thumbs-upped Evan's messages.

"I feel so gross! I need a quick shower first," Olivia said to Ruby as she ran up the stairs and peeled off her damp clothes. After a three-minute shower, Olivia pulled out a pair of black SKIMS high-waisted underpants from her lingerie drawer—comfy, no seams, and very stretchy. She wiped some clear-color deodorant on. *Four swipes should be enough*, she thought. Sweat level was currently seven.

She picked out a flowery purple and white tank top from the closet and then went to look at her bras to decide what would be the best fit for under the shirt. She chose a white sports bra style because the shirt was clingy, and she didn't want her back fat to bulge out from the typical bra straps. She took the towel off her wet hair and pulled the bra over her head and arms, but then suddenly, she was trapped. It had rolled up around her armpits. *Nothing new*, she thought. This had happened before. In the summer humidity, putting on tight clothes or bathing suits was always challenging. She struggled a bit more, but she was almost immobile.

"Just stop and take a deep breath and don't freak out, Olivia," she said to herself. Her arms were pinned straight up. She tried to bend them, one at a time, and reached her hand down under the opposite armpit to untangle the bra.

She was stuck. She walked over to the bed, sat down, and then laid back, with her legs dangling on the floor, trying to calm down. Maybe the bedspread would soak up some of the water from her dripping hair. At least she was at home and not in a dressing room, trying on something that was too tight. *That* had happened before plenty of times that she'd rather forget.

Deep breaths. You've got this! She said to herself, trying to calm down and concurrently pumping herself up.

"Alexa, play soothing music!" she yelled out. Ruby jumped up on the bed and started licking the lotion on Olivia's hands.

"Ruby. No! Stop! That tickles," Olivia yelled, wiggling around, trying to sit up. "Stop! UGH!" Worst case scenario, she would ask Siri on her phone to call Ray for help.

Olivia finally was able to push Ruby away with her knee. She sat up and tried a different tactic. She focused on the front of the bra and tried to pull it down in the center, to cover her breasts. After a dozen times of tugging on it, she was able to work her way from the center to the sides and get the front situated. Next, it was time to move to the sides and back.

After about five more minutes—that felt like five hours—Olivia was dressed. She really needed *another* shower, though. She turned on her fan and went to stand in front of it. She blotted her face with a towel. Next, she swept some foundation on her face, along with a little eyeliner, mascara, and her absolute favorite LANEIGE lip mask. She put her wet hair up in a clip, slid on her favorite hot pink Crocs and went to the kitchen.

"Oh, crapola! Where's my phone?" Olivia yelled out. She zoomed around the house, looking in all the usual places. It was nowhere to be found.

She suddenly remembered that she could use her watch to ping it. She stood still and listened carefully. The sound was coming from upstairs. Like a detective zeroing in on a clue, she quietly climbed the stairs and tapped the locator icon again. It was coming from the linen closet.

"Oh, Ruby, now I remember! It was from when I pulled out a new bath towel and then they all came tumbling down. I had to set down the phone to refold."

Finally, Olivia walked over to Andrea's place, carrying a tote bag with a bottle of wine and two cold beers.

"What. A. Day!" she said out loud as she knocked on Andrea's door. Harry opened it with a huge smile. His face looked even better in the light of day. Olivia felt a flutter in her stomach as their eyes locked. Harry reached out to grab the bag from her hand. He put his hand on her back as she walked past him into the house.

Tingles. The attraction was there. She was starting to sweat again. Figured.

"I owe you a drink, or two, or three!" Olivia said as she took the wine out of the bag. "Andrea, did you hear that Harry is my hero? He helped the FBI arrest my felon ex-husband today!"

"Hon. Oh my gawd! I. Am. Beside myself," said Andrea, patting her ample chest region. "Lookie here, dearie! I just recorded the news clip. Harry showed me how to use my phone to make a video of the part where he's on the tram in the chase. I need to send it to the rest of the family!" Andrea looked down and started tapping feverishly on her phone, her reading glasses were barely hanging onto the tip of her nose.

"So, let's get a drink, and we can put our stories together," said Harry, grabbing two wine glasses from the cabinet. Olivia looked at the various bandages on Harry and hoped he wasn't too badly hurt from the tram chase.

They gathered in the living room and turned down the sound on the TV. Andrea listened to Olivia's story with wide eyes and her mouth agape. Every once in a while, Andrea would sway back in her chair and say things like, "You can't be serious! That did not happen! I don't believe it. Thank the heavens above he's finally arrested!"

"Harry, what were you doing on the Boardwalk in the first place? How did you realize it was Evan on the runaway tram?" Olivia asked. "It all seems so unlikely!"

"I know! I was trying to get some GoPro video of the crowds on the beach and the Boardwalk. Just to use as B-roll in my videos. As I was walking back from the beach, Gran texted me she saw some guy trying to steal your car and that Ray and Evan had run off after him!"

Andrea chimed in. "I was out watering my plants and heard a commotion over by the parking lot. I saw Ray and Charlie running over there. Then, I noticed Evan banging on your car door. I had no idea what was happening, but I pulled out my phone to get a video," she said, holding out her phone for Olivia to see.

Olivia took the phone and tapped on the "play" icon. "Oh my gosh! What in the world is Luke doing, speeding out of the parking lot like that! He is insane!" Olivia was glad Andrea had the video because otherwise she would never have imagined how it all played out. Also, she needed to get this video to the police. "Andrea, can I forward this video to myself?"

"Sure thing, hon. Glad to be able to help out," Andrea replied. "Maybe I should start my own TwitTok account and be an investigative reporter?" They all laughed.

"TwitTok?" Harry belly laughed as grabbed his stomach and hunched over gasping for breath. "You mean Twitter or TikTok? I'm gonna veto that idea, Gran! Don't want you to get yourself into trouble and be *canceled!* Back to my superhero story now, ladies. So, I read the text from Gran but not really much I could do at the beach, right? But then I heard the tram horn honking. I turned around, and it was speeding right at me. If I hadn't moved, it would have hit me for sure. I need to download the footage so we can take a look," Harry said as he pulled out his GoPro from his backpack. "Honestly, this could go viral!" Olivia scooted closer to him and watched as he played the footage and fast forwarded to try to get to the right spot.

"At first, I admit, I didn't even realize Evan was there. I saw the police horses coming at a full gallop and figured I could try to help out. I was thinking maybe it was a medical emergency with the driver or something like that. I never imagined it was a hijacked tram! I didn't see Evan until right as I was about to jump onboard and then realized it was the same guy driving the tram who had stolen your car. Perfect timing, I guess!"

"Harry. You're on TikTok, right? You need to upload that clip and then send the link to the local news stations. Or maybe even national news?" Olivia said, excitedly. "Let me research the right accounts and hashtags while you get the clip ready."

Harry and Olivia drank the entire bottle of wine, which was only two glasses each, but Olivia felt more relaxed. It was easy to talk with them, Olivia thought. She felt like one of the family. Speaking of family, she looked at her watch and realized her parents would be there in about 30 minutes.

"Hey, I need to go over and clean up my place. Luke messed things up and I want to try to get everything in order before my parents arrive," said Olivia. "Can you both come to Ray's second birthday party this evening? We're going to set things up on the picnic tables outside by the pier. I heard that they'll be serving homemade Puerto Rican delicacies!"

Olivia looked down at her phone and read off the things that Evan had texted her: "Mofongo, empanadas, cuchifritoes, and flan de queso, which is a cream cheese dessert. I don't know what half of it is, but it sounds delicious!"

"Yes! We'll be there. I know Ray's family well and would love to see them again. I've been to Puerto Rico a couple times and the food is amazing. Much of the cuisine centers around plantains—they're kind of like smaller bananas," said Harry. "I love to travel and try new foods. And I also love to cook." He winked at Olivia.

Good Lord! Harry was an expert at flirting. Olivia was smitten. She would change into something sexier and do up her make-up and hair.

Luke was detained. She couldn't imagine he had anyone who would pay a bail bond for him. Was she finally free to live her life?

CHAPTER 56
Ray

> Ray's Mama to Ray:
> Happy Birthday, Ray Ray!!!! We hope you're doing something fun today!

We wish we could be with you but we look forward to seeing you next month up here in NYC. I'll FaceTime you later when dad is back home.

Ray to her Mama:
Thanks Mom! I miss you all so much! I wish we were together too. It's been a very crazy day so far but I'll fill you in when we talk later. *Hugs*

Ray put her phone on the kitchen counter and got a glass of water. She took a long sip and then picked up her phone, walked over to the sofa, and sat down with Charlie. She let out a huge sigh of relief.

Listening to Evan during the tram chase was mentally exhausting, and she couldn't imagine how Evan was feeling right now. Would this be the end of Luke craziness? Ray's stomach was still queasy. Her face was flushed. Her shirt was drenched in sweat. Charlie had been such a good boy, just sitting there quietly while Ray explained the situation to the officer, and they listened in on the scene at the Boardwalk.

Ray was suddenly ravenously hungry. She got up and grabbed a banana. She should meditate to calm down. She turned on the TV and found a meditation yoga session on YouTube. She unrolled her yoga mat for the second time of the day and sat on the floor trying to clear her mind.

Ray tried her best to concentrate on the 30-minute yoga session, but her mind was reeling. At the end, still not feeling very relaxed, she rolled up her yoga mat and walked upstairs to take a shower. When she got out, she heard a commotion downstairs. Charlie was barking excitedly. Maybe Evan had come back? Ray put on her new sexy short, bright blue silk robe and walked down the stairs.

When she reached the bottom of the stairs, she heard a loud, "Surprise!"

If Ray was surprised last night, at this moment, she was completely stunned! Obviously, her parents had a key to the beach house and had let themselves in.

"Venga! Mama! Dad! Abuelita! Abuelo! You're all here," Ray said. "I can't believe it!" Ray ran over to her mama and gave her a huge hug.

"Ven aquí, mi amorcito linda! Happy birthday! We wanted to come and surprise you! Evan helped us arrange it," her grandmama said. She grabbed Ray's cheeks and kissed the tip of her nose.

Ray looked down at her robe and reached around and tugged down the back. Though it was super short, it wasn't revealing her butt cheeks at least. She grabbed the tie around her waist and pulled it tighter.

Ray hugged each one and by the end, her smile was so big her cheeks were hurting, and tears were flowing freely from her happy eyes… for the second day in a row.

"I'm so happy you could all come," she said for the third time. "I just got out of the shower, so I need to change! But after that, I need to fill you in on what seems like a million things."

"I'm gonna go out and bring in the rest of our stuff, Ray Ray. Then you and I can hit the beach? So put on your swimsuit! I've been dreaming of riding in some waves the entire hot and sticky drive down here," her dad said. "It's been way too long since I've gotten the boogie board out!"

Ray's dad spent his youth as a quintessential beach bum. He used to be a beach lifeguard back in the day. Along with a surfboard, he had one of those fancy heavy duty boogie boards from the Ron Jon Surf Shop. The Anders Beach Closet, as they fondly called it, housed all of the umbrellas, canopies, chairs of various sizes, boogie boards, sand toys, the beach cart, coolers, blankets, sand games, frisbees, footballs, etc. Back when Ray was younger, she couldn't believe the amount of stuff they lugged to and from the beach. Nowadays, Ray took a backpack chair and a light umbrella, along with a small tote bag. Long gone were the days of needing three baskets full of beach toys and games.

"I'll stay here with your grandparents, and we'll rest up. When you're back from the beach, I'll give you a hair trim, sweetie. It's getting a little long for you, no?" Ray's mom said as she reached out to check the length of her hair.

"Yes, Mama. I was just thinking I needed a haircut," said Ray, as she grabbed her mother's hands and gave them a squeeze.

"How's Andrea doing?" Ray's dad asked. Andrea hadn't lived there nearly as long as Ray's grandparents had, but they'd become even closer over the past decade or so since Andrea had moved to the beach full-time for retirement.

"She's as fit as a whistle," Ray said. "I'll text her to let her know you all are visiting and ask her to stop over. Let me change into my suit now." She pulled away and went upstairs, careful to pull her robe down to cover her backside as she went up the stairs.

Ray paused as she was about to enter her bedroom, overhearing her mom and dad talking.

"Now Johnny, you need to keep Ray Ray occupied at the beach for at least three hours! Not a moment less. It will take us at least that long to decorate and get all of the food prepared," Gloria said. "And whatever you do, don't tell her about losing your job yet. It's her birthday and we need to keep happy thoughts!"

"Will do, Glor. I'm on it!" Ray heard her dad's steps coming up the stairs and quickly entered her room and closed the door.

Her dad lost his job? Why were they keeping it a secret from her? Ray felt worry stream through her body as a dozen scenarios crossed her mind. Her parents lived comfortably, but things in New York were expensive. Her mom didn't make much as a stylist, and she didn't think her dad's salary was anywhere near what new graduates were making right out of college. They must be worried about money.

And so much for her mom and her grandparents wanting to rest after the long drive down from New York. Those little sneaky sneaks, planning a birthday celebration for her! She hadn't realized how much she had missed seeing their smiling faces in real life. Should she move to Brooklyn to be near them like they'd begged her to do so many times? No. That wasn't the life she wanted, was it?

Ray to Evan:
OMG. My family is here to surprise me for my birthday!!! I'm headed to the beach with my dad momentarily. Good luck with the police! When will you be back? Xoxoxoxo

CHAPTER 57
Luke

Luke sat in the back of the SUV as they drove to D.C. After he'd been taken into custody at the beach, he was transported to the local police station where he was photographed and fingerprinted. They tried to obtain a voluntary statement from him, but he exercised his right to remain silent. His online network had published a list of lawyers that were on board with representing defendants in the January 6th Capitol breach. He recalled one firm that was based in D.C. and phoned their office but had to leave a voicemail.

His ankle was on fire, and he'd also bruised his shoulder. He had a few minor cuts on his face. They'd strapped an ice pack to his ankle and one to his shoulder, but they were barely cool at this point. Luke closed his eyes and wished he was dead. How had it all gone to hell like this? Why did he try to escape? It just made things a million times worse.

Now he had a series of other charges to deal with—breaking and entering, burglary, passport fraud, vehicle theft, assault, hijacking public transportation, reckless driving, public nuisance, menacing behavior, fleeing and evading arrest, and even jaywalking. He couldn't remember the entire sordid list.

Luke *had* gone into the Capitol building on January 6th, but only briefly. He entered after the initial violence and once he was in there and took in the frantic scene, he turned around and walked back outside. He stood on the steps in solidarity. But no matter if the election was stolen or not, it was clear things were completely out of control, and he wanted no part in the violence. He was happy to fight the good fight online from the safety of his home office. However, he wasn't prepared to be a political mercenary. Now, he'd lost everything—his job, his money, his family, his friends, his wife, his freedom. *How had it come to this?*

He closed his eyes and tears silently streamed down his cheeks forming wet spots on his shirt. His arms were restrained so he couldn't wipe them away. His chest started heaving as a tragic sob escaped his mouth. Luke shut his eyes as tightly as he could stand doing and held them closed. He was embarrassed by the involuntary display of emotion.

The agent in the front passenger seat turned his head to look back and said, "We should be there in about 45 minutes."

"Pull it together, man!" he whispered to himself as he slammed his head back against the car headrest. And then again. And again, for a third time.

The drive seemed to last an eternity. With each mile, Luke's mind fell deeper and deeper into a maze of what-ifs. What if he hadn't married Olivia? What if his mom hadn't died so young? What if the pandemic never happened? What if he never became obsessed with politics? What if he had minded his own damn business and just lived his own damn life?

Where would he be right now? *Definitely not sitting in the back of a cop car being interrogated by the FBI.*

He was just a regular guy—or at least he had been a regular guy. He caught a glimpse of his face in the car's rearview mirror. He looked haggard and much older than his 27 years. He hadn't shaved in a few days. He had a large bandage on his forehead from the tram crash. He could feel grains of sand in his hair. He was uncomfortable on every level. Physically and mentally, he was on the verge of a complete breakdown.

PART 4
Friday, August 11, 2023
A few weeks later.

CHAPTER 58
Evan

Evan's computer pinged and he clicked out of his WordPress window. He opened his email window. The subject line was, "WAFN = We Are Fake News!"

"Say, what?" he said to himself as he clicked to open the full email. "Whoa. No way."

The email was from the legal team that was investigating WAFN for a class action lawsuit. Evan immediately forwarded the email to his boss and then messaged her on Slack as a heads-up. He wondered what this meant for his company and the new website he'd launched last month.

Evan's phone vibrated and he picked it up, thinking it might be his boss calling. They had a policy at work where they wouldn't say anything controversial over email or in written messages, they'd make an old-school voice call. It wasn't her, though.

Brandon to Evan:
Bro! Check out this pic of Michael Jordan! Just saw his boat go by for the Marlin fishing comp

"Very cool boat," Evan said to himself as he clicked on the picture and spread his fingers to zoom in and check out Air Jordan up close.

Evan to Brandon:
No way! That's lit! I heard rumors he was in town for the big tourney

Evan's Uncle Jack regularly crewed with one team or another for the annual White Marlin Open and he was out there today. Back when Evan was young, before his dad died, his dad (Justin) and Uncle Jack (Justin was Jack's older brother), would take Evan and Brandon along fishing and crabbing with them almost every weekend during the crabbing season—normally from April into December along the East Coast. There was no fancy way to remember it like there was for oysters—eat them only in months with the letter "R"— which meant September through April.

For a while, after his dad died, Evan had stopped fishing completely. It was just too depressing. But once he was in college, he started back at it. He'd gone out as a deckhand in the marlin tournament for three years in a row while he was on summer break, before he had a full-time job.

Those were the summers when he was also in the beach scope business. He would walk up and down the beach wearing his red swim trunks, carrying a camera, trying to get families with small kids or groups of young girls to take photos. The scope business had skyrocketed since he was a kid. It used to be those small keychain scopes with little photos or typical photo prints. Nowadays, they print photos on anything and everything.

This year was the 50th anniversary of the White Marlin Open, and things were more hyped than ever. Nearly 400 boats would hit the waves in competition for more than $10 million. The tournament awarded prize money for catches of white marlin, blue marlin, tuna, wahoo, dolphin, and swordfish. Local folklore claimed that FDR coined the name "The White Marlin Capital of the World" in 1939 after he had a momentous day of fishing in Ocean City.

It was unusual, but today was the last day of the week-long tourney and not a single legal-sized white marlin or blue marlin had been caught. So far, the biggest fish brought in was a 265-pound tuna.

Ray to Evan:
Good morning! Still ok for me and Charlie to come and stay with you this weekend and experience the small-town charm of Historic Berlin? Gonna show me the sites where Runaway Bride and Tuck Everlasting were filmed? Xoxo

Evan quickly thumbs-upped the message. His boss was calling.

"Hey. Yeah. Totally crazy, right? I mean we knew that the entire project was super sketchy—especially after we found out most of the article commentary was bogus," Evan said.

"All of our communications and documentation may need to get turned over to the authorities. I contacted our company lawyer and she's gonna want to talk it through with all of us. So, Monday, we'll need to have an in-office meeting," Mary Ann said.

"Ok. Cool. So, what to do with the website for now? Should I take it down?"

"Just keep it online, but stop all work on it," Mary Ann replied. "We won't make any decisions until Monday."

Evan hung up and shook his head in disbelief. It had been such a crazy summer. To top it off, there was a resurgence of COVID underway. The CDC was saying another booster shot should be available in the fall, along with the annual flu shot. Seemed like every fall, people would need to get both shots as a standard procedure. Forever. COVID wasn't going away anytime soon.

He had a deadline at the end of the day. He needed to clear his mind and get back to work. Evan's current work project was for a marijuana dispensary located in Salisbury, Maryland. As of July 1, Maryland's recreational cannabis law gave adults 21 or older the right to possess up to 1.5 ounces of cannabis flower, 12 grams of concentrated cannabis, or a total amount of cannabis products not to exceed 750 mg THC.

Personally, that was not Evan's scene, but many of his friends were ecstatic about the new law and had parties in celebration over the past month. He'd taken some time to talk with his friends while he was mocking up options for the website he was working on, kind of an informal focus group. There were tons of stock images of weed, but Evan was planning to swing by the actual dispensary and take some photos next week for the final prototype.

This was the first weekend Ray would be coming to stay at his place, which seemed long overdue. His mom was having a BBQ, and they would go there together tomorrow. Evan thought there may be some kind of announcement about an engagement because his mom was acting very weird. Well, much weirder than usual. Vernon's daughter and her family were also coming, and they were all staying at his mom's house. Jack, Brandon, and Raymond would also be there. It was the first big family party since before the pandemic.

Evan looked at the clock, stood up to stretch, and then walked to the bathroom. It was almost lunch time. He had several chores on his to-do list for the lunch hour. He needed to get the *good* sheets on the bed and the *good* towels in the bathroom. Fortunately, most of the stuff in his place had been initially sourced by a girl so it was decorated well and had all the necessary niceties, Evan thought. It didn't give off a typical cheesy bachelor pad vibe.

After Ellie left, Evan put his own distinctive touch in some of the decorations in the apartment. He'd hung up some music-related artwork, mostly abstract jazz lithographs and illustrations. He put his guitars on display stands in one corner of the living room. The turntable was sitting front and center on a new table next to the TV. He had a stack of LPs that he'd started collecting again over the past few months. He'd hung up more speakers, attached to the ceiling, around the entire room.

It was a nice apartment. He felt comfortable, but Evan was lonely. Sure, he had Ray, and they texted almost nonstop each evening. Working from home each day, he felt isolated. Some days during the week, he never left the apartment complex. He'd normally go down to the gym first thing in the morning, which was on the first floor. But most of the time, he was the only person there. He wasn't used to living alone. In fact, this was the very first time he hadn't had a roommate in his entire life.

Evan did a quick set of 20 jumping jacks and then made a PB&J sandwich. He opened the *Garena Free Fire* app to get a quick game in before he had to get back on his computer. Aerosmith's *Shook Me All Night Long* was playing on his sound system. It was a good day. He snapped a selfie and texted it to Ray.

CHAPTER 59
Olivia

It was Friday, and in her normal teacher life, it was always TGIF—but in her waitressing life, the weekend would go by in a complete daze. Olivia had to smile nonstop. Answer the same questions. Repeat the exact same phrases. Over and over and over again. The money had been good, but waitressing at the beach out in the hot sun, or in the cold rain, or in the brisk breeze was not easy. It was exhausting. Her nose had become permanently red, no matter how much sunblock she applied.

School was exhausting in a completely different and much more rewarding way. Olivia loved fine tuning the lesson plans, grading homework, and helping with the extracurriculars. The school's active shooter drills, she would try to block out.

The first day of school was the Tuesday after Labor Day. The countdown was on! Olivia would set up her classroom next week. New Teacher Orientation was the coming Monday and her last day of work at JJ's was on Sunday. She'd told him that she'd be available to fill in if he was shorthanded, but nothing permanent on the schedule until next summer. Even then, though, Olivia had no idea what she'd be doing after one full school year. It was very fluid. She was willing to help out on busy fall weekends. Being a teacher was not just a 9-5 job. She'd have all sorts of commitments that fell outside of the school day.

And there was Harry. It had only been a few weeks since she'd met him, but things had progressed quickly. Last night, after they'd had a romantic dinner watching the sunset from the top of the reimagined Embers restaurant, they'd discussed going on a vacation together.

They'd gotten very caught up in the excitement of planning a vacation and ended up booking a special cruise deal on a sailing from Baltimore to Bermuda for the week leading up into Labor Day weekend. Being spontaneous was never something Olivia had trouble with. She was always living in the moment—but thinking about it now, she couldn't believe she planned an expensive vacation with someone she barely knew! It seemed so extravagant and irrational, but Harry wanted to take advantage of his unlimited vacation time being jobless. He'd offered to pay for the cruise tickets and Olivia would pay for any incidentals and excursions. Harry assured Olivia that he had been saving up for a vacation over the pandemic and could afford the cost.

Olivia sat on the sofa with her laptop and searched for tours in Bermuda. Ruby was curled up on the floor with her head resting on Olivia's foot. After compiling a list of about a dozen potential excursions, Olivia changed her focus to Luke. She did a quick Google search—like she did every few days—

and saw a news update. He had not posted bail, and his trial had been scheduled. Olivia assumed she would be contacted at some point soon to serve as a witness. Then, hopefully, she could put this entire exhausting episode behind her and move on with her life.

Olivia to Ray:
You won't believe this, but Harry and I are taking a cruise over Labor Day!!!!!

Can you watch Ruby for me? It's for 5 days.

She grabbed a handful of cheese puffs from the huge jar her mom had brought with her a few weeks ago. They were not quite stale yet. Olivia forgot how much she loved them. They were low sugar, so that was healthy, right? She had a stack of napkins handy in her lap.

The local news played in the background on her TV. They were showing the fish weigh-in for the White Marlin Open.

"Oh, look! It's the boat that Jack's on, Ruby! They finally got one! A marlin. And it's so freaking huge!"

Olivia turned up the sound and hit the record button. "O.M.G. There's Jack!"

Olivia to Ray and Evan:
Jack is on tv right now with a freaking huge fish!! I wonder if they won? OMG!!

The news switched over to something about the first Republican presidential candidate debate. Olivia turned down the sound again. Next, she navigated to the Maryland Elections website and submitted a form to be an Election Judge. The next Primary Election Day would be Tuesday, May 14, 2024. General Election Day was scheduled for Tuesday, November 5, 2024.

Olivia's Mom to Olivia (with picture):
Dad and I finally saw Barbie last night! You were right. It was transcendental!

I want to go and see it again. We both wore pink.

Also – There's a conservative group on campus trying to get people to boycott Barbie for being too woke. Don't they understand that their behavior is basically saying, "Hey – I'm misogynistic!"

Olivia's Mom to Olivia (with picture):
Also, I saw us on the local news last night! It was so late that I didn't want to text you. They were showing coverage of the crowds for the Beyonce concert rain delay. And there we were - all blinged out and soaking wet! LOL. The photo is a little grainy, but if you zoom in you can tell it's us!

Olivia to Mom:
OMG! That's so funny! That concert is still giving me life! So good!

Glad you finally saw Barbie! What a spicy pink outfit, Mom! You guys look sooooooo cute! Love the kenergy from Dad. Anyone who doesn't like the Barbie movie clearly doesn't understand the struggle women deal with every single day in this patriarchal society! Makes me so mad.

BTW, Evan's Uncle Jack may have caught a huge fish at the Marlin Open? Just saw HIM on the local news!!!

So – you won't believe this, but I'm going on a cruise with Harry over Labor Day before school starts!!! I have to go to work soon but TTYL about it all!!

Mom to Olivia:
That's so great honey! Your dad and I really liked Harry when we met him last month. He's smart, and funny, not to mention very handsome. TTYL.

Olivia 'hearted' the message and put her phone down. The disjointed text conversation had made her mind spin. She would never tell her mother this, but she'd lost track of the number of drunk customers at work who had gotten handsy with her like they had some kind of male-given right to touch a woman whenever they wanted? Olivia wasn't the kind of person to make a huge scene at work, but Jack had a policy where he—or Raymond—would immediately talk to any rowdy/inappropriate customer and ask them to leave. He'd bring their bill and some takeout boxes and ask them to pay and leave. So for that, Olivia was thankful.

She had to get ready for work and take Ruby out! Her last Friday. Fish Friday. They had a special on the catch of the day sandwich. If Jack had caught that ginormous fish, the bar would be really hoppin' today. The official weigh-in was six blocks south of JJ's so a lot of the crowd would walk over afterward for drinks and/or dinner.

As Olivia was walking back to her townhouse with Ruby, she saw Andrea struggling to get up the steps to her front door, carrying two large tote bags, one in head hand.

"Hold up, Andrea! Let me help you with those bags," Olivia said as she hurried over to the stairs. "You shouldn't be trying to carry such heavy bags! What do you have in here, anyway? They must weigh a ton," exclaimed Olivia as she tried to carry the bags in one hand and keep hold of Ruby's leash in the other.

"Don't you worry one bit about me, Olivia. I've got this covered," said Andrea, as Ruby tried to get her head into one of the bags, sniffing anxiously. "Just sit the bags down right here while I unlock the front door."

Olivia peaked into the bags as Andrea dug around her huge pink flamingo purse to find her keys.

"Are you having a party without inviting me, young lady?" Olivia smirked as she saw both bags were filled with junk food.

Two big tubs of Dolle's Candyland caramel popcorn, two boxes of saltwater taffy, and what looked like it could be a couple pounds of fudge. The other bag was full of what looked like three two-liter bottles of Coke, and many bags of cookies and chips.

"Don't you mind my eating habits, dearie! I'm having a little party later tonight with my friends from the senior center. We're going to watch the latest season of *Bridgerton* because Harry just got my TV hooked up on Netflix."

"Ok. Well, fortunately, I have other plans tonight because I *do not* need to watch Bridgerton with you and your friends. Andrea. No offense," laughed Olivia. "Whelp, I've gotta get to work now. Have fun with your friends tonight! Remember to pace yourself with all that junk food!"

Olivia put Andrea's bags inside the front door and then tugged on Ruby's leash and turned to walk down the steps as her phone buzzed in her pocket. *What in the world!*

CHAPTER 60
Ray

Ray had Charlie out at the pet area behind the building when her phone started vibrating in her pocket multiple times in a row. She wondered if it was a work-related incident as she tapped it on.

Jack to Evan, Brandon, Mary, Ray, Olivia (with photo):
Hi All. Apologies for the mass text but heads-up that we reeled in a nearly 650-pound blue marlin! It could be a huge winner in the tourney. Let's see how it goes. Keep your fingers crossed!

Evan to All:
DAMN!!! That's HUGE!

Fishing for compliments? Don't be KOI!

Brandon to All:
FINS CROSSED

Olivia to All:
Oh man! That fish got SCHOOLED!! I just saw you on the news!!

Ray laughed as she read the immediate responses that were pinging in. She tried to think of something clever to write and Googled fish puns. She tapped on the *!!* for Jack's initial text and then *HaHa* for each response.

Ray to All:
Very e-fish-ient work, Jack! Hope you get GILLIONS of dollars!

Ray walked back into her place and grabbed the mail out of the box. There was a padded envelope package at the front door. She must have just missed the delivery person or else didn't notice it when she walked by on the way out.

She looked around and didn't see anyone nearby. She grabbed the envelope. It felt like a huge packet of paper. The return address was California. Her ex-boyfriend, she wondered?

The two seagulls flew onto the front steps and hopped around for a moment and then sat on the bottom step, content to relax in the pleasant breeze. Ray glanced over at them and said, "You two must have gotten your fill of snacks on the beach today? Now it's time for a siesta, huh?"

Charlie was used to the birds by now and didn't make a fuss when they hung around the house. If any other strange birds flew nearby, though, he'd be barking up a storm.

Ray walked inside and opened it up. It *was* from her one and only ex-boyfriend, Arnold.

"What the heck?" Ray started reading the papers and her phone buzzed, indicating an incoming call. Arnold was calling her right now?

"Hey, Ray. I saw that you should have just gotten my delivery. I know how analytical you are, so I wanted to send the details to you first and then call to explain."

"Hi. Arnold. Yes. I just opened it. What's up?" Ray's heart was beating so fast, and she tried to remain calm. She hadn't talked to Arnold in ages, and hearing his voice brought back a flood of memories.

About 45 minutes later, Ray hung up the phone and looked out the window. The seagulls were sitting on two wooden pilings on the dock. It was windy and overcast and the water had a greenish tint to it. Sunset would either be a real beauty or a total bust, depending on the cloud formations at dusk.

She went upstairs and picked up her overnight bag. She got Charlie's tote bag and walked to her car. The drive to Evan's place was longer than usual with the Friday night traffic.

As she drove, she thought about the conversation she just had with Arnold... which led her to think back to the discussion with her parents the day after her birthday. Her parents had approached her about selling the beach house and moving in with them. The beach house was worth a lot of money that would help them get by while her dad looked for a new job. At his age, he was experiencing ageism in the job hunt, he said. He was seemingly overqualified for almost everything he applied to, and shortsighted younger managers were feeling threatened—not wanting someone so experienced on their staff. So many employers wanted cheap entry-level labor. Gen X was falling off left and right as they desperately tried to hang onto the corporate ladder.

Ray's grandparent's place in Brooklyn was old and it was in desperate need of a series of minor renovations to make it more accessible for her grandparents, adding handrails and ramps, pull-out cabinets, lower shelves. Her dad wanted to install some new tech to help automate things for voice command or a mobile app. It added up.

Ray was torn. She could hardly imagine selling their beach house where her family had made so many amazing memories. Her dad loved the beach house as much as—or maybe even more so than she did—but he was trying to be smart and make a rational decision for their family's future.

Over the past few weeks, Ray had been considering her options. She loved living at the beach house. And now that Evan was in her life, she had even more reason to stay put. Ray had saved enough money for a downpayment on the beach house—she could buy it from her parents. But would they let her do that and take her money? In the back of her mind, though, she wondered if moving to New York was a better option? She could spend time with her family and also be a big help. They had a third room. She could make it a bedroom/office combo.

She was feeling so confused, but after her conversation with Arnold, she felt like she had a third option in the mix. If she could potentially double her salary, her parents couldn't say no to her buying the beach house, right?

When Evan opened the door to his apartment, Ray fell into his arms. *Can't Stop Lovin' You* by Aerosmith was playing on the sound system.

They kissed, and Evan led her around the room in a dance, seemingly channeling a Chmerkovskiy brother from *Dancing with the Stars*. Very sexy and smooth.

"I missed you, Ray," Evan whispered in her ear. "What's on your mind? You seem distracted."

"First, you know how much I love you, right? And didn't you say it was your dream to go surfing in California?" Ray asked, raising her eyebrows in worried anticipation of his answer.

"Yes, of course. I love you too, babe. And, yes, I'd love to take a vacation to the West Coast," Evan said as he tried to spin her around somewhat awkwardly because she was so stiff.

"Your job is normally 100% virtual, right?" Ray asked next. "Could you work remotely for a few months in a row?"

"Um. Yeah. I guess so? What are you getting at, Ray?" Evan said as he pulled her into a closeup nose-to-nose embrace.

"Out of the blue, I just got an opportunity to be VP of Product Development for a new app that would help identify fake news and other artificially developed content," Ray said. "It would be absolutely amazing for my career. They want to launch it in time to help monitor the election next year. The only issue—if you even call it that—is it would entail a kick-off in-person in California—Silicon Valley—for three to six months starting in October. Once everything is established, I wouldn't need to be there on site full-time."

"Ok. So, are you asking me to come with you? Or visit?" Evan said as Ray stepped back and put her hands on his arms.

"I'd love for you to come with me," Ray said, quietly as she rubbed his arms, up and down "You could work from there and surf at Linda Mar State Beach. That's in Pacifica, California. They will put me up in a long-term corporate rental near there. It's plenty big enough for both of us. It is a dream job for me, paying way more than my current salary."

"I feel like I should take some time to think about it, shouldn't I?" Evan laughed. "But my initial thought is 'Hell yeah!' But my brain says I need to talk with my work first. Obviously, we haven't been together for very long. I know I love you. This would be a big decision. So, I guess I need some time to think about it?" Evan picked Ray up and swung her around. "But congrats! This is huge news. I'm so proud of you, Ray!" Evan said. "Tonight, we celebrate!"

Evan was already planning to take Ray out to dinner at his favorite Berlin restaurant, but having a reason to celebrate would make it much more fun. Berlin's claim to fame, as some called it, was its picturesque Main Street. It was lined with trees and dozens of retail shops, galleries, antique stores, restaurants, live music venues, coffee shops, bakeries, butcher and local seafood market, sweets, and more.

After dinner, they walked around and popped into the various shops. Ray bought a dish towel with a cartoon sun that said "Ray of Sunshine" on it. They shared a waffle bowl sundae at Island Creamery, which Evan told her had been voted the best ice cream shop in America.

"Want to wish on a shooting star tonight, Ray?" Evan asked when they finished their dessert. "We can make your dreams come true."

"Well, my dreams are indeed coming true! You mean that August meteor shower that's going on now, right? I keep seeing posts about it online," Ray said.

"Yep. And we are right next to the best place to watch in all of Maryland."

Evan went on to explain that Assateague Island was a certified dark sky spot. The best place to watch the Perseid meteor shower. It was almost at peak viewing time. Evan had his camera and tripod in the back and would try to get some pictures of the Milky Way.

Jack to All:
Whelp. It's oh-FISH-ial!!!! $$$$$$$$$$$

Not sure about the final numbers, but the fish will bring in more than $6 million in prize money!!!!!

"Oh. My. God! Six million dollars!" Evan said. "For one damn fish!"

Ray looked at him with wide eyes. "I'm totally speechless!" She looked at her phone.

A series of messages made their phones buzz and beep.

Jack to All:
Looks like the celebration at Mary's tomorrow night will be a little more #Boujee than usual! LMAO $$$$

Saturday, August 12, 2023
The next day.

CHAPTER 61
Ray

Charlie had been anxious all night, being in a different place. They eventually shut him out of the bedroom because he kept whining and pacing around the room. Ray saw sunlight coming through the side of the curtains and got up to take him for a walk so he wouldn't end up having an accident.

"Hey, Charlie Boy. You're such a good doggie, aren't you?" Ray said as she opened the bedroom door and rubbed his back. She slid on her shoes and walked out the front door and down the three flights of steps. Charlie was tentative since he wasn't familiar with this routine.

Once they got to the ground floor, Ray walked over to the grassy area by the parking lot, which was next to a bunch of stinky garbage bins. Not as charming as her beach house, for sure.

Charlie made quick business of it, and they were on their way back up the stairs in less than three minutes. Once back inside the apartment, Ray decided to take a better look around at things. She'd been there only a few times and had never taken the time to examine the place. She refilled Charlie's water bowl and looked around the kitchen.

Evan's ex did have a good sense of style, Ray had to admit. The place was fresh and sophisticated. Lots of high-end kitchen appliances and the dishware was on point. It looked much more up to date than Ray's beach house. Ray started to make coffee. Now that she was up, no use disturbing Evan and trying to go back to sleep.

The meteor shower last night had been a real showstopper. They'd watched at least two dozen meteors with huge tails. Evan was able to get a bunch of good Milky Way shots with his fancy camera.

While watching the stars and having a lot of quiet time for contemplation, Ray decided she would take the new job. With or without Evan coming to California, the offer was too good to turn down. Sure, she'd be bicoastal and would probably have regular late calls due to the time difference. She would have more than enough money to buy the beach house from her parents. They'd be disappointed with her decision to stay in Maryland, but she had to make this decision for herself, and this summer, she was happier than she'd ever been in her entire life!

Ray planned to give her two-weeks' notice at her current job on Monday. She felt a pain in the pit of her stomach just thinking about it. She loved her team so much. To add to her anxiousness, Olivia didn't know this yet, but she and Evan wanted to go on the cruise with her and Harry. Evan had plenty of vacation days, and Ray would be done with her work. Ray thought Olivia would be happy to have a couple's vacation, but she wasn't totally sure. Evan's brother had offered to watch both dogs for them while they were away.

Ray to Olivia:
Good morning! Can you and Harry come to Evan's mom's house tonight for dinner?

Jack says he can drive you both with him (and he'll let you off work early).

Also, can you give me a call when you get a chance? Want to fill you in on something.

Don't worry – no criminal activity involved. LOL

Ray and Evan had originally planned to chillax and catch up on streaming shows. They had the first two episodes of the new season of *Only Murders in the Building* to watch. Also, they needed to catch up on *What We Do In The Shadows*. Evan had recently followed all of the related WWDITS accounts on Instagram for her. Gizmo's set trailer tour fascinated her! Last weekend, Ray and Olivia had zoomed through the sixth season of *Too Hot To Handle* and both had declared that it was the best season yet.

But now, Ray felt like she had a million things to do if she was really switching jobs and heading to California next month. And a cruise to boot? *Who even was she now?* She hardly recognized her life.

She had never gone on a vacation without her family. Not that she would go crazy, but she didn't have to worry about her parents judging her attire or her food or drink choices. She could wear revealing bikinis and eat desserts with every meal and drink a bottle of wine every single day. Not that she *would*. But she *could* if she wanted. And she was sure that Olivia would encourage her to do such things.

Ray wondered how she would cope with being away from Olivia for a few months. How would Olivia react? Ray had finally found a best friend, and now she was abandoning her! She hoped Olivia would be happy. And she also hoped Harry would stay local because they made such a cute couple.

After Ray confirmed Olivia was okay with the cruise plan, she and Evan would go online and purchase the tickets. But now, it was a yoga session for Ray. She took off her slides and propped her phone onto the coffee table so she could see it from the floor. She didn't want to try to figure out how to cast the video to Evan's TV.

Ray finished yoga right as her phone vibrated. Olivia was calling on FaceTime. Ray crossed her fingers and answered with a big smile.

CHAPTER 62
Evan

Evan woke up and saw Ray was not in the room. He could barely hear the serene voice of a yoga instructor coming from the living room. He decided to stay in bed and let her finish her session. He picked up his phone.

Brandon to Evan:
Hey Bro – Can you pick up beer and wine for the party today? Jack said he might be late so I want to be sure that we have enough drinks to kick it off.

Mom to Evan:
Good morning!! Can you bring your big cooler and that fancy blender of yours? I want to make some frozen drinks for the party.

Evan thumbs-upped both messages. He had an Instagram notification Ellie had posted something after a long time. He opened it, scrolled through his feed, and saw a group of photos of Ellie getting extra friendly with some dude. He probably should have removed her from his friend list, but he had assumed she would be the one to do it. They were in bathing suits at a pool. A "Bob" was tagged. The guy was super dorky, but they looked happy. He clicked on "Unfollow" and then went back to the news feed.

He saw an advertisement for "hims." Evan wondered how much that company must spend on advertising. Every day, he'd see multiple ads on social media and on TV. Now they had chewable mints for ED?

Evan hadn't been on Insta in a few weeks and was just seeing Olivia's post from their *Barbie Movie* outing. "Damn, Daniel! We look so frickin' good," Evan laughed, and he swiped through the 10 pictures Olivia had posted from their #Barbenheimer double-feature extravaganza.

Harry had gone with them at the last minute, and he totally brought Black Ken to the Dojo Casa Mojo Home, or whatever they called it. Olivia's get-up had her looking exactly like Margot Robbie. It was uncanny. As a couple, Olivia and Harry understood the assignment. They got props from at least a dozen other viewers at the theater.

Evan and Ray also wore pink, but they just didn't have the attitude to go with it. Because of Ellie's cruel laundry prank, Evan had his pick of pinkish clothes to select from for his outfit. He wore a white shirt that appeared tie-dyed pink with matching shorts that were also previously white. Although they had more reserved looks, Evan still thought they looked *snatched* as Olivia told them repeatedly. Last week, Harry helped Olivia film a parody "I'm Just Ken" video for TikTok. Apparently, it had taken off with nearly 10,000 views, the last Evan had heard.

After they watched the movies, they stopped at Dumser's Dairyland for ice cream and had a frank discussion about gender roles and recounted their favorite parts. Ray joked that she had experienced the "listen to me play the guitar for 30 minutes phenomenon" with Evan, and Evan had owned up to it and promised to do better.

Evan closed the app and went to Google to do a quick search. He typed in "Surfing at Linda Mar State Beach." As he read the search results, his excitement began to build. He would need to get a new wetsuit because the water was cooler, and the waves were so much bigger.

Next, he clicked on the link to the live webcams. A series of beach views came up. It was still early in the morning out there, so the video was a little hazy and dark. On the site, the waves for today were categorized as a *Sick Day*. Evan laughed out loud. He would love to be a *California Surfer Dude*. He would tell his family to watch him on these live feeds. He heard

Charlie let out a quick bark from downstairs and looked at the time.

He jumped out of bed and went into the bathroom to take a shower. About 10 minutes later, he walked out of the bathroom and saw Ray on the bed in a sexy hot pink nightie. *I Don't Want to Miss a Thing* by Aerosmith was playing on the Bluetooth speaker.

"You like? I bought this cowboy hat and new nightie during my hot pink Barbie shopping spree and didn't even get a chance to put it on last night!" Ray said as she stood up and ran her hand down over her hips. "But first, I have some devastating news about your night guard. Charlie got hold of it and chewed it up. I hope, hope, hope it was not one of those really expensive custom ones you got at the dentist?"

"What? Oh damn!" Evan said, walking over to take the mangled plastic from Ray's hands. "That cost me over three hundred bucks!"

"Oh my God. I'm so sorry! I'll pay to replace it," Ray said as she shrunk down onto the bed. "I should have thought to warn you. Dogs go crazy for mouth guards and retainers… all the saliva on it. I'm really so sorry!"

"Psych! You got played!" Evan yelled, grabbing Ray up off the bed. "That was just one of those cheap ones you mold yourself in boiling water. It cost less than 20 bucks," Evan laughed and clapped his hands together.

"Ok. Yes. Let's clap for you. You got me. Well done," Ray laughed, but her face was bright red with embarrassment.

"I must say that I was very, very disappointed when I woke up to see that you weren't still in bed beside me, darlin'."

Dancing Queen started playing. Evan pushed Ray's back up against the bedroom wall *and dot, dot, dot.*

CHAPTER 63
Olivia

Olivia knew she should get up to take Ruby outside, but the bed was so comfortable, and she didn't want to wake Harry. They were face-to-face on their sides with his arm wrapped around her bare torso. She didn't make a move to grab her phone from the bedside table, even though she'd heard it vibrate a few times.

She'd been staring at his face. His chest. His huge arm muscles. His sexy shaved head. He had quite a few moles on his head. One was quite large right above his left ear. One was on his lower right cheek, mostly covered by his short beard stubble. One was below his right eye near his nose. It kind of looked like a tear falling from the corner of his eye. It was adorable.

Olivia thought back to last night—the first time Harry had stayed over for the entire night. They leisurely walked down the Boardwalk, hand in hand. *Swoon.* He had such nice strong, big hands. They ate dinner at a new place called Cheese Wheel Pasta that everyone had been raving about on Facebook. The fresh pasta was excellent. Carbs be damned! Olivia had a side of mouth-watering fresh bread.

Afterward, they rode the Ferris wheel right at sunset. Then, they went to the arcade for a bit before finally heading to watch a live band at the Purple Moose Saloon. They ended up staying until closing time and it was an exceptionally long and lonely walk north on the boards so early in the morning.

Was she moving too fast? Maybe. She was throwing caution to the wind. It felt right. Nothing had ever felt so right.

Ruby let out a loud whine and Harry's eyes popped open. "Good morning! How did you sleep last night?" Olivia asked.

"With my eyes closed," Harry deadpanned.

"You dork," Olivia said, tickling the side of his stomach. Olivia rolled on top of him and then straddled his lap, put her hands on his cheeks, and leaned down to give him a quick kiss on his lips.

"I need to take Ruby out," she said. "Can you stay in bed and wait for me? Pretty please?"

"Ok. But if you want to tap this smokin' bod again, you need to bring back up some coffee with you," Harry laughed.

"You got it." She hopped off the bed in one swift jump. "Ten minutes tops. You know I have no chill!" Olivia screamed as she sprinted out of the room.

Exactly 12 minutes later, Olivia arrived back in bed with two insulated mugs of coffee and two donuts.

"You're two minutes late," Harry said.

"You did *not* just time me, did you?" Olivia laughed as she picked up her strawberry shortcake donut and took a bite. "You get the French toast donut. It's the last one."

Harry picked up the donut and took a bite, with a groan of appreciation. "So, Wonder Woman, are you ready to take to the friendly skies tomorrow? The parasailing place texted asking me to confirm our appointment."

"Yes. And no. I'm definitely freaking out!" Olivia said with a huge sigh. "But if you're with me, it will be okay. It's like on *The Bachelorette*—overcoming fears will bring us closer together, right?"

"Yes. Indeed. You know I want to get as close to you as I possibly can," Harry said as he put the empty plate on the bedside table and pulled Olivia into his lap.

They didn't get out of bed again for two more hours.

Mom to Olivia:
Good morning!! Are you excited for your last weekend of work at JJ's?

I found the most gorgeous hat for your cruise. It should arrive at your place on Monday. I also got you a couple other fun surprises.

Can you even believe the Maui fires! Such a tragedy!!

And DID YOU SEE THE NEW GOLDEN BACHELOR PREVIEW? Gerry. Seems like a total hottie. LOL

Also - do you think that Michelle Obama manifested the Barbie movie in her book?

FYI, Dad and I are going to a Jim Henson exhibition today at the Maryland Center for History and Culture in Baltimore.

Ok. Last text. I promise! I asked ChatGPT for the best excursions in Bermuda for you. Check your email for the list.

Olivia hearted, exclamation pointed, and thumbs-upped her mom's numerous texts.

Olivia to Mom:
Have fun today! I've got a full weekend and can't wait to wrap things up at JJ's! It's been a lot! I'm so exhausted! TTYL

Olivia had to get ready for work ASAP. After her long sexy night with Harry, her face was flushed, and she was completely exhausted. She could barely walk down the stairs. Harry was still in bed but was planning to head to the Ocean City Farmers Market to get some B-roll for the short documentary he was making. They'd meet up later at JJ's to go over to Evan's mom's party. Harry had mansplained to Olivia that "B-roll" is footage you use in a video as filler when you're editing parts together to make it more interesting. She was an *influencer*, so obviously she already knew that.

Olivia got on her bike and winced as she started slowly pedaling out of the parking lot. Her muscles were burning. On the bright side, she was super excited to hear about Jack's award-winning fish! How much money would he get? She had no idea how those things worked.

When she arrived at the restaurant, two local news crew vans were parked outside. It looked like one was doing a live shot. Jack was talking into a microphone and absolutely beaming. She pulled out her phone and took a few photos and then started recording a BTS video. She figured it would be a fun behind-the-scenes view for social media, showing all the huge cameras and crew members.

Once the news crews had left, or else got seated for lunch, Jack called everyone together in the kitchen for a quick update.

"First, I want to thank all of you for keeping the place going all week while I was in the tournament," Jack said. "It paid off. Not sure if you knew, but I was the one who pulled in the massive fish. We all signed an agreement at the start of the week about how we would split the proceeds. Given that it was me reeling in the line, I got the majority of the winnings while the rest was split among the remaining crew members."

A slew of congratulatory statements were shouted out and then Jack continued. "What it means for us here is that I want to expand things for next year. Over the off-season, we'll do some upgrades to the existing place and add on a new interior room behind the building, and we can be open year-round if we want." A loud round of applause broke out, with a few whoops and hollers from Raymond.

"Can we get some of those sick heating towers?" someone asked. "What about that system where you can text people when their table is ready?" someone else yelled out.

"Those fancy high-powered hand dryers for the bathrooms!" Olivia added, with a smirk. "And floor length mirrors! And more merch! And a selfie station! And advertising for social media? Oh, yeah! Those airplane sign things on the beach!"

Jack laughed. "Please email me *all* of your suggestions! I'm open to absolutely anything and everything. And to top it off, I'm giving everyone on staff as of today a $5,000 one-time bonus."

Everyone jumped up and started screaming. They joined together in a huge group hug and started jumping up and down. It was cheesy and it was overwhelming. Olivia started tearing up.

As the group broke apart, she turned and hugged Raymond tightly. He picked her up and swung her around, almost making two circles, when he lost his balance and stumbled, both landing on the kitchen floor with a thump.

"Oh, my goodness, Raymond! We'll have to use all our bonus money on medical bills," laughed Olivia, with tears running down her cheeks and rubbing her elbow.

Jack helped them both stand up. He stood in the middle, his arms around them.

"I couldn't have done it without all of you helping me out all summer," said Jack with tears in his eyes. He walked around the kitchen and shook each employee's hand. "You guys are the best. Thank you. Each and every one of you. This win was for you, brother!" He tapped his hand on his heart and then saluted the photo of himself with his brother Justin that was hanging on the wall, hence the bar's name: JJ's by the Bay. "Ok. Back to work, fam! It's still the summer season for another month!"

They went back to work, and Jack had Raymond tell everyone that the next round of orange crushes was on the house. Olivia took photos and videos all day as she served. The energy in the air was extremely exciting. The shots she got today would make for awesome social posts throughout the rest of the summer.

The rest of the day sped by in a flash and before Olivia knew it Harry had arrived, and they were headed over to

Evan's mom's place. Olivia had told Ray she'd love for her and Evan to join them for the cruise. With the bonus money, Olivia would feel much more comfortable with the cruise expense. In fact, she was going to pay for the unlimited drink package and the swimming with dolphins' experience. Life was a journey to experience to the fullest, and she didn't want to keep it low-key anymore.

CHAPTER 64
Evan

Evan and Olivia arrived at his mom's place before most people and helped them finish setting up the folding tables outside and putting down the newspaper. Evan started a fire in the firepit and got the grill ready. Jack stopped by Hoopers for a bushel of crabs. Hoopers had a kitchen fire break out the previous weekend, but fortunately they were back in business after a few days.

Along with the steamed crabs, they'd have burgers, hot dogs, corn-on-the-cob, and coleslaw. His mom had gotten a Smith Island Cake, made famous on the Eastern Shore because of their eight thin layers, instead of the more traditional four cake layers. Vernon's daughter, Diane, brought Baltimore's best local cookies—Berger Cookies and Otterbein's Cookies. Evan's mouth was watering just thinking about the desserts. Olivia and Harry brought a bucket of Fisher's Popcorn, a bag of Hoop Tea, and a 12-pack of hard seltzers.

Soon, they were all sitting around two long tables, hands all gooey with Old Bay and mallets pounding the table, sounding like woodpeckers in a disjointed melody.

"Whoa! Look at this bug, people!" Evan exclaimed. "I think it's that spotted lanternfly that's been all over the news! We're supposed to kill it, right? It's invasive?"

Everyone stopped their conversations and looked over at the bug, which was flitting around the platter of corn-on-the-cob. Olivia ran over and started taking photos and a video. "Squash it, Evan! I'll record you doing it," Olivia said, as she excitedly bounced up and down.

Evan grabbed the ear of corn and flicked the red-spotted bug off onto the picnic table and then swatted it ceremonially with a wooden crab mallet, saying, "I sentence you to death, invader!"

After the bug excitement, Evan's mom grabbed a roll of paper towels and wiped her hands off. She stood up and called Vernon over from the grill.

"Everyone, gather around. Vernon and I have an announcement to make! I doubt this will be a shocking surprise," Mary said, clapping her hands together. "Vernon and I are engaged!" She pulled the ring out of her pocket, put it on her finger, and held up her hand to show off the ring.

During the rowdy cheer of congratulations, Vernon bent down and reached under the picnic table, pulling out a box with plastic cups and two bottles of champagne on ice. He popped the corks, and Mary poured the glasses while Diane passed them around.

"Let's toast to my beautiful Mary. My love! My everything! I can't wait to be yours forever. Cheers!" They kissed to a round of applause.

Next, Brandon stood up. "We love you, Vernon, and know how happy you make Mom. That's a hard act to follow. But Raymond and I also have an announcement. As many of you know, we've been knee-deep in the adoption process. I'm happy to let you know that we were just connected with a smart and beautiful young woman who has agreed to give us the honor of adopting her baby boy. She's not due until next year. Fingers crossed it will all work out!"

Another round of congrats went around the table, and Mary gave her son a long hug.

Evan stood up next. "Coincidentally, Ray and I also have an announcement!" Evan paused and looked around the table at each person to extend the dramatics.

"Ok. Stop it with your concerned looks! We're *not* engaged and we're *not* having a baby, folks! Sorry to disappoint you! Ray has been offered an amazing new job and will have to go to California for a few months this fall to get started. I've agreed to go with her. So, let's give a big congrats to Ray!" Evan held up his almost empty glass and started the third toast of the evening.

"You're coming?" Ray asked as she put her arm around him.

"Yep. Cleared it with work just a bit ago," Evan said as he leaned over to give her a quick kiss.

Jack stood up. "Well, y'all already know my big announcement. Yee-haw! I'm now a multi-millionaire! And we definitely need to do a huge-ass toast to that!"

Jack signaled Raymond, who pulled out a bottle of cristalino tequila and started pouring it into the empty cups.

Everyone laughed, and Raymond started chanting, "Money, money, money…" Everyone joined in, and Diane's kids started dancing around the table. Soon, there was an impromptu conga line going around the yard. Nobody noticed the two seagulls watching on, perched up on the roof.

PART 5
Monday, September 4, 2023
Three weeks later. Labor Day.

CHAPTER 65
Ray

Ray sat on the balcony looking out at the sunrise coming up over the Atlantic Ocean. The waves were huge. The remnants of Hurricane Idalia had passed by yesterday, but the water was still churning as the storm went out to sea. Prayers up for all of those in Florida affected by the hurricane Ray thought as she closed her eyes and put her hands together at her chest.

Ray had been taking her motion sickness medicine every day and had put a motion sickness patch behind her ear, and she also wore bracelet sea bands. She didn't want to risk getting seasick. *Always be prepared.*

Their cruise ship was supposed to be docked this morning in Baltimore, but the Chesapeake Bay had been "closed." Ray had come to learn that if the waters of the bay were rough, they wouldn't allow boats to enter. Their ship had been waiting at the mouth of the bay since last night. It was listing from side to side quite a bit, but she'd never felt scared by the rocking motion. Trying to eat dinner last night had been quite an adventure. And the performers in the variety show were all forced to sit on chairs instead of doing their typical dance routines.

From Ray's point of view, though, the irregularities added some excitement to the adventure and made it more memorable. She wasn't feeling sick and had no job to go to tomorrow. She was content sitting on a rocking boat.

Now Olivia on the other hand, had gone from the highest of highs while they were in Bermuda, to the lowest of lows when she found out that Jimmy Buffett had died.

Ray thought back to the scene. On Saturday morning, they continued their daily ritual of eating at the breakfast buffet on the top deck. They'd all had custom omelets. Ray liked the fruit. Olivia liked the pastries. Evan and Harry loaded up on all the breakfast meat.

They'd just finished eating—three plates worth for the boys—and were looking at their cruise apps, trying to figure out their plans for the day. Evan and Harry wanted to go to the sports trivia game. Olivia wanted to go to the spa for a facial. Ray declined Olivia's offer to join her at the spa—she hated having strangers touch her. Ray wanted to relax in the sun on one of those round wicker two-person cabanas and finish reading her murder mystery book.

Olivia was the only one with external internet access. She had purchased the Wi-Fi package because she said that she had to monitor emails from school. But everyone knew that she just wanted to keep up with her social media content. As they were all looking at their phones, Olivia shouted out a shrill "Oh no!"

Everyone was startled. People at nearby tables also looked over, clearly eavesdropping to see what was going on. Olivia had been right in the middle of taking a sip of her iced coffee. She coughed and sprayed a mouthful across the table.

"What's wrong?" Harry said, clearly worried, wiping the coffee droplets from his arms.

"What happened, Liv?" Evan asked as he grabbed her arm.

"It's Jimmy Buffett," Olivia said softly and paused, her eyes welling up with tears. She couldn't continue the sentence. She stared at her phone in a daze. It was like she couldn't say it out loud because that would make it true. She turned her phone for them to see, and whispered, "He died."

"No way. Wow. I'm shook," Evan said, pushing back his chair and looking up into the air. "I knew he had postponed his concerts this summer and wasn't well, but I had no idea how serious it was. Damn."

Ray had thought something horrible must have happened from Olivia's initial reaction. Not that it wasn't a big deal, but Ray was almost relieved to find out it was not a personal tragedy.

Olivia let out a sob and said she had to text her mom. Her mom replied immediately and said that she'd heard the news but had been hoping Olivia wouldn't find out so she could continue to enjoy her cruise.

Ray felt like an imposter in this conversation because although she liked his music, she hadn't ever gotten attached to celebrities. She wasn't a fan of crowded concerts. She didn't understand the attraction of tailgating for hours in the hot sun and then sitting on the lawn for a couple more hours listening to music. Basically, watching the performers on the big screen and barely being able to see them on stage from so far away. And the concertgoers would sing so loud that you could barely hear the actual singer. To top it off, the concert shirts were more money than the actual tickets, in many cases.

News spread like wildfire on the cruise ship. Everyone was shaken up, to say the least. Manny, the cruise director, switched things up on the itinerary, calling it the *Jimmy Buffett Labor Day Weekend Show*. They offered discounted margaritas for the rest of the cruise and the pool band played Buffett music all weekend long. At night, they had *Margaritaville Karaoke* and gave away prizes for the best parrot head outfits. When they went to eat lunch, they found the waitstaff had removed all the shakers of salt from the dining room. Olivia started crying when she noticed. "Salt… salt, salt," she whispered.

After a few hours of doom scrolling and showing everyone her videos and photos from various Buffett concerts, Olivia had declared she was done with her mourning period, and she posted a heart-worthy dedication to him on social with the hashtag #RestInParadise.

Olivia told everyone to put on their Hawaiian shirts. They'd drink margaritas and hurricanes in memoriam. Olivia had come prepared; she had parrot earrings and a small stuffed parrot for her shoulder because that was part of her normal vacation get-up. She ended up winning the *Best Parrot Head* prize, which was coincidentally a huge stuffed parrot. Ray took photos and a short video from their table as Olivia accepted her award on stage.

The sun was fully up, and Ray noticed the ship had finally started moving into the bay. She read her book and waited for Evan to get up. She didn't want to disturb him since they'd gone to sleep late last night, taking full advantage of the final night of their all-you-can-drink beverage package.

She finished reading her book and set it down. She saw a couple of seagulls fly by. She wondered what city they were passing by. Suddenly, the two birds landed with a quick swoop onto the lifeboat below her balcony. Ray looked at them. They looked at Ray. She took a quick breath.

"No. It can't be…" She shook her head in disbelief. She closed her eyes and opened them again, looking at the birds. One without a foot. One with a little growth on its beak. *Her seagulls.* They looked back at her, tilting their heads back and forth. Ocean City was not so far away, she thought as she looked over to the land on the right, starboard side. The Eastern Shore.

"Grammy. Pop-Pop. I know this can't really be you two, but on the very slim chance that it is, I want you to know that I love you very much and I miss you terribly. Thank you for everything you've done for me. I know you wouldn't want me to stop living my life just because you're gone. I feel like my life is finally beginning to take shape. Thank you for watching over me. I love you both so much," Ray whispered to the two seagulls as her eyes welled up.

The birds sat there, in no hurry to move. Ray looked at them and picked up her phone to take a photo. "My very own *guardian an-gulls*."

CHAPTER 66
Olivia

Olivia woke up suddenly, startled from a bad dream. She had a huge headache and her stomach was gurgling. How many hurricanes did she have last night, she wondered. *Note to self— don't forget to hydrate today.*

She closed her eyes and tried to block out the terrifying visions from the recurring dream of running her car into Luke. This time, he had sprung out of nowhere and was standing on the hood of her car wearing a ridiculous Roman gladiator costume and started shooting a machine gun at her through the windshield… that's when she woke up. Every time it was a little different, but she always woke up in reaction to some kind of violent attack, her heart rate increased, and her face flushed. Nightmares or not, though, this secret was going to stay a secret *forever*.

She felt the subtle swaying of the boat and lifted her head and looked outside. The ship was moving, and it wasn't rocking as much as it was last night. Harry was still asleep. Olivia looked at her award-winning parrot prize, smiling. She would take it out to the balcony to get a good picture so she could text it to her family. She opened the balcony door and tried to close it quietly.

Once she was outside, she thought she heard mumbling coming from the balcony next door—Ray and Evan's connecting cabin. She tiptoed across the small balcony and peeked through the gap by the balcony divider and saw Ray sitting in the chair, holding her phone up in front of her.

Olivia popped the parrot out in front of Ray's balcony and in her best parrot voice said, "Ahoy, Matey! Yo, ho, ho! Batten down the hatches! Ray Ray want a cracker?"

Ray jumped up and her book fell to the floor with a thud. "Livvie! Oh my God. You scared the crap out of me, woman!"

The girls leaned out over their balcony railings and started laughing uncontrollably. The seagulls started squawking, they were technically Laughing Gulls, after all.

"What's going on out here?" Evan said as he opened the balcony door, eyes still sleepy, hair a mess.

"Just some early morning shenanigans," Olivia said as she shook her parrot up and down. "Right, J.B.?" she asked the stuffed animal.

Ray held her phone out. "Liv, look. This photo has the stuffed parrot and my two seagulls!"

"That's so cute!" Olivia said as she took the phone away from Ray to examine the photo. "I'll text it to myself."

Olivia's balcony door opened, and Harry came out singing, *Come Monday*. He grabbed Olivia in a huge hug, dipped her back and kissed her hard on the lips. "I always want to be holding you tight, my sweet Livvie," he said as he lifted her back up. Olivia smiled the biggest smile she had all summer and kissed him again. The boat abruptly swayed, hitting a big wave and they lost their balance momentarily.

All four looked out across the Chesapeake Bay. Olivia took a few awkward group photos of them leaning out over their respective railings. Their perfect vacation was almost over. Their crazy summer was almost over, too.

CHAPTER 67
Evan

Ray was in the shower and getting ready to go to breakfast. Now that they were in the bay, Evan finally had internet access. He sat on the balcony and used his phone as a hotspot and powered up his laptop.

He had to enter the draft picks from his Fantasy Football live draft, which they'd done right before heading out for the cruise. He'd been running a league for years now as the commissioner. He'd only won one time, but every season he took it very seriously.

He knew everyone would be anxious to set their teams before the first football game on Thursday. Evan had drafted Lamar Jackson as his QB, having faith that this was the season that the Ravens would get back to the Super Bowl.

They were going to an Orioles game before heading back home, assuming this ship ever docked back in Baltimore. The Os were in first place in the American League.

Evan pulled up a playlist. Aerosmith's *Home Tonight* started playing.

A gust of wind came up and his new Bermuda baseball cap blew off his head and landed on top of the lifeboat below. He stood up and leaned down over the railing to reach it. Just out of his grasp. He started inside to grab something to try to reach it. As he opened the balcony door, he noticed a seagull pushing the hat closer and closer with small taps from its beak. Another seagull—with only one foot—watched on.

Evan was perplexed. *Do birds normally do this kind of thing?*

He reached down to grab the hat when it got close enough. "Ah. So. Um. Thanks, bird?" he said with a salute after he put it back on his head. The birds squawked and then flew away.

Evan went inside as Ray was coming out of the bathroom. "Hey, the strangest thing just happened! My hat blew off and landed on top of the lifeboat. And, unless I'm hallucinating, a seagull rescued it for me?"

Ray's eyes widened and glistened with unshed tears. She walked over and hugged Evan tightly. "That is a story for another day," she said.

You never knew how the summer was going to play out, Evan thought.

2023 was one for the books.

Next in the Ocean City Seagull Series

Throw out your bicycle helmets and grab your candy cigarettes, because next up in the *Ocean City Seagull Series* is a flashback to life in Ocean City, Maryland, in the 1980s. We'll dive into Uncle Jack's origin story. Jackson Michaels and his brother Justin were lifeguards and ruled the beach in their heyday, but life didn't turn out quite like Jack always imagined it would.

ACKNOWLEDGEMENTS

It's been my lifelong dream to publish a novel. So many writers say that—but for me, it's been a true and persistent longing. As a professional writer of articles, content, and marketing communications, I've always considered myself a writer. But I wasn't an author—and that's what I wanted most. Over the years, I helped others promote their books while quietly dreaming of doing the same for myself. I started and stopped countless manuscripts, often wondering if I just wasn't meant to write long form.

When the world began to emerge from the worst of the pandemic, I realized we were living through a monumental moment in history—one worth capturing. And what better setting than my perennial happy place, Ocean City, Maryland? This book is a post-pandemic slice-of-life story, grounded in 2023, and I hope it serves as a time capsule of real-life sentiment from an era we're still processing. Some readers may not be ready to revisit those times just yet—and I understand. This isn't a breezy beach read, a classic romance, or a tidy mystery. But I hope it's a little bit of all three: relatable, thought-provoking, and, above all, enjoyable.

There are many people who helped me find the courage to see this project through. While it would take far too many pages to thank everyone who's influenced me, I want to highlight those who championed this book over the past two years.

First and foremost, Kip—my loving partner. You've been with me every step of the way, offering unwavering support as

I overanalyzed every single aspect of the publishing process. From walking the streets of Ocean City with me as scenes unfolded in my imagination, to scouring bookshops and Amazon listings with me for cover inspiration—you've truly lived this story right alongside me. Writing a novel means carrying it around in your head 24/7, and you never once asked me to put it down.

To my children, Korina and Ryan—thank you for your endless patience and insight. You answered hundreds of questions about 20-something life in 2023. You explained the latest slang, social media habits, phone games, and even helped fine-tune the cover design. You also introduced me to BookTok and Bookstagram, which made this 50-something mom feel like maybe she could pull off a book launch in the digital age.

To my parents, James and Cheryl—thank you for raising me with books and for supporting my leap from architecture to journalism at the University of Maryland. You've always believed in me, and without your influence, I wouldn't have pursued a writing career. Our shared love of reading and our summer tradition of going to Ocean City have shaped me in more ways than I can count.

To my sister Kelly, and her family—Rob, Owen, and Hallie—thank you for being a wellspring of funny stories and joyful chaos. Kelly, we've always been a creative team. From writing parody songs and making VHS skits to library marathons, you've always fueled my imagination. Your help with character development, especially sensory details, brought the story to life in vivid color.

To my current and past pets: Luna the rough collie, and rescue cats Penny, Mango, Snuggles, and Sunny—you inspired the furry friends in this book more than you know. You follow a long line of beloved Arford pets who made life better just by being near.

To my editor, Malory Wood—this book might never have left the draft stage without you. Your guidance on story flow, character arcs, and formatting helped shape the final product. And thank you to my Ocean City neighbor and fellow author, Katherine Ruskey, for introducing me to Malory.

To Marc Emond—thank you for creating the stunning cover art. As the longtime cartoonist for the *OC Today Dispatch* and the artist behind Stinky Beach Studio, your work captured the spirit of Seagull Street perfectly. I'm honored to have your painting represent the heart of this book.

To my first two beta readers beyond the family—Maura and Kelly—thank you for your honest feedback and willingness to power through that early draft. Your insights helped make the book stronger. Also, special thanks to Maura for her guidance on the book cover design.

To the friends who helped me stay motivated, reviewed rough drafts, offered plot advice, and weighed in on cover designs—Wendy, Carrie, April, Dianne, Suzanne, Eric, Kiati, Kelly, and Alison—thank you for your support!

To all the friends, neighbors, and colleagues who encouraged me—you helped make this dream a reality.

And to Executive MBA Cohort 9 at the University of Maryland's Robert H. Smith School of Business—thank you for pushing me to think bigger. Without that experience, I wouldn't have founded Red Hill Creek Enterprises. I hope to help others publish their dream books one day, too.

Finally, to the Town of Ocean City, Maryland—thank you for being the place where memories are made. Whether you're a visitor or a lifelong local, this book is for you.

BOOK CLUB QUESTIONS

1. What was your favorite part of the book, and why did it resonate with you?

2. Was there a character or moment that frustrated you? If so, why?

3. Did any scenes make you laugh or cry? What emotions did the book stir in you?

4. Which character's journey surprised you the most?

5. Were there any quotes or passages that stood out to you? Why?

6. The book explores different perspectives and perceptions. How did it make you think about authenticity in your own life?

7. How has your perspective on post-COVID life evolved over time? Do you think the book accurately captured that period?

8. The book blends slice-of-life, romance, and mystery. Did one element stand out more to you? Would you have wanted more of either?

9.   What role did the setting (Ocean City, Maryland) play in shaping the story? Could it have taken place anywhere else, or was the location essential?

10. What kind of vacations did you take growing up? What's your dream vacation?

11. Did the title *Welcome to Seagull Street* hold any deeper meaning for you by the end of the book?

12. If this book were made into a movie, who would you cast in the main roles?

13. What do you think happens to the characters after the final page?

14. Would you recommend this book to a friend? If so, what type of reader would enjoy it most?

ABOUT THE AUTHOR

Alissa Arford is a Maryland native who grew up in Parkton and graduated from Hereford High School. A proud third-generation Terp, she earned both her journalism degree and executive MBA from the University of Maryland—continuing a family tradition that now includes her two kids as fourth-generation Terps.

With a career spanning journalism, digital marketing, and branding, Alissa has held senior leadership roles in professional tech consulting firms, SaaS finance apps, nonprofits, and higher education. Throughout her career, she has combined her love of writing, technology, and strategy to create compelling brand narratives and data-driven marketing solutions.

No spot holds a more special place in Alissa's heart than Ocean City, Md. Her earliest and fondest memories are of summers spent on its sandy shores: building sandcastles, jumping waves, and enjoying classic Boardwalk treats like Dumser's ice cream, Fisher's caramel popcorn, and Thrasher's fries. She splits her time between her home in Ellicott City and Ocean City, where she creates new memories while honoring old traditions.

Photo by Ben Baker-Lee

LEAVE A REVIEW

Thank you for reading!

I hope you enjoyed *Welcome to Seagull Street!* If this story resonated with you, I'd love to hear your thoughts. Reviews help other readers discover the book and mean the world to new authors like me.

If you have a moment, please consider leaving a review. Your feedback makes a difference! Thank you for your support and for being part of this journey.

Stay in touch by subscribing to my newsletter at alissaarford.com.

Contact me at alissa@alissaarford.com.

Follow me at on Facebook, Instagram, TikTok, Bluesky, YouTube, and Threads.